PRAISE FOR
FLYING WITHOUT A NET

"[E.M Ben Shaul] knows her Judaism and she knows her Torah and she manages to bring those together with a modern love story and show us that 'love is love' and sometimes we have no control over who we love and why."

—Amos Lassen, *The Jewish Advocate*

"A truly amazing story about love and religion that will stay with me forever. I loved, loved, loved it and highly recommend it. Undoubtedly one of my favorite books this year."

—From Top to Bottom Reviews

E.M. BEN SHAUL

flying without a net

interlude **press** • new york

For Michael, who encouraged me when I wasn't at all sure about any of this, and for E and Y, who made this whole process that much more interesting.

אם תרצו, אין זו אגדה

תֵאוֹדוֹר הֶרְצֵל—

If you will it, it is no dream

—Theodor Herzl

author's note

DANI AND AVI HAVE LIVED in my brain since 2003, before the Massachusetts Supreme Judicial Court ruled that marriage equality should be the law in Massachusetts. Because of the discussions that were going on during that time, I wondered what it would be like to see all this change going on around you but to know that, because of your faith, you might still be left out. At that time, very few resources were available to LGBT Orthodox Jews. That has changed for the better. For more information on Jewish LGBTQ resources, please visit the following sites:

- Eshel: http://www.eshelonline.org
- Keshet: http://www.keshetonline.org
- A Wider Bridge: http://awiderbridge.org

May this blog post by Rabbi Steven Greenberg on the subject of Leviticus 18:22 be helpful, not only to Orthodox Jews, but to LGBTQ people of all faiths and those who love them:

- http://blogs.timesofisrael.com/
  silence-is-not-ok-when-torah-is-painful

walking many paths

It turned out to be the best random errand Dani Perez had ever been dragged along on, but he had no way of knowing that at the time.

At the time, he was annoyed, exhausted, and starving. And it was all Rafi Weiss's fault.

"Meet me in Harvard Station," Rafi had said. Even though they were talking on the phone, Dani pictured Rafi's brown eyes twinkling. "We can work at my house, if you don't mind running a quick errand with me first. And then you can just walk back to your place when we're done."

"How quick?" Dani asked, knowing Rafi and his "quick errands."

"Five minutes. Promise—*b'li neder*. And then I'll make sure you get real food."

"I didn't think you meant to make a solemn vow there, Rafi. And when you say 'real food' you mean…" Rafi's definition of food tended to run toward chips and soda more often than not, and Dani really needed protein, having survived all day on—chips and soda.

"I'll make you dinner, so we'll both be able to eat it." For all that he was a junk-food junkie, Rafi was also a great cook, so the offer of a Rafi-cooked dinner was real incentive. And Rafi kept strictly kosher, so his offering to cook meant no logistical gyrations to find food that would make both men happy.

The whole ridiculous errand started because Rafi and Dani had a presentation to prepare for a local Hadassah group—a brief history of Israel and the Arab-Israeli conflict. The Hadassah group did one of these every year, to attract new members. Rafi was the Arab history maven; Dani was on the program because, he told himself, he was a sucker. The fact that he was Israeli and had served in the Israel Defense Forces made him an easy choice to speak on the current situation in the Middle East. He wasn't a subject expert, but he did keep up to date with the situation in Israel and the region more than many people he knew.

Rafi had said that the only time he could meet to go through Dani's slides was on Tuesday evening. So Dani had shown up, as requested, at the subway station near Harvard University and now here he was, being dragged down Massachusetts Avenue in Cambridge, Massachusetts, in the heat of mid-July to a room that Dani was positive wouldn't be air conditioned, just so Rafi could drop off some sheet music for his a cappella group.

They turned off of Massachusetts Avenue and headed down Dunster Street, which Dani was glad to find was much less busy than the combination of people, cars, and buses had been moments before. It was summer in Harvard Square, however, so construction was going on at just about every corner, and the jackhammers made it no quieter.

"We'll go back the other way, via JFK Street," Rafi said, speeding up to get through the construction zone.

Dani pulled a handkerchief out of his backpack and wiped his brow. "Rafi, it's ninety degrees and humid. I know you have some sort of unnatural cooling system in that curly hair of yours, but some of us just get a summer buzz cut and hope for the best."

Dani ran his hand over this year's version of his short-cropped hair, which he still wasn't used to, even though he got a similar haircut every summer. He adjusted his sunglasses and jogged to keep up with Rafi's pace. Rafi was Dani's height, but he had longer legs and was walking much faster than any sane person would in hot weather.

"If this stuff is so important that they get it tonight, why don't you have rehearsal?"

"We're on hiatus for a couple more weeks." Rafi turned to look at Dani as they turned onto Mount Auburn Street. "But Moshe and Avi really wanted to work on the new arrangement of 'Erev Shel Shoshanim,' because Moshe's brother and his fiancée want to use it as the bride's processional at their wedding, and since I had the sheet music handy, I promised I'd drop it by. It'll seriously take just a few minutes."

If Rafi didn't have such a ridiculously busy schedule to begin with, Dani never would have agreed. But Rafi was notoriously hard to pin down, so anyone collaborating with Rafi quickly learned to take advantage of coincidental free time whenever possible.

"Okay," Dani finally said. "But I'm going to hold you to that 'just a few minutes.'"

"No problem. Really."

Dani and Rafi entered the Harvard Hillel building. Dani had been at the new Hillel building for a couple of events in the twenty years since it had been built, but he was still amazed by the grandeur of the building. He admired the stately staircase and the curved windows that showed the patio just beyond as he and Rafi climbed to the second floor.

"They really just let you meet here?" Dani asked.

"Yeah," Rafi said. "One of the perks of Moshe being faculty—when classes aren't in session, he can use the building as long as there's not something already scheduled there. And since they have a halfway-decent piano, it's a great rehearsal space for us. C'mon, they're in the back room."

They crossed the hall toward one of the small meeting rooms. It was wood-paneled except for the expanses of wall that were filled with bookshelves. A piano sat in the far corner of the hardwood floor, and around the room were small tables with two or three chairs. Dani figured the room was usually used for study groups. Two guys were bent over one table, which was covered with piles of papers.

"No, more of a salsa beat. Can't you imagine it?" one said, scribbling furiously on the top paper.

"Salsa? For 'Ani Ma'amin'? Are you nuts? You take a lesson from one of the greatest rabbis in Jewish history, turn it into a song—"

"I didn't turn it into a song; it's been sung to various melodies since the 1940s. You can't pin that one on me."

"Be that as it may. You'd be the one turning it into a salsa tune."

"I think it'll work. If Kolainu B'Yachad can do it to 'Kah Ribon,' we can do it to 'Ani Ma'amin.'"

"'Kah Ribon' is a *Shabbat* lunch song. People do all sorts of things to Shabbat lunch songs."

"Uh… guys? I brought the sheet music," Rafi said, cutting off the discussion.

Both of the men looked up. "Cool. Hand it over," the first guy said, coming around the table with his hand outstretched.

"You're welcome, Avi," Rafi said, grinning.

"Thanks," the guy—Avi—responded.

As Avi came better into view, Dani had to control his desire to just stare and drool. Avi virtually matched his physical ideal for a guy—tall, slim but not too thin, long fingers. Light brown hair about a shade lighter than Dani's own, greenish-blue eyes nothing like Dani's brown ones. He was dressed casually in jeans and a "Here Comes Treble" T-shirt. And when Avi turned to pick up a notebook from a side table, Dani noticed the knitted *kippah* on Avi's head.

"Hey, Avi? This is Dani. He was kind enough to let me drag him along on the way to my place."

"Hi," Dani said.

"Hi," Avi responded, much more quietly than he'd responded to Rafi.

"You've got to forgive Avi," the second guy said. "He's shy when he's not on stage."

"*Moshe!*" Avi yelped. A very cute blush worked its way up Avi's face.

"Hi," Moshe said, coming toward them. He stood next to Avi, and Dani was struck by the contrast between the two. Avi towered over Moshe, who was probably no more than five-foot-seven. While Avi had light hair, light skin and blue eyes, Moshe had the dark curly hair, darker complexion, and deep brown eyes that Dani knew from some of his Moroccan friends. "I'm Moshe, the brains of this organization."

"Yeah, right, like you think so," Rafi said. The two of them began bantering, and Dani took the opportunity to look at Avi while Avi watched Rafi and Moshe. Dani had been right that he was tall—at least three inches taller than Dani's own six-foot-two.

"So," he said to Avi after a minute or so, "I take it you're involved with this group?"

"I'm one of the founders. And I sing baritone." Avi blushed again.

"That's cool. Would you mind if I came by a rehearsal some time?" Dani had no idea why he asked that, but if Avi was one of the founders of the group, then it was important to him. And if it was important to Avi, then Dani wanted to know more about it.

"Yeah… I mean, no. I mean, it's fine if you want to come by rehearsal some time. We'll only be meeting here for a couple more weeks, until the students come back. After that, we'll probably be meeting at my place in Coolidge Corner. The Hillel is usually booked straight through the *yomim tovim* because the holidays take up the whole month by the time we get through Rosh Hashana, Yom Kippur, Sukkot, and Shmini Atzeret and Simchat Torah. Eventually we'll find a new rehearsal space for the rest of the academic year," Avi said.

"Hey, Dani, get a move on. I thought you were hungry!" Dani hadn't noticed, but Rafi and Moshe had stopped bickering, and Rafi was at the doorway.

"Coming," Dani called back. He looked at Avi one last time. "It was a pleasure meeting you. I hope to see you again."

"Thanks," Avi almost-whispered. "Come back soon." He quickly turned to join Moshe over the stack of papers.

Dani and Rafi headed toward the subway station.

"What was all that about?" Rafi asked as they walked down JFK Street. They had to dodge around the usual foot traffic of people going in and out of the shops in Harvard Square and the occasional groups of students who were staying around Cambridge for the summer. Unlike other areas of Massachusetts heavily populated by students, Harvard Square never seemed to quiet down.

"All what?" Dani asked.

"The whispering with Avi."

"I was only whispering because he was whispering. And, not that it's really your business, but Avi... intrigues me. I'd love to get to know him better," Dani replied.

"Dani, Avi's... not what you're looking for. Really."

Dani didn't know if Rafi meant that Avi was straight, or involved with someone, or both.

"Is it okay if I make a new friend, Dad?" Dani asked, unable to keep the sharp tone from his voice.

"A new friend is fine. Try for a new conquest and I think you'll hurt Avi more than you can even imagine." Rafi stopped walking and, with a stern look in his eyes, turned to face Dani. "And I will not allow it. Keep that in mind."

"I will, Rafi. I promise."

"*B'li neder*," they said simultaneously.

FIFTEEN MINUTES AFTER GETTING TO Rafi's house, Dani remembered.

"Hey, Rafi? Have you seen my sunglasses?" He rummaged through the bag he'd thrown onto the one chair in Rafi's tiny living room.

"You were wearing them when we went into the Hillel building, but I don't think you wore them on the way out."

"I had them in my hand when I was first talking to Avi. I may have put them down on the piano, but I don't recall." Dani would be the first to admit that he had been somewhat distracted, and the whereabouts of his sunglasses had been low on his priority list.

"Let me give Avi a call and ask if he saw them." Rafi pulled out his phone and dialed before Dani had a chance to think about it. "Oh, voicemail. Okay, I'll leave him a message. Hey, Avi, it's Rafi. Did you happen to see Dani's sunglasses? There's a chance he left them on the piano. If so, give me a call and let me know, okay? Thanks." He hung up and turned back to Dani. "I figured it would be easier on Avi for me to be the go-between than just telling him to call you directly. If he calls me, I'll give him your number and tell him to call you. But this is more likely to get a response."

"So what's Avi's deal?" Dani asked.

"No deal; he just doesn't like the phone much, especially with people he doesn't know."

Dani suspected there was more to the story than that, but he let it drop.

DANI WOULD HARDLY EVER GET up early on Sunday morning to go into downtown Boston. But after an extended series of phone messages, he and Avi finally found a time to get together so that Dani could get his sunglasses back. And despite the inconvenience, Dani wasn't going to turn down an opportunity to see Avi again.

So that's how Dani found himself at the entrance to the Boston Public Library at ten-thirty on one of the hottest July mornings the city had seen that year. Of course, to compensate for the heat, he'd chosen the coolest, most breathable clothing he owned—a light blue loose-weave polo shirt and khaki shorts, no socks, and his standard sandals.

Avi was already standing in front of the McKim building of the library when Dani came around the corner from the subway exit. He was dressed like Dani, but his shirt was red, his shorts were black, and he was wearing sneakers instead of sandals. Dani was amused that Avi was standing in front of the statue personifying science while reading *The Great Partnership: Science, Religion, and the Search for Meaning*. If he had known Avi better, Dani would have asked if the choice was deliberate.

"Hey, Avi," Dani said, reaching out his hand. "Dan Perez. Thanks for finding my glasses."

Avi looked up from his book and smiled and then shook Dani's hand firmly. "Hi, Dan," he said. "Thanks for coming to meet me here."

"Sorry it took so long to find a time to meet."

"I'm sorry I couldn't bring your sunglasses to you at work. Had I been in the Cambridge area at all this week, it might've worked out, but since I was out in Burlington all week, it just wasn't feasible before Shabbat."

Dani grimaced. "Yeah. Sorry again for calling you on Shabbat. I really should know better." While most of Dani's Jewish friends were

not observant and would answer the phone on Saturday, Dani should have figured out why Avi wouldn't answer.

"Eh, no problem. For one thing, I leave my cell phone off over Shabbat, so it didn't even ring and bother me. Second, it sounded like you'd lost complete track of what day it was by the time you left the message."

"Yeah, it's been one of those weeks. Working crazy hours trying to fix last-minute bugs can really mess with my sense of time. But I usually know when it's Shabbat."

Avi nodded. "Anyway, I've got your glasses," he said. He pulled an eyeglass case out of his backpack, opened it, and handed Dani his sunglasses.

"Thanks so much." They had taken care of the business that had brought them there, but Dani was loath to leave so quickly. And Dani remembered that Avi had said in his phone message that whatever was bringing him to Copley—of course Dani couldn't remember what it was—didn't start until eleven. "Hey," Dani said, glancing up and down Boylston Street for something he could invite Avi to do for the short time he had available. *Thank God for Starbucks.* "Do you have time for a cup of coffee?"

After glancing at his watch, Avi said, "Yes, I have about twenty minutes before I have to meet the tour I'm working. And an iced coffee would be perfect."

"Great."

They crossed the street and entered the—*todah la'el,* air conditioned—coffee shop. Avi claimed an empty table by leaving his backpack on a chair. He came to where Dani was standing at the end of the ordering line.

"Do you want me to order your iced coffee?" Dani asked. "I'm not sure how comfortable I'd be just leaving my bag unattended like that." Dani wasn't willing to attribute it to his experiences while living in Israel, but he had an aversion to unattended packages and parcels, even if he knew their origin.

Avi shrugged. "Eh, I'm not concerned, but sure—get me a medium, sweetened, with space," he said, pulling his wallet out of his pocket.

Dani waved him off. "My treat. Really. I appreciate your finding my sunglasses; buying you coffee is the least I could do."

"Thanks." Avi gave Dani a shy smile and put his wallet back in his pocket. "I'll be over there." He pointed to the table where he'd left his bag.

"I'll be just a minute." Dani turned toward the counter, but, purely for aesthetic appreciation, he tried to keep his eye on Avi as he walked back to the table.

Once the drinks were ordered, Dani sat at the table. "It shouldn't take too long. You've still got about fifteen minutes, right?" he said.

"Well, I like to be there early, but we're meeting at the entrance to the outbound T stop, so it's only about a two-minute walk from here. I've got time."

The kid at the counter gestured to Dani, who got the drinks and then returned to the table. Avi took a long drink from his coffee, then smiled. "First coffee of the day is always the best," he said.

"This is only your first?" Dani asked, grinning. "To get up this early on a Sunday, I need at least two—one right before my shower and one right after. So this one," he gestured at his cup, "is three. I'll probably have at least two more today, though I am trying to cut down on my caffeine intake."

"Wow. One more after this and I wouldn't be able to sleep tonight. Two more and I'm bouncing off the walls and babbling rather incoherently. I haven't done more than that since college."

"So," Dani said after another sip or four, "what is it that you do, anyway? I know you said in phone messages that you interpret and that you use AJ as your professional name, but what do you interpret, and why do you have a 'professional' name?"

"I'm an ASL—American Sign Language, that is—interpreter, and a lot of people find 'AJ' easier to sign," and here he made a quick hand gesture, "than either 'Avraham'"— a longer hand gesture—"or even 'Avi'"—a mid-length hand gesture. "When I was given my name sign, my instructor asked me for my initials and decided that 'AJ' was a good designation for me."

"Name sign?"

"A shorthand, so to speak, to designate a person within the Deaf community. They tend to be very community-specific, meaning that if I were to move, say, to New York and there was already an AJ in the community, some adjustment would be made to my name sign— placement, movement, something to differentiate between me and this theoretical other AJ. My friend Dalia's name sign is a 'D' handshape done at the side of the face, near the eye, because Dalia's eyes are so strikingly blue. My sister Chava's name sign is a 'C' handshape combined with the sign for 'funny' because Chava has a wicked sense of humor." Avi blushed. "Sorry for going on like that."

"No, I'm really interested. So your sister's an interpreter, too?"

"No. Chava's Deaf."

"Oh," Dani said. "That was going to be my second guess."

There was a brief pause, then Avi said, "Thank you."

"For what?"

"Not spouting some sort of platitude or expressing your sympathy for my sister's Deafness."

"It's who she is. There's no reason to put a value judgment, positive or negative, on it."

"That's such a refreshing attitude."

Dani shrugged. "I'm a sabra born to two Anglo parents who was one of the few *Ashkenazim* among a majority-*Sephardi* group in army basic training. I learned early on that judging someone based on differences— disability, religious beliefs, ethnic background, whatever—was a really bad idea. And I just try to apply that across the board."

"It's a nice change, that's all," Avi said. He looked at his watch. "Look, I hate to do this, but I've got to run and meet the tour group." He pushed back his chair, stood, and grabbed his backpack and the remnants of his coffee.

Dani stood up as well. "I'll walk you over there. I've got to catch the T back to Park Street, and I can cross the street there as easily as here."

"You sure?" Avi asked.

"Positive." Dani picked up his bag, and then he and Avi headed out of the coffee shop. "So what's the deal with this tour?" Dani asked.

"Well, my friend Steve is a local tour guide, and periodically he'll do a special interpreted tour. I try to support those as much as possible, so I often sign up to be the interpreter and bring as many friends as I can drum up. Today, for instance, I'm bringing both my siblings and my friend Dalia."

"So you have two siblings? Are they both deaf?"

"No. Jake can hear, but he's fluent in ASL. And, anyway, Steve is going to be talking the whole tour. Hearing people will be there; it's just that we make this one accessible to the local Deaf community as well."

"That's really cool."

They approached the meeting place at the corner of Boylston Street and Dartmouth Street, in front of the Tortoise and Hare statue near the finish line of the Boston Marathon, and Avi looked around. "No sign of them yet. Figures."

Dani looked at his watch; it was 10:55 a.m. "I'm sure they'll be along soon. The T's probably running slow."

"Probably." Avi looked around again.

"Hey," Dani said. "Do you mind if I stay and keep you company until they show up? I'm really not looking forward to heading home to an afternoon of laundry and grocery shopping."

"Sure. I have a book with me, but waiting *with* someone is better."

"Thanks," Dani said.

They waited only a couple of minutes—while they talked about the rain that had fallen every Saturday since the beginning of summer and how it made even the briefest outing annoying—before three people approached.

"Hey, Av," the man in the triad said.

"Hey, Jake," Avi responded. He then did something that looked like a salute toward the two women. They signed back something to him, and he gestured to Dani.

"This is Dan Perez. He's a friend of Rafi Weiss." As he spoke, Avi signed as well. Dani figured he was telling the women what he had just said. Avi paused, then turned back to Dani. "Hang on. Rafi introduced you as Dani, but you introduced yourself as Dan. Which do you prefer?"

"Either is fine. I tend to introduce myself as Dan, but family and close friends call me Dani. It's really Daniel, but no one calls me that unless they're pissed at me."

"Dan," Avi said, "this is my brother Ya'akov, my sister Chava, and my friend Dalia." He gestured toward the women as he spoke their names. Chava was a petite brunette with long, light-brown hair pulled into a single braid down her back. Dalia was taller and blonde, with wavy, shoulder-length hair. And it was quite obvious that Ya'akov and Avi were brothers. Were it not that Avi was about four inches taller, they could've been mistaken for one another.

"Nice to meet you all," Dani said as Avi translated.

"Good to meet you, too," Ya'akov said. "You joining us on this thing?"

"I wasn't planning on it, but Avi's been telling me a bit about the tour, and it sounds really interesting." And the opportunity to spend at least part of the day with Avi wasn't something Dani wanted to turn down.

Ya'akov relayed what Dalia was signing. "Yeah, please join us. There's bound to be plenty of space."

"Dal, we'll have to check with Steve, really," Avi said while signing back to Dalia.

"But he'll say yes," Dalia said, again through Ya'akov.

"Dal…" Avi started, but Dalia glared at him, and Avi stopped whatever protest he was about to voice. He turned toward Dani. "Dan, if you're really interested in joining us, I'll check with Steve. And Dalia's right—he's bound to say yes."

"I'd love to." And despite the heat, it was true.

Avi pulled a baseball cap out of his bag. "You'll want this, even if you don't think so now."

"Thanks." Dani double-checked his bag to make sure his water bottle was full and then took the proffered hat and put it on.

Steve, the tour guide, was more than happy for Dani to join. It was a small group, most likely due to the extended heat wave. Dani found the information interesting and very well presented. Was Avi planning to do any more of these? *Maybe I could find reasons to join in.*

And that's how Dani ended up learning more than he had realized there was to know about the buildings in Copley Square. He had never known that MIT had been on the site of what was now an office building near Clarendon Street or that the same building had once housed the Boston Society of Natural History—which, as Steve pointed out, was now the Museum of Science. But, more importantly, he had learned a great deal about Avi, both from how he interacted with his siblings and Dalia and also from things that they—with Ya'akov's assistance when necessary—said about him. Dani doubted that Avi had wanted him to know, for example, that he had been afraid of the T-Rex at the Museum of Science when he was a kid, even if the story was told with affection.

He still had much more to learn about Avi, but now it seemed possible that he would have more opportunities to do so. Avi had seemed comfortable having coffee, so Dani decided he would see whether Avi would say yes to repeating the experience.

2

an afternoon at the improv

As soon as he returned to his apartment after the walking tour, Dani took out his phone.

"'Alo?"

"Dudu?" He needed his brother's perspective on things and, while he was setting himself up for future teasing, he couldn't imagine confiding in anyone else. "It's Dani." He slid off his shoes in the front entryway and then turned left into the living room.

"I knew that. No one—except you and Ima—has the *chutzpah* to call me 'Dudu' anymore. And you're definitely not Ima."

"If your brother can't call you by a hated childhood nickname, who can? Anyway, I need your advice." He sat down on the blue-and-grey striped sofa and put his feet up on the oak coffee table, pushing away the latest issue of *Entertainment Weekly*. Dani had furnished his first apartment with pieces from his parents' basement combined with items he'd gotten on Craigslist, and even though he could now afford fancier furniture, he kept the comfortable pieces that he liked. His overall décor was best described as "eclectic," though he usually described it as "yardsale chic."

"You *need* my advice? That's different. Usually you completely ignore my advice and then live to regret it."

"It's a different situation; it's something I've never experienced before."

"Who is he?" Dudu asked.

"How the Hell did you jump immediately to the thought that I was calling you about a guy?" Dani took his feet off the table and sat up.

"I know you. Who is he?"

Dani sighed. "Friend of Rafi Weiss. One of the guys in his choral group." He stood up and headed toward the large glass sliding door that opened onto his balcony. He mentally debated between talking with Dudu from the balcony or from the air-conditioned apartment and settled on going outside.

"How'd you meet him?"

"Remember how Rafi *schlepped* me down to Harvard on our way to his place last week? It was to drop off something to Avi."

"The mystery guy's named Avi, eh? So, what—we're talking lust at first sight?"

"Dudu, he's—you remember that guy, Shai, that I knew in basic training?"

"The tall one with the gorgeous hands? You talked about him for *months* in your letters. How could I forget?"

"Physically, Avi's all that and more. He's gotta be at least six-foot-four, lanky but not too skinny. I'd love to see what's under that shirt he was wearing."

"Dani, slow down. No visualizing him naked until you've at least had dinner with the guy. Hell, at least until you know he's interested."

"That's one of the problems. I spent three hours with him today, and I got absolutely nothing from him directly. He's an enigma."

"So is it just his looks that attract you?" Dudu asked.

"At first, yeah. Hell, Dudu, the guy's *gorgeous*. But now that I've actually talked to him, seen him interact with other people, I really want to know more about what's inside the massively attractive wrapping."

"He's not a gift box, Dani."

"I know that. Really, I do. And, I'll admit it, the first impetus to learn more about him came from the fact that Rafi was warning me off him. But he's fascinating, and I want to know more."

Dani sat on one of the two green café chairs that were just the right size for his small balcony. From his perch he could see the edge of the small park and the benches filled with couples, young and old.

"So ask him out. Not like you haven't done it before, hundreds of times."

"Not *hundreds*, but I get your meaning. No, though. Avi's different. He's… I don't know. There's something about him—other than Rafi's dire warnings—that tells me to step lightly. Like he's an easily frightened deer, and moving too quickly will just make him bolt."

"You must be attracted to this guy—you're talking in clichés and Disney images. Lust always fogs your brain, Dani, and you end up doing stupid things."

"And that's exactly what I want to avoid this time. I don't want to rush things; I don't want to bulldoze him. Friendship is good. Friendship that grows into something more, even better. But…"

"But first you have to find out if he's gay?"

"That's part of it. First I have to get past *them*." Dani shuddered just to think about it.

"Them? Giant-ants-from-that-silly-science-fiction-movie-out-of-the-50s-Them?"

I never should have let Dudu loose on my DVD collection, Dani thought. "No, you idiot. *Them*, Avi's people. His Three Wiseguys. His brother, sister, and friend Dalia. Even just from our short interaction it was clear that these three watch out for Avi and would protect him from anything. Let me tell you, they scare me."

Dudu laughed.

"What are you laughing about?" Dani asked, shifting in his seat. Being laughed at by oneself is bad enough; being laughed at by one's younger brother is downright humiliating.

"I've never heard you this flustered so early in a relationship. It's cute."

"*Cute?* You call this cute? Avi's got guard dogs, and my concern is *cute?*"

"Dani, calm down. You're a suave guy. You can charm them easily, and if that doesn't work, you're a highly trained weapons expert, remember?" Dudu was still laughing, the asshole.

16

"Suave and charm isn't what's called for here, Dudu. The Wiseguys aren't that gullible. They're watching out for Avi's best interests, and they're not at all convinced that I'm in Avi's best interests." Hell, at this point, *Dani* wasn't convinced he was in Avi's best interests. "Therefore, I need to go slow and easy. And I have no fucking clue how to do slow and easy."

Dani stared at the street below. He stood up and leaned against the railing. A dog walker passed with a standard poodle and three greyhounds on leash; their tails began to wag as she approached the park.

"So now you have to ask yourself a question." Dudu paused, which Dani assumed was for dramatic effect. The dork.

"And that would be…?" Dani prompted him, swearing he'd kill Dudu—slowly and painfully—if he said, "Do you feel lucky, punk?"

"Is he worth your learning how to do slow and easy?"

"Fuck, yes."

"So why are you bothering me, then?" Dudu asked. There was humor in his voice, though, so Dani knew he didn't mean it literally.

"I just needed to hear my thoughts out loud, I think. I needed to say these things to someone, to get confirmation that I wasn't crazy, that this might be something worth pursuing, even though it might require me to completely change how I approach relationships."

"You're not crazy, Dani. And, you know, changing the way you approach relationships might not be a bad idea. Since you came out, have you been in any relationship that lasted more than six months?"

"No. The longest relationship I've had with a guy was about four months, with Binyamin. But he moved to Amsterdam; that wasn't my fault."

"True. But what about the guys you've dated who *haven't* moved overseas? Why didn't those relationships last?"

"Myriad reasons, but I get your point," Dani said as he went back inside his apartment. Slow and easy might be just what I need. Especially if he's straight and Dalia's his girlfriend. Though quick and obvious might be a less painful way to find out he's not at all interested."

"Or the fastest way to convince him that you're not the guy to date."

"So how do I keep from being the bull in the china shop and destroying every possibility of something coming of this?"

"Dani, I'm going to deny that I ever said this if it comes up in the future, but you're really a thoughtful guy, sensitive to others' feelings. So I can't see you completely ignoring Avi's feelings and pushing him into doing things he's not ready for. More likely, honestly, is you holding back, being too cautious and not reading the signs he's trying to give you. If he is interested, he'll let you know somehow. You just have to be receptive to those signs when they come along."

"How'd you get so insightful, brother-of-mine?" Dani asked.

"Too many fucked-up relationships, I guess. And years of therapy."

Dani didn't comment; there was more truth to that last part than either of them talked about.

"So," Dudu continued, "are you gonna take advantage of any of this sage advice from your brilliant and much-beloved brother?"

"I'm going to give it a try, if Avi's at all interested. Now I just have to figure out how to find that out."

"Here's a bold suggestion. How about you *ask*?"

"What, like 'Hey, Avi, do you sleep with guys?' That's not really subtle or slow or easy, Dudu."

"No, but 'Hey, Avi, do you want to have coffee again some time' *is* subtle, and you might be able to, based on his response to your question, determine whether it'll be two friends just going for coffee or two guys on a first date."

"Good point. Thanks, Dudu; I really appreciate this. I feel like a kid asking out his first girlfriend… or boyfriend. But this just feels different. From what Rafi said, Avi's more inexperienced than anyone—male or female—that I've ever lusted after."

"So you'll call him?"

"Yeah. Right after I get off the phone with you."

"Cool. Let me know what happens, won't you?"

"Sure will," Dani said. "Hey, Dudu? I owe you one."

"You sure do. Make me dinner some night this week?" Since Dudu was in graduate school in computer science, all of his free time was spent

either in the library or in the computer lab. Real meals only came his way when he got someone to cook for him or take him out, and more often than not, that someone was Dani.

"Sure. You name the night."

"I'll let you know, okay?"

"Okay." Dani paused. "Love ya, kid." Dudu hated being called "kid" just slightly less than he hated being called Dudu.

"Yeah, I know. You're an idiot, you know that? But if this becomes something real, you'll let me know, right?"

"You'll be the first."

"G'night, big idiot brother."

"G'night, twerp."

They hung up, and Dani stared at his phone. He was going to call Avi, as he'd told Dudu. But he wanted to be sure of what he was going to say. He just about had his thoughts in order when the phone rang in his hand.

"Fuck. Talk about bad timing," Dani said to the empty apartment. He answered it without looking at the caller ID. "Hello?" he said, a bit more harshly than he usually spoke on the phone.

"Uh… Dan? Is this a bad time?"

"Who is this, please?" Dani asked, even though he thought he recognized the voice.

"It's Avi, Avi Levine? From the walking tour?"

"It's good to hear from you, Avi. Sorry about my tone just now; what can I do for you?"

Dani could hear Avi taking deep breaths. When the pause was longer than expected, he worried that Avi wouldn't continue, but he didn't want to rush him.

Finally, Avi spoke again. "I know we didn't have much luck last week, trying to find a time to get together, and I feel really bad about making you come out on a Sunday morning just because I've got a whacked-out schedule. I'm going to be in Government Center all of next week, and I was wondering if you'd like to meet for lunch one day at the Milk Street Café, my treat. Sort of as an apology for *shlepping* you out into the heat early on a Sunday morning."

Dani couldn't swear that Avi took a breath at all during that whole speech. But he decided not to comment on it and just answered the question. "I'd love to. How's Tuesday?"

"Tuesday?" Avi repeated, and then there was another pause, but it was shorter. "I'm working in Government Center on Tuesday morning, so that would be perfect. Want to say twelve-thirty?"

"That works for me," Dani said. "I've got a meeting that ends at noon, but it shouldn't take me more than twenty minutes to get from my office to Milk Street. I'll call you if I'm running late."

"Great. I'll see you then."

"I look forward to it," Dani said. "Thanks for calling, Avi. And thanks again for the tour this afternoon."

"You're welcome. I'm glad you could join us."

"Maybe we could do it again some time."

"I'd like that," Avi said.

Dani tried to think of something else to say, because he didn't want to hang up yet, but then his door buzzer rang. "Ah—Avi? That's my doorbell. I've got to go. I look forward to seeing you Tuesday for lunch."

"As do I. Be well."

"Thanks. Bye." Dani hoped he didn't sound too abrupt, especially given how he had answered the phone; he wanted to throttle whoever was on the other side of the door, though of course the visitor had no way of knowing they were interrupting.

"Bye," Avi said, and they hung up.

Of course, when Dani went to the door, no one was there. Presumably it had been UPS buzzing to try to get a signature, because a package sat inside the vestibule. Dani sighed at the lost opportunity to talk to Avi, but he comforted himself with the thought that they'd have more time on Tuesday.

ON TUESDAY MORNING, DANI TOOK a little more time than usual choosing his clothes. He was aiming for something between his usual T-shirt and

jeans and an outfit that would make his coworkers think he was going to an interview. In the end, he went with a blue button-down and a pair of khakis, which had the advantage of being comfortable but still slightly fancier than his usual work clothes.

When his meeting ended sooner than scheduled, he hoped he could be early to meet Avi and thus not make Avi worry he was being stood up, but, true to form, he got caught in a subway delay and got to Downtown Crossing with just enough time to get to the restaurant without being late. He walked as fast down Washington Street as he could without running over tourists stopping to look at maps as they tried to find their way to the Freedom Trail. When he reached the corner of Washington and Milk, he kicked into a jog, knowing he was calling it close. As he passed the yarn shop next to the Old South Meeting House, he spotted Avi standing in front of the restaurant, wearing a dark blue button-down shirt, black pants, and loafers, reading something on his Kindle. His black messenger bag was hanging from his left shoulder, and as Dani watched he absently adjusted the strap.

"Hey, Avi!" Dani called out, and Avi looked up from his book. "Sorry if I'm a bit late. I had to wait forever for the Red Line."

"Actually," Avi said, pulling out a pocket watch, "you're right on time." He stuck his watch back into his pocket and his Kindle into the pocket of his bag and smiled at Dani. "So... have you ever been here before?"

"I've had their food at various work things, but I really didn't know they were kosher. That is, I figure they're kosher or you wouldn't have recommended them."

"They try to be subtle and attract clientele other than just the kosher-keepers. And I've seen people without *kippot* on their heads having business meetings here, so it seems to be working. Anyway, the food's good, so that's the place's main selling point."

Avi's voice wobbled; Dani was quickly learning that meant Avi was nervous, so he pulled open the door and gestured for Avi to precede him. After just a couple of minutes they were heading for a table.

"When you eat in one of the few kosher restaurants in town, the chance of running into an acquaintance is pretty high," Avi said, leading

Dani toward the back of the seating area, away from the door. "And ever since this place renovated and expanded their menu, I find that I run into people almost every time I come here."

The space was lit almost completely by natural light coming through the floor-to-ceiling windows that formed the outside wall of the restaurant. Even in the back corner, the space was well lit. Dani hoped he didn't spill any of his tomato soup on his shirt; he wasn't usually a clumsy eater, but he felt more self-conscious than usual. The salad he had on his tray was safer than the soup. Had Avi chosen a salad without soup for a similar reason?

"So," Dani said, "what is it that you're up to today? Do you frequently have jobs that take you to Government Center?"

"I go wherever the job is," Avi said. "I find myself travelling all over eastern Massachusetts, and some weeks I'm in Worcester one day, Dennis the next, and Lawrence on the third day. There aren't enough interpreters to fill all the jobs that people want us for, so we get gigs all over. During the school year, I have a relatively steady stream of business from the various colleges and universities, but during the summer and winter breaks, it's much more random."

Something else had piqued Dani's interest. "Do you always carry a pocket watch? It's kind of cool. I love pocket watches, but I know that if I wore one I would lose it within fifteen minutes." He hoped the question didn't sound like a non sequitur.

"The one I use was my grandfather's. He gave it to me when I graduated from college. At the time, I didn't know just how much use I'd get out of it. But I hate having a watch on while I'm signing—it distracts me, and that is very bad for an interpreter. So I started carrying a pocket watch, and now it's what I use exclusively."

"So, it's handsome and practical. That's just cool." Dani ate a couple more bites of his salad, hoping Avi would pick up the conversational thread, and he was pleased when Avi did so.

"My siblings liked meeting you on Sunday, as did Dalia," Avi said. "I seem to remember you mentioning a brother on the phone; do you have any other siblings?"

22

"No," Dani said with a smile. "I just have the one brother, Dudu… sorry, he prefers Dave these days. He's three years younger than me. When we were younger, we were really competitive. But now that we're older, we've actually become very close, much to our mother's surprise." Dani chuckled, then continued. "Actually, I had just gotten off the phone with him yesterday when you called."

"Oh?"

"Yeah. He'd just suggested that I call you to invite you out for coffee again, and I was about to dial your number when my phone rang. That's why I was a bit brusque when I first answered the phone—I didn't want to delay calling you because of some random caller."

"You were talking to your brother about me?" Avi asked, but his tone was more one of pleasure than of confusion.

"He's the one I go to when I need to talk something out, need to figure out how to approach a situation."

Avi smiled at that. "It sounds like he serves a similar role for you as the Gang does for me."

"'The Gang'?" Dani asked.

"Jake, Chava, and Dalia. I've called them the Gang of Three since I was in high school."

"So you and Dalia have been together for, what, fifteen years?" Dani hoped his disappointment didn't show on his face. If Avi and Dalia had been a thing since high school, there was no way Avi would be interested in anything Dani had to offer.

"Actually, longer. She joined our class in tenth grade, and I was one of the only people who could communicate with her without the interpreter. So she and I ended up becoming friends very quickly… and lab partners, and study partners, and so forth. We spent so much time together, it must have seemed to my parents like Dal had moved in. She's protective of me, for reasons I'm not totally clear on. She's the youngest of six, and the only girl in the family, so it might be that she liked having someone to boss around when we were younger; now it's just nice to know I always have someone in my corner. And she was a good friend to Chava, too, when we were younger. Chava was going through the awkwardness of

puberty compounded with her discomfort with being different because she's Deaf. Dalia became Chava's mentor in many ways, showing her how to turn her differences into strengths."

Dani nodded. "I can see how that would be valuable for both of them. But can I ask you something that's totally not my business?" Dani figured that if he had no chance, he might as well ask the obvious, if possibly offensive, question.

"Uh… sure. But I reserve the right not to answer."

"Perfectly reasonable," Dani said. "So why haven't the two of you gotten married yet? I thought Orthodox Jews married younger than most. Two *dati* people dating for over fifteen years but still single? Haven't your parents—or hers—pressured you?"

Avi smiled, and when he spoke, it was clear from his tone that he'd answered this more than once. "No, Dalia and I aren't dating, and we never have dated. Everyone seems to think we are, though, when they first meet her. It's just that—outside my immediate family—Dalia's probably the woman I'm most comfortable with, and most people interpret that as us having a romantic relationship. So if you're interested in her, I'm in no way an impediment."

Dan smiled back. "It's not Dalia that I'm interested in."

"Huh?"

Dani took a deep breath and then made his—possibly, no, probably, idiotic—pitch. "I may be completely wrong here, and you have every right to be offended if I am, but maybe you and I have enough in common to perhaps see where this might go—friendship or something more."

Staying completely silent, Avi blushed and looked down at the table.

Oh, shit.

Dani had come up with a list of don'ts for this lunch—don't blatantly ask Avi if he's straight; don't pressure him into anything; don't jump the gun.

And now he had violated all three of those in one breath.

"Avi? You okay?" Dani asked after a minute of silence.

"Yeah, just overwhelmed," Avi said, not looking up from the table. "I… I don't know what to say. I don't know what you want me to say."

"Tell me the truth. That's all I ever ask. If you're not interested, let me know. If you decide that you don't want to even maintain a friendship with me, I'll understand. Hell, it wouldn't be the first time I misread someone."

He sat waiting to find out just how quickly Avi would tell him to fuck off.

But Dani was in for a surprise.

"Okay," Avi said, looking Dani directly in the eye, "here's the truth. You didn't read me wrong, but you did."

At Dani's confused look, he continued. "Here's what I mean: yes, for the past year I've been trying to figure out what I'm really looking for, and more and more I realize what I'm looking for is a relationship with a man rather than with a woman. And the fact that there's a whole aspect of my religious background that complicates the dating-a-guy thing is another wrinkle I can't even begin to unpack for you at this point."

Dani's shoulders fell; he tried not to frown.

"But, and this is the key," Avi continued, "I have no experience, and I have no idea what, if anything, you might expect from me. And I don't want to be pressured or cajoled or wheedled into anything before I am ready. So if you're prepared for that, then fine—let's see where this goes. But if you're not ready to go at my speed, let's forget this conversation ever happened and just see if we can be friends." Almost immediately, his blush now deep red, Avi looked back down at the table.

How should I respond? Everything that came to mind sounded so clichéd. Dani wanted to tell Avi that he wouldn't rush him, that Avi could set the pace, that all he wanted was for Avi to be comfortable. But Avi had no reason to believe him, and Dani didn't want to just be spouting pretty words that Avi could dismiss.

Avi was clearly uncomfortable, though, and Dani was not at all happy that he'd caused most of it. He had to fix this, and fast, before this relationship was the shortest on record.

"Avi," Dani said softly. "Hey, look at me. It's all right."

Avi looked up, but still wouldn't meet Dani's eyes.

"I don't expect anything other than friendship. Honestly." And Dani was surprised to find that, despite his lust, he really meant it. If Avi and he ended up as just friends, that would be fine.

Avi opened his mouth, but nothing came out.

"That doesn't mean that I won't be thrilled if this builds to something more, but I'm not going to rush you."

Avi finally spoke. "Are you absolutely sure?"

"I can't promise I won't accidentally move too fast for you, but I will definitely slow down the minute you say so. Trust me, Avi. Pressuring you isn't on my agenda."

"That's good to hear, though the thought that you have an agenda is a bit frightening."

"I didn't mean it that way," Dani said. "I just meant that, well, I like you. A lot. And I'd like to see where this goes, if anywhere. So pressuring you would be counter-productive."

Avi smiled shyly at Dani. If Avi kept looking at him that way, Dani was going to have a real problem with the "slow, no pressure" thing. But he controlled himself, sparing a moment for the thought that Dudu would be proud.

"So where does that leave us?" Avi asked.

"I don't see that anything has to change. We can go for coffee, meet for the occasional meal, maybe do the occasional movie, walking tour, concert—things friends do together. And then see what happens. No rushing, no pressure, just us following our own path. Is that okay?"

"I think I can live with that."

They sat silently, and then Dani looked at his watch. "Oh, shit. I've got to go; I'm meeting with my boss at two-thirty and I am completely unprepared." He grabbed his backpack as he stood up.

"Well," Avi said once they were outside. "Thanks again for meeting me for lunch." He blushed. "And thanks for what you said. I really am interested; I just don't know what I'm doing."

"That's okay. We'll figure this out as we go along."

Avi reached out with his right hand, as if to shake Dani's hand.

"Hmm," Dani said with a smile, holding Avi's outstretched hand loosely, "is there something in your universe between a handshake and a hug? 'Cause I think we've moved beyond one but not quite to the other."

Avi half-smiled at Dani. "I'm really not sure."

"Eh," Dani said, "we'll improvise." He tugged lightly on the hand he was holding, and Avi walked a couple paces toward him. Dani put his arm around Avi's shoulders and squeezed lightly.

"Improvisation," Avi said. "I can live with that."

After a final squeeze, Dani let Avi go. If he stayed any longer, he was going to miss his meeting. They walked to the corner of Washington Street, where they had to go in opposite directions.

"Have a good rest of the day, Avi. I'll call you tonight and find out how it went."

"I look forward to it."

Dani turned left toward the T while Avi headed toward the courthouse. Already Dani was planning their next get-together. It had to be somewhere public, so Avi wasn't spooked, but cozy, where they could talk.

Eh, Dani figured, he could always improvise.

chance encounters of the stressful kind

Two weeks later, when Dani's phone rang at nine a.m. on the first Sunday morning in almost a month when he could sleep late, he considered ignoring it. But he *was* awake, even if he was still in bed; he should get up sometime. He grabbed his phone and glasses from the bedside table.

"Hang on, hang on," he mumbled as he put on his glasses and hit the green button to answer. "Hello?"

"Dan? It's Avi; I hope I'm not calling too early."

"No, no worries," Dani answered, sitting up. It wasn't like Avi to call unexpectedly. "Is everything okay?"

"Everything's fine; thanks for asking. I've got some errands to run, and I know you've been crazy busy for the past couple of weeks, so I don't want to impose or make you rearrange your schedule, but I was wondering if you were interested in meeting me for coffee or lunch or something. You could even run errands with me, if you felt like it, though now that I'm saying it, that sounds like a ridiculous idea."

"Avi, relax. Breathe. I'd love to run errands with you." Dani was surprised to find that it was true. He usually hated the idea of running errands, but, perhaps because they weren't *his* errands and they entailed time spent hanging out with Avi, spending the better part of the day going

in and out of stores actually sounded like fun. "What are the errands you're planning to do?"

"Well, I've got to pick up some sheet music from Rafi, so we could get coffee near there if you felt like it, but I also need to go the Israel Book Shop and return a set of *tzitzit* that don't fit, so maybe if you were with me we could go get lunch, if you felt like schlepping out to Brookline today. Not that you have to. Schlep out, I mean. If you wanted to just stay in Cambridge."

Dani took a brief moment to imagine what Avi looked like wearing just the four-cornered, fringed prayer shawl that was usually hidden under his shirt. He shook his head to clear it and then said, "Avi, I want to spend the day with you. I'm happy to pick up the sheet music and have coffee and then do your exchange at the book shop and eat lunch. I didn't have any real plans for today, so I'm glad you are suggesting some. What sort of timing are you thinking of?"

"Well," Avi said, "I just got back from *Shacharit*, so, while I've got my morning prayers out of the way, I'll need about twenty minutes to have breakfast and get some caffeine into my system so that I'm not a complete bear, and then I'll drive to Cambridge. So figure an hour total, in case I'm slow or there's traffic?"

"Perfect. That will give me a chance to get up and dressed and organized for a day of errands."

"I *did* call too early; I'm sorry," Avi said, interrupting Dani's train of thought.

"No, not at all. I was awake; I just hadn't gotten up yet. So, yeah. The time it will take you to get ready will be just enough for me to shower and dress and have breakfast. Let's say ten thirty in front of Pandemonium?"

"It's a good thing I'll be driving and not on foot," Avi said. "Between Pandemonium and Rodney's Bookstore that block is kind of a dangerous place for me; I tend to come home with books I had no idea I wanted."

"Same. Would you rather we meet somewhere else?"

"No, in front of Pandemonium is fine." Avi chuckled. "It's not like I'd be able to find parking today. But we'll have to do the bookstores another time, though I have to warn you that I get quite absorbed. Actually, that

might be a valid warning for the errand at the Israel Book Shop, just so you know."

"Consider me warned. I'm easily absorbed there, too—so many books, so little time, as the T-shirt says."

"Excellent," Avi said. "So I'll see you in about an hour in Central."

"I'm looking forward to it."

They said their goodbyes, and then Dani perched on the edge of his bed trying to decide what to wear. He wanted something that was comfortable for walking around but not as *schlump*-y as his usual running-errands clothes. He finally settled on a pair of blue cargo shorts and a blue and green striped polo shirt, plus his Tevas. Perfect for running errands or having coffee with one's boyfriend-of-sorts.

As he showered, Dani considered the day to come. Coffee and errands and lunch with Avi seemed like a great way to spend a Sunday: low stress, no explicit expectations, just what they needed to get to know each other better. What could be more perfect?

"AND THEN HE SAID—OH, HANG on."

"That seems like a really odd thing for Moshe to say, honestly."

"No, you goof," Avi said, waving to someone. "The car that just honked at us, the driver is my mom. She's pulling into the parking spot right in front of the Book Shop; I've got to go say hi."

Well, Dani thought, *so much for simple and stress-free*. He had rarely met the parents of anyone he was dating, and never this early in a relationship, but he could understand why Avi couldn't just keep going as if he hadn't seen his mother. Dani had to walk a bit faster to keep up with Avi's long-legged stride, but soon he found himself standing next to Avi as a man and woman in their mid-sixties climbed out of a sporty silver Toyota.

"Dan, these are my parents; Ima, Abba, this is Dan Perez." Dani heard a slight hesitance in Avi's voice that he had already learned to associate with nervousness.

"Nice to meet you," Avi's father said. "Call me Yoni." Looking at Yoni, Dani knew where Avi got his height. Yoni was an inch taller than Dani,

but their height was where the similarity between Yoni and Avi ended. Yoni had red hair, a short-cropped red beard, and brown eyes.

Avi's coloring he got from his mother. She had the same light brown hair, from what Dani could see of it wisping out from her headscarf. Her eyes were the same shade of greenish-blue as Avi's. However, she was only a bit more than five feet tall; she had to stand on her tiptoes to give Avi a kiss on his cheek.

"And I'm Ilana," she said. "Though Avi would probably tell you to just call us Ima and Abba."

"Well, when I was in high school, it felt weird to introduce my parents as Yoni and Ilana, but 'Mr. and Mrs. Levine' felt just as weird. So I figured I'd say they were my Ima and Abba and leave it up to them to tell my friends what to call them. They didn't take the bait, though, so a huge number of my high school and college friends call my parents Ima and Abba."

"Makes sense to me," Dani said. "I'm Daniel to my parents when they're annoyed at me, but most people call me Dan or Dani."

"So, what brings you to this part of Harvard Street on a Sunday afternoon that you could be spending at the Arboretum?" Avi asked, and to Dani he sounded a bit less tense.

"Your father needs a book for his class that he says can only be found here, and I figured I'd poke at the history books and see if there's anything I can incorporate into eleventh-grade European history to give the kids a bit more of a rounded perspective."

"My mom teaches history at Brookline High and my dad is a constitutional law professor at Boston University," Avi said.

"And what is it that you do?" Ilana asked Dani.

"I'm a software developer at a company in Cambridge," Dani responded.

"And how do you and Avi know each other?" Yoni asked.

"Through Rafi Weiss," Dani said. "Rafi and I used to work together, and—"

"And Dan was with Rafi a couple of weeks ago and left his sunglasses at the Harvard Hillel. I picked them up and made sure that they got back to Dan," Avi said, and that nervous tone was back.

"Oh, wait," Yoni said. "Chava mentioned having met some friend of Rafi's recently. Was that you?"

"Yeah, that was me. I went on a walking tour with her and Ya'akov and Dalia that Avi was interpreting. It was fun, but next time I go on a walking tour I should consider the weather. It had to have been the most humid day so far, and I was guzzling water like you wouldn't believe."

"This summer's been brutal, hasn't it?" Yoni said.

"I'm going to remind you of this in January when you're complaining about the cold and wishing it was summer," Ilana responded, and it was clear to Dani that this was a conversation they'd had many times.

"Anyway," Avi said, interrupting his parents' good-natured squabbling and gesturing at the bag he carried, "I'm going to go and exchange these tzitzit for ones that fit better."

"Do they even sell ones your size?" Ilana asked.

"The *beged* doesn't reach all the way down to my waist, but it's better than nothing, and the tzitzit themselves hang down long enough not to be awkward. I call that as good a win as possible without special-ordering custom-made tzitzit."

"Makes sense to me," Ilana said. "Though how I ended up with such tall boys, I'll never know; your father promised me children who would fall between his height and mine."

"You fed and watered us on schedule and used appropriate fertilizer," Avi said, and again it was clear to Dani that this was an old conversation. "I love you, Ima. Love you, Abba. I'll probably FaceTime with Chava this evening, so I'll talk to you if you're around."

"Okay, we'll talk to you later. It was nice to meet you, Dani."

"Nice to meet you, too." He shook Yoni's hand and began to offer his hand to shake Ilana's as well but then remembered that it might make her uncomfortable if she was *shomeret negiah* and didn't touch men outside her immediate family. But he didn't want to insult her by *not* shaking her hand, so he stood there awkwardly with his hand half extended. He was glad when Ilana took his hand and shook it.

"Maybe we'll see you again soon," she said.

"I hope so." Dani replied.

Avi went into the Book Shop and Dani followed mindlessly, mulling over the interaction with Avi's parents. He stood next to Avi at the sales counter as Avi and the sales clerk—whose name apparently was Lilach, and whom Avi had apparently known since at least high school, given the way she was teasing him—discussed the tzitzit that Avi needed to exchange. When Lilach headed to the back, Dani shook himself out of his thoughts long enough to ask Avi, "How'd you end up with the wrong size in the first place?"

"Chava picked them up for me, and even though she had a note telling her what to get, she still managed to walk out of here with the medium rather than the extra tall," Avi said. "And there's no way a medium is going to fit me."

"You sure it was Chava who made the mistake and not whoever sold her the tzitzit in the first place? Because, you know, it would be hard to miss that you're, what, six foot four?" Dani didn't want to say, *Because Chava is deaf and might not have been understood,* but that was what he was thinking.

"Six-five, actually, and Chava told me she didn't check the label, just pulled the one from the lowest shelf, where she assumed the extra talls would be."

"Ah, thus reinforcing my philosophy of 'never send your sibling to shop for you without explicit instructions.'"

"Yeah, I was desperate and didn't have much of a choice." Avi shook his head. "It was a week of rehearsals and all-day interpreting gigs and shredded tzitit... it wasn't pretty. And she *had* explicit instructions, or so I thought."

"Should I even ask how your tzitzit got shredded?'"

"It was a horrible subway train door accident combined with an already kind of old set. It's also why I'm so *m'dakdek* about tucking them into my pants now."

Dani's mind wandered as Avi talked about the fringes he apparently now was very careful to have running down the inside of his pants legs rather than hanging out. He was grateful that he didn't have to respond immediately when Lilach came back with three sets of tzitit for Avi to

look at. He left Avi to his decision making and wandered around the store, noting the variety of books available. He tended to think of all Jewish bookstores as being pitched at Orthodox people only, so it surprised him to find Conservative and Reform books shelved side-by-side with the traditional texts and a whole section devoted to weddings, which included books on framing same-sex marriages within a Jewish context.

After a few minutes he wandered to the register and was pleased to find that Avi was finishing his transaction.

"Find anything interesting?" Avi asked.

"Actually, yes. I'm going to have to come back and poke around when I have more time."

"We'll add it to our list of bookstores to visit on a day when we have lots of time and expendable cash reserves," Avi said, smiling.

"Sounds like a plan," Dani responded. As they walked out of the store, he asked, "So, lunch?"

"*Yes*. Shopping always makes me hungry. Is Chinese okay? I've been in the mood for scallion pancake for days."

"Chinese sounds good."

He let Avi lead him across the street to the block of kosher restaurants and then waited until they were seated and Avi was looking at the menu before he asked the question that had been on his mind for the past half hour.

"You're not out to your parents, are you?" he asked very quietly. He looked briefly at the ten other tables in the restaurant; he could see all of them from his vantage point, and, while none of the other patrons seemed to be paying any attention, Dani didn't want to say anything too loudly.

Avi sat up ramrod straight, took a swift glance around the restaurant, and then whispered, "Not yet. I keep trying, but it's such a difficult conversation, and I truly don't know how they will react."

"How explicit have you been?"

"Not too explicit. For one thing, I'm only now being particularly explicit with *myself* about what I want," Avi said, blushing. "And my parents… we haven't really talked about sex since I was in high school.

So the idea of starting that conversation is terrifying in itself, and then the possibility that they'll hate me for it… I just—"

"I understand," Dani said, sorry that he had started this line of conversation. "I really do. I know I'm one of the lucky ones because my parents were completely accepting. And we didn't have the *halachic* implications hanging over us."

"Oh, don't even remind me of that. I haven't even *started* figuring out my counter-arguments if they start down the road of what the Torah says about forbidden relationships." Avi ran his hand over his hair, knocking his kippah slightly askew. "I still have no clue what I will say if—when— they start quoting me chapter and verse."

"Maybe they'll take it better than you are anticipating."

"Maybe," Avi said, though his tone indicated that he wasn't particularly optimistic.

"No matter what happens when you talk to them, whenever that is, call me after, okay?" Dani hoped it would be sooner rather than later, but he wasn't going to push. He hated being someone's dirty secret, though he knew—or, at least, he thought he knew—that Avi would never think of him that way.

"I shall. And thank you."

"Anyway," Dani said, finally looking at the menu, "enough serious conversation for now. What's good here?"

"I've never ordered anything here I haven't liked," Avi answered, settling more comfortably into his chair.

"So order a couple of your favorites," Dani said, gesturing for the waitress, "and I'll follow your lead."

Tefilah: God, Open My Lips

Are you there, God? It's me, Avi.

Forgive me; that was overly glib. That will be just another thing I have to atone for on Yom Kippur. But this is new to me, so please, Hashem, bear with me.

I've known my whole life that I could add a request, a bakasha, *in the* Shmoneh Esrei *as a personal prayer. But I've never really done it, not this way. Not for something like this.*

And I'm torn. Because I'm balancing one of Your mitzvot *against another one. I learned "Honor your father and your mother" from the time I was tiny. It's so important that You put it in the* Asseret HaDibrot, *as the bridge between the commandments that are about issues between people and God and the ones that are between two people.*

But my heart guides me in a way that many would say goes against Your will. I do not believe that. I do not believe that You would make me in Your image and create me in such a way that I have physical and emotional attraction to men but then declare what I feel an abomination.

That is not the Hashem I was taught to love. That is not the God of my ancestors, Abraham, Isaac, and Jacob.

So I hope You will help me find my way.

I am discovering more about myself every day. My parents have always been there in the past to guide me through my confusion. But this... this confuses me but would confuse—and possibly anger—them even more.

My mother is driven by another of your mitzvot: *"P'ru ur'vu"—be fruitful and multiply. She wants me to marry. To settle down. To have children. I want to do all of those things, too. But while she has an image of my future* wife, *I have a vision of my future* husband. *She tries to make a* shidduch, *she tries to set me up with girls she thinks I'll get along well with. And she's right; we invariably do. I've ended up with a number of friends because my mother wants me to meet a nice girl. There just isn't a spark. There's no physical attraction.*

But how do I tell her? How do I tell them both?

In the old days, this sometimes caused parents to sit shiva for their children, mourn for them as if they were dead. Parents would live the rest of their lives as if their child was *actually dead. I cannot picture my parents reacting that way. But I am afraid I will hurt them.*

Please help me find a way to talk to my parents. And please allow us to keep our relationship intact. Hashem, s'fatai tiftach ufi yagid tehillatecha; open my mouth that I may declare your praise.

a time of innocence, a time of confidences

It all started so simply.

"Hey, Avi," Dani said, "let's stay in and watch a movie next Tuesday night."

Since Avi had been on BU's campus all day, Dani figured he'd be on board with this plan. The first few weeks of the school year had been extremely busy for him, and they were just leaving a concert at the Paradise, blocks from where Avi had been working.

"Oh, that sounds like heaven," Avi said. "How's this? I've got a gig in Brookline, and I can pick up stuff to make dinner. You can meet me at my place, and we can watch something on Netflix."

"Would you be willing to bring dinner instead and come to my place?" Dani asked. "I've got a ton of DVDs, and that would give you an opportunity to see where I live. One of these days, I'll have to figure out a way that I can cook for you."

"Some Sunday, when we have lots of time, I can teach you how to make food that I can eat. The *kashrut* stuff can be tricky, but it's not impossible. For Tuesday, though, either I'll make something or pick up takeout."

"Works for me."

✡

AFTER WORK ON TUESDAY, DANI went back to his apartment. He showered and changed into a soft red short-sleeved polo shirt and jeans, then neatened his apartment. After all, it was the first time that Avi was visiting and, while he didn't figure Avi would mind the bit of clutter—mostly unshelved books—around his living room, he did want to wash the dishes in the sink and put away the ones in the dishwasher. He was just finishing when Avi called.

"Okay, they're finishing our order now, so figure I'll be there in about half an hour, provided the traffic isn't against me."

"Excellent. I'll see you then," Dani said. It took some time to find the paper goods he had stashed, and he had just finished setting the table when the buzzer sounded.

"Who is it?" He figured it had to be Avi, but since Lockdown Friday after the marathon bombings, Dani had become more security conscious.

"It's Avi."

Dani pushed the button to unlock the downstairs door. A couple of minutes later, Avi knocked on the apartment door, and Dani let him in. Dani figured he hadn't wasted any time before ordering dinner, because he was still wearing what Dani had come to think of as Avi's interpreting uniform: a dark shirt, dark or neutral pants, and dress shoes.

"Hey, Avi," Dani said. "It's good to see you." He led Avi to the kitchen and gestured for him to put the bag of takeout on the table. As soon as it was down, he pulled Avi into a hug. Avi seemed startled, but then he reciprocated, wrapping his arms around Dani and holding him for a few seconds.

When they pulled back, Dani said, "I'm sorry, Avi. That was a bit more than you were probably expecting."

"Well, yes," Avi said, "but it wasn't at all unwelcome." He paused and then asked, "Rough day?"

"Long day. Too many bugs and not enough days left before the release to fix them all and get them tested. Project management is asking for an extension, but we've already asked for one, so who knows what the answer will be."

"You sure you want company? I'm happy to leave you dinner and head home if you'd rather."

"No, Avi. I'd rather have dinner, watch something, and enjoy the evening with you."

"If you're sure…"

"I'm positive," Dani said, taking the containers of food out of the bag. "Now, I've got the table all set with paper plates and cups and plastic forks and stuff. It's a clean tablecloth and we can use paper napkins. I bought new drinks that I haven't opened, though I'm not even sure that's something you needed me to do—"

"Dan, relax. I'll be able to eat and drink. It's all good." Avi brushed Dani's hand with his fingertips, and while it was an innocent touch, Dani recognized it for the intimate gesture it was meant to be. "I tell you, people who don't keep kosher spend more time stressing about how they can feed those of us who *do* keep kosher. I do appreciate it, Dan. I truly do. But I don't want to be yet another thing that causes you stress. I'd much rather be the one in charge of food instead of making you worry about how you're going to feed me."

Dani stood and stared at Avi and then said, "That may be the most I've heard you say all in one breath since our first lunch when I asked whether I was misreading you."

"I… I have opinions that I usually keep to myself, I guess. But when people make assumptions about me, I can't let the assumptions stand when they're dead wrong."

"If they're only sort of wrong, though, you let them keep assuming?" Dani asked, and even as he asked he wasn't sure whether he meant it as a serious question or a way to defuse the situation.

Avi looked thoughtful and then said, "If they're only sort of wrong, it depends on how much energy I want to expend." He picked up two food containers and moved to the table while Dani got another couple of containers.

"Have a seat," Dani said when he came out of the kitchen and found Avi still standing by the table.

"I didn't want to sit where you usually do, and I couldn't figure out…"

"Sit anywhere," Dani said with a smile. "I'm not at all picky about where I sit. When I got my first place I had only one chair, so that was where I sat, but I'd move it around the table if I wanted to. Once I had a couple more chairs, it made things more complicated because then I had to actually decide where I wanted to sit instead of just sitting wherever the chair happened to be." He gestured at the chair to Avi's right. "C'mon. Have a seat."

They were quiet while scooping the Chinese food onto their plates, with the exception of the occasional "Pass the rice, please," and "Oh, this looks good." Once they were settled and eating, however, Dani reopened the earlier conversation.

"So, you don't need to correct people's misapprehensions of you?"

"I've never found it necessary for everyone to understand me. In fact, more often than not I've found that people don't understand me and are mostly unwilling to try. So I just let them believe what they want to believe, unless it hurts me or someone I love." Avi ate a couple more bites and then said, "I've always been different. I'm an Orthodox Jew. I'm unusually tall. I'm a strictly observant *frum* gay man. I don't fit into any standard box, and that makes people uncomfortable. In high school I thought it was on me to fit in, to change myself to fit people's expectations. Then, in college, I thought it was on me to change people's perceptions, to make *them* change. But it's *exhausting*, trying to make everyone change. So, people can believe what they believe. As long as it doesn't cause me or my loved ones harm, what do I care?"

Dani chewed his mouthful of food slowly. He didn't really know how to respond, but he thought he should say *something*. Avi had clearly been through a lot of self-evaluation and knew his own mind.

"Okay, I can understand that," Dani said. "I just get really frustrated by people making up their own ideas about me, about what I believe, about who I am. So my instinct is to dispel any myths or misinformation that people have."

"Don't you get tired, tilting at windmills? Trying to combat the world's ignorance one person at a time?"

"It's *tikkun olam*, Avi. We strive to repair the world. Sometimes we can do it by affecting many people at once. But sometimes we have to take on the task one person at a time." He paused. "This, though, wasn't the conversation I was hoping to have tonight. It's too weighty a subject for a night intended for relaxation and the consumption of light entertainment."

"I'm sorry. I didn't mean to ruin the spirit of the evening."

"You didn't ruin anything, Avi," Dani said, hoping his tone was reassuring. "I'm very glad we can have this sort of conversation. I just thought we both could use an evening of less-weighty subjects."

"I appreciate that. But at the same time you're right—it's very nice that we can have this sort of conversation. So maybe we should put a bookmark in it here, watch our movie, and then maybe pick up the conversational thread if we're still feeling up to it?"

"That sounds like an excellent plan," Dani said. "Now, to the matter of a movie."

They took some time to look through Dani's collection of DVDs, debating the various merits and demerits of the movies that caught their eyes. They finally settled on *The Breakfast Club* and settled on the sofa to watch.

About ten minutes into the movie, Avi said, "As much as I have always loved this movie, it never spoke to my high school experience. Even when I watched it as a high school student, it didn't resonate with me."

"At all?" Dani asked, pausing the film.

"The archetypes spoke to me. But the trappings themselves, the high school setting, it was so divergent from my high school experience."

"What do you mean?"

"Well, first of all, we didn't do detention. And especially not on Saturday. So, fundamentally, the plot of the movie hinged on a situation that was foreign to me."

"Okay, but still the relationships…"

"Weren't like relationships I saw in my school. I mean, I went to a coed school, so there were girls in my classes, and I had friends who were girls, but only after high school, when I could see the characters

as archetypes and not just as the characters themselves, could I map my experiences to any part of the movie."

"But, I mean, all high schools, seemingly, have these people," Dani said. "Didn't you have the brain, the athlete, the criminal?"

"The brain, sure. Many of us were the brain. We had basketball teams, one girls' varsity and one boys' varsity, so we had the athlete. But the criminal? Not really. Well, we probably did, but nothing was known, just like I couldn't honestly tell you if there were any gay kids in my school. There likely were. Hell, I *know* there was a gay population there because *I* was there, though I didn't have a name for why I didn't fit in. But most of the rest of it? Completely foreign."

"Hang on," Dani said. "When did you first realize… I mean, I've known I wasn't interested in girls since I was about fourteen, though I didn't think about what that meant until later in high school."

"You came out at fourteen?"

"I wouldn't say I came out then. Not by a long shot. I just knew that all of the guys were obsessed with the bodies of the girls in our class, and I was more interested in staring at Shuki, who sat three desks away from me."

"When I was fourteen, I was completely flummoxed by the fact that my male friends were lusting after the girls in our class. I couldn't think of the girls that way; they were my friends, and the idea of kissing them was like the idea of kissing Chava. Later in high school, I began to dream about kissing the boys instead of the girls, but I suppressed those feelings as much as possible. In college, well, in college I was in serious denial. I dated a bunch of girls, but obviously nothing came of that. And then I faced the reality of who I am, accepted it, and now I'm here."

"You kind of glossed over a lot there," Dani said.

"Well, they're not my stories to tell. Not completely, at least."

"Can I ask some questions, and you answer what you're comfortable with and tell me if you're uncomfortable?"

"We can try that," Avi said. "I'm not deliberately holding back; it's just not something I'm used to talking about."

Dani turned off the movie and settled into the sofa. "So, you dated girls in high school?"

"I went to a very rigorous high school. There were two patterns: either you dated within the community or you didn't date until college. I dated a bit within the community, but it was not dating like anyone outside the frum community would define dating. I mean, I took girls to the movies, to concerts, to dinner, whatever, but it was so innocent. We all were either *shomer negiah*, and therefore wouldn't touch each other in a sexual way before marriage, or were too sheltered to know what a mainstream date was like."

"Not every teenager is sexually active," Dani said.

"True, not every. But many. Not in the community I grew up in, not in the community that I still live in, but your average mainstream American teenager? Most of them have at least experimented beyond the point I have even now that I'm thirty-three years old."

"Okay, so you went out with girls in high school. I presume you continued in college?"

"Yeah," Avi said. He sat in silence and then stood up. "I need some water." He walked to the kitchen table, picked up his water, and on his way back to the living room asked, "Should I bring yours as well?"

"Sure, that would be great. Thanks so much."

He watched Avi turn around and then he listened as Avi took both water glasses into the kitchen to refill them. The sound of running water was relaxing. It also gave Dani some white noise to cover the sound as he released frustration with a semi-growl. Avi was harder to get to talk than some of the Army lifers he knew through his reserve duty.

When Avi came back, he handed Dani his glass and sat on the couch. "Thanks. I just was getting parched."

"No, it's fine. And I'm sorry if you feel like I'm interrogating you."

"Maybe a little bit." Avi sighed. "It's just… I get asked about my dating history a lot, and I've never found a good way to talk about it. It's been especially hard recently, since I realized just *why* I hadn't ever found 'the right girl' and that what I was feeling was not going to get me

in trouble with the *beit din*." Avi paused and then said, "Well, as long as no one tells them."

"Would the beit din really punish you for being gay?" From what Dani knew, the religious courts didn't get involved in people's day-to-day lives unless they were potential converts to Judaism or they were party to some matter that had come before the court.

"Not for *being* gay, but maybe for acting on it. Though for them to find out I would have to tell them about it, which I would have no reason to do, and they would likely need witnesses to my gay acts, so it's highly unlikely that they'd actually… Oh, never mind. It was a ridiculous line of thought, mostly brought on by bad dreams. The only contact I've ever had with the beit din was as an interpreter."

Dani decided not to pursue it further, though he was simultaneously fascinated and horrified by the idea of modern religious courts imposing punishment for someone being gay. So he tried another tack. "You get asked a lot about your dating history?"

"Oh, yeah. I'm thirty-three, frum, and unmarried. Everyone wants to know what might be wrong with me that I'm not even in a serious relationship. So they subtly—or not so subtly—ask who I've dated before, what kind of woman I'm looking for, where I've tried to meet people, all that. Some of them have even tried to ask for specifics on my actual sexual history, not that it is any of their business."

Dani considered his next words carefully. His relationship with Avi was new enough that he didn't have a clue as to whether there would be serious potholes in his next avenue of inquiry, and he really didn't want this to be a conversation that ended Avi's desire to be with him. Just the opposite—if Dani navigated this successfully, he and Avi might have a chance at a path toward a deeper relationship.

Boy, that was a lot of travel metaphors all at once, Dani thought, internally laughing at himself.

"What?" Avi asked.

"'What, what?" Dani replied.

"You had a slight smile that really didn't match the tenor of my last statement, unless you find people being nosy about my sex life amusing."

"No, I just had a thought that didn't in itself amuse me, but that made me think of something else that was humorous. I'm sorry; nosy people poking into your love life is not at all funny. I should know because I have been through a similar thing."

"It sucks, doesn't it?"

"Very much. Especially when the people in question claim—Hell, believe—they're doing it for your own good out of the goodness of their hearts."

"'Everyone has a *bashert*,' they say. But I have to tell you—even if I believe that everyone has a destined mate, which I'm not one hundred percent sure I do, I can't believe that some person who barely knows me will be the one who knows who my bashert might be." Avi shook his head. "*If* we each have a destined mate, I can guarantee you that the person who will introduce me to him will be someone I know and love, not someone who doesn't know me."

"And what do you say when they ask?"

"What do I say to the prying busybodies? I find the nicest way possible to tell them to go fuck themselves, if you will excuse the language." Avi huffed out a breath and rubbed his hands over his face.

"I think that's the first time I've ever heard you swear," Dani said.

"I tend not to swear unless the situation deserves it; overuse of expletives takes the power away from the words. But people who butt into my personal life, into my *sex* life, and think they deserve to know? They deserve nothing but my contempt."

"And what would you answer if *I* asked?" Dani asked, knowing he was approaching dangerous territory. "Hypothetically, that is."

"It would depend on how and why you were asking. If you were asking so that you and I can find a baseline where we are both comfortable so that we can figure out what this relationship is going to be, then I can't say that I would be comfortable, but I would answer as honestly as I can. If you were asking because you want to pressure me to go beyond where I am comfortable, I'd tell you to go to Hell." Avi stood up and started to pace between the sofa and the wall-mounted television. "When we've been dating a while, which, you know, we haven't really talked about. Are we

even dating? If we're not, my sexual experience, or lack thereof, is none of your damn business. If we are, then it does become your business when we decide that it's time for us to move forward in our relationship. But if you are asking solely out of prurient interest, then forget it." Avi was almost out of breath at the end and, while he stopped pacing, he stood next to the armchair rather than sitting next to Dani.

Dani took a deep breath and let it out slowly. "Wow. That's… that's a lot to unpack. Let's take this apart slowly." He patted the cushion next to where he was sitting. "Come on back, if you want. I'm fine if you don't, if you'd rather stand over there. But if we're going to have this conversation I'd rather have you sitting next to me."

Avi seemed to weigh his options carefully, but then he walked back to the sofa and sat next to Dani, though not as close as he had been. Dani itched to take Avi's hand, but he didn't want to disrupt the fragile calm.

"All right," Dani said. "First, the conversation that maybe should have happened—no, that definitely should have happened already. In my mind, yes, we are dating. Whether you want to put more labels on it, whether you want to call yourself my boyfriend, that's up to you. But I definitely consider us to be dating. I've been thinking of you as my boyfriend for a while now, and I know Dudu thinks of you as my boyfriend."

"Dudu? You've told your brother that you and I are dating?"

"I have; I hope that's okay."

"I… I just don't… I've mentioned you to the Gang of Three since the walking tour, but only briefly. I guess it would be okay with you if I tell them we're dating?"

"It definitely would. And I'm sorry if you have been feeling at loose ends, like we hadn't defined our relationship and therefore you were hanging in the balance with me. That was never my intention."

Avi nodded at that, so Dani continued.

"My interests in your relationship history—and, mind you, it's in your relationship history much more than in your sexual history—is *because* you and I are dating. I don't want to make you uncomfortable; at the same time, I don't want you to feel like I'm holding back either. So we have to, for lack of better terminology, determine a relationship baseline."

"It's going to be a very rudimentary baseline," Avi said.

"This isn't about rudimentary or sophisticated, Avi. It's just about us, about what we—*each* of us, *both* of us—are comfortable with."

Avi was silent, and Dani struggled not to fidget. "You're saying all the right things. I like everything you are saying. But… I have to admit to being nervous. I'm putting a lot on the line here." Dani started to speak, but Avi raised his hand to stop him. "I'm not saying you aren't doing the same. But you've got experience that I don't. I'm a child compared to you when it comes to sexual experience. Forget sex, when it comes to *romantic* experience. I'll tell you about my background, but you have to be aware that it will seem so innocent. And I know it's not a competition, but there's I worry you are going to give up on me when I prove—and I know I will—to not be ready for whatever you want from me."

"Please don't sell me short," Dani said. "Please have more faith in me, have more trust in what we could have together. Trust that I will listen to you, respect your boundaries." He reached out then, finally giving in and taking Avi's hand. "I'm going to screw up. I know that. I'm sometimes impulsive, and I'm not always rational about things that are important to me. But if we can talk about things, then we can find a path that suits us both." *Again with the travel metaphors*, Dani thought, suppressing the same smile that had almost gotten him in trouble earlier.

"I can try, but that's the best I can offer," Avi said. "This is all foreign to me. Not just the intimacy itself—and, yes, I'll give you the five-minute explanation of my dating history—but the whole concept." He adjusted his kippah two or three times, which Dani had come to recognize as a nervous tic, and sighed. "I want to tell you. I really do. I just… I'm just not sure I have the appropriate vocabulary. And part of me is worried you'll think I'm too much of a lost cause and you'll want to find someone else. I *like* you, Dan. A lot. More than might be good for me. But I'm scared, too."

"I understand, Avi. You and I are still getting to know each other. I see this conversation, and the ones that I hope will follow it, as yet another way to learn about each other. There's not going to be a quiz, there isn't anything you need to memorize, it's not an intellectual pursuit. It's about

us, about what we want to have together. And that's all that should matter. Trust me when I say I sympathize that it is scary to change the way you think about yourself, how you see yourself. But also please trust me when I say that if we make this work, it could be wonderful."

Dani paused, hoping he hadn't just completely messed up. This whole thing, this *relationship*, now that he was definitely calling it that, was full of potential pitfalls, and just when he thought he'd navigated the worst of it, it got scarier. But he still felt the same as he had in that first conversation with Dudu about Avi—this could be the best thing that ever happened in his life.

"I want to make this work," Avi said. "And I'm not deliberately holding back. I'm just really not used to talking about this. I've had thirty-three years' experience with *not* talking about my sexuality and sexual experiences and only a couple of months' experience actually talking about anything related to it." Dani started to interrupt, but Avi must have seen his startled expression and said, "I don't mean my parents never talked to me about sex or that they kept their sex lives completely secret. After all, I have two younger siblings, so I knew where babies came from when I was pretty young. But we talked about my generation's sexuality in purely hypothetical terms. I wasn't having sex in high school; I wasn't even having sex in college. I've *kissed* a total of three girls in my life, the only women I've ever seen naked were my sister and her friends and that was totally by accident and *completely* horrifying, and I only began to realize in the past year or so why it is that I find the thought of girls' nudity so off-putting now as I did when we were kids. I thought I had never grown out of my 'girls are icky' stage, but it's only recently that I realized that I never had the opportunity to have an 'oh, dear God, guys are really hot' stage.

"I've never felt the things I feel when you and I are together, and I don't have words for those feelings, which totally terrifies me. And you, with your gorgeous face and your amazing body, totally terrify me, but in a good way, I think. But I don't know what to do with any of those feelings, and—I'm doing it again, rambling on and getting myself all spun up."

"Avi, relax. Take a deep breath and listen to me. I told you this at our first lunch, and I'll tell you as many times as you need to hear it. I will not rush you, I will not ask more from you than you are ready for. At least, not intentionally. I can't promise that I won't accidentally move faster than you're expecting. But if I do, *please* tell me. We should be able to talk about everything and anything that is important to us. And the unimportant things, too."

"I'll try. That's the best I can promise."

"That's all I ask."

Avi flipped his hand over within Dani's grip and squeezed gently. "Thank you."

Dani squeezed back, feeling the tension in Avi's body begin to relax. It was a start.

Tefilah: Create for Me a Pure Heart

In these, the earliest hours of the day after Yom Kippur, please, Hashem, hear my request.

My heart is torn. I am caught between love of You and Your mitzvot and love of myself. Love of myself and love of my family. Love of my family and, perhaps, the possibility of love for another man.

I know. It's too early for me to call any feelings I have for Dani anything other than friendship. And I know that from the perspective of halacha, *of Your laws, there is no sin involved in thoughts, in feelings.*

But what if those thoughts, those feelings, cause others pain? What if by my actions, or at least by my consideration of future actions, I am causing pain to another person.

To my parents? To my family?

I stood next to Abba at shul *all day. We sat in the same seats that we have used for as many Yom Kippurs as I can remember. But I was a different me from the person I have been. And when we struck our hearts with our fists and asked forgiveness "for the sin we have*

committed with false denial and lying" and "for the sin we have committed by disrespecting parents and teachers," I couldn't help but look over at him and also think about Ima sitting in the women's section on the other side of the mechitzah. When they find out, when they learn that I am not exactly the son they think I am, when I tell them that I am still their Avi and I hope they can still love me, how will they react?

I have friends who have left Your path when they could not find a way to reconcile their love for You with their love for another man. I do not want to turn away from all of Your laws, from the way I have been taught, and from the life I have grown up loving. But I fear that my parents will reject me outright when I tell them.

I should have more faith in them. I should have more faith in You. Please, Hashem, help me to have faith.

Lev tahor be'rah li, Elokim—God, create for me a pure heart. Al tashlicheni milfanecha—do not send me away from before You.

step forward, step back, run like hell

A WEEK LATER, DANI SAT in the canvas-walled *sukkah* in Avi's postage-stamp backyard while Avi finished up in the kitchen.

"I hope you don't mind *yom tov* leftovers," Avi said, coming down the back stairs carrying a platter of chicken. "I never know how many guests I'm going to end up with, so I always cook extra." He put the platter on the table. "Just a couple of things left to bring out."

"There is never anything wrong with leftovers," Dani said, following Avi back into the house. "Especially ones that smell this delicious." He took a bowl of roasted cauliflower, broccoli, and carrots from the counter while Avi picked up a bowl of rice, and they went out to the sukkah.

Avi had a small, prefabricated sukkah appropriate for himself and a few guests. It was six feet wide, ten feet long, and eight feet tall, allowing him to put in a folding table and eight chairs, nine if the guests were comfortable being a bit more crowded. Its roof was made of bamboo mats, which allowed the rain to come in and allowed people inside the sukkah to see the stars at night. The walls of Avi's sukkah were blue, and he had put up a few decorations: paper chains near the roof around the four walls, which were traditional but often impractical in New England fall weather; a laminated poster of Jerusalem; and a laminated card with the traditional blessing said before eating a meal in the sukkah.

Once they were settled with food on their plates, Avi said, "Hang on a sec; I need to do the *ushpizin*."

"Ushpizin?" Dani remembered there had been an Israeli movie by that name that took place during Sukkot, but he couldn't remember exactly what the title referred to.

"Tradition has it, seven famous biblical figures come to the sukkah, one for each day of the holiday: Avraham, Yitzchak, Ya'akov, Yosef, Moshe, Aharon, and David. Since tonight is the third night of the holiday, tonight is Ya'akov's night, which would traditionally mean that I'd be feeding my brother Ya'akov dinner. He uses the ushpizin as an excuse almost every year as a way to bum a meal off me."

"Any chance he's going to come by tonight?" Dani asked.

"No, he's working tonight. He's a doctor in the emergency department at Beth Israel. So it's not out of the realm of possibility that he'll come by tomorrow morning after he gets off shift. Sometimes I wake up and find him sacked out on my sofa. My place is closer than his when he's got just a short window to catch some sleep outside the hospital." Avi pulled out a small book that Dani recognized as a *birkon*, the book with the blessings that were associated with meals. Avi said a couple of quick paragraphs in Hebrew; Dani understood the words, but was not familiar with the prayer itself. Avi then said the blessing in honor of eating in the sukkah then put the book aside. "Okay. Let's eat."

After they started to eat, Dani said, "So how was work today?"

"Exhausting," Avi said. "Even though I was careful with my wrists Monday and Tuesday, giving them plenty of rest and using my splints the way I'm supposed to in order to prevent repeated-stress injuries, I found the first day back to work exhausting. And with the holidays the way they are, this whole month is full of stops and starts, which just exacerbates everything. But I'll be okay. I'm good about icing and taking my anti-inflammatories when I need them." He took a sip of water and then said, "And how was your day?"

"Relatively uneventful. We're getting to the end of the Agile sprint, so I've got to demo what I've done at the beginning of next week, and of course it's got bugs. So I'm now on a bug hunt. But no big deal; people

almost expect the end-of-sprint demos to be bug fests." He took a bite of chicken. "Oh, Avi. This is delicious. I need to get back to cooking and not just living off frozen stuff and whatever takeout I happen to grab on my way home."

"If you want, I can give you pointers on quick dinners you can make with minimal effort. I've spent years collecting recipes."

"We should cook together some night. What do you think?"

"Sounds good to me."

"It'll likely have to be here," Dani said, "because my kitchen is…"

"Not so me-friendly, yeah. I could make it work, in a pinch, but you're right that doing it here makes more sense." He looked at their immediate surroundings. "Well, not *here*, because it's hard to cook in the sukkah. But yeah. Not next week, because it'll be right after the end of the holidays, but maybe the week after?"

"That should work."

They continued to eat and catch up. They had a short debate on the current state of US-Israel relations, but Dani was careful to keep his strongest opinions to himself. Fighting over world politics could wait until their relationship had built a stronger foundation.

"You in the mood for dessert? Some tea, maybe?" Avi asked as they stacked the dishes.

"Tea would be wonderful. Today was gorgeous, but now that it's getting darker, it's definitely starting to feel like October."

"We've been quite spoiled this year. Sukkot with weather in the seventies is such a gift for those of us who eat all our meals out here. I draw the line, though, at sleeping out here."

"Does anyone sleep in the sukkah in New England?" Dani asked. "I can't imagine it's at all comfortable."

"Some do. I am not one of them. I can give up lots of creature comforts, but sleeping outside in Massachusetts in October? I don't find that a meaningful way of observing the holiday."

"Makes sense. Sleeping outside can be fun, but not when there's a reasonable chance that the temperature will dip below freezing. I can't

imagine that the rabbis who wrote the Talmud intended for people to freeze in the name of a mitzvah."

"I agree," Avi said. "There's a lot of leniency when it comes to *pikuach nefesh*, and if not sleeping outside in New England in October isn't potentially life saving, I don't know what is."

They brought the dinner dishes and the serving platters and utensils into the kitchen, and Avi put on the kettle. "Tea inside or outside?" Dani asked.

"Inside, I think," Avi said, taking off his jacket and draping it over a kitchen chair. "Feel free to get comfortable in the living room; I'll bring the tea in soon."

Dani walked into the living room and took off his coat. The room was huge, almost twice the size of the living room in Dani's apartment. There were bookcases along three of the four walls, and the fourth had a fireplace with windows on each side. A wide-screen television hung on the wall between two sets of bookshelves on the wall that met the hallway to the front door. A comfortable-looking, forest green sofa sat across from the television, and chairs were set in conversational groups around the room. Piles of papers sat on a couple of the incidental tables. Dani took a closer look at the one closest to the sofa and found that it was a stack of in-progress sheet music.

After draping his coat over the back of a chair, he looked at the books. They seemed to be divided by language and then by subject. Avi had one whole bookcase dedicated to religious books: a set of *shas*, the books containing the Talmud and the major commentaries; a shelf of books containing multiple annotated editions of the *tanach*—the canonical books of the Hebrew bible—and commentaries; some more modern commentaries on the classic texts. The next bookcase contained Jewish-themed books in English: books on running a traditional Jewish household, books on Jewish bioethics, a book called *Kosher Meat* that clearly wasn't about cooking. Dani pulled that one off the shelf to look at more closely.

The next bookcase contained mainstream fiction from many genres, including science fiction, fantasy, and mysteries. And the last bookcase contained non-fiction books.

"There are more in my bedroom, including the majority of my professional books," Avi said, coming back into the room and startling Dani.

"Sorry, I didn't mean to be nosy. I just love looking at people's book collections."

"No, it's fine. All of the books out here are for public consumption." Avi must have noticed the book Dani was holding, because he suddenly went red. "That one, I thought was in the bedroom. That one's the Gang of Three's fault. The Sunday following our walking tour, they lured me with the promise of a bookstore crawl and ended up 'educating' me, as they put it. Thanks to that outing, I am now the confused owner of way more books on gay sex than I ever thought were published. Not that I thought about it. Before, I mean. Those books don't leave my room."

"You bought books on gay sex?" Dani asked, surprised and pleased.

"Jake, Dalia, and Chava picked them out. They did most of the loading of my basket, and I just paid for the pile, trusting them completely. That may have been my first mistake. I was quite surprised when I got home and started to read them. But Jake had a point—he said that I needed to educate myself, and he was right that books would be a much better means than just using Google and flailing around the Internet. So I am now the proud owner of a large collection of books that intimidate me."

To Dani, books themselves couldn't or shouldn't be intimidating, but that wasn't a debate that he and Avi should have now. So he said, "That's a smart approach. I mean, you probably do research about most new things you take on, so why not this? Especially this, which is such a huge change in your life."

"That was basically the Gang's argument, as well," Avi said. "And, though I hate to admit it, they were right. While I may not be quite ready to just sit down and read any of them cover to cover, it is comforting knowing that I have resources at the ready when I want to look at them."

They stood looking at Avi's bookshelves, with Dani pointing out books that he'd read or books he owned but hadn't read or books he thought Avi might like because of books that were on the shelves. Avi, in turn, recommended books for Dani to read or sheepishly pointed out books

on his shelves that he had only skimmed or that he'd always meant to read but hadn't gotten around to. It was not surprising to Dani that he and Avi had reading tastes in common, but he was also happy to be able to expand Avi's reading horizons.

While they were still discussing books, the kettle whistled. "I'll go get the tea," Avi said. "Be right back." He gave Dani a kiss on the lips and then immediately pulled back.

"Dan, I—"

Dani moved his hands up to hold Avi's shoulders and leaned close. "Avi," he whispered, capturing Avi's lips with his own. He started to deepen the kiss when he realized that Avi was completely unmoving. Dani pulled back and saw that Avi's face was expressionless and his eyes looked scared.

"Avi?"

"I… I've got to go."

Avi walked briskly toward the door, grabbed his wallet off the table in the entryway and a hoodie off the coat rack, and left. Dani stood by the bookcase, completely flummoxed. He had a ringing in his ears, intense and painful. The kettle was still whistling, so he walked into the kitchen and turned off the flame under the kettle, but then had no idea what to do. He walked back into the living room and sat on the sofa.

What the Hell had just happened? He thought the evening was going so well, that he and Avi were learning a lot about each other. It was great, and then for a brief moment it was *perfect*, and then… nothing. Worse than nothing. Avi had run away from his own home, in reaction to something Dani had done. Or had he? Dani hadn't initiated the kiss, though he had participated fully. In truth, he had done more than that. He'd deepened the kiss, or at least tried to, after Avi initiated it. So had he scared Avi off completely?

Dani scrubbed his hands over his face and tried to think. He couldn't predict where Avi might go; while they were learning more about each other every day, they had never broached the topic of what Avi would do in a fight-or-flight situation. And chasing Avi down when he was upset was likely the stupidest thing he could do, anyway. If Avi was freaked

enough to run, he probably needed some time to think without Dani breathing down his neck.

But Dani was a guest in Avi's home, even if Avi wasn't there. So he wasn't going to do anything he wouldn't do if Avi was there. So no snooping around, even if it meant that he was missing a golden opportunity to learn more about Avi. And he couldn't leave, because he couldn't lock the door behind him, and even in Brookline he didn't feel comfortable leaving the door unlocked. Staying seemed to be his only option. But how long Avi would be gone was a complete mystery. Dani groaned and pulled out his phone.

"'Alo?"

"Dudu, it's me."

"Didn't you tell me we'd have to find a new squash night because Wednesdays were now your Avi nights?"

"Yeah, well…yeah."

"That was informative," Dudu said, a laugh in his voice.

"Sorry. It's been an odd night."

"It must be, if you're calling me instead of having dinner or whatever with Avi."

"I was having dinner with Avi. In fact, we'd finished dinner and were up to tea and conversation," Dani said. "But then it got weird."

"Weird how?" Dudu asked.

"I'm now alone in Avi's home, and Avi is God-only-knows-where, having run out on me with no explanation."

"He ran out? Was there any precipitating event?"

"Kind of?" Dani said.

"Okay, you're making very little sense. Walk me through the relevant part of the evening, and we can try to figure out what happened."

"We had a really nice dinner in his sukkah, and then we decided to have tea and dessert inside. He was putting things away from dinner, and I was perusing his bookshelves, and then we were talking about books. Suddenly he kissed me, I kissed back, and then he ran out."

"Before I try to unpack that, I have a simple question. Have you tried to call him?"

"That didn't occur to me. Isn't that stupid?"

"Not stupid. You're not thinking completely clearly."

"That's true enough."

"Okay, so give him a call, and then call me back."

"Thanks, Dudu. I'll talk to you in a couple of minutes."

He hung up and dialed Avi's number. It rang once through the receiver of his phone, and then he heard it ringing in the room with him. He walked toward the source of the sound and found Avi's phone on a side table next to one of the piles of paper.

Shit.

Dani dialed Dudu's number again.

"'Alo?"

"Avi left without his phone."

"Okay, so you can't call and get a feeling for his current mood. I guess it's time for plan B."

"What's plan B?"

"You hang out in his place until he comes back."

"Don't take this the wrong way, but plan B sucks."

"And you have a better idea?" Dudu asked.

"No, not really. Other than maybe calling Ya'akov and finding out where Avi runs to when he needs to. But I don't have his contact info, so I'd have to break into Avi's phone to get his contact information, and I *really* don't want to do that. So it seems like you're right, and my best plan is to sit here and read this book that I pulled off Avi's shelf and hope that Avi comes home before it gets too late."

"How long has he been gone?"

"Uh…" Dani looked at his watch. "Seven minutes, maybe? I called you the first time just a few minutes after he left."

"Not long enough for you to be too worried yet, then."

"No, except that he *ran away from me*, Dudu! We had a lovely dinner, we were heading toward a nice evening, and then suddenly he kisses me, freaks out, and runs away from me. What am I supposed to do with that?"

"Be patient with him. You know he's new to this; you know he's not as experienced as you. You told me you were prepared to go slow and easy."

"I have been. I still am, I think. Remember—he kissed me. I wasn't going to make a move toward kissing him until we'd been dating longer, because I didn't want to freak him out."

"Okay, so start there. He is, presumably, working through some really strong feelings that are not like anything he's dealt with before. He may not have the words to express what it is he's feeling, or if he does have the words he may not have been able to access them when he was freaking out about having kissed you. So his running makes some sort of sense. You don't have to like it, but at least be sympathetic to it."

"I can be sympathetic. I *am* sympathetic."

"But you don't truly understand it."

"No, I don't. Because I've never felt what Avi is feeling. I mean, I've felt early-relationship nervousness, but I've never felt the need to run."

"But here's what you have to remember. It doesn't matter what you would have done. What matters is what you do when he comes back. And I promise—he will come back. So when he comes back, what are you going to do?"

"Give him a hug, tell him I'm glad he came back, and try not to yell at him for scaring the crap out of me."

"That sounds like a good start."

"Thanks for letting me talk it through, Dudu. You always seem to be able to help."

"I understand you. And I can be more neutral than you can."

"True enough." Dani sighed. "Is this going to get any easier?"

"The more you and Avi get to know each other, the smoother it will become, I'll bet. I can't promise there won't be other hiccups, but you'll learn what makes him nervous, what makes him want to bolt. And he'll learn about you."

"Thanks, Dudu. I should probably let you go, but I really appreciate you taking the time."

"Any time, Dani. Love you."

"I love you, too."

They hung up, and Dani sat back on the sofa and opened the book he'd taken from Avi's shelf. He was part way through the second chapter

when he heard footsteps on the front porch. He itched to stand up and greet Avi at the door, but at the same time he wanted to give Avi a chance to approach him on his own terms. He just hoped that Avi didn't mind that he'd waited for him to come back.

After a few moments, the front door opened. Avi walked in and slipped off his shoes, and then he turned and hung up his jacket. He seemed to be lost in his own thoughts. After a minute, Avi turned and said, "I'm sorry."

Dani stood and walked toward Avi, who was still standing by the closet. "You have nothing to apologize for," he said. "I'm sorry if I freaked you out."

"It wasn't you," Avi said, almost in whisper. "I freaked *myself* out. And I'm sorry I ran out on you. But thank you for staying."

Dani came closer and took Avi's hand. "I'm glad you came back. Can I… can I give you a hug?"

"I'd love that," Avi said, falling into Dani's embrace. They stood near the closet, holding each other, and Avi buried his face in the juncture between Dani's neck and shoulder. "I'm so, so sorry," he whispered again.

"Shh, *motek*. It's all okay." Dani kissed the side of Avi's head. "If you want to talk it out, I'm happy to listen. If not, though, I'm happy to just hold you."

"Hug first; talk after," Avi said, still speaking into Dani's neck.

"Works for me." Dani rested his cheek against Avi's head, breathing in his scent. "I'm glad you're back," he said again.

"I'm glad you're here," Avi responded.

They stood in the hallway, simply holding each other, and then Dani pulled back. "Your hands are cold. Let me make that tea we didn't have."

"It's my house, Dan. I can make the tea."

"Please, let me help." In that moment, Dani wasn't sure if he was talking about the act of making the tea or with Avi's current anguish, but either way he wanted to be helpful.

"Thank you for turning off the heat and not letting it all boil out," Avi said, turning on the flame.

"You're welcome," Dani said, rubbing Avi's back as he passed behind Avi to get the sugar. "It took me a minute to figure out that's what I was hearing, to be honest." He went to get the milk and then remembered they'd had meat for dinner. Knowing Avi, though, there'd be coffee lightener that contained neither meat ingredients nor milk ingredients. "You have any *pareve* soy milk for the tea?"

"In the fridge. Pareve pitcher is in the middle cabinet."

They moved around each other, preparing a tray with two teacups, some tea bags, the milk pitcher, and the sugar, and then they stood silently and waited for the water to boil. Dani didn't want to rush Avi, and it seemed Avi was waiting until he was more settled to start the conversation.

Once the kettle whistled, Avi poured the hot water and then carried the tray out to the living room. He and Dani settled themselves on the sofa and only after they had each taken a first sip of tea did Avi say, "Again, I'm so sorry."

"Oh, motek, no need to apologize. Clearly something spooked you; I'm just hoping it wasn't something I did."

"It's clichéd, but it's completely true that it's not you, it's me," Avi said. He took a deep breath and said, "I'm a planner. I'm a guy who rehearses conversations in my head before I open my mouth and anticipates multiple possible scenarios so that I am not caught off guard. I don't really do things spontaneously, not really, though that is changing somewhat. But the important things, those I think through and analyze and contemplate and ponder before acting. And then tonight…" He took a long sip of his tea and made a vague gesture with his unencumbered hand.

"Tonight you spontaneously kissed me. And it didn't fit your mental map of the evening, and it freaked you out."

"Exactly," Avi said. "I'm not at all saying I regret doing it; in fact, now that we've kissed, I plan to kiss you often. But in that moment, I couldn't deal. I panicked, I didn't think, and I ran. And, I hate to say it, but I can't guarantee I won't have a similar reaction to something else in the future."

"Do me a favor?" Dani put down his teacup and took Avi's hand.

"Mm?"

"Tell me if you're freaking out. We maybe should set up a non-verbal signal in case you can't actually formulate the sentence, but please just let me know. I can't help if I don't know what's going on."

Avi put his teacup down and faced Dani. "I'll try. I can't promise I won't panic, but I will do my best to talk instead of running."

"Thank you," Dani said. "Can… is it too soon for us to try this again? I mean, I don't want to do anything to make you uncomfortable, but I'd really, *really* like to kiss you again." Dani couldn't remember being this hesitant to kiss someone, but he didn't want to scare Avi into running again.

"I think that would be all right, as long as I know it's coming."

"So, no spontaneous kissing?" Dani asked.

"For now. Give me a bit of time to get used to it, and then spontaneous kissing will be more than welcome. But for now, if it's all right with you, I'd appreciate a warning."

"I can live with that," Dani said. "I'm going to kiss you now. There might be hugging involved, as well, though no guarantees on that front."

He framed Avi's face with his hands. Then, shifting himself so that he was perched on the edge of the coffee table, he slowly closed the gap between himself and Avi.

"Last warning," he whispered against Avi's lips.

"Bring it on," Avi whispered back.

They kissed slowly, taking the time to learn the shape and feel of each other's mouths. They restricted themselves to the movement of lips against lips, enjoying the simple intimacy. After a few minutes, Dani pulled back and was gratified when Avi tried to chase Dani's lips with his own.

"You doing okay, motek?" he asked.

"Mm," Avi responded, his eyes still closed. "I like that."

"The kissing? I like it, too," Dani said, grinning.

"Well, yes. That I like a lot. But I meant when you call me motek. I've never been a big nickname guy, well, except for my name, I guess, but… you've called me motek three times tonight, and I like how it makes me feel."

"I'm the opposite," Dani said. "I am a nickname kind of a guy; I'm glad you aren't bothered by it."

"I'm not against nicknames," Avi said, leaning his forehead against Dani's. "I'm just not usually good at them, so when people don't come with built-in nicknames, I just tend to call them whatever name they're introduced to me with."

"Which explains why you still don't call me Dani, why you introduce me as Dan to everyone?" They were getting away from the kissing that had been so wonderful, but if this conversation was what Avi needed, then they'd have the conversation.

"Would you prefer I introduce you as Dani?" Avi asked.

"Honestly, I don't care. But I wouldn't mind you calling me Dani. Or whatever else you're inspired to call me. If you're ever inspired to choose a nickname for me."

"Now you're rambling," Avi said, pulling back to smile at Dani. "Maybe we should be occupying our lips elsewise?"

"'Elsewise,' he says," Dani said, chuckling softly. "I'll show you 'elsewise'… if that's okay. I mean, would it be okay with you if we took this a bit further?"

"Yes, I think it would. Thank you for the warning, and please accept my apology in advance if I flinch a bit at first. It's not… I'm not…"

"I understand, motek." Dani moved close and peppered light kisses across Avi's lips; Avi reciprocated kiss for kiss. Dani licked gently at the seam of Avi's lips, hoping for a positive response. When Avi moaned and opened his mouth, Dani pressed forward, flicking his tongue into Avi's mouth. Avi responded by wrapping his arms around Dani's waist, but then he pulled back.

"Avi…" Dani whispered.

"I'm not stopping; I just want us to get more comfortable. This position is going to kill my back after a couple of minutes."

"Would you find it weird if we both lay down on the sofa? I don't want you to feel like I'm rushing you or anything. I want you to be comfortable with this, but I also want, well, for you to be comfortable." Dani realized he wasn't making himself clear. "I mean…"

"I understand what you mean, and it's very sweet of you to worry. I think lying down might be best. But would it be okay with you if I were on the outside, closer to the table than to the back of the sofa?"

"That would be fine," Dani said.

In the end, Dani stretched out on his right side facing out, and Avi, his feet dangling over the arm of the couch, lay facing him.

They lay there just looking at each other, and then Dani kissed Avi lightly. Avi immediately opened his mouth under Dani's, and Dani deepened the kiss. After a minute of kissing, Avi let out a sound.

"Everything okay, motek? Was that an endorsement or a complaint?" Dani was already starting to feel aroused just from the kissing, and Avi was probably feeling something similar, which might or might not be a good thing.

"Is it all right if the answer is both?"

"What's going on?"

"This, the kissing, is wonderful. The fact that I'm losing feeling in my left wrist is the problem. And I think I'm starting to get a cramp in my hip."

"Don't worry, motek," Dani said. "We don't have to have all the answers immediately. We're going to have to figure this out as we go, I'm afraid. Let's see what we can come up with."

Avi shifted and sat up, and Dani sat next to him on the sofa, taking Avi's hand in his.

"I'm sorry it's not so straightforward with me," Avi said.

"Shh, motek. It's an issue with everyone, figuring out comfortable positions. From where I sit—well, lie—the big issue is how tall you are."

"It's been a problem most of my life, to be honest. I never thought of it getting in the way of my love life, though."

"You need a longer sofa, maybe. Perhaps a sectional without arms."

"So you're moving out of software and into interior design now?" Avi asked with a laugh.

"Considering the week I've been having, it has a lot of appeal."

"Thank you," Avi said in an undertone. "For not leaving, I mean. And for being gentle with me."

"I'll be here as long as you'll have me," Dani said. "Even if it means trying to figure out where things go without messing up your *kashrut*."

"I'll teach you the organization of my kitchen, and you'll be fine." He kissed Dani's cheek. "But no, really, I appreciate it. I feel like anyone else would've left after I ran out and I'd never have seen them again. I'm half surprised you didn't."

"I told you I was willing to go at your pace, and I meant it. If your pace includes waiting while you take a walk to clear your head, I can't argue with that. Everyone needs their own coping mechanisms, and I'm not going to tell you that mine are any better than yours. I just got worried because you didn't have your phone, and I had no idea if you had your keys. And I'm glad you came back relatively quickly, though I would have waited as long as necessary. Which reminds me… I should give Dudu a heads-up that you're home."

"You called Dudu? I… I guess I shouldn't be surprised; I realized I didn't have my phone when I went to call Jake."

"It's nice to find someone who is as close to his siblings as I am to mine; it often feels like I'm the odd one in my circle of friends because I genuinely get along with my family. But Dudu and I have been close since we were kids, and we got even closer after we both had been through *Tzahal* and, because of Army duty, had a shared vocabulary for things that most people in our lives in the States don't even have context for."

"Jake and I weren't all that close when we were young. We're less than two years apart, though we were two grades apart, and that led to some friction when we were younger. But once Chava came along, and when it was obvious that she'd need more attention from our parents than Jake and I had, he and I bonded over… I wouldn't call it our shared abandonment, per se, though it felt like it when we were in middle school," Avi explained. "But we got close, since we could depend on each other. Chava we both adored from the get-go, even though she was the reason that our parents weren't there for us as much. And then Dalia rounded out the foursome; we're something of an odd group, but we're there for each other no matter what."

"They've been supportive of your coming out, right? Because having that support structure? Absolutely vital."

"They've been amazing. It was probably hardest for Dalia; part of her likely thought she and I were going to get married someday. I mean, part of *me* thought that would happen, mostly because of family pressure. But I think she believed she could make me want to be married to her. She was one of the first people I came out to, and she and I had a rough six months or so, while I was trying to make sure that these changes I was making in my life, the admissions I was making to myself, were really how I felt and what I wanted."

"While I was going through my own issues of identity—which, mind you, is still an ongoing process, but this was at the very beginning— Dalia had a hard time accepting that I meant it, that I really am gay," Avi continued. "For something that had absolutely nothing to do with her, she took it really damned personally, and she saw it as a personal insult that I had come out to her. But ever since she's worked through her own issues, she's been nothing but absolutely supportive. Jake and Chava, they were supportive from the get-go. They told me later that they'd known for a while that something was wrong in my life, that I had been unhappy for a very long time, and they were just glad I had found my way to happiness."

"You're lucky to have them," Dani said.

Avi nodded. "I am."

Avi eased his hand out of Dani's and stood up. "I'm sorry it's gotten so late. I should let you go home, and I should finish neatening up and get to bed. Again, I'm so sorry for how I reacted." He gave Dani a quick kiss on the lips, then reached out his hand to help Dani up. They walked to the door, where Dani grabbed his coat from the rack and shrugged it on.

"Thanks for coming," Avi said, opening the door. "I'm sorry, again, for the weirdness earlier."

"Forget it, motek. It's all fine." Dani moved to give Avi a kiss, waiting until he saw a tiny nod before he actually kissed him.

"Have a good night; be safe getting home."

"I'll text you, if you want."

"I'd appreciate that."

"We'll talk tomorrow?"

"Sounds good."

Dani went down the porch steps and then turned to wave to Avi before going to his car. Avi waved back, and then Dani got in his car and drove the twenty minutes to Cambridge. After he pulled into a space in front of his building, he texted Avi. *I'm home. Heading inside and to bed. Sleep well, motek.*

Sweet dreams, Avi texted back.

Sukkot was *zman simchateinu*, the time of our joy, according to the prayers of the holiday. Dani thought the ancient rabbis who wrote those prayers might just have been on to something.

the core of the matter

THE WEEK AFTER SUKKOT SEEMED even worse to Dani in terms of Avi's schedule than all the holiday-filled weeks preceding it. Dani understood, he truly did—Avi had missed a lot of work time and a lot of practice time with Kol Ish because of the holidays and now had to play catch-up with his own life.

But it didn't mean he liked it that Avi never seemed to have any time to talk, let alone to get together.

"I'm sorry, Dani," Avi said on the phone on Tuesday night, an hour after the holiday ended. "I'd love to see you tonight, but I've got a sink full of dishes and two loads of laundry facing me before I can even think about going to bed. Given that it's already nine o'clock, I can't imagine you'd want to schlep all the way to Brookline just to watch me do dishes and laundry."

"I actually wouldn't mind watching you do dishes and laundry; I'd even help, seriously, motek. We haven't talked since Sunday, and while, yeah, that's not so long, I've gotten kind of addicted to talking to you every night."

"If you really want to, and you don't think you'd be bored or feel it was a waste of time to come out, then sure. I'd love to see you." As he said the last part, Avi's tone softened, and Dani smiled.

"Give me about twenty-five minutes, and I'll be there."

"If I don't answer the first time you ring, call my cell. I don't always hear the bell over the water, but the phone I hear."

"Sounds good to me. I'll be there soon."

THE TRAFFIC WAS LIGHT, so about twenty minutes later he was pulling into Avi's driveway. He got out of the car and jogged up the path to Avi's front door and then rang the bell.

"You made good time," Avi said, opening the door. He gave Dani a quick peck on the lips and then stood aside.

"Almost no traffic this time of night, motek."

"Good point." Avi headed toward the kitchen, and Dani followed. He draped his coat over one of the chairs at the kitchen table and then sat in another one as Avi went to the sink.

"Tell me how I can help you reset from yom tov," Dani said. "I came to help."

"You're helping just being here and keeping me company. I'm sorry I was resistant to your coming over."

"I get it; this is a crazy month. But it's almost over."

"That is true. And as of tonight, all the holidays are over. I've got nothing to worry about, holiday-wise, until Pesach."

"What about Chanukah and Purim?" While Dani knew that the next major holiday was in April, when Passover came, there were a number of minor holidays in the next six months, and it would surprise him if Avi didn't at least observe some of those holidays.

"Chanukah is just candle lighting every night, so that's not a big deal. Maybe I'll make latkes, if I have enough time to grate the potatoes and make the pancakes, but I haven't done it in years because they're no fun to make for just one person and I didn't have time to have people over. Purim, yeah, but what? I make *mishloach manot* packages for a couple of friends, send the other gifts of food through the shul's fundraiser, and go to hear *megillah* on my way home from work on the *erev* and on my way to work in the morning so I hear the reading of the Book of Esther

twice. So, my next real holiday stress is Pesach. And for the next month, there's absolutely nothing, not even a minor fast."

"So you'll be free more often?"

"Should be." Avi put down the pot he'd been drying and walked over to Dani. "Thank you for being so patient with the craziness of my schedule. I bet you never imagined dating a dati guy." He pulled the closest chair closer to Dani's chair and sat down.

"To be honest, no dati guy I knew would have admitted he would be interested in dating a guy, let alone been open to any overtures I might have made."

"There's a lot of that attitude, unfortunately, still in the dati community. Within the Modern Orthodox segment of the dati community, though, things are getting a little better—slowly, but they're getting better."

"I still don't understand how you can be any type of dati and gay and keep your sense of identity. One of your selves, for lack of a better word, thinks your other self is an abomination." Dani knew his tone was challenging, and he didn't mean to put Avi on the defensive, but it was a question that he really wanted answered.

"I wasn't really thinking we'd have *this* conversation tonight," Avi said, his tone both less defensive and more hurt than Dani had expected. "And there are assumptions in your premise that are both offensive and uninformed. But if you need a high-level answer, the best I can tell you is that the two 'selves,' as you called them, are less in conflict than you think. There is nothing *assur*, nothing forbidden, about anything that I have done. *Halacha* does not mandate how you should think; the Law guides how you should act. And even if you interpret the passage from *sefer Vayikkra* as strictly as possible, there's still no *issur* in me kissing you, which is all we've done so far. If we ever decide to move toward the specific act that is the subject of that *passuk* in *Acharei Mot*, then I will have to do more research, talk to understanding rabbis, whatever. But for right now? My two selves are in perfect sync. And both are more than a little annoyed with their boyfriend, even while they greatly appreciate his coming over to help clean up from yom tov." Rant over, Avi kissed Dani and then walked back to the dish rack.

It was clear to Dani that Avi had figured out some of the answers he hadn't had back in August. But he still hadn't answered Dani's fundamental question.

"Motek, I don't want to argue with you, but I don't understand. I mean, you say it's not a problem according to *halacha* to live as a gay man, and that you haven't violated any prohibition in the Torah, but at the same time you haven't truly integrated your two lives." Dani took a breath and let it out slowly. To some extent, Avi's point had merit, but if he was going to be involved long-term with Avi, he needed to comprehend how Avi approached this. "Beside your family, how many people in the dati community know you're dating a guy?"

"Dalia knows," Avi said.

"She's family, or the closest thing to it."

"Okay," Avi said, and his tone got sharper, "well, the members of Kol Ish know."

"So that's five other guys."

"Why are you being a jerk about this, Dani? I can't imagine that you rushed out of the closet when *you* were figuring out *your* sexuality. I can't imagine you announcing to all of the guys in your platoon that you were gay; I can't imagine it would have gone over well at all." He pushed himself out of his chair and walked back to the sink, turning to face the sink and away from Dani.

"*Tzahal* doesn't care if you're gay or straight or whatever." Dani took another moment to pause and take a breath. This was not what he had wanted for this evening, and it was really his own damn fault. "But I hear what you're saying, sort of."

"Well, that's a step in the right direction," Avi said, his tone sharp. "I am glad that my life choices are beginning to meet with your approval."

"That's not what I mean, Avi, and you know it." Dani sighed in frustration. "I don't want to be put in the position of having to deny who I am. I don't want to be shoved back into the closet because you aren't comfortable telling people you're gay."

"I shouldn't have to make important choices about how I live my life because of what *you* need! It has to be about what *I* need!" Avi snapped,

turning to face Dani. "And I'd never ask you to go back into the closet; that's not what I'm saying. This isn't *about* you. This is about *me*, about how I live my life. A life that, yes, I really, *really* want you to be a part of. And I do know that the decisions I make, or don't make, have impact on your life. But the impact they have on my life is so much greater." Avi's body rigid, his eyes flashed with anger. "I cannot and will not rush the difficult decisions in my life to please someone else. This is true for how fast you and I will progress in our intimate relationship, and it is true for how soon I will let people know about my sexual orientation. It will all happen, but at *my* pace. And if you can't or won't wait for me to come out to people at my own pace, then how can I trust that you'll wait for me in other things?"

"The problem is, I know your community. They're going to try to marry you off, because they don't *know* you and I are dating. Because if they knew you were dating someone, they'd back off. But no one knows, because you haven't said anything to your parents." Dani's heart beat fast as he realized he had admitted one of his fears.

Avi took two steps away from the sink. "My parents know I'm dating you. They know that I'm serious about who I am and that this isn't a phase or something to try to steer me away from. They accept that I'm gay, that I'm not interested in women. It's true that it's all new to them and that they have to reevaluate everything they thought they knew about me. But they're willing to learn, and I'm trying to educate them as I educate myself. And they try to educate their friends." His eyes softened a bit, as if he could see the anxiety in Dani's heart. "There are and will be bumps along the road, I know that. But you can't paint the whole frum community with one brush just because you've had bad experiences with individual members of it. We don't all think with one mind. The people who have said things to you were assholes, but there are assholes in all communities. I've met software developers who are assholes; does that mean that all software developers are assholes?"

"Software developers don't have a shared dogma," Dani said, though it sounded lame even to his own ears.

"Neither do Jews. You know that. Hell, neither do Orthodox Jews. Neither do *Modern* Orthodox Jews. It's the old joke—two Jews, three

opinions—but it's not a joke, not really. *Halacha* gives us guidelines for how to live, not how to think. And how we think shapes how we practice our Judaism, which means that each person's observance is individual, unique. Yes, there are commonalities, but we don't all adhere to the same way of thinking. And, yes, you'll find frum assholes who will say that homosexuality is completely and absolutely assur. But that is not a mainstream viewpoint. You'll find some modicum of acceptance in almost every frum community."

"That has never been my experience."

"That may be true," Avi said, "which sucks. I mean, the dati community you know, or knew, must have been filled with really obnoxious, closed-minded assholes. But not all frum people, at least not the ones that I associate with, are that way."

"You say that without having tested the theory, since you haven't come out to all of them yet."

"I don't have to come out to every single person I know to expect that they won't be jerks about it. And I won't associate anymore with anyone who is. I don't need people in my life who will constantly judge who I am." Avi sighed. "And, on the flip side, I don't need people in my life who will pressure me to make decisions I'm not ready to make. When you promised you wouldn't rush me, we were talking about our sexual relationship, yes. But it has to extend to this, to the pace at which I choose to come out. I'm not ashamed of my relationship with you, and I'm not going to hide my involvement with you from anyone, whether we are out together or if I am asked if I'm in a relationship. But at the same time, it's not like I'm going to rent the billboard on the corner of Washington and Comm Ave and advertise our relationship, either. It's a personal thing, and I want to keep it a personal thing."

Dani took a deep breath and then said, "All right. I hear what you're saying. And I am sorry for pressuring you about this. I just…" He stopped, trying to figure out how to explain it to Avi without getting Avi angrier. He stood up and took one step toward Avi. "All of the dati people I knew before I came out, they all thought that gay people were an abomination. And while, yes, I'm learning that not all dati people feel that way, I still

have trouble understanding how someone can identify as dati and gay. I mean, yeah, halacha doesn't mandate thought, just action. But how many people know that? How many people *practice* that?"

"A lot of people know. Think of it this way. Halacha has a lot to say about kashrut. But not everyone keeps the same type of kosher, even among the dati community. So, for example, I don't hold that you have to only eat *glatt* meat or *chalav Yisrael* milk, but other people do. That doesn't make my type of kosher any less legitimate than their type of kosher. The people who only eat glatt or chalav Yisrael won't eat the food I make, but that's because of how *they* interpret the rules. In my experience, most of them don't believe I'm not keeping kosher; they just hold by a greater stricture."

"We have a difference of opinion on how to interpret the law," Avi continued. "Judaism allows for that; we have a long tradition of different communities having different standards, all of which are considered legitimate interpretations of halacha. Same with this. My interpretation of halacha has no problem with my being gay and my being frum. Someone else's opinion of halacha may not be as inclusive, but those people may also say I don't keep kosher enough or that the fact that I have a television in my house or an Internet connection means that I'm not frum. I disagree. My *community* disagrees. If they don't like my interpretation of halacha, they can leave me to my life. I'm not going into their houses and saying they have to be accepting of my kashrut standards, but at the same time they cannot come into my house and tell me that I cannot eat my own food to my own standards of kashrut."

Avi stopped and took a breath. Dani closed the distance between them and took Avi's hand. "Okay, motek, I get it," he said. "I think. I mean, it's still a huge thing for me to work through, since I have been so used to the dati community that I know judging me simply for whom I choose to love. I just… Until I met you, I had never met an Orthodox Jew who was open-minded about gays. So I admit it will take me some time to adjust my biases. Please be patient with me, motek."

"We'll be patient with each other," Avi said, bending for a kiss.

Tefilah: Willingly Accept Our Prayer with Compassion

Aveinu Malkeinu—our Father, our King—hear my voice.

Words are my livelihood, but they fail me now. And my voice is my instrument, but it is silenced by my emotions. I cannot express what I need to express, but in the silence of my prayers, I hope You can hear me.

I usually turn to my parents, to their understanding, when I am in a difficult situation. They have been my support, my foundation, when I am unstable. But at this moment, they are the cause of my instability. You, we say, are our Rock and our Redeemer. Please be my rock at this time of uncertainty.

My heart is with Dani; I know it is. But my heart is also with my parents, and they have made my heart hurt and my brain confused. I thought they had accepted that I was dating a man, even if they didn't understand it. But now they are questioning. And I am questioning.

Not my feelings for Dani; I would never question those. But my relationship with my parents, which I thought I would never have reason to question. Because they now are backing away from their unconditional acceptance of my relationship with Dani. And while I am glad to not have to hide it from them anymore, it was easier when they didn't know.

Please, Hashem, guide my heart, so that I can find a way to have the love of my parents despite my feelings for Dani. Guide their hearts, so they may find a way to love and accept me despite their uncertainty about my new identity. Help us to find a way that our love for each other can survive the turbulence of the changes in my life. Let them see how wonderful a person Dani is; let them come to understand the depth of feeling I have for him.

Aveinu Malkeinu, chus v'rachem aleinu. Kabel b'rachamim uvratzon et tefilatain. Our Father, our King, have pity and be compassionate to us. Willingly accept our prayer with compassion.

accidental encounters

Positives, Dani said to himself later. *I have to remember the positives that came from all of today's excitement. Number 1: Avi's fine. Shaken up; in some pain; a little twitchy about getting back on his bicycle after his ankle heals. But overall, fine. Number 2: The Levines and I have come to something of an agreement—they'll try to get to know me and I'll try to get to know them. Not that we're all buddy-buddy now, but progress has been made. Number 3: Avi's fine.*

It had started with a phone call while Dani was at work…

He hadn't checked the caller ID when he picked up because he was still concentrating on the lines of code he was debugging.

"Dan, it's Jake. Everything's fine."

"Well, that's good to hear." Dani had paused, letting his brain catch up. "Wait. When people call and say everything's fine, something's not fine. What's going on?"

"It's Avi," Jake had said. "He's here with me at the hospital."

Dani had immediately started making a mental list of what he would have to do before leaving the office for the rest of the day. Any conversation that started that way—especially when there was an emergency room involved—ended with Dani leaving the office, and he'd gotten it down to a science. For reasons he still wasn't clear on, though it likely had to

do with his IDF training, he was seen among his circle of friends as *the* guy to call in an emergency. After, of course, they'd called 911.

"What happened?" he asked, striving to keep his voice calm as his heart rate shot through the roof.

"You know that stretch of Comm Ave, right by the BU Bridge? Where, if you're heading away from Kenmore Square, you turn to get onto the bridge?"

"Yeah?"

"Well, as he tells it, Avi was riding toward that turn-off onto the bridge, got clipped by some idiot in an SUV, and ended up flying over his handlebars and into the street. Lucky for him, the cars behind saw it happen and stopped before anyone else hit him."

Dani swallowed all of his immediate questions. He figured that Jake wouldn't be this casual if anything were seriously wrong with Avi. So Dani let him continue his explanation.

"To her credit, the idiot driver—a BU sophomore, it turns out—pulled over and called an ambulance. She stayed with Avi till the ambulance arrived, and then she and the EMTs did a good guilt trip on him until he agreed to get in. He's seething more about that—and the damage to his bike—than about his injuries."

"Injuries?" Dani asked, as calmly as possible.

"He'll be *fine*, Dan. I promise. He's in the best hands. I've made sure of it. He's more annoyed than anything else right now."

"Jake, what injuries?"

"Some contusions and abrasions, and he likely sprained his left ankle when he flew off the bike. He's just been taken down to get his ankle X-rayed, and he was giving everyone hell while they made him wait. Really, Dan, he's fine."

"I'm coming to see him." There was no question. It's not that he didn't trust Jake, but he needed to see for himself that Avi was all right.

"I anticipated as much. You know how to find us, right? Just go straight to the emergency entrance. Tell them to page me if you don't see me."

Dani looked at his watch. If all went exactly right, he could be at Beth Israel in fifteen minutes. Realistically, though...

"I'm leaving right now. Provided I can catch a cab quickly, I'll be there in half an hour."

"Dan, relax. He's fine."

"I know that. But I need to see him."

Jake sighed. "See you in thirty."

Dani hung up and sent quick e-mail to his boss telling him that he was leaving, even though with their open office plan it wouldn't surprise him if his boss had overheard some of the phone conversation. Then he grabbed his backpack and cell phone and strode toward the elevator. As he quick-walked through the building's lobby, he heard someone call his name.

"Gotta go. Medical emergency. Send me e-mail," Dani said, not slowing his pace as Jason, one of his coworkers, caught up with him.

"What's up?"

"Boyfriend. Bike accident. Got a call from the hospital. Gotta go." He hoped Jason would realize he wasn't trying to be rude but that he was just in a rush.

"Where you headed?"

"Beth Israel."

"Want a lift?"

"Really?"

"Hell, yes. Not like I've got anything pressing." Since the company's software release had gone out the previous weekend, things were calmer in the office than they'd been in months.

"Thanks," Dani said.

The morning commute had ended, so the trip to the hospital was quick. As Jason drove up to BI's front door, he asked, "Do you want me to come in with you?"

"No, thanks. I appreciate it, though. Please let everyone know I'll be back when I can, though it most likely won't be until tomorrow morning."

"Sure. Call me when you know anything, okay?"

"Will do. Thanks again." Dani got out of the car and ran into the hospital. He was afraid that Jake had been downplaying Avi's injuries. He needed to see Avi. Now.

Dani stalked to the emergency department's admissions desk. "Get me Dr. Levine," he said.

"Which Dr. Levine, sir? And what is the nature of your complaint?"

"Dr. Ya'akov Levine. And my complaint is that you haven't paged Dr. Levine for me yet."

"Please calm down, sir. Dr. Levine is with a patient." She handed Dani a clipboard. "Please fill out this form, and then have a seat. You'll be seen as soon as possible."

"You don't understand," Dani said, struggling to keep his voice even. "Dr. Levine called *me*. I want to see him, and I want to see him *now*."

One of the security guards approached. "Is everything okay, sir?"

"No," Dani said. "This… *person* is keeping me from seeing Dr. Levine."

Dani felt a hand on his shoulder. "What?" he snarled, whirling to face the new obstacle.

"Hey, Dan," Jake said, smiling. "You done intimidating people and ready to see Avi?"

"Oh, thank God," he said. "Take me to him. Please."

Jake led Dani around the admissions desk, to an area partitioned by curtains. He pulled back the third curtain.

"Hey, brother-mine, you've got a visitor."

"If you called Ima and Abba, I'm gonna kill you, banged-up or not," Avi said.

"I hope you won't kill him for calling me," Dani said. Now that he could see Avi, hear him joke with Jake, Dani was beginning to calm down. But he needed to be closer.

"Hey, Dani" Avi said.

"Hey, yourself," Dani responded. "You okay?" Stupid question, he knew, but he was at a total loss.

"A bit achy. Hungry."

Avi and Dani looked at each other. Dani absorbed the fact that Avi was, in fact, all in one piece, looking bruised and scraped but not too bad. He was sitting up on a gurney, wearing a hospital gown and his kippah, with his legs hanging over the edge—no socks or shoes, with a bandage wrapped around his left ankle.

"I'll be right back," Jake said, backing out of the cubicle. Dani barely noticed.

He wanted to go to Avi, to hold him and know that he was really fine. But he perhaps Avi would feel awkward with Dani expressing affection here, in a public place.

"Dani?" Avi's voice interrupted Dani's thoughts.

"Yeah?"

"I'm glad you came."

"Are you for real?" Dani asked. His tone was sharper than it should've been, but now—knowing Avi was fine—he was free to panic.

"What?"

"Avi, you were in a fucking *accident!* What sort of friend, let alone boyfriend, would I be if I didn't come? I'm never too busy for you. Never." Now Dani did walk over to Avi's side. He ran his hand lightly down Avi's arm. "Oh, God, motek. When Jake called, I…"

"Flipped out?" Avi said, a small grin on his face.

"I was *going* to say 'dropped everything.' Nothing waiting for me at work is so important that I'd choose it over you."

"I'm glad you're here," Avi said.

Dani was trying to figure out exactly how to respond when the curtain parted and Jake came in followed by a colleague.

"Dan," Jake said, "this is Nancy Sullivan. She's the best orthopedist we've got."

Everyone exchanged hellos, and then Dr. Sullivan turned to Avi.

"So," she said, "your films showed exactly what I expected—it's sprained, but nothing is broken. I'll prescribe you some high-dose ibuprofen and give you a pair of crutches, and then you can clear out of here."

"Thank you," Avi said.

She scribbled on her prescription pad, then handed the page to Avi. "I'll send this to the pharmacy; pick it up on your way out, okay? As soon as they bring the crutches, you can go, so feel free to get dressed."

"Thanks, Nancy," Avi said. "Make Jake bring you by sometime when he comes over; it seems I only see you professionally these days."

"Yeah," she said. "You've got to stop that, you know."

"I'm trying," Avi responded.

"That you are," Dr. Sullivan called over her shoulder as she left.

Jake walked back toward the entryway of the cubicle. "I've got real sick people to treat; I trust you'll take care of him, Dan?"

"Yeah," Dani said. "As soon as they spring him, I'll get a car to take us back to his place. I'll make sure he gets lunch, as well."

"Uh, guys? I'm sitting right here. I can take care of myself." Avi sounded more peeved than Dani had ever heard him.

"Avi, please. Let me do this."

"Yeah," Jake said. "How often do you get someone at your beck and call? And be glad it's Dan and not, say, Ima and Abba."

"Point."

"Okay, then. I'll leave you two alone," Jake said. If I don't see you before you leave, Avi, I'll come by after work. Actually, I'll come by after work even if I do see you before you leave."

"How late are you working tonight?" Avi asked.

"Only till four; I should get to your place by four-thirty, no problem."

"Bring dinner, will you?" Avi asked.

"Yeah, I can do that," Jake said. "I'm assuming three of us?"

"Yeah," Avi said, looking at Dani. "Three."

"Thanks, Jake," Dani said.

He left, and Avi started to ease himself off the gurney. Quickly, though, he winced and froze in place.

"Need a hand?" Dani asked. He wanted to help, but at the same time he didn't want to crowd Avi.

"Yeah," Avi said. "I'd appreciate that."

Slowly, to prevent as much pain as possible, they got Avi dressed. Dani tried his best not to stare at the bruises on Avi's chest and side; he figured Avi was probably self-conscious enough knowing Dani was seeing him naked.

As Avi finished dressing, the occupational therapist came in bearing crutches. It took a while, but eventually she and Avi came to an agreement

about the height and comfort of the crutches, and, after she confirmed that Avi did, in fact, know how to use them, she left.

Dr. Sullivan came back to sign Avi's discharge papers, reiterated the need for him to rest the ankle, and left.

"So," Avi said.

"So," Dani responded. "Let's go and get your meds, and then I'll get us a car home. I got a lift from work; I didn't want to take the time to get my own car."

The trip to the hospital pharmacy was fairly quick, and there were a number of cars around, so in much less time than Dani had feared, he and Avi were dropped off in front of Avi's house. It took a bit of maneuvering to get Avi out of the car, and Dani felt horrible about the unavoidable pain, but soon they were standing on the sidewalk contemplating the walk up the path to the porch.

"Give me your keys," Dani said.

"Huh?" Avi replied, clearly not completely engaged in reality.

"If you give me your keys, I can open the door so that you don't have to fish for your keys while dealing with the crutches."

"Makes sense," Avi said. "I'm sorry—it's a bit more painful than I'd anticipated, and all I really want to do right now is get inside, sit on the couch, elevate my foot and put ice on it, and take my meds." He pulled out his keys and handed them to Dani.

"Do you want me to walk with you, or do you want me to go ahead of you and open the door and give you a clear shot to the sofa?"

"Go up and open the door. It's going to take me a couple of minutes to work my way up, and then I'm going to need to collapse, so, yeah. An open door would be perfect."

"Okay, I'll go." Dani gave Avi a quick kiss. He got Avi's door open and had the lights on before Avi had made it to the bottom stair of the porch.

"You okay?" Dani asked, looking out from the doorway to where Avi was leaning against the railing of the porch stairs.

"Give me a sec; I just need to rest a moment."

"No rush whatsoever. Once we're inside, I'll set you up on the couch and then I'll make lunch."

"Thank you," Avi said quietly. "For coming down to get me, for rescuing me from the possibility that I'd be left in the care of my parents, or, worse, Dalia."

"She that bad?"

"She hovers. Even more than Ima does."

Dani thought a minute. "I take it you've experienced this before?"

"Yeah," Avi said. "Remember, I've known her for more than half my life. I encountered Hovering Dalia most recently last summer, when I sprained this same stupid ankle falling off the same stupid bike; she appeared most vociferously about five years ago when, well, I sort of missed the fact that I had appendicitis."

This wasn't something Dani wanted to hear about while standing on the porch. "You ready to go inside?"

Avi straightened up. "Yes. I really need to sit down and put my foot up."

Dani let Avi precede him into the house. Avi moved as quickly as possible toward the sofa while Dani dropped his backpack and Avi's under the coat hooks. He detoured into the kitchen to pull an icepack from the freezer, and, by the time he joined him, Avi was already ensconced with his foot up on the mahogany coffee table with a blue and grey striped pillow cushioning it.

"So," Dani said, sitting next to Avi on the sofa and arranging the cold pack on his ankle. "Tell me about your appendix."

"What's to tell?" Avi asked. "I presented with atypical symptoms; no one, including Jake, thought it was anything to worry about."

"Apparently, though, that changed," Dani said, trying not to freak out about something that had happened in the past and that had left no discernable side effects.

"Yeah," Avi said. "My inflamed appendix eventually ruptured—thus causing me to feel much better—until I started exhibiting the symptoms of peritonitis. I was with Chava at Ima and Abba's, and she called Jake, who told her to get me to the hospital as soon as possible."

"And?" Dani asked.

"And I spent over a week in the hospital, constantly on IV antibiotics, and then they sent me home. I spent the following two weeks flat on my back, trying to regain my strength, and then the next six months still feeling not-quite-myself. Eventually, once they'd deemed me healthy enough, I went back into the hospital so they could remove the remnants of my appendix."

"Avi, you're lucky to be alive," Dani said.

"So I've been told. Repeatedly. During the two weeks I was home but still sick, I had Dalia here, hovering and worrying and trying to get Jake to readmit me to the hospital. I love her dearly, and I know she worries only because she cares, but…"

"I understand. And I'll try my best not to hover." Though Dani knew he'd worry. He couldn't promise not to worry.

"Thank you."

"So," Dani said, "you said you were hungry?" Food—the Jewish family's panacea.

"Famished. Didn't have breakfast, because my bagel was in my backpack when I fell— and is thus still in Jake's office."

"I brought your backpack home, actually. It was with the rest of your stuff that they gave us at discharge. I just figured you wouldn't want it weighing you down," Dani said.

"Oh, thanks. The bagel… it's probably disgusting by now, but if it looks okay, can you put it in the fridge?"

"I'll grab it on the way to make food. You sit." Dani handed Avi the remote from the corner table, "And I'll scrounge in your fridge and see what I can come up with."

"Thanks," Avi said, settling deeper into the sofa.

After standing for a minute in the living room doorway to make sure Avi didn't need anything else, Dani went back to the hallway, retrieved the rather sad-looking bagel, and then went into the kitchen to see what he could scare up for lunch.

He took a quick look in and around the sink. The rack sitting on the bottom the sink was blue. The sponges sitting by the edge of the sink

were blue. And the dishes resting in the dish rack had a blue decoration around the edge. "Blue's *chalavi*, right?" he called to Avi.

"Yeah," Avi said. "But if you find *fleishig* leftovers you want to heat, feel free to switch it over. The red rack under the sink is for fleishig, and the sponges should be there, too. Left cabinet is fleishig dishes, and if you're really motivated you can put the blue ones for milk that are in the drainer into the right cabinet. There's sink cleanser and a sponge on top of the microwave if you're going to switch from one to the other."

"Nah," Dani said. "Defeats the purpose of a good scrounge if you have to work too hard for it. By the way, I'm tossing the bagel." He opened the fridge and rummaged around. He found the makings of a good salad and a couple of vegetable omelets. Not gourmet food, but enough sustenance until Jake showed up with dinner.

Once lunch was ready, he brought it to Avi in the living room. When they finished eating, it was twelve-fifteen and Dani was at a loss as to what he should do. He'd been invited for dinner, but he didn't know how Avi felt about company when he felt crappy or whether Avi really wanted him hanging around for four hours.

He was trying to figure out how to ask when Avi spoke up.

"Hey, Dani?"

"Yeah?"

"Up for a movie marathon? You'd have to change the DVDs, 'cause I'm not really in any shape to do so, but if you're willing, I've got tons of stuff."

"We could just watch on Netflix; that way neither of us would have to get up," Dani said. "Got anything specific in mind?"

Avi thought for a minute. "How do you feel about an afternoon of space-related movies—*Apollo 13*, *The Dish*, and, if there's still time, *October Sky*?"

"I've never heard of *The Dish*, let alone seen it," Dani said.

"Let's start with that one, then," Avi said. "You're in for a treat, if you like movies about heroic geeks doing everything wrong but it all turning out okay."

"Sounds like my kind of film," Dani said.

And Avi was right—it was a wonderful movie. That guy who'd been in the live-action version of *The Tick* was one of the stars, and it was a perfect way to relax after the morning they'd both just had.

They finished *The Dish* and had just moved on to the beginning of *Apollo 13* when Avi's doorbell sounded.

"I'll get that," Dani said, pausing the video.

"Meanwhile, since we're paused anyway, I'm going to go use the bathroom. It might take a while. And feel free to ignore the door. It's probably Jake bringing dinner. He's got keys; he'll probably just let himself in and he's ringing the bell to warn me."

"But what if it's just some random door-to-door guy?"

"If we ignore him long enough, he'll go away," Avi said, levering himself off the sofa.

A minute or so later, Dani heard a key turn in the lock followed by two sets of footfalls in the entryway and muffled conversation.

"You think Jake brought Dr. Sullivan?" Dani asked Avi, who was still moving slowly down the hallway.

Avi shrugged. "Could be."

At the knock on the door jamb, Dani looked up.

And came face to face with Avi's parents. He immediately got up and walked over to the doorway.

"Hello," Ilana, Avi's mother, said. She sounded as surprised to see Dani as Dani was to see her.

"Where's Avi?" Yoni, Avi's father, asked. He was carrying a large pot and he looked perturbed.

"Heading toward the bathroom; he might be a while," Dani responded, more brusquely than he had intended. He tried to make up for it. "Can I take your coats?"

Ilana shrugged out of her red windbreaker and handed it to Dani without a word; after setting the pot temporarily in the corner, his father handed over his dark gray topcoat with a curt, "Thank you."

"Hey, Jake, c'mon back. We'll eat in here," Avi called from the kitchen.

"Jake isn't here yet," Ilana called back as she headed in his direction. Yoni picked up the pot and followed her. Dani hung up the coats and

then followed everyone else into the kitchen, where he found Avi sitting at the kitchen table with his foot up on a second chair.

"Ima?" Avi's bewilderment was palpable.

"Jake called Chava, who told us what happened. We figured you wouldn't want to be alone, so I cooked up a chicken soup for you, and we've brought it over."

"Thanks," Avi said, "but I wasn't—I'm not alone."

Avi's parents turned to look at Dani.

"Jake didn't tell us you were here," Yoni said.

"Jake called me right after it happened; I couldn't not go to the hospital."

"That doesn't explain why you're here now," Ilana said. Her tone rankled, but Dani understood that she was worried about Avi.

"Ima," Avi said, "I couldn't get home on my own, and I wasn't going to hang around at the hospital until Jake was off work."

"And you couldn't pick up the phone and call one of your parents?"

"You were in class, I thought. So was Abba. There was no reason to disrupt your day." Avi's argument wasn't going to go over well, but Dani wasn't in a position to help.

"So instead you called *him*?"

"*He* has a name, and it was Jake who called him." Avi looked quickly toward Dani. "Not that I don't appreciate you dropping everything and coming over. Really."

"But why did Jake call *him?*" Ilana asked, more pointedly.

"Because he knew Dani would want to know? Because he knows Dani's an important part of my life? If you were in an accident, *chas v'shalom*, wouldn't you want Abba to come to the hospital?" Avi's voice was getting softer with each question, which Dani knew was a bad sign.

"That's different," she said.

"Why?" Avi asked.

"He's my husband. Of course he should be with me."

"Dani's my boyfriend. Would you feel any different if it were Jake or Chava who was injured? *Chas v'shalom.*"

"It's not the same," Ilana said.

"Why?" Avi asked again.

"Because…" she started, but then she didn't continue.

"Abba? Do you feel the same way?" Avi asked.

"Well," Yoni said, "I think what your mother means is that we hoped that you would have called us. That we wouldn't have had to hear from Jake, through Chava, that you'd been in an accident."

"I understand that," Avi said, "and I'm sorry I didn't call you. But Dani was with me, and I knew he could take me home. I really didn't see any reason to bother you."

"It wouldn't have been a bother," Ilana said. "Right, Yoni?"

"Right," Yoni said. "And, well…"

"Yes?" Avi wasn't rude, but his tone was less than deferential.

"We're just… uncomfortable with the idea of you and Dan as a couple. It's not you, Dan," he said, turning to address Dani directly.

The longer this conversation continued—the longer Dani was witness to this struggle between Avi and his parents—the more uncomfortable he became. He wanted to leave, but he was afraid that would just reinforce whatever misconceptions the Levines might have about him. So he'd stayed, but he had tried to be as invisible as possible. And now he was being pulled directly into the conversation.

But Yoni seemed oblivious to Dani's discomfort. He continued speaking, turning back to Avi. "And it's not even the fact that you're both men. It's just…"

"It's just *what*?" Avi asked.

"All these years, your mother and I had a pretty good idea of who you were. And now we find we were mistaken, so we need time to assimilate this… this new definition of you. I'm sorry if we come across as unfriendly, Dan," he said, turning to Dani yet again.

"Can you understand how trapped I feel right now?" Avi asked. "I don't want to have to choose between you; I don't want to be put in that position."

"We're not asking you to choose," Ilana said. "We're just asking you to give us time. We need time to get to know Dan, to understand who he is. We worry about you, Avi. We want only what is best for you. So

we're nervous about your relationships. It wouldn't matter if you were dating a woman; we'd still be nervous. Give us time to get to know Dan for who he is, how he fits into your life."

"You asked for time after the *yomim nora'im*," Avi said. "It's been *months* since the High Holy Days that Dani and I have been dating, and you've barely talked to him at all."

"We should rectify that," Ilana said. "Dan, please understand, it's nothing about you personally. In fact, would you like to join us for Shabbat lunch this week? We'll have time to talk, get to know each other."

Dani wasn't sure it would help, but maybe it was a step in the right direction. "Thank you," he said, "I appreciate it."

As Dani was trying to figure out what to say next, the doorbell rang again.

"*That* must be Jake," Dani said. "I'll go let him in." He wanted to get away for a minute; maybe that would allow the tension in the room to decrease just a bit.

He opened the door, and this time it was actually Jake, who was armed with what smelled like takeout Chinese.

"Hey, Dan," he said, "where can I put this?"

"You say that like I know Avi's kitchen," Dani said. "Eh, we'll find a place. Not like he's going to be getting up and moving stuff around much."

"How's he doing?" Jake asked.

"He was in a lot of pain when we first got back from the hospital, but he took his meds and was resting the ankle. He hasn't moved much since we got back here—I set him up on the sofa, and for most of the afternoon we've been vegging and watching space movies. Well, until about fifteen minutes ago, when your parents showed up."

"Oh," Jake said.

"Yeah, *oh*."

"How'd that go?"

"Well," Dani said, "there hasn't been any blood yet, but only because I've been restraining myself. I've been telling myself that they're only being this way because they're worried about Avi—both because he's hurt and

90

because they don't know me and can only imagine that I'm corrupting their precious darling."

"Aren't you?" Jake asked with a grin.

"Not nearly as much as I'd like to," Dani said. "God, how I want to."

"Do you want it enough to make dealing with Ima and Abba worth it?"

"Hell, yes."

"Okay, then. That's all I need to know."

"But, seriously, Jake—we've done nothing more than hold hands and kiss, and your parents look at me as if I'm gonna tear Avi's clothes off and do him in the middle of Harvard Square."

"Don't worry, Dan—they looked that way at Chava's first boyfriend, too. It's not you; they can't get their minds around the idea that we've grown up, that sometimes we do things that they're not completely ready for."

"Are they this harsh with your girlfriends?" Dani asked.

"No, but that's because, in their minds, I should be married already. Every girl I bring home is a potential bride, and thus a potential source of grandchildren."

"Ah," Dani said. "I'm familiar with that phenomenon. It's how my parents look at Dudu's girlfriends, and he's not even thirty yet."

"So this thing with my parents, it should just resolve itself once they get to know you."

"Yeah, they sort of said that. They even invited me for Shabbat lunch. You'll be there, right? To be a buffer, just in case?"

"Yeah, I'll be there, don't worry. I'm off this weekend, so I'm gonna take advantage of my parents' hospitality as much as possible."

"Anyway," Dani said, "they're probably wondering what happened to us."

"You ready to go back in there?"

"Not sure, but I don't want to leave Avi alone for too long."

They reached the kitchen just in time to hear Avi's father say, "Are you sure you trust him? He looks at you like he's planning something."

"Yes," Avi said. "I do trust him. More than you apparently trust me. I'm an adult. I can conduct myself in a relationship in an adult manner.

That includes being able to say no to things I'm not comfortable with, but it also includes me saying yes to things I do want, things I am comfortable with."

"How do you know what you're ready for? How can you know what you're getting yourself into with him?" Avi's mother asked.

"How can I know what I like, what I'm comfortable with, unless I try? I trust Dani; he's not going to do anything I'm not comfortable with. I'm a better judge of character than you give me credit for."

"He's much more experienced than you are, especially with *this*," Ilana said.

"How experienced were you when you married Abba?" Avi asked.

"That's not important," Ilana responded.

"Why?" Dani asked, knowing he was about to get himself into trouble. "Why is Avi's lack of experience any more important than yours?"

Dani heard Jake's indrawn breath and Avi's whispered "Dani…" but he plunged ahead. "Avi's an adult; he's able to make his own decisions about who he wants to get involved with. He's smart enough to know how to protect himself, and he deserves the respect of his parents. He's…" There was nothing else Dani could say without either incriminating himself in their eyes or seeming to pressure Avi. Dani looked at Jake, pleading with him to stop this before Dani said something he shouldn't.

And, thank goodness, Jake stepped up. "C'mon," he said. "We're all a little—or more than a little—frayed right now. Let's not say things we shouldn't. It won't help Avi at all, and I know, at the crux of it, that's where all this is coming from." Dani could understand why Avi called Jake the family peacemaker. "Let's go eat, and you'll get a chance to talk this out when we're all more relaxed."

Avi's parents exchanged a glance, and then Ilana said, "You're right, as usual, Jake. And we're sorry, Avi; we really don't mean to be so harsh with you. We're just… still figuring out what all this means, what it's all about. We need time, and we'll try to get to know Dan if he'll give us the same courtesy."

"Of course," Dani said, trying to look as non-threatening as possible.

"Thank you." Ilana paused, then said, "Come on, Yoni; let's let these three have dinner together out from under the watchful parental eye. Avi's in good hands."

"I promise," Avi said, "that next time I'll call you first thing."

"Let's hope there *isn't* a next time," Dani said, looking pointedly at Avi.

"From your mouth to God's ears," Yoni said. "Take care of yourself, Avi. Or, if you can't, let these two take care of you."

Dani took that as an endorsement of his continued presence in Avi's life, even if Yoni hadn't meant it that way.

After another few minutes of getting Avi settled on the sofa again and quick instructions on reheating the soup, Avi's parents left, with Jake walking them to the door.

"That went... well, I guess," Dani said.

"I'm sorry about all that, Dani. They're good people, really. They're just..."

"They're just concerned about you, which I understand and respect. But they'll have to learn to get used to this 'new you' and all the peripherals that go with that."

"You're more than a peripheral, Dani," Avi said.

"Oh, you sweet-talker, you," Jake said, returning to the living room. "So, now that all the melodrama is over with, you guys ready to eat?"

They had a pleasant rest of the evening, with Avi and Jake telling stories of past injuries and past incidents interspersed with random chat on other topics, other non-parent-related topics.

All told, Dani was more comfortable with how he fit into Avi's life— Avi had stood up to his parents on Dani's behalf, which Dani doubted he'd had to do for any previous friendship.

And Dani had hope that he and the Levines would come to a consensus about how he fit into Avi's life. He wasn't going to give Avi up just because Yoni and Ilana couldn't picture their son in a relationship with him. This relationship, as new as it was, was too important.

into the lion's den

It was just lunch, right? No reason to feel this deep, gut-level fear. No reason at all.

But it wasn't going away. Dani was nervous. Hell, he was beyond nervous; he'd gone all the way to sheer, unadulterated panic.

It didn't help one bit that he wasn't completely comfortable in his clothing. He was much more dressed up than usual for a Saturday—suit, button-down shirt, tie, kippah, the whole "I'm an upstanding citizen, not a threat to your way of life" costume. But he'd agreed to meet Avi and his family at their synagogue and to go to Avi's parents' for lunch. And he didn't want to start the afternoon by embarrassing the Levines in front of the rest of the community.

Of course, he wasn't going to make it obvious that he was anything more than a lunch guest, at least until they were alone at the Levines'.

By the time Dani got to the synagogue, services were finished, and people were milling around the social hall nibbling on whatever had been put out for *kiddush*. He stood in the doorway for a minute, hoping to spot Avi or Chava, but he didn't see either one. Screwing up his courage, he moved farther into the room. Long tables in the shape of an X dominated the middle of the room. Many people were gathered around them filling their plates with vegetables, kugels, small pastries,

and fish salads. Dani ambled toward the left corner of the room where the drinks table was set up. He was amused to find that he could choose soda, water, whisky, schnapps, vodka, or seltzer all from the same table. Desperately wanting the whisky but realizing it wasn't a smart idea, he poured himself a cup of soda. He then walked back to the food table and jockeyed for position among the people who seemed to have parked themselves by their favorite items.

"Hey, Dani," Jake said, coming up next to him. "Damn, but you clean up good."

When Dani had gone for lunch at Avi's during Rosh Hashanah, he'd worn dress pants and a button-down. And his job's dress code was basically "come to work dressed." So this, the suit-and-tie combo, was reserved for special occasions—like *bar mitzvah* ceremonies and weddings—and job interviews. This Shabbat seemed more like an interview than anything else, which was part of what prompted Dani's clothing choice. And he was glad *someone* was impressed, even if Jake was already on Dani's side.

"Thanks," Dani said. "You should see me in my tux."

Jake smiled. "Maybe someday. You never know, right?"

"You never know," Dani repeated. He could think of a couple of situations in which Jake would be present and he would be wearing his tux. Not many, but a couple.

Anyway.

He looked around the room. At least three hundred people milled about. The men were all in suits and ties. The women all wore dresses or skirts and blouses, and many of them wore hats or headscarves. "Was there a *simcha* this Shabbat, or do you get this kind of crowd every week?"

"Big *macher*'s daughter's getting married. *Aufruf* was today. Thus the crowd." He gestured to the elaborate kiddush set out. "And the food. Go snag yourself something; I'll let Avi know you're here."

"Thanks, Jake," Dani said, pushing away from the wall and moving toward the tables with the food. He made polite mumblings at people wishing him *Shabbat shalom* but tried to stay away from people who looked as if they might try to engage him in conversation and away from people who were on the hospitality committee, who would ask if

he needed somewhere to eat lunch. Dani appreciated that they went out of their way to make newcomers welcome, but he was feeling awkward enough without having to explain himself to total strangers.

Finally, however, he reached the food table, snagged himself a couple of pieces of cake, and plotted his path to slink back toward the wall.

"*Gut Shabbos*, Dan."

He turned to find Gedaliah, one of the tenors from Kol Ish, behind him. Gedaliah's diminutive height and boyish face made him look as though he was barely eighteen, though Dani knew he was in his early thirties and had a wife and three kids. He was blond and blue-eyed; a boy with identical coloring, who couldn't have been older than two, was riding on his shoulders.

"Shabbat shalom, Gedaliah," Dani responded.

"What brings you to this neck of the woods?"

"Lunch with the Levines."

"Ah," Gedaliah said, nodding.

"Yeah."

"I saw Avi here a second ago." Gedaliah seemed unsure what to say, which was understandable. After all, Dani was probably the last person Gedaliah anticipated running into at shul.

"Yeah," Dani said. "Jake went to find him, tell him I was here. I'm gonna…" He gestured toward the wall where he'd been lurking.

"Enjoy," Gedaliah said. "And good luck with lunch."

"Thanks."

Dani snatched one last piece of cake from the kiddush table and went back to his hiding-in-plain-sight place by the drinks.

And that's where Avi found him.

"Hey," Avi said. His tone was overly casual, but his facial expression betrayed much more fondness.

"Hey, yourself. Shabbat shalom."

"Shabbat shalom, Dani."

Dani looked Avi up and down, indulging himself as much as he could, given the setting. Avi was wearing a dark blue three-piece suit with a

white button-down shirt and a navy tie with small treble clefs on it. The suit was perfectly fitted on Avi's body.

"How's the ankle?" It bothered Dani to see Avi walking with a cane, but, boy, did it beat the crutches!

"Like it was when you asked right before Shabbat—still a bit tender, but healing. Stop *hovering*, Dani; you're beginning to remind me of Dalia."

"In my own defense, I warned you I was gonna be this way," Dani said.

"Yeah, but I didn't know you meant it to quite this degree." Avi paused. "Trust me, Dani, okay? I've been through this before. My ankle will heal."

Dani knew that, intellectually. Emotionally, however, was a completely different story.

"I'll try, Avi. That's all I can promise, okay?"

Avi smiled. "That's all I'm asking."

Dani noticed a row of upholstered chairs along the wall of windows that separated the social hall from the synagogue's permanent sukkah frame. "Do me a favor, then?"

"Yeah?"

"Come sit with me until your family's ready to leave. I just—"

"Yeah, sure," Avi said. He sounded as though he was doing this solely to humor Dani, but that was good enough.

They made their way slowly to the line of chairs, not because of Avi's injury but because they were stopped every five steps by someone else wanting to greet Avi and ask how he was healing. He always introduced Dani—in a "this is my friend visiting from out of town" way, not a "this is my boyfriend; someday I want him to jump my bones" way—and Dani just nodded politely.

Eventually they got seated. Dani itched to take Avi's hand, but it was probably the worst place to do so.

"What are you thinking?" Avi whispered to Dani.

"That I want be alone with you," Dani whispered back.

Avi blushed.

And, of course, that's when Dalia came over. She signed to Avi and he signed back, but he didn't interpret. From his gestures, however, it was

obvious to Dani that she was teasing Avi. To get the heat off Avi, Dani waded into the fray.

"Hey, Dalia," he said, trusting that Avi would interpret. "Shabbat shalom."

"Gut Shabbos, Dan."

"How's school?"

"Annoying. End of semester stuff. Grading and other crap. Students who didn't show up all semester now expect me to give them decent grades. And don't think you can distract me so that Avi won't have to tell me how you made him blush." Even in Avi's voice, the comment was pure Dalia. And now Avi was blushing even deeper.

"Later, Dal. Not here." Avi's tone brooked no argument, and Dani assumed he was putting the same conviction into his signs. Dalia nodded, and the subject was dropped.

Not long after, Chava joined them, followed by Jake. "Ima says that she and Abba will be ready to go in a couple of minutes," Jake said. "I'll go grab the coats; you should stay here so that we don't have to reassemble everyone once Ima and Abba are set." He went to the coat room, leaving the four of them looking at each other.

"So," Dani said to Chava and Dalia, "you're both going to help me out this afternoon, right?"

Avi translated what Dani said, then continued to interpret when Dalia responded.

"As much as we can."

"My parents are being unreasonable," Chava added. "There's no reason that they should accept my dating Jeremy without reservation but give you and Avi so much *tzuris*." Chava and Jeremy had met about two weeks ago. Avi had expressed some concern about the relationship, but he was trying to be as supportive of Chava as she was being of him and Dani.

"Chava, they just have my best interests in mind, really," Avi said, clearly discomfited.

"That doesn't give them the right to decide whom you should date," Chava responded.

Avi lowered his voice to a stage whisper; clearly this was a conversation that was better left unvoiced, but Dani was glad that Avi kept him part of it. "They're not deciding; I'm deciding. They're just expressing their opinion, which, mind you, I don't agree with one bit." He paused. "Look, this isn't the time or place for this discussion. I'm glad you're comfortable with Dani and me being together, but I don't want this to become a point of contention between you and Ima and Abba. I won't do that to you, and I won't do that to them."

Before the conversation could get any more heated—or Avi could get any more agitated—Jake returned with an armful of coats. "Any movement on the parental front?" he asked.

"Not while you were gone," Dani responded, "but I think they're headed this way." He stood up in anticipation of leaving and to show respect to the Levines. It was best to start the afternoon on his best behavior.

"Shabbat shalom," Dani said as they approached.

"Gut Shabbos, Dan," Yoni said, and Ilana echoed the greeting.

"Thank you again for inviting me to lunch."

"We should have done it a while ago," Ilana said. "I'm sorry we didn't." She looked at the assembled multitude, then continued. "Seems like we've got everyone; shall we head out?"

They put on their coats as they moved out of the social hall. The group got stopped a couple more times by friends who wanted to convey Shabbat greetings, but within just a couple of minutes they were walking toward the Levines' house.

Dani tried to keep up with the multithreaded conversation going on around him during the ten-minute walk from the shul to the Levines' house, but he was distracted with worry about the upcoming meal. This was, he thought, make-or-break when it came to his relationship with Avi's parents and, potentially, with Avi. Just as Avi had said to Chava, Dani didn't want to put Avi into a position of having to choose between him and his parents.

Dani couldn't call that one, and he knew himself—if it came down to it, he would encourage Avi to not reject his parents, even if doing so would mean Dani would have his heart torn out.

Caught up in his own concerns, Dani yelped when he felt a hand on his shoulder.

"You okay?" Jake asked quietly.

"Yeah," Dani said. "No… yeah… oh fuck. I have no clue."

"You're overthinking. Just let this be lunch. Don't think about any implications or repercussions you've decided will result. Damn…" he sighed. "You're so much like Avi sometimes, it's no surprise the two of you are so right for each other."

"It's just…" Dani shook his head. "Avi's become so much a part of my life already. But at the same time, he's been part of your parents' lives for his whole life. I just don't want…"

"I know," Jake said. "It's just that you don't want to lose Avi, but you don't want him to have to choose between you and our parents. But, by the same token, neither do my parents. They know the score; they know—much as they don't want to think about it—that Avi would choose you over them in a heartbeat. So—despite everything you're thinking—they're bound to try to make this as comfortable as possible. They'll go out of their way not to make trouble, not wanting to alienate you and thus alienate Avi. Why the Hell else would they have invited all the rest of us? They want you to be comfortable, so that they can get to know who you really are."

Dani thought about that. "I hope you're right."

"Trust me," he said. "I know their tactics. You should've seen them when I brought home my first serious girlfriend."

"How old were you at the time?"

"I was a college freshman. So there I am, eighteen and dating seriously for the first time, and I bring Andrea home for Pesach. The first night is fine—there's lots of people at the *seder*; lots of people who can run interference if my parents get difficult or if Andrea starts feeling uncomfortable. I'm terrified, however, about what will happen at lunch. It's supposed to be just family, and I'm really convinced that my parents are going to give Andrea the third degree, ask her all about her plans for marriage and family. But they surprise me. Instead of making her feel like a specimen on a slide, they draw her out, make her feel comfortable

talking about what she's majoring in, why she's chosen her field. By the end, they had gotten to know her, they respected my choosing her, and they had gotten to know more about me through getting to know her."

"So? *Nu?* What happened with Andrea?" Dani asked.

"She eventually realized that she hated being a biology major, switched to advertising, and after college she stayed in Chicago. She's married, has four kids under the age of six, and is working for the *Sun-Times*."

"But it's different for us, for Avi and me. If I have my way, this will be it for me. No more playing the field, no more stupid, meaningless flings with people who don't really want to know who I am, no more inequitable relationships in which I care more than he does, or he cares more than I do, or any of that shit. I want this..." Dani sighed. "I think I want this to be permanent. Hell, I *know* I want this to be permanent. But Avi's... well... I don't want to pressure him, and I don't want to rush him, and I don't want to accidentally hurt him. And all that anxiety and all that pressure and all that fear inside me just amplifies when I think about the fact that, with their disapproval, your parents could take all that out of my hands, make it no longer my decision, *our* decision, but *theirs*. And that frightens me more than anything." Dani had no idea why he was spilling his guts to Jake, but he felt better having said all of it out loud.

"Look," Jake said. "My parents are going to, ultimately, have one concern and only one concern—whether you're going to treat Avi well."

"Hell, yes, I am," Dani said.

"So you're fine. No matter what else they throw at you, remember that their real goal is to answer that one question. Everything else is just leading up to or dancing around that question. Show them that Avi's happiness, Avi's wellbeing, comes first, and they'll love you."

"Thanks, Jake," Dani said. He would have said more, but they were almost at the house, and the elder Levines were within hearing distance.

At the house, Dani turned and saw Avi, Chava, and Dalia deep in conversation about a hundred yards behind him. He stopped at the front door. He didn't want to enter the house alone, and he also wanted to make sure that Avi was okay after the walk from shul.

"You and Jake sure were intense," Chava said.

"It was nothing," Dani said. Not that he wasn't planning to tell Avi all about the conversation, but he didn't think Avi wanted to interpret it for Chava and Dalia while he was hearing it for the first time.

"So," Avi asked Dani, "you ready?"

Dani took a deep breath. "I think so." And he was surprised to find that he meant it.

"Then let's go. I could really use an Advil, and I need to take it with food."

They moved into the house, and Dani immediately took Avi to the living room to sit and take the weight off his ankle. For each argument Avi mounted, Dani had a counter-argument, which is how Dani eventually found himself tearing lettuce and slicing tomatoes for the salad. Dani was informed that this was traditionally Avi's job, but when he explained that he didn't think it was in Avi's best interest to be standing for that long, Ilana just smiled, handed him the vegetable knife, and pointed him to the proper cutting board.

Once the salad was completed, and Ilana had confirmed that all of the food on the hot plate was warming properly, Yoni called people to the table. One by one, they found seats around the large table in the Levines' dining room. The table was set with a white tablecloth overlaid with a lacework tablecloth. On top of that was laid a clear plastic table cover to protect everything from potential spills. Fine china and sterling silver flatware were set at every place. In the center of the table was a decorated cutting board with the Hebrew phrase carved into it that translated as "For the Sabbath and Holidays."

As Ilana entered the dining room, she placed two loaves of challah on the cutting board and then placed a cloth over the bread. The cloth was decorated with the same Hebrew phrase. After they'd completed the preliminaries—the blessing of the Sabbath over a cup of wine, the ritual hand-washing, and the blessing over bread—lunch began.

"So," Yoni said, and Dani braced himself for the onslaught of questions, "what did you think of the rabbi's *drash*, Jake?"

Each week, in the middle of Shabbat morning services, the rabbi gave a sermon. The rabbi of Yoni and Ilana's synagogue had a general pattern:

he would start with something in the news or something from a television show or movie he had seen, connect it to something in the week's Torah reading, and then tie it all together with thoughtful analysis that built on analysis of the Torah portion by one of the great Jewish scholars.

Jake shot Dani a look that he couldn't understand and then launched into a critique of the rabbi's lesson. Dani couldn't say that he followed it—either the rabbi's original argument as Jake presented it or Jake's counter-argument—as he was too busy being thankful for this momentary reprieve.

Someone kicked Dani under the table; from the angle, he figured it was Chava. He looked at her, and she gestured toward Avi.

In an attempt to be subtle, Dani looked at Avi out the corner of his eye. And he was shocked to find that Avi was blatantly watching him rather than paying attention to his brother.

"… And that's why I think his interpretation of Ibn Ezra on that passuk is not as relevant to modern society as he was describing." Jake wound down his explanation and looked toward his father.

"Ah," Yoni said. "What I meant was, did you think that he was getting better at keeping it to fifteen minutes." There was laughter around the table, though the full meaning of why was lost on Dani.

The first course—gefilte fish and the salad Dani helped make—was served, and the interrogation began.

"Dan?" Ilana began, "what do you see yourself doing in five years?"

Avi's reaction was immediate. "*Ima*! I thought I asked you not to make this like a job interview; we're supposed to be having Shabbat lunch, and lunch only."

"One of your complaints when we were at your place last week was that we haven't gotten to know Dan well and that we're unfairly judging him based on preconceived notions. How are we supposed to know who Dan is if we don't ask him?"

"But…" Avi started.

Dani didn't want this turning into a fight, so he said, "No, it's a reasonable question." He thought. "Well, the computer software sector is getting more stable, but there are still some uncertainties, so while I

hope to still be employed as a software engineer, I know there are no guarantees in my business. I hope that, even if I am not programming in five years, I will be doing something both personally satisfying and fiscally responsible."

Dani wasn't sure they'd buy that—after all, it sounded weak even to Dani himself—but Ilana nodded, and then Yoni took his turn.

"Dan, how many people have you dated?" Dani noted that he didn't ask specifically about the men, which surprised him.

But he answered honestly. "I've had three serious relationships, and—given how young I was then—in retrospect I can't say that the first two were really serious. I thought they were; I was convinced of it at the time. But now that I know what real relationships are supposed to be like, I can't count any more than one." He wasn't going to mention the casual flings he'd had, because not only weren't they relevant, they weren't the Levines' business. Dani knew he wasn't going to screw around on Avi, and that was all that was important.

"Abba," Jake asked when Dani finished, "how did your students do this semester?"

"We have other questions for Dan," Yoni said.

Jake smiled. "But he's not being allowed to taste Ima's cooking. Give him a break, let him fortify himself for the next round of questioning, and then you can bring out the truth serum, okay?" Jake said it jokingly, but Dani appreciated Jake's willingness to interfere.

Ilana and Yoni asked a couple other questions between the fish course and the main meal. They were pointed and probing, but at no time did Dani feel they were inappropriate.

Over the main course, they got more subtle. Instead of direct questions about Dani's intentions toward Avi and Dani's future prospects, they asked him about the current situation in Israel, whether his extended family was all safe, and other questions meant to determine his stance on the current political atmosphere in Israel. Not knowing from the outset where Ilana and Yoni stood on the topic, and knowing that there were many valid positions, Dani found the conversation stressful. However,

it turned out that his views and Avi's parents' views were in alignment, so Dani found himself relaxing.

By the time they reached dessert, it seemed like the oral part of the exam was over, as conversation turned to the Patriots' prospects—on which he had no input whatsoever—and whether or not the winter was going to be as harsh as last year's.

After dessert and the blessings after the meal, everyone adjourned to the living room for more conversation. They sat around the room on comfortable chairs and a couple of sofas, except for Chava and Dalia, who sat on the living room floor and started setting up for a game of *Settlers of Catan*. Again the topics were random and didn't approach anything near the level of questioning that Dani had anticipated. The scariest part was when they veered into the topic of the presidential election. They agreed on many of the issues. But since Dani was not automatically supporting the one Jewish candidate, he was worried they'd see that as a sign that he was unfit for their son.

At around three-thirty, Yoni looked at his watch. "If I'm going to get to *Mincha*, I'm going to have to cut this short. We'll have to have you back again, Dan."

"Thank you," Dani said, standing up. "Both for lunch and for… well…"

"Not forbidding you from ever seeing Avi again?" Yoni responded, and his smile was more genuine than any Dani had seen from him.

"Well, yeah," Dani said, and Jake, Chava, and Dalia laughed as Avi turned bright red.

"We know it's been… awkward at times, between you and us, and we wanted to rectify that," Ilana said.

"We'd had this idea," Yoni continued, "that we'd sit you here under the harsh lights of the dining room and grill you on your intentions toward Avi."

"Which, in fact, you did to some extent," Chava signed and Avi interpreted.

"We did, didn't we? But… and I think Ilana will agree with me," Yoni said, turning to Ilana, "we've seen how you interact not only with Avi

but also with Jake, Chava, and Dalia. And as much as it's still going to take us some time to get used to the idea, you've shown that you really do care about Avi, and that's really all we care about."

"Thank you, sir," Dani said.

"Please," he said, "call me Yoni. Not even my students call me 'sir' anymore."

"Thank you," Dani said again. He wasn't sure what to do now; it was clear that lunch was over, but he wanted to get some time alone with Avi, to decompress.

Avi seemed to understand. "Hey, Abba? I'm not sure I'm up to shul again today. I could really use some downtime for my ankle—I want to go home, put up my foot, and ice it again."

"Sounds like a good plan," Jake said.

"You could do that here," Ilana said.

This time it was Dalia who had a suggestion. "He'd be more comfortable at home, and Dan can make sure he gets there safely, can't you, Dan?"

Dani nodded, unwilling to wade into the complex negotiations that were obviously going on.

"I can get home okay myself," Avi said.

Chava kicked him in response—in his good leg.

"Actually, on second thought, maybe it would be best if Dan walked me home."

"It's a plan, then," Jake said. "Give me a minute, Abba, and I'll be ready to go with you. Thanks for lunch, Ima."

"You're welcome, Jake," Ilana said.

Within a couple of minutes, Jake, Yoni, Avi, and Dani had their coats on and were ready to leave.

"Thank you again," Dani said to Yoni and Ilana. "I really do appreciate your hospitality."

"You're welcome any time," Yoni said, and Ilana nodded in agreement.

"Thank you," Dani said, though he felt silly for saying it yet again.

They finally said their goodbyes and their Shabbat shaloms, and then Yoni and Jake headed back toward the shul and Avi and Dani headed slowly toward Avi's house.

Once they were inside, and Avi was settled on the couch with an ice pack on his ankle, Dani said, "Well, that wasn't as bad as I thought it would be."

"What were you expecting?" Avi asked.

"The Spanish Inquisition." Dani realized as it came out of his mouth that he'd given Avi the straight line for a Monty Python reference, but Avi resisted.

"Has it really been that bad?" Avi asked.

Dani thought. "Not really. I know it's only because they love you. And today was actually very nice, once we got past the oral exam."

"You passed, though. And they're tough graders."

"Especially when it comes to you, I think."

"It would be the same for anyone dating Jake or Chava; it's not just you."

"Yeah," Dani said. "Jake said essentially the same thing."

Avi chuckled.

"What?" Dani asked.

"He's such a *yenta* sometimes."

"Yeah, but he's doing it for our own good, so I can't get too angry at him for meddling."

"True."

They were both silent for a couple of minutes, and then Dani said, "So…"

"'So,' what?"

Nothing Dani was thinking was at all appropriate for him to say: *So now that your parents no longer think I'm going to corrupt you, am I free to begin corrupting you; so now that we've lived through lunch with your parents, are you at all ready for a meal with my parents; so can I take you out somewhere and wine and dine you publicly?* Instead, he said, "So… with Shabbat ending so early these days, d'you want to go catch a movie tonight?"

"Yeah," Avi said, smiling.

It was normal, it was stress-free, and it was just what they needed.

plenty to be thankful for

DANI LOVED THANKSGIVING. THERE WAS just so much about the holiday
that made him happy—good food, spending time with family, the
acknowledgment that winter is coming. And this year there was something
else: he was going to share his favorite secular holiday with Avi.

Thanksgiving was odd in his parents' house. Both of Dani's parents had
moved to Israel as children—part of the *aliyah* wave of the early fifties—so
they considered themselves more Israeli than American. But as immigrants,
they embraced the quintessentially American observance of Thanksgiving
as a way to celebrate the country they'd chosen. So Thanksgiving in Dani's
parents' home, for as long as Dani could remember, involved turkey and
stuffing and all the traditional Thanksgiving foods—the ones that weren't
blatantly non-kosher; while the Perezes had never kept kosher, certain
foods were never brought into the house. And any and all relatives who
happened to be in the area were invited.

After the meal, which always began right around three, everyone sat
in the living room with a fire blazing. Various traditions had sprung
up over the years—card games were played by uncles and cousins and
anyone else who wished to join; the relatives who did handcrafts would
knit or crochet or whatever while catching up on family gossip; Dani
and Dudu usually played guitar or piano to entertain the masses. The

specific rituals varied, depending on the makeup of the crowd, but the spirit of togetherness and thanksgiving was ever-present.

Any year that a dati family member was expected be in town, accommodations were made for them. So Avi's joining the Perezes wasn't any extra burden, just a question of logistics. Dani's parents had a number of dati friends in the neighborhood, and one or another was always willing to let them use their kitchen. Since Dani's cousin Batya had moved to Allston the previous May and she was dati, Dani's mother had asked if she'd be willing to donate her kitchen to the cause. Batya agreed, so the Sunday before Thanksgiving had found Dani's parents, Dani, and Dudu gathered in Batya's small, but serviceable, kitchen to review exactly who would cook what and when. Batya had been willing to make her kitchen available every evening for cooking, refrigerators had been cleared out to accommodate all the food being prepared, and the Perezes' dati neighbors had given Dani's parents a key to their house so they could heat up everything on Thursday, since the neighbors were spending Thanksgiving with their kids in western Massachusetts.

Yes, everyone cooked. Penina Perez firmly believed that her boys should not leave home without basic life skills, so they'd learned to cook. And for Thanksgiving, everyone pitched in, and each of them had their specialties. And by the end of Sunday afternoon, they had a plan for preparing their traditional Thanksgiving dinner in a way that Avi would be able to enjoy.

Each night that week, when Dani spoke to Avi, after regaling him with the latest progress on the cooking, he tried to reassure him about the upcoming gathering. Avi seemed much more nervous than Dani thought the situation warranted, but he assured Avi that he would be welcome.

Thursday morning, Dani got to his parents' house around eleven.

"You're late," Penina said in greeting as Dani hung his coat on the hook inside the front door. "Please take all the coats off the hooks and put them on Dudu's bed. Then I'll need your help with setting the table."

"Sorry, Ima," Dani said. "I was on the phone late last night and then overslept."

"With your young man?" Penina asked, her blue eyes twinkling.

"Yes, Ima, with my 'young man.'" Dani leaned down to kiss Penina on the cheek as he walked past her toward Dudu's room.

"This one's serious, isn't it, Dani?" Penina asked.

"Yeah," Dani said. "I really think this one could be it. If he'll let it be."

"A cautious one, your young man is?"

"He is. But I think you'll really like him if he lets himself relax." Not that Dani thought Penina wouldn't like the shy, reserved Avi that the public sees, but he hoped Avi would relax enough to show the real Avi, the one Dani was beginning to think he could fall in love with.

Dani carried the coats upstairs to the room that used to be Dudu's. Coming down, he paused on the stairs to soak in the atmosphere of the house. Dudu and their father had come home from their errands while Dani had been upstairs. From his position on the stairs, he saw his father starting a fire in the fireplace in the living room, as he did every year. He heard his mother asking someone to go get something from the basement, and he heard Dudu's laughter in counterpoint to whatever his aunt Rachel was saying. He took a moment to look at the pictures on the stairwell wall. The old pictures were interspersed with newer ones; one recently added might be his dad, his brother, or himself at age three or so, since all three of them had looked so alike at that age. This felt right; this felt like home, even though he hadn't lived here in over a decade.

"Dani, don't stand there daydreaming; I need you," Penina called from the kitchen.

"Coming, Ima." Dani went into the kitchen to see what Penina needed.

"So what does your young man do?" Penina asked while handing paper goods to Dani.

"He's an American Sign Language interpreter and a singer."

"So he's smart *and* talented."

"Yes," Dani said, amused by this interrogation; this was the most interest Penina had shown in any of Dani's partners since he'd graduated from high school. "He's good-looking, too."

"Eh, that's secondary, Dani. Looks aren't everything, you know."

"Yeah, yeah, I know. But it doesn't hurt, either."

"True," Penina said, fluffing her auburn curls and mock-preening.

"Anyway," Dani said, trying to move—temporarily—away from the topic of Avi. "Do you already have a seating chart, or am I on my own?"

Penina laughed. "Of course I have a seating chart. How else could I guarantee that you and your young man would be as far away from each other as possible, so that Abba and I can interrogate him at our leisure?"

"I hope you're kidding," Dani said, thinking about the Shabbat meal he had spent with the Levines. "I think that would scare him so much he'd never want to see me again."

"Don't worry, Dani. I'm kidding. I sat you and Avi next to each other, with Dudu right across so that there's a chance Avi will feel vaguely comfortable."

"Thanks, Ima," Dani said. "I really do appreciate you letting me invite him."

"He's important to you; you're important to us. What more do I need to know?" She smiled. "But if you don't have that table set before people start to get here, I'll find reasons to keep you in the kitchen all afternoon, keeping you from having any time to enjoy his being here."

"I'm going, I'm going," Dani said.

Knowing better than to assume that his mother was bluffing, Dani set up the tables and chairs right away. The Perezes went all out when it came to Thanksgiving dinner. So not only did the main dining room table have to be extended with all the available leaves so it would seat twelve, two card tables were set up in the living room for the kids. Fall-themed tablecloths, plates, napkins, and cups were laid out on each table where people would eat. Orange plastic forks, knives, and spoons were set at each place. The buffet table was covered with another fall-themed tablecloth, and a large cornucopia was set in the center. After half an hour, Dudu came to help Dani.

"I like this," Penina said, coming into the dining room.

"Child labor?" Dani asked, and Dudu chuckled.

"You're not children anymore, Daniel," she said. "No, seeing my two sons helping each other instead of whacking each other with whatever they could."

"We're not children anymore," Dudu said, smiling at his mother. Dudu shared his mother's coloring and his brother's build. While he usually wore the graduate student uniform of sweatpants and a T-shirt covered with a zippered hoodie, today he had taken time to put on a button-down shirt and a pair of khaki pants.

With the two brothers working together, setting up the tables was straightforward, and they finished about one. Since people usually started showing up at one-thirty—leaving plenty of *shmoozing* time before the meal actually began—when the doorbell rang at one-fifteen, Dani knew who it had to be.

"I'll get it." He figured Avi would be less nervous if Dani was the first person he saw.

Dani took a deep breath, practiced, "Hey, Avi, glad you could make it" to himself, then opened the door.

"Hi," Avi said.

"Hey, Avi," he said. "I'm glad you could make it." *Good,* Dani thought, *I did that without saying anything improper*. He opened the screen door and held it as Avi walked in.

"Sorry I'm so early," Avi said, blushing.

"Eh, don't worry. It's only fifteen minutes. And, anyway, it just means you'll be put to work in the kitchen. Hope you don't mind."

"I'm happy to help. Just tell me what to do, and I'll do it."

Oh, the things Dani thought and then suppressed—and the accompanying mental images. But he just shook them off and said, "Ima's in charge and she'll definitely have something you can do."

Dani gave Avi a half-hug and a quick kiss, and Avi reciprocated. "I'm really glad you came," Dani whispered.

"I'm scared to death," Avi whispered back, "but I'm glad I came. Is this what you felt like when you came to my parents' place for lunch?

"Worried they'll take one look at me and declare me unfit for their son? Definitely. But you have nothing to worry about—my parents will love you. I know it."

"I hope you're right," Avi said. "Anyway, no need to delay the inevitable. Let's go before I completely chicken out and run in fear."

"Relax, Avi. They'll love you. Really."

They went into the kitchen, and, without turning around Penina said, "Dani, please go down to the basement and get more aluminum foil."

"How can I help, Mrs. Perez?" Avi asked.

Penina turned around immediately. "Hi, Avi," she said, smiling widely and reaching her hand out to shake Avi's. "It's lovely to meet you. And please call me Penina."

"Thank you for having me," Avi responded and he was blushing again.

"You're more than welcome. It's a pleasure to meet you. I've heard so much about you from Dani that I feel like I know you already." Dani knew Penina was bluffing, but he also knew she wanted Avi to feel as comfortable as possible as soon as possible.

"Thank you," Avi said again.

"So, nu, Dani? Things aren't going to bring themselves upstairs. Please go get the foil so I can put things into the oven. Avi, if you don't mind, could you get the platters down from that shelf?" Penina gestured to the uppermost shelf in the kitchen cabinet, where they'd stashed the platters and utensils borrowed from various dati relatives.

"Uh, sure," Avi said, immediately complying with Penina's request.

"Dani, *now*, please," Penina said.

"Going, Ima," Dani said, and went.

After a minute, Avi's laughter drifted down the stairs to Dani, and Dani knew that Avi had to be talking to Dudu. He was pleased that Avi was comfortable with his brother. Avi and Dudu had hit it off the first time they'd met, for reasons that were not clear to Dani, but he wasn't going to complain.

"Dani," Dudu said when Dani came back into the kitchen, "you never told me that Avi told such good stories."

"He's a natural," Dani said, and Avi blushed.

"Dani, stop putting Avi on the spot and give me some help here," Penina said.

"Sorry, Ima; sorry, Avi," Dani said.

"It's okay," Avi said. "I'm getting used to it." He smiled.

Dani, Avi, Penina, and Dudu continued to get the food prepared as Ben, Dani's father, worked as doorman and chief greeter to the onslaught of relatives. Ben was tall, almost as tall as Dani, and was the source of Dani's brown hair and eyes. After removing their coats, each new arrival came into the kitchen to say hello to Penina and to offer their help. For the most part, Penina sent them to relax in the living room, but one or two—the competent ones, the ones who understood the complex nature of preparing kosher food in a non-kosher kitchen—were allowed to stay and help. With each new arrival, Avi got more and more quiet, only responding to questions posed directly to him.

By the time the fifth set of relatives came through the kitchen, Dani knew it was time to either get Avi out of the kitchen or make the relatives go away. He caught Penina's eye and indicated Avi, then gave her a pleading look Dani hoped she'd understand.

And, as always, he shouldn't have worried. Penina glanced at Avi, then looked at Dani and said, "Why don't you go find some extra napkins, just in case? I think they're upstairs in the closet." Dani recognized it as Penina's way of giving Avi and Dani some time alone, because both she and Dani knew that there were no napkins in that closet. But Avi didn't know that, and the relatives didn't know that.

"Avi, can you lend me a hand?" Dani asked, heading toward the hallway and the stairs.

"Sure," he said.

Upstairs Dani bypassed the closet and led Avi toward what he still thought of as his room. When Dani left for college, his parents had turned the room into a combination office and guest room, but it was always available when Dani needed it. While Penina had put up new curtains and removed the Superman duvet from the bed, there were still certificates of achievement and other high school memorabilia hanging on the wall. To Dani, it still had the right mix of "his" room and his mother's office to make it seem he still belonged there.

"Wait," Avi said, hanging back as Dani tried to pull him into the room. "Your mother asked for…"

Dani cut him off. "It was just a ruse, Avi. She knew I wanted to get out of there, and I knew you needed to get out of there, so she sent us on an unnecessary errand. No need to worry—she'll carry on just fine without us for a while. Now come and sit down and relax; you looked ready to crawl into one of the cabinets and pull the door shut behind you."

Dani led Avi toward the bed and then sat on the edge. He patted the bed next to himself. "C'mon, sit down. You look like you're ready to fall over."

"I… but…" Avi blushed and gestured with his expressive hands, then tried again. "I'm not sure… I just don't…" He threw his hands in the air and sighed. "I'm going to sound like an idiot when I say this, Dani, so please try not to laugh."

"I wouldn't laugh, Avi. Honest."

"Thank you. So…" Avi paused, and Dani wondered for a minute if Avi was actually planning to continue. "I'm really out of my depth here."

Dani figured that anything he said now would freak Avi out even further, so, after taking a glance around the room, he stood up, pulled out the desk chair and moved it to face the bed. He then sat back down, across from the chair.

"That better?" Dani asked, gesturing toward the chair.

"Much. Thanks." Avi sat in the chair. He was still close, but there was apparently enough distance that he was comfortable. Dani could already see Avi relaxing.

They sat and just looked at each other. Dani had no idea what to say or do; his only goal had been to get Avi away from the crowd that was unsettling him. And Avi didn't seem as though he had any idea what to say or do. So they just continued to sit and look at each other.

Finally, Dani broke the silence. "How are things with your parents?"

"They're trying," Avi said. "I would like to think they'd be this way with any relationship I was in, regardless of my partner's sex. At this point they still try to think of you as just a very close friend, sort of like Dalia, only male."

"Don't push them," Dani said. "My parents took a long time to realize that I meant it when I said I was more interested in men than in women.

And I think there's a part of Ima that still hopes I'll find a nice girl and settle down, though she completely accepts who I am."

Avi looked worried. "Are you absolutely sure I should be here today? I mean, if she's not comfortable with…"

Dani interrupted him. "Avi, stop. Remember, I came out almost fifteen years ago. My parents have had plenty of time to work through any problem they had about me dating guys. She's thrilled you're here, and she's very glad I'm in a stable relationship. I was a bit irresponsible after I first came out and, to be honest, for a good long while after that. Ever since then Ima has been watching my relationships somewhat warily."

Avi was silent, then said, "I just don't know how to talk to my parents about this. They seemed perfectly comfortable when I first told them about you, but then, they began asking me whether this was really the choice I wanted to make. And they don't seem to understand that it's not a conscious choice. It's not like I woke up one morning and said to myself, 'Hey, what would it be like to date guys? I should experiment!' I think they still hope that I'll 'get over' this 'phase' they think I'm going through. I want to tell them all about you, get them to understand why you're so special to me. But I just can't. And then I worry that, if I don't tell them how important you are to me, you'll start to think I don't care for you. And I do. More deeply than I ever thought possible."

Avi paused, but Dani didn't say anything, even though he longed to. He knew Avi still had more to say, and, if he interrupted, Avi might lose his nerve.

"I dream. Of you, of us. Of things I can't even put words to, feelings and emotions that I don't have even the slightest idea what to do with. And I wake up aching, wanting, and not knowing how to deal. Barely even knowing what it is that I really want. I'm not ready for any of it. And I feel sometimes that I'm holding you back, that you'd be happier if I were more experienced. And I'm going to shut up now before I embarrass myself even more."

"Shh, Avi, motek, don't worry," Dani said, hoping to dispel some of Avi's fear. "I'm happier with you than I've ever been with anyone else, regardless of your experience or lack thereof." With Avi, Dani knew he

was finally learning what real relationships were, what it meant to be with someone for the long term. "I want this to be comfortable for both of us. We'll find our way, at our own pace." Dani knew he had said that to Avi before, but he was beginning to understand that Avi needed to hear it often, that he needed the reassurance that Dani was happy with how the relationship was proceeding.

With his left hand, Dani grasped Avi's right, which was resting on his right knee. Avi jumped slightly, but then he relaxed into the chair.

"This okay?" Dani asked.

"Yeah," he said with a small smile. "It's fine... it's good... I like it." He blushed and stopped talking.

"Avi, it's fine to tell me what you like and what you don't like. Otherwise, I have no way of knowing, okay?" Dani knew that Avi had minimal experience with romantic or sexual relationships of any sort, but more and more he was realizing just what that meant for them as a couple.

"Okay," Avi said. "And I have to thank you."

"For what?" Dani asked.

"For rescuing me back there. I get up in front of hundreds of people on a regular basis, either to perform or to interpret, but I just can't handle crowds. I get all tongue-tied, and I begin to feel like everything I say sounds ridiculous, so I just stop talking, and then I feel even more ridiculous. And I know this is your family, and I know they're very likely people I'll get along with, but I just... freeze up, I guess."

"It's okay, Avi. My family can be a bit much when it's just the four of us. Throw some additional relatives in, and it can be a madhouse. We've got some time before anything except appetizers will be served; if you want to just sit up here and relax, that's fine."

"No," Avi said, shaking his head. "I don't want to hide. I just... I need to prepare myself before going back down there."

Dani stood up, but he didn't let go of Avi's hand. "Do you want privacy? Should I go downstairs and wait for you?" Dani didn't want to leave Avi, but if it would be better for Avi, then Dani would give him space.

"No," he said. "I want you here with me." Avi tugged on their joined hands. "Come on; sit back down. This shouldn't take too long. And, anyway, it's odd for me to do this while you're standing over me like that."

Dani sat, and Avi closed his eyes. He took a couple of deep breaths, then sat, unmoving except for the fingers that lightly stroked against Dani's. Dani doubted Avi had any idea how much the unconscious gesture aroused him. He started to breathe harder, and his heart rate sped up. He shifted so that Avi wouldn't notice that he was getting hard; he didn't want, during this time that he was supposed to be allowing Avi to relax, to make Avi more nervous.

After a few minutes, Avi opened his eyes. "Okay," he said. "I think I'm good to go down."

"You sure?"

"Honestly, no. But I'm going to try."

"We should have a signal," Dani said. "You know, if you need to get away again?"

"Did you play spy games as a kid?" Avi asked, smiling broadly for the first time since walking into the house.

"Uh… yeah, I did," Dani said. "I'd be the Mossad agent, and Dudu was the criminal I was sent to track and apprehend."

"Anyway," Avi said. "I don't think we need any verbal signal—you seemed very good at picking up on my need to escape before."

"Mostly because I was watching you very closely."

"Then keep doing that," Avi said. And he blushed again, so Dani knew he meant it.

They stood up, still holding hands, and walked out of Dani's room and down the hall. At the top of the stairs, Dani slowly drew his hand out of Avi's. "Not that I don't want to hold your hand," Dani said. "But I can only imagine what Doda Nechama would come up with if she noticed. She'd tell Batya, because Batya and her mother talk about everything, and by the end of dinner everyone would be speculating about our wedding."

"Not that I don't want you to," Avi responded. "And you're completely right."

They went back to the kitchen. Penina looked up from her final preparations, nodded and smiled at Dani and Avi, and then returned to her task. Avi and Dani made sure that all the serving utensils were arranged and brought out the last of the table decorations, keeping themselves busy until Penina said it was time to gather the troops in the dining room.

Dani was pleased that during the meal Avi was able to relax enough to talk not just to him and to Dudu but also to some of the others. Penina must have had Dudu's help with arranging the seating, or she was psychic, because she seated just the right combination of cousins with Dani and Avi, and Avi was able to find topics of conversation to share with them.

After dinner, everyone went into the living room. Dudu headed straight for the piano bench; Dani glanced at the corner to make sure his guitar was nearby and then led Avi toward the sofa closest to the piano.

Eventually, Dudu switched from classical to more modern music, playing a mix of Israeli and American folk songs. Avi's tension seemed to seep out of him as he infused himself with the music. It didn't take long until Avi was humming along or singing under his breath.

"Hey, Avi," Dudu called out, "you wanna join me here?"

"You play much better than I do," Avi responded.

"Fifteen years of piano lessons will do that to a person," Dudu responded dryly. "What I meant was, I'll play, and you'll maybe sing something for us?"

Avi walked to the piano. Dani followed, walking around the bench to grab his guitar while Avi and Dudu talked. "You sure this is okay?" Avi asked Dudu. "It's a family gathering; I don't want to intrude."

"What? And you're not family?" Dudu grinned. "Of course you wouldn't be intruding. Come on, *habibi*, sing one song with me."

Dudu played Dani a middle C and he tuned his guitar while Dudu and Avi negotiated what song to do.

They finally decided to sing Paul Simon's "Me and Julio Down by the Schoolyard." When they finished that, Dudu started playing the intro to "Al Kol Eleh" by Naomi Shemer, and Dani joined in.

"That's dirty pool," Avi said. "I can't resist Naomi Shemer; I've been singing her songs since I was in kindergarten."

"So, nu? Sing with us."

Avi sang, which led to Penina requesting "Yerushalayim Shel Zahav," another Naomi Shemer song. Avi sang that one, too.

Soon the family was calling out requests, and Dani, Avi, and Dudu complied if at least one of them knew it. When cousin Ofir requested "Ana BaKoach" followed by "HaMalach HaGoel Oti," both from the liturgy, only Avi knew the songs, and everyone was treated to his voice, a cappella. The impromptu concert only stopped because Avi's voice was giving out. He blamed it on lack of time to warm up; Dudu and Dani blamed it on their Aunt Devorah's continual requests for annoying bubblegum rock songs.

When the last of the guests had finally left, and Avi and Dani had finished helping clean up, they collapsed onto the sofa. Dudu sat on the piano bench but didn't play.

"Thanks for everything," Avi said. "I've had a wonderful afternoon." He was stretched out as much as he could with his arms along the back of the sofa and his legs extending a good way under the coffee table. Dani had his arms along the back of the sofa, too, so that Dani and Avi were almost-but-not-quite leaning on each other.

"I am so glad you came," Dani said quietly.

They sat there, just listening to Dudu as he puttered, putting away sheet music and arranging things the way he liked them. Penina and Ben came into the living room bringing cups of mint tea for each of them. They sat and shmoozed until Avi declared that if he didn't go home soon, he'd fall asleep on the way.

Dani walked Avi to the door and gave him a hug and a discreet kiss goodbye and then watched as Avi walked to his car, got in, and drove off.

Penina came up behind Dani and looked out the screen door with him.

"I liked him," she said. "He's… different from your previous young men."

"That he is," Dani responded.

"It's good," Penina said, nodding.

"Yes," Dani said. "It is."

Tefilah: May the Sayings of My Mouth Be Acceptable to You

Hashem, I depend on Your understanding not just what I say but also what is in my heart. I come before You struggling for words, struggling to be understood.

Until now, I had believed that Dani understood what I intended, even if I did not express myself clearly. He asked questions and probed for the source of my distress when I could not coherently form the thoughts into words. But now I fear that he and I are destined for miscommunication.

Dani means well. He likes me; he may even be coming toward loving me. But he needs to, above all else, understand *me. He needs to give me time to form the thoughts I need to form, to express what I need to express. If he cannot do that, I cannot see us having a future together.*

Hashem, please guide me toward the right words. Help me to convey the meaning that Dani needs to hear. Find for me the proper terms with the correct meanings so that he and I understand each other fully. Please do not let us get derailed because of a lack of communication.

You in Your wisdom created the languages of the world to prevent man from reaching God at the Tower of Babel. Perhaps You can create for me a language that Dani will understand unquestioningly, so that he does not turn to the well-meaning but misguided words of others as his guideposts for understanding my needs.

May the words of my lips match the words of my heart. May You hear me and help Dani to hear me.

Yihyu l'ratzon imrei fi v'hegyon libi lifanecha Hashem tzuri v'go'ali—may the sayings of my mouth and the meditations of my heart be acceptable to you, Hashem, my rock and my redeemer.

there's nothing like a midnight doughnut run

WHILE DANI BELIEVED HE AND Avi had come to an understanding, he was still unsettled as Shabbat afternoon shifted into *motzei* Shabbat. *We need to do something fun.* The first step, though, was getting Avi to agree.

"So," Dani said, formulating a plan even as he began to speak, "almost the end of Shabbat."

"And?" Avi asked.

"So, with Shabbat ending so early these days, d'you want to go catch a movie tonight?" With luck, going out and seeing a movie together would dissipate the remaining stress that was between them.

"Yeah." Dani heard the tension in Avi's voice despite the affirmative answer.

"So, good. After *Havdallah*, we can look online and see what's playing where."

Dani and Avi spent the last hour of Shabbat relaxing and reading, both trying to reconnect in that comfortable place they were in on Thanksgiving. There was still work to be done, but Dani began to feel that they would be able to overcome the damage he'd accidentally done to the trust between them.

"How's this for a plan?" Dani asked after Shabbat ended and Avi did *Havdallah* to formally end Shabbat. "We'll take a cab from here to my

place so that I can change into something more appropriate for a movie night, and then we'll take my car to the Somerville Theatre. They're playing *Denial*, which I've heard wonderful things about."

"We can take my car, and then we won't have to pay for a cab or worry about how I'll get back home after the movie," Avi countered.

"All right, then." Dani smiled. "So, you go change and I'll call the theater and see if they've got tickets left, and then we can leave."

"Sounds reasonable to me." Avi put away the candle and spice box and rinsed out the kiddush cup and then went to his room to change out of his suit.

"Hey, Dani?" Avi asked as he came out of his room a few minutes later, much more comfortably dressed in jeans, a YU sweatshirt, and sneakers.

"Yeah?"

"You hungry?"

"Not particularly; you fed us really well at lunch." Also, stress tended to make him not want food, and, even though the stress was fading, his appetite was likely to be diminished for a while longer.

"Okay. We can always get snacks at the movies. I should be *pareve* by then," Avi said.

Dani did the mental math. They had finished lunch before three, so by the time they were buying movie snacks, Avi would be able to have dairy again, which was good because the kosher offerings at the local movie theaters skewed toward the chocolate variety.

"Works for me." Dani said. He looked Avi up and down. "You look good."

"Thanks," Avi said, blushing slightly.

"So," Dani said. "I'll just grab our coats while you close up, and we can head out."

"Okay," Avi said. He efficiently made his way around his house turning off lights that had been left on over Shabbat and making sure he had unplugged the hot plate.

Dani returned, carrying his dress coat and Avi's parka.

"I guessed which coat you wanted." Avi had a ton of winter coats, so Dani took his best guess based on what the weather had been earlier.

"That's fine," Avi said. "They're forecasting forties, right? A veritable heat wave."

There was a bit of traffic, but they got to Dani's apartment with sufficient time for Dani to change and for them to get to the movie without rushing.

"Sit, Avi. Relax while I get changed. D'you want a drink or something?"

"No, thanks. I'm fine."

"I'll be just a couple of minutes," Dani said. He started loosening his tie as he headed to his room. When he got to his room, he hung up his suit, tie, and dress shirt, making a mental note to get his suit cleaned. Now that he and Avi were spending so much time together, it was possible that another suit-wearing opportunity would arise sooner than he would otherwise anticipate.

Dani walked into the living room dressed in jeans and an MIT sweatshirt. "You made the outfit look sufficiently comfortable that I figured I'd follow your lead," he said, smiling at Avi.

"Makes sense to me." Avi said, pushing himself out of the chair he was sitting in. "So, you ready?"

"Yeah. Your car or mine?"

"If you don't mind, let's take yours."

"That's fine. The meters aren't enforced on this street after six, so you can just leave your car where we parked it."

They put their coats on, with Dani switching to a less-formal coat, and headed out to the street. Dani had been lucky on Friday and had managed to get a parking space less than a block from his apartment.

"Sorry to make you lose your prime space." Avi said. "I feel guilty; I get spoiled by having a driveway and not having to troll for street parking every time I take my car out."

"S'okay. If I'm lucky, it'll still be empty when we get back. Having the resident sticker helps with that."

They drove from Dani's place to the theater, which was only a five-minute trip in perfect traffic. However, this was Saturday night in Cambridge. So it took them close to fifteen minutes to get there. The

theater had a parking lot, though, so they wouldn't lose additional time searching for a street space.

"So I'll drop you off in front of the theater, and then I'll find a space," Dani said as they approached the parking lot.

"I'll be fine walking from wherever you park the car, Dani. My ankle's completely better."

"Yeah, but this way you can get the tickets, and I'll find you either in the line or in front of the theater."

"Oh, okay."

Dani handed Avi ten dollars, which Avi pocketed. They were still working out the logistics of who pays for what when. The usual rule was that whoever made the invitation did the paying. But for something like this, a joint "why don't we" kind of decision, the rules were less cut-and-dried. Sometimes, one bought the tickets and the other bought the snacks. In this case, if they could get the tickets and the parking accomplished simultaneously, who cared who paid for what?

Dani dropped Avi in front of the box office and then pulled into the parking lot. By the time he found a space and got back to the front of the theater, Avi was standing on the sidewalk watching for him.

"So," Dani said, walking up to Avi and accepting the ticket Avi was holding out, "snacks."

"Yeah," Avi said. "It's been more than three hours since lunch, so I don't have to worry about avoiding *chalavi* snacks. What's is your opinion on Goobers?"

"I'm for them. And how about some Twizzlers?"

"Works for me."

"How's this for a plan?" Dani asked. "You go grab us some seats; I'll get the food."

Avi handed Dani back his ten dollars. "Okay," he said, then strode off down the hallway. Dani went to the concession stand and got their agreed-on snacks, plus two bottles of water, and then went to find Avi. Avi tended to take seats farther toward the back because of his height, so he didn't bother looking in the front few rows. Once he located Avi a couple of rows from the back, he went up the stairs.

"Hey, motek," Dani said as he approached where Avi was sitting on the aisle.

"Hey, yourself," Avi said, smiling. "Hang on, I'll get up." He stood and let Dani go into the seat next to him and then sat down again. "I hope you don't mind being on the aisle like this; I know many people like the middle seats in theaters, but there's never enough space for my legs unless I'm on the end."

"No problem; any seat is good as long as I'm not in the first row craning my neck."

As they waited for the film to start, they talked about the predicted cold snap, Dani's pending design review at work and why he wasn't quite ready to present the product enhancements he was designing, Kol Ish's upcoming performance at Faneuil Hall as part of the City of Boston's Chanukah celebration as the theater began to fill.

Almost exactly at the posted start time for the film, the lights went down and the "pre-show entertainment"—what most people would call commercials—began. As soon as the lights were lowered, Dani took Avi's hand and squeezed his fingers lightly.

THE MOVIE GOT OUT AT almost eleven-thirty. And there was only so far that Goobers and Twizzlers could stretch. Yes, the movie was interesting. Yes, it was captivating. In fact, Dani hadn't noticed *during* the movie just how much time had passed. It was only after, when the lights came up, that he noticed how late it was.

And how long ago lunch had been.

"Remind me," Dani said as they walked out of the theater, "to never suggest movie-without-dinner when the movie including previews is more than two hours long, okay?"

Avi laughed. "I was so full from lunch. I had no clue I'd want food again tonight."

"But, y'know, I can't really, honestly, say that I want real food."

Avi was quiet for a minute, and then he said, "'Not real food' is about all I can get in the Cambridge area; all of the kosher restaurants are in

Brookline. And anyway, they're all closed now. What were you thinking of?"

"How do you feel about a brief road trip?"

"How brief?" Avi asked. "I hate to say it, but it's already been a long day."

"Fifteen minutes, tops? At least to get there. How long we're there, well, depends on a number of factors."

Dani watched the series of minute changes in Avi's expression as he mentally weighed the pros and cons of following Dani's lead.

Finally, Avi said, "Okay, I'm game."

They walked to the car, and Dani drove toward Mass Ave. After a ten-minute drive, Dani said, "There—that's where we're going," gesturing to the Doughnut Stop Believin' sign mounted on the otherwise nondescript building tucked away on a side street just past Porter Square.

"They just opened a couple of weeks ago, and they have a good *hashgacha*; I checked. I thought we could check them out, try their doughnuts, so that we have some options for *sufganiot* in case we can't get any anywhere else in time for Chanukah."

"You planning on staging a taste comparison of jelly doughnuts from all of the various kosher sources in the Boston area?"

"What, you don't like the idea?" Dani asked, grinning. "A new, kosher doughnut shop opens a month before the canonical doughnut holiday, and you expect me to not check it out?"

They got in line, checking out the sign that listed all the types of doughnuts available that evening. Since it was late, the selection was more limited than it might have been earlier in the day, but there was enough variety to require some thought. Ultimately, Dani decided on a chocolate glazed and Avi chose a Boston creme. Each grabbed a bottle of milk from the cooler, and then they went to find a table. While the seating in the store was limited, most people were getting their orders to go because of the late hour, so there were a few places to sit.

For the first couple of minutes, there was no conversation between Dani and Avi—they were both just enjoying the freshly made donuts.

They were lost in their thoughts, so they were startled when a voice came from Dani's left.

"Hey, Dani; hey, Avi."

Dani looked up and saw Shlomo Lindenbaum, a member of Kol Ish, standing next to the table. Shlomo was shorter than Dani, but still pretty tall. His straight brown hair flopped down into his eyes, and he pushed it aside absently as he spoke.

"Hi, Shlomo. Did you have a good Shabbos?" Avi asked.

"I did, thank you. And you?"

"Shabbat was lovely, thank you," Avi said.

"Have you met Sharona?" Shlomo asked, gesturing to the slight blonde woman standing next to him.

"Hi, Sharona," Avi said. "I'm Avi; Shlomo and I are in Kol Ish together. And this is my boyfriend, Dani."

"It's nice to meet you both," Sharona said, nodding toward Dani. Dani noted that Sharona didn't bat an eye at the information that Avi was gay. "What brings you out this evening?"

"We saw the new Rachel Weisz movie, and at the end we both realized that we were starving, and what better for late-night food cravings than doughnuts?" Dani said.

"The man speaks truth," Sharona said.

Two other couples came over, and Sharona said, "Dani, Avi, these are Sarah and Lior and Tamar and Scott. Guys, these are Dani and Avi; Avi sings with Shlomo."

Pleasantries were exchanged, and brief small talk was made. It turned out that Dani had worked at the same company as Scott's brother, which was why Dani thought that Scott looked familiar. And Lior and Avi had met once before, though it had been a number of years ago.

"We can get a bigger table if you want to join us," Dani said.

"Nah," Sharona said. "We don't want to crash the end of your date. It's hard enough to go on a date in Brookline without running into people from the frum community when you go out to dinner; it's totally not fair for us to disrupt your evening more than we already have."

"See, Dani," Avi said, his tone joking, "I told you it wasn't a vast conspiracy that every time we go out to dinner we run into someone I know."

"It's inevitable," Lior said. "There's a very limited number of kosher restaurants. So the probability that you'll run into someone you know who is also out to dinner on the same night is pretty high."

"Exactly," Sharona said. "Which is why we should let them have some time to themselves. C'mon, Shlomo. You'll get a chance to catch up with Avi at rehearsal on Monday."

The group said goodnight, and Shlomo, Sharona, and their friends left. Dani watched them go, and then turned to Avi.

"Avi, please let me apologize again for thinking you were ashamed to introduce me as your boyfriend. I—"

Avi put up his hand, and Dani stopped talking.

"Dani, it's fine. I understand why you might've thought that, as I said before. But now you have proof. The people I know don't care whom I date. They just want me to be happy." He licked his fingers, where there was a bit of glaze remaining. "And I have just finished a magnificent doughnut, so I am very happy."

Dani laughed. "And even without the doughnut?"

"Even without the doughnut, I would be happy, as long as I was with you."

Dani leaned across the table and gave Avi a discreet kiss.

Avi gave Dani a cheeky grin. "But the doughnut makes it even better."

Tefilah: Blessed are You, Who Has Such Phenomena in His World

We say, Hashem, that you created humans in Your image. Yet we believe with complete faith that You have no corporeal body.
If You did, and it looked like Dani's, well, then.

Is it chillul Hashem—*desecration of Your name—to say, "Good going"? He is…gorgeous. And I finally perhaps understand what people mean when they talk about human beauty. I mean, I've appreciated good looking people before. But this is the first time I've been up close and personal with another man's body. With Dani's body, specifically.*

And he is…amazing.

Dani is as beautiful on the outside as he is on the inside. And while I knew that he was a very handsome man, I had not thought about what that might mean for his physique. He is the physical embodiment of the fantasies I did not know I had. As Shlomo HaMelech—King Solomon—wrote in Shir HaShirim, *"As an apple tree among the trees of the forest, so is my beloved among the sons; in his shade I delighted and sat, and his fruit was sweet to my palate."*

I understand Shir HaShirim, *the Song of Songs, much more now. I can relate to the lover who is basking in the beauty of their beloved, who is so struck by the appearance of the one who is in their heart that they wax poetic, that they write the most epic of love songs.*

"My beloved is mine, and I am his, that feeds among the roses."

I have never completely understood all the blessings we have for all the random occasions of life, but the one for seeing a beautiful person or creature now resonates with me. Baruch atah, Hashem, Elokainu melech haolam, she'kacha lo ba'olamo—blessed are you, Hashem our God, King of the universe, who has such phenomena in His world.

many splendored things

"You sure you're good with this?" Dani asked Avi as they pulled into the resort hotel's parking lot on the day before New Year's Eve. "If you are having any second thoughts, we can cancel and go home. No harm, no foul." That wasn't totally true. They'd be out the hotel deposit and the deposit they'd given for the company organizing the kosher New Year's getaway that brought them to Vermont, but Dani considered that a small loss for Avi's comfort.

"I'm fine. I've gone through the second, third, and even fourth thoughts, but this feels right, us getting away for a couple of days."

"Okay, then, good. We'll park and get registered and settled, and then let's look at the brochures they sent and see what we want to do this afternoon."

They parked the car and unloaded their luggage onto a luggage cart brought over to the car by a resort employee. They followed the man and the luggage to the hotel's front desk and got their room assignment and then continued up to their room.

The resort employee opened the door and put the luggage in the room, accepted the tip that Avi handed him, and then said, "Enjoy your stay."

"Thank you," Avi responded and then followed Dani inside.

Their suite was small but beautiful. The door opened onto a sitting room with a couple of cream-colored sofas and a small dining table with chairs upholstered to match the sofas. From there, a doorway led into a bedroom with a single king-sized bed and a bathroom.

"Is this going to be okay with you?" Dani asked.

"The room? It seems fine to me."

"There's only one bed. We're going to have to share," Dani said.

"I thought that was one of the points of this get-away. Us having some time away from the craziness of our regular lives, getting a chance to relax together, explore our intimacy?" Avi was blushing, which Dani took to mean that there was more explicit terminology going through Avi's head than he was comfortable saying out loud. That was all right; Dani could work with "explore our intimacy" as a starting point.

"Do you have a preference as to side of the bed?" he asked.

"Not really," Avi said. "I'll take whichever one you don't want."

"Okay, so you take the right as we face the head and I'll take the left."

"Works for me," Avi said, placing his suitcase on the right side of the bed. He immediately started unpacking his luggage into the closet and dresser; Dani opened his luggage but didn't unpack much, pulling out only what he thought he would need soonest.

"So," Dani said once they had everything set up as they wanted it, "it looks like starting tomorrow there's a number of group activities. This evening there's a lecture we could attend on the history of the area, or we could go for a walk around the resort, or we could sign up for some spa time, or we could go for a swim…"

"All of the choices are a bit overwhelming," Avi said. "We've got three days here; we don't have to do everything at once. The walk around the resort sounds nice, though. Tomorrow night will probably be more New Year's themed, so we might want to do the exploring tonight in case we want to participate in any group activities tomorrow night."

"Yeah, as long as the weather holds, I say let's do that. They've even provided a map of suggested scenic routes, so we don't have to worry about getting lost."

They put their coats on and started out on a walk that the brochure estimated would take about forty-five minutes. Since they kept stopping and looking at the scenery, however, they were out for about an hour and a half, and by the time they got back it was beginning to get dark and they were ready to warm up.

"The brochure said there's a café open basically all the time. Want to go get a warm drink and sit by the fire?" Avi asked Dani as they walked back into the hotel lobby.

"Oh, yes," Dani said. "Warm is good. Something warm to drink and a fire to warm us up is doubly good."

They went to the café and chose a table with two comfortable chairs. A waiter took their order for two hot chocolates and a fruit platter. Dani reached across the table, took Avi's hand, and squeezed it gently. Avi squeezed back.

"I'm glad we're here," Dani said.

"I am, too."

"We're here for three days. Do you have anything specific in mind that you'd like to do? Did you have a chance to look at the day trips?"

"I know that skiing is the big draw here, but given my ankle, there's no way I'm going skiing. I hope you don't mind, Dani."

"I've never been a huge skiing guy myself, motek. Don't worry. And I figured you wouldn't have any interest in skiing. There are so many non-skiing-related activities—outlet shopping, antique stores, art galleries and artists' studios, lots of options. We can play it by ear, day to day. No reason for us to be over-planning on our vacation."

"I'd like to be able to take it on a day-to-day basis. I want to enjoy this vacation, not feel like we have to rush from thing to thing."

Their server came with the fruit plate and their hot chocolates, and they each took some berries and melon. Dani waited for Avi to say his *berachot* and take his first bites before he picked up the conversational thread; he knew that if he didn't wait, Avi would get involved in conversation instead of eating, because he wouldn't want to pause just to say the blessings, but he also wouldn't eat without saying them first.

They spent some time catching up, discussing the things they hadn't had time to talk about during the busy days leading up to their vacation. They discussed Avi's Chanukah concert with Kol Ish, which Dani had attended and loved. It was the first time that Dani had attended a full, formal concert by the group, and he was impressed not only by how Kol Ish sang and performed but also by the passion of their fans.

"Do fans ever bring you things, like they do at arena shows? Do you ever have fan interactions that concern you?"

"I've gotten all sorts of things from fans. They're usually adorable and harmless—drawings of us done by kids who have heard our music in their day schools, little tchotchkes like clay treble clefs, that sort of thing. I've been propositioned a number of times, and I've had a couple of women ask if I wanted to date their daughters, but nothing actually scary. It's weird—I'm really shy with people I don't know, as you experienced when we first met. But when I'm meeting fans in the lobby after shows, I don't feel the same social anxiety. Maybe it's because I have a set role when meeting fans; maybe it's because I'm with the other guys in the group and they know me. I've never really tried to figure it out."

"The afternoon we met, I was completely amazed by you," Dani said. "Have I ever told you that? I asked Rafi about you, and he wouldn't tell me anything because he wanted to protect you. He only gave me your contact info after I threatened to make him figure out how to get my sunglasses back from you."

"I'm so glad he did finally give it to you," Avi said. "I choose to believe that we would have found a way to get back in touch, but it likely would have taken longer."

"You were interested in getting in touch?" Dani was surprised. He had never thought that the instant attraction he'd felt might have been mutual.

"I was. But I wasn't going to track you down or even ask Rafi for your number. Some would say it was *bashert*, that it was meant to be, that you left your sunglasses behind so that you'd have a reason to call me. I mean, Rafi most likely wouldn't have given you my number just so you could ask me out. I know him well enough to know that."

"You're right. He wasn't going to give me anything. And that's why the first call about my sunglasses came from him, not from me. But since *you* asked Rafi for *my* number, that started the whole series of events that brought us here, which I'm very glad about." Dani took a sip of his cocoa and ate a bit of fruit.

"I am, too. I was terrified, I'll tell you that. Before I called Rafi back, I was planning to give back the glasses the next time I saw him, and have him give them back to you. But there was something about you that kept tickling the back of my brain. I tried to ignore it, but the more I tried not to think about you, the more prevalent you became in my thoughts. So when I called him, I asked for your number. And, as you said, that was what brought us, ultimately, to this point."

Dani raised his cocoa mug in a humorous salute. "To Rafi, who brought us together."

"To Rafi," Avi agreed, clicking his mug against Dani's.

"We owe him at least a good bottle of wine, if not more."

"We can throw in a fruit basket."

They sat in comfortable silence, enjoying each other's company but staying in their own thoughts. Dani thought about the past six months, the tumultuous journey that brought them to this place; he wouldn't change anything if it meant that he wouldn't have ended up here.

By the time they finished the fruit, it was approaching dinner time.

"I'm not really hungry right now," Dani said. "How about you, motek?"

"The snack we just had will tide me over for a while, but I'm likely to want something later." Avi pulled the schedule of events out of his backpack. "This says that dinner is available buffet-style from six-thirty until eight-thirty and that the kitchen will be open for room service until eleven-thirty."

"Okay, so we can relax for a while now and figure out food later, if that's what we want."

"Yes, that looks completely feasible."

"So let's do that," Dani said. "We can go back to the room, relax for a while, take a look at what activities we might be interested in for tomorrow—or not, as the case may be. And then, if we're hungry before

the buffet is over, we can come back here or we can order food up to our room if it's after the buffet closes or if we're just not in the mood to come down."

"That all sounds perfect," Avi said, standing and picking up his backpack.

Dani stood up as well, and they made their way to the elevator and up to their room.

When they were in the suite, they took off their winter gear and put it away, hanging coats in the closet and lining up their boots near the door. Avi took a couple of things out of his satchel and placed them on the coffee table in the sitting room and then went into the bedroom. Dani puttered around the sitting room for a few minutes to give Avi time alone to get himself comfortable, and then he went into the bedroom as well. Avi had changed out of his jeans and into what looked like the softest pair of sweatpants that Dani had ever seen. Avi had also traded in his button-down shirt for a T-shirt with "One in Every Minyan" on it and a picture of ten guys sitting in shul, one of them wearing a pink kippah. He was lying on the bed with his ankles crossed, and his book was out, but he wasn't reading it.

"Nice shirt," Dani said.

"Thanks. It was a gift from Jake."

"Mind if I join you?" Dani asked after a moment.

"Sure."

Dani dug a pair of sweats and a Tzahal T-shirt out of his bag and stepped into the bathroom. He hoped that in not very long he'd be able to dress wherever was most convenient, but for now he was willing to step away in order to make Avi comfortable. Once he had changed his clothes, he went back into the bedroom and pulled a book out of his backpack. He sat on the edge of the bed, waited to see if Avi would say anything, and then he lay down and opened his book. After a minute, Avi slid his hand across the space between them on the bed and gripped Dani's hand.

"Hey, motek," Dani said quietly.

"Hi," Avi said, matching Dani's tone.

"How're things?"

"Good. Really good. I can't believe how comfortable this bed is."

"And you?" Dani both wanted to take Avi's statement of comfort at face value and also double-check that Avi was truly okay with the sleeping arrangements. And since Avi had stressed how much better it was if Dani asked rather than assumed, even if it took away some of the spontaneity, Dani was learning to be better about asking.

"I'm… getting there," Avi responded, clearly understanding the unspoken part of Dani's question.

"You want to read or do you want to talk?"

"Is there a third option?" Avi asked, rolling over and kissing Dani lightly.

"Is this… are you…" Avi making the first move was not at all what Dani had expected, and it left him flummoxed.

"Let's see where this goes. I mean, wasn't this part of the point of this trip?"

"It wasn't a main focus for me," Dani said.

"I know. And I love that. But I'm feeling like maybe this is what we're here for, at least to some extent. We're away from all our usual stressors, we're in this lovely suite with this magnificently comfortable bed… Shall we see where we go from here?" Avi kissed Dani again, putting more intent into it.

Dani returned the kiss and used the tip of his tongue to part Avi's lips. When Avi opened for him, he rolled on his side and moved his hands up to clasp the back of Avi's head, trying hard to straddle the line between supporting and directing.

They shifted into a position that allowed them to kiss freely without either of them losing sensation in their arms. This meant that Avi was lying flat on his back and Dani was lying on his stomach and was draped across Avi's chest, with his legs still on the bed itself. Dani figured that aligning their hips was a bit more than Avi might be ready for, though he wouldn't stop it if that was the way it went. Avi caressed Dani's back while Dani stroked Avi's neck. Avi moaned into the kiss and shifted his hips restlessly while his hands strayed to the edge of Dani's T-shirt. After

another minute of kissing, Dani felt a tug on the hem of his shirt and pulled back to look at Avi.

"Everything okay, motek?"

"Too much fabric. Can't feel *you*," Avi said.

Dani withheld the chuckle that threatened to bubble up. Avi clearly lost all of his substantial facility with words when his brain was lust-clouded. "Should I take off the shirt?"

"Mm," Avi responded.

Dani shifted so he was sitting on the edge of the bed, facing away from Avi. As quickly as he could, he shucked off his shirt and tossed it toward his luggage, though he missed his target by a significant distance. He turned back to Avi, who was now shirtless as well.

"Oh, motek," Dani said on a startled exhale, taking in Avi's bare torso for the first time.

"I know," Avi said, blushing. "I look like pre-serum Steve Rogers. Ima keeps telling me I'm too thin."

"You're magnificent," Dani said. "And even post-serum Steve has nothing on you."

"I'm bony. I don't work out, so I don't have any abs to speak of. I…"

"I think you're gorgeous," Dani said. "Is it all right with you if I…"

He reached out one hand but didn't make contact with Avi's skin until Avi nodded and whispered "Yes."

Dani appreciated the verbal confirmation of the nonverbal approval. "I'll go slow, but if you want me to slow down even more, let me know."

He kissed Avi again while he moved his right hand onto Avi's left pec, tracing it lightly with his fingertips. Avi moaned and arched slightly into Dani's touch, which Dani took as encouragement. He moved his fingers closer to Avi's nipple, skimming just above it. Avi moaned louder, then pulled away from Dani's lips.

"Come *on*, Dani. Stop teasing," Avi said.

Dani relented and brushed Avi's nipple lightly with his index finger.

"Mm," Avi said. "Feels good."

"I'm glad," Dani said, and then he began kissing his way down Avi's neck and across his shoulder blade until his lips met his fingers. He lapped once at Avi's nipple and then paused.

"More," Avi said. "Please."

Dani sucked on the nipple he had been teasing and moved his fingers to the other side to start teasing that nipple. Avi shuddered and moaned again.

"Still doing okay?" Dani asked, looking up at Avi.

"Beyond okay," Avi responded breathlessly, shifting his hips restlessly. "Just… do something."

"What sort of something?" Dani asked, his tone teasing.

"Touch me. *Please.*"

Dani resisted the urge to point out that he had been touching Avi and instead asked, "Is it okay if I move a bit… south?"

"South is good. Touch me, Dani, please. I can't… I don't…" Avi's frustration was clear both in his voice and on his face.

"Shh, motek. Relax. It's okay; I understand." Dani hoped he sounded comforting and not patronizing; as new as this territory was to Avi, it also was new to Dani. And he didn't want to fuck this up.

Dani moved his hands to the waistband of Avi's sweatpants and inched the pants slowly down Avi's hips. He left Avi's underwear in place, figuring that Avi would be less stressed if he still had something keeping him from being totally exposed to Dani's eyes. And Dani was surprised to find that he was completely fine with that. He eased Avi's sweatpants down and over his feet and then tossed them to the side. He slid back up the bed, stroking Avi's legs gently on his way.

"How are you doing, motek?"

"Doing okay. Thanks for checking. Still *need you*, though. Trust me that I'll stop you if you're going too fast."

"All right," Dani said, moving back to the position he'd been in and kissing Avi.

This time, as he started to kiss Avi, he moved his hand to the front of Avi's underwear. He stroked Avi on the outside of his boxer briefs, and Avi whimpered.

"Still good?" Dani asked, pulling back from the kiss and stilling his hand.

"I… I think so. I'm, oh, God, I'm enjoying this physically. But… But mentally, I think I need us to slow down just a tiny bit."

"Want to go out to the sitting room, or get dinner, or something?" Dani didn't want to completely put on the brakes, but if that's what Avi needed, he'd go with it.

"No, not that dramatic. But maybe exposure parity? Take off your pants and maybe just lie beside me for a couple of minutes?"

"I can do that." Dani got off the bed, took off his sweatpants and left them on the floor near the side of the bed, and then lay on the bed again next to Avi, though he made sure they didn't touch. "Okay," he said. "Tell me how you want to proceed, if you do."

"I do. I'm just not sure exactly what I want. What we were doing was wonderful, felt wonderful. I'm still just figuring this all out, and I only know what I want based on when I know it's too much. And then I feel like I'm stringing you along, even though I know you've said I'm not."

"I'm fine with you figuring things out as we go along," Dani said. "And I'm also fine with you thinking you're okay with something until we get deeper into it and then you wanting to slow down or stop completely. I will do my best to ask before I do anything new or different."

"Thank you for being so understanding," Avi said. "I mean, this can't be at all easy for you, to go at my pace when you're already…" He gestured toward Dani's groin and blushed, which Dani interpreted as referring to his only barely flagging erection. Avi himself was still visibly hard, as well.

"Consent isn't just about me asking you to go to bed with me and you saying yes. It's about me making sure you are as interested in what we are doing as I am. It's about us being partners in this because otherwise what's the point?"

"That sounds so…. businesslike. I mean, *I* definitely appreciate that this is how you feel, but do you find that this approach lessens your ability to get guys to go to bed with you?"

"Okay, there's no good way to say this, but it worked with you, and you're the only one I'm interested in having go to bed with me. And,

anyway, any guy that wouldn't want to work under those rules isn't a guy I'd want to get intimate with. I'm all for spontaneity, but even a late-night pickup in a bar with a stranger involves a discussion of consent. Hell, a late-night pickup in a bar with a stranger should involve as much discussion of consent as does a long-term relationship."

Avi ran a finger down Dani's chest. "Is it okay if I do this?" he asked.

"Oh, motek, that's wonderful," Dani responded. And it was—the simple touch from Avi, as innocent as it was, was more erotically charged for Dani than some of the most skillful blowjobs he'd had over the years.

"Can I…" Avi asked, and Dani was quick to nod.

"Yes, motek, yes. Anything you want." Dani had no clue what Avi was going to want, but whatever it was, he was up for it.

Avi rolled onto his stomach and shifted around until he was in the same position on top of Dani as Dani had been on top of him. Dani closed his eyes to focus on the touch, on the feeling of Avi's hands on his bare skin, but that meant that he had no warning before Avi's fingers danced across his chest. He felt a light tug on the ring in his left nipple, and he almost opened his eyes check the expression on Avi's face, but he decided not to.

"That okay?" Avi asked.

"Mm," Dani said. "Really good."

Avi's hands continued to explore Dani's chest, tentatively at first but then more boldly, which Dani took to mean that Avi was gaining confidence. Dani was just starting to really relax into the touches when he felt Avi's lips on his chest, and his eyes flew open.

"Motek?"

"This okay?" Avi asked, pulling away slightly.

"Oh, it's more than okay. It's just totally unexpected. *Good* unexpected," he rushed to add, "but unexpected."

"All right, then," Avi said. He gave the lightest of licks to Dani's right nipple.

"Nngh, motek, do that again," Dani said, his breath coming quicker.

Avi repeated the light flick of his tongue against Dani's nipple and then moved to the left nipple and did the same thing.

"Oh, motek, so good."

Avi seemed hesitant as he used his right hand to tease at Dani's right nipple as he lapped at the left. Dani was quickly reduced to just a few words, relying instead on moans and the occasional request for "more" or "like that." Avi's touches became bolder, more confident, as Dani encouraged him with soft sighs and gentle direction. Avi started moving down Dani's chest, kissing his way toward Dani's waistband.

"Not that I'm not enjoying this, motek, but I don't want you to find yourself in deeper than you expected or wanted," Dani said, using what felt like his last two remaining brain cells to string together a coherent sentence.

"Expectations are not something I'm working with at this point," Avi said. "This is totally uncharted territory for me."

"I hear that," Dani said. "Do you want to switch places again? Maybe being on the receiving end some more will allow you to judge where your comfort zone lies."

"It's possible," Avi responded, shifting off of Dani and lying down next to him.

"Please, promise you'll tell me if I'm doing anything that makes you uncomfortable."

"I will. I very much liked what you were doing before."

"So more like that, then?" Dani asked, shifting onto his stomach.

"Yeah," Avi whispered.

"Can I try something? You might like it, you might not. If you don't, I will stop immediately. If you do, we'll keep going."

"Go ahead," Avi said, and Dani was somewhat surprised he didn't ask for further clarification, given how vague Dani's request was.

Dani crawled off the bottom of the bed and walked around to stand at Avi's side. "Move over just a tiny bit, please," he asked, and Avi shifted toward Dani's side of the bed. Dani climbed back onto the bed and placed one knee on each side of Avi's hips. Not wanting to make Avi uncomfortable by pinning him down, he rested most of his weight on his knees.

"This okay?" Dani asked.

"So far, so good," Avi answered, closing his eyes.

Dani shifted a bit more of his weight onto Avi's legs and kissed Avi deeply. Avi returned the kiss with equal fervor, chasing Dani's tongue with his own when Dani began to pull back. Dani placed his hands on Avi's chest and started stroking slowly around his nipples as he had before, remembering how much Avi had enjoyed it. Avi arched into Dani's touch and placed his hands on Dani's wrists.

"Too much?" Dani asked.

"Not enough. Please touch me harder, or faster, or *something*. It's like I'm chasing something just out of sight, something I can't quite identify but that is vital. I mean… I know I'm not actually chasing something, but I'm *chasing* something." Avi shook his head. "That made no sense."

"I understand, motek," Dani said, increasing the pressure of his touch against Avi's skin. The circles he was drawing around the buds of Avi's nipples became smaller and smaller until he was flicking Avi's nipples to the random rhythm that was running through his head. He wanted to keep Avi guessing when the next touch would come, which might help him keep focused enough on Dani that he wouldn't be overwhelmed by the sensations. After a few minutes of this, Dani moved one of his hands toward Avi's waist. He didn't have a plan, per se, and he was prepared to follow whatever path and pace Avi set for them.

Dani traced the waistband of Avi's boxer briefs with one finger. "Is this okay?" he asked for what felt like the hundredth time that evening, but he really didn't care. He just hoped that Avi didn't mind him interrupting the flow of things so frequently.

"Yeah," Avi gasped, his eyes still closed. "You can… go under them, if you want," he said. Avi took a deep breath, let it out slowly, and then made a noticeable effort to open his eyes. He pushed himself up onto his elbows and looked directly at Dani. "Just a warning, though. I'm totally in the weeds about this, Dani. This is stuff I've never even thought about doing until very recently. So, yes. It's fine for now, and I'm giving total consent to this. But I may change my mind in the middle, and I trust that if that happens that you'll understand that we need to stop

whatever it is we're doing. It might be just momentary, or I might need more of a break."

"That's completely fine, motek. You say go slow, I'll slow. You say stop, I'll stop. I'm just enjoying being here like this with you."

"All right, then," Avi said with a smile. "I'm all yours." He lay back and closed his eyes again.

Dani removed his finger from the edge of Avi's waistband and instead kissed Avi. Easing Avi into the next stage would be better all-around than just going for it, even if they had been at this pre-foreplay stage for a good half hour or so. It wasn't how much time they had been in bed that was important, he reminded himself, it was the extent to which Avi was comfortable. He knew this. He *did*. But did it make him something of a dick to want to be able to move forward just a bit faster? It probably did, he acknowledged, though he also had to admit that he was enjoying getting to completely know what Avi's reactions were to almost every single touch.

After a few minutes of kissing, Dani smoothed his hands over Avi's chest and followed the motions with his lips. Since Avi's nipples were a sensitive spot, Dani made sure to spend time there, enjoying the push-pull of Avi getting simultaneously more relaxed and more aroused as his body reacted. He kissed his way down Avi's sternum, dancing his fingers across Avi's smooth skin as he moved closer to Avi's waist. And this time, when he reached Avi's waistband, he slid his fingers underneath.

"Lift up?" he asked quietly, not wanting to jar Avi away from the sensations.

"Mm?" Avi responded.

"Your hips. If you lift them just a bit, I can slide your boxers down… if that's okay."

Avi nodded and canted his hips, giving Dani enough clearance to slide the boxer briefs down his legs just enough to allow Avi's erection to spring free. Dani sat up and straddled Avi's legs, so he had a good view of Avi from head to hips, and he took a moment to simply admire Avi's body. He continued to touch Avi gently as he looked at Avi's broad shoulders and long torso tapering to his narrow waist. With one finger he traced

the slight dusting of hair that started just below Avi's navel and ended in thick curls above his now-hard dick.

"Oh, motek, you're…" He paused, temporarily running up against the limitations of English. "*Nehedar.*"

"Magnificent," Avi mumbled, then paused. "S— sorry. Thank you. I… thank you."

"You are, though. Magnificent. And more. I'd use the words of the *paytanim* to describe your beauty if I didn't think you'd consider it both sacrilegious and too flowery. Those mystic poets really knew what they were talking about, though." Dani pressed a kiss to the inner corner of Avi's hip, right above his thigh. Avi arched his hips toward Dani's mouth, so Dani kissed Avi there again, swiping his tongue in a vague line toward Avi's groin.

Avi moaned Dani's name, so Dani repeated the motion with his tongue and moved his hand to encircle the base of Avi's cock. When Avi didn't object, Dani began jacking Avi slowly, giving him time to get used to the sensations. Not that Dani didn't think Avi did this to himself—though he wasn't sure at all—but the feel of someone else's hand for the first time was something to get used to.

Dani kissed the tip of Avi's dick, again giving him time to get used to the feel of Dani's lips. Avi's hips jerked upward, dislodging Dani's loose grip, but then he gasped, "Sorry!" and lay back again, supporting himself on his elbows so he could look at Dani.

"Don't apologize for reacting to things that feel good," Dani said. "I can take it if you fuck my face a bit."

Avi blushed at Dani's words, but he nodded his assent. Dani said, "Are you ready for me to try this again?"

"Yeah," Avi said, laying his head on the pillow and closing his eyes yet again.

"You can watch me if you want," Dani said. "Some guys like watching their partners go down on them." He hoped he didn't sound defensive; he didn't mean it in a defensive way. He truly wanted Avi to know he could watch. But he also wasn't sure why Avi kept closing his eyes.

"Is it weird to say that I want to experience how it feels without being distracted by how gorgeous you are?" Avi asked. "Combined with the fact that I'm a little nervous that I'll be weirded out watching you suck my penis. So for both my pleasure and my sanity, having my eyes closed seems to be the way to go. If that's okay with you, that is."

"It's fine with me as long as it's fine with you," Dani said. "You can always watch another time." He wrapped his hand around the base of Avi's cock and kissed the head. This time he was prepared for Avi's hips to jerk upwards, so he opened his mouth and let Avi thrust inside. He sucked lightly around Avi's cock head, letting Avi control the depth and speed of the thrusts.

After a couple of minutes, Dani cupped Avi's balls with his other hand. Avi whimpered and then froze.

"Dani, I'm... Hang on. Wait, please. Please stop," he said, almost begging.

Dani immediately pulled his mouth off Avi's cock and sat up. "Is everything all right, motek?"

"Yes—No. Not really. I mean, it all felt good, but I... it felt *too* good, and I can't... I need..." Avi sat up, swung his legs around until he was sitting on the bed, and then tried to stand up, but his underwear was around his knees. He wiggled it up and then managed to stand. As he readjusted his briefs around his hips, he said, "I'm sorry, Dani," and walked to the doorway of the bedroom, which connected to the sitting room. At the doorway he turned to face Dani again and said, "I just... I need some time to think, to process. Please."

"Take all the time you need, motek. I'll be here when you are ready to talk, if you want to talk, or to just hold you, if that's what you want, or whatever."

"Thank you, Dani. I'm sorry."

"No need to apologize. Please just let me know if you need anything."

"I will. Thank you." Avi turned back around and walked out into the sitting room, closing the bedroom door behind him.

Dani put his sweatpants on. No reason to be sitting here in his boxers if Avi was in the other room, he figured. After he stood up to pull his

pants back up over his hips, he walked back to his own side of the bed, grabbed his book, and lay back on the bed. He didn't know how long he would be waiting. He didn't do waiting very well. Waiting alone especially sucked.

After about half an hour, he got up. He was thirsty and, while he didn't want to crowd Avi while he was processing whatever he was processing, he also didn't feel comfortable trapped in the bedroom. The mini-fridge with bottled water and fruit juices was in the mini-kitchen off the sitting room, and maybe he could go out and get himself a drink without disturbing Avi.

Dani walked to the bedroom door and cracked it open just a tiny bit, enough to get a view of the sitting room. Avi was sitting on one of the overstuffed chairs, his bookbag at his feet and a large tome on his lap. His glasses were riding low on his nose, and he had clearly run his fingers through his hair a number of times. He was running his finger down a page of what looked to Dani to be a book of *responsa* and was mumbling to himself. As Dani watched, Avi put one finger in the page he had been reading and flipped to the back of the book, looking closely at a page. He nodded once and then flipped back to the page he'd been on.

Quietly pulling the bedroom door open just enough to leave the room, Dani crept to the mini-kitchen and got a small can of seltzer and then went back to the bedroom. He pushed the door open just a bit farther and cringed at the squeak. Dani spun around to see if it had disturbed Avi. And it had.

Avi placed a scrap of paper as a bookmark, closed his book, and looked up, straightening up when he saw Dani standing in the bedroom doorway. "I... I'm sorry, Dani."

"I'm sorry, motek. I didn't mean to disturb you. I'll go back to the room and give you more time."

"No, that's all right. I can't say for sure if more time will be at all useful to me. I've done a lot of thinking and some reading, beyond what I've already done, I mean. Reading tonight, here. And I need to talk to you about some stuff I've been trying to figure out since you and I started dating, something I've really been studying closely since we first kissed.

It's… well, I can't say it's particularly simple or straightforward, but it's been on my mind for months now, and we really need to talk about it before I can go any further with you sexually. I'm sorry, but I hit a wall tonight, and I need to work this through."

"All right," Dani said, walking over to the sofa, and gesturing for Avi to come sit next to him. Avi put his book on the coffee table and sat next to Dani. Dani put his hand on Avi's leg. "Clearly this is something that's been on your mind. Let's talk it out."

"Okay, so. You know there's a *halachic* prohibition on wasting sperm. That is the mainstream interpretation of the sin of Onan in *Beraishit*."

"I'm following you so far," Dani said, tracing abstract patterns on Avi's thigh with his fingers.

"And from the time I was little, I had been taught that both masturbation and condom use were assur because of the sin of Onan. But as I see it, both masturbation and condom use are essential parts of being a safe, sexually active gay man in the twenty-first century. And I know that there must be opinions out there in the big sphere of *responsa* that I would be able to find that would say that condom use is *pikuach nefesh*. Most likely there's also *teshuvot* that deal with masturbation, though I would think that would be harder to justify. And then there's, well…" Avi was silent, but he was turning bright red.

"Yes, motek?"

"Fellatio is an issue, as well. For similar reasons," Avi whispered.

"Oh, motek. I'm not going to tell you I don't enjoy oral sex, because I do enjoy it. It's actually one of my favorite things, both giving and receiving. But if you decide it's something you can't do, I'll understand."

Dani knew the words were what Avi wanted to hear, and he wasn't lying, not completely. But he really, *really* hoped Avi would figure out a way to have blowjobs be permissible. Because Dani was very eager to show Avi how good one could feel, and he wanted to know what Avi's mouth would feel like on him. He could wait, though, until Avi was ready. He was getting used to waiting, and, as odd as it had seemed to him at first, it actually did increase his enjoyment of the things that they did do. Knowing that Avi had thought, and possibly researched, and

definitely analyzed how he felt, and had decided that there were things he could be comfortable with made each new sexual act that Avi initiated that much more thrilling.

"But, see, that's the thing. The more research I do, the more it seems that there are ways to allow just about any sexual act you and I might engage in, except for actual penetrative anal sex. And even that, I'd bet, there would be some workaround, though that would take research I really, *really* am not yet ready to do."

Dani nodded as if he completely understood what Avi was saying, though in truth he was incredibly confused. But then he realized that he was doing both himself and Avi a disservice by not speaking up, and he owed it to Avi to be as honest as possible.

"Hang on, wait. I'm completely confused here. Are you saying that oral sex—me going down on you, you going down on me, whatever—is still in the realm of possibility or not?"

"I'm saying that six months of knowing that everything I thought I knew was not necessarily completely correct is not enough time for me to throw out the conditioning of a lifetime. I'm not saying I was brainwashed or anything. But look at it this way: For years we believed that cutting carbs out of our diets would keep us thin. But then we learned that we need some carbs to give us energy. It isn't an easy thing for someone who has avoided carbs for their whole adult lives to realize that they now can—and should—have some carbs. My situation is similar. For much of my formative years, and continuing with various *divrei Torah* and other sources of learning in my adult life, I've been told that it was *halachically* problematic to ejaculate for reasons other than procreation. P'ru u'rvu is the mitzvah that is drilled into the minds of all dati girls and boys from the time they are old enough to know what it means. So for me to now internalize the idea that it might be permissible to ejaculate and have it not be assur, for it not to be connected to p'ru u'rvu? That is going to take some time for me to assimilate."

"I've been working on it, since before we met, in fact. But it was all theoretical. Now it has gone from a hypothetical to *Halacha l'ma'aseh*, and I have to allow myself to indulge, as it were," Avi continued. "Believe

me—I truly enjoyed what we were doing, and I would love to do it again. I just have to keep reminding myself that it is permitted, that it isn't something I would have to account for on Yom Kippur."

"All right," Dani said, "that's a lot to take in. I mean, I can see how it would take you time to reset all your thinking. It's a good thing, though, yes? Ultimately, I mean. And I'm trying my best not to be selfish, but to me it sounds like this opens up a whole realm of possible experiences that you had previously thought was off limits, but now turns out to be available to you. Which I hope you would include me in, as you see fit."

"Of course you'd be involved," Avi said. "I want you to be involved. I want to explore everything with *you*. This isn't just for me. Part of it is, yes. Part of it is very personal. I started studying this before I met you, and even if I hadn't ever met you I would most likely be learning everything there is to know about how to fit my identity as a gay man into my identity as a dati man. But the actual, hands-on, *Halacha l'ma'aseh* parts of it? I probably wouldn't be working through the day-to-day practicalities of the changes to my religious life that my sexuality brings with it with nearly as much urgency as I am now."

"There's no urgency, Avi," Dani said. "I don't want you to make decisions you're not completely comfortable with because you think there's some rush. When I said I was happy to wait for you to be ready, I meant it."

"You might be willing to wait, but *I'm* not, Dani! Especially now that I've started exploring what is possible. Feeling you touch me like that tonight, seeing how I can make you feel, what I can make your body do, knowing what you can make mine do… I want to know more. I want to feel more. And so I need to get my overly analytical brain to join the party, to get it to understand that this is permissible and pleasurable, not something to be studied and picked apart."

"Don't be so hard on your brain, motek. I love your brain and how it works. I love the way you look at things from every angle, get the pieces to all fit, be in harmony. It's the part of you that allows you to make such beautiful music, to get all the disparate parts of the chorus to

work together as one. I love your passion, how you throw yourself into everything you do." Dani paused, having temporarily run out of words.

"That's sweet, Dani. I… I'm not sure how to respond, honestly. Your passion for my brain is impressive. A little odd, but impressive."

"I'm expressing myself badly, motek. My thoughts are all over the place, and I'm expressing myself very badly. There is one thing, however, that I need you to know. I'm not telling you now because I want something from you, or because I want you to do something you're not ready for, or because I think you need to hear it, or anything like that. It's something I probably should have said months ago, but I didn't, and I don't have a good reason for why."

Avi looked at him, concern plain on his face. "What is it, Dani? Are you all right?"

"I'm fine. I just now realized that I really need to tell you."

"Tell me what, Dani?"

"I love you. You're… you are the best person I've ever met, and I'm proud and humbled to call you my boyfriend."

He paused. Why was all of this spilling out now? It's not as if he hadn't known, probably since Avi's bike accident, that he loved Avi, but he hadn't been ready to say anything. And what he'd said to Avi was true—he wasn't saying this because he expected to receive anything in return or to hear anything specific from Avi.

He wasn't sure what Avi would say or how Avi would react. The silence, though it had only been seconds long, was making Dani twitchy.

"Avi?" Dani was terrified that Avi would consider his declaration of love manipulative, as a ruse to try to get Avi back into bed, which it wasn't at all. "I… I don't expect you to say it back. I don't want you to feel compelled to express feelings you don't actually feel just because I said it. It's just that, while I was sitting in the bedroom trying to give you space and time to process, all I could think about was how much I wanted to wrap my arms around you and hold you and make you comfortable and happy."

"Oh, *chamudi*, I…" Avi put his head on Dani's shoulder. "I love you with all my heart. I feel like I've loved you forever." He sat up and shifted

151

so that he and Dani were face to face, and then he raised his hands to frame Dani's face and kissed him.

"Come, *chamudi*," Avi said when they broke apart to breathe. He stood up and offered a hand to Dani, who took it and allowed himself to be pulled back up. "Let's go to bed."

Tefilah: And Your Love, May You Forever Not Remove It from Us

Hashem, when the rabbis of old wrote the prayers, they wrote a lot about Your love for us—for the Children of Israel and for all Your creations. But love can take many forms.

Dani told me that he loves me. And I love him. But is love enough to surmount the issues inherent in our relationship? Is our love strong enough to endure possible censure from my community, which I hope someday will be our *community?*

We have already been intimate in ways that many would tell me that You do not approve of. I have experienced a level both of joy and of pleasure that I never imagined, that I never thought possible. I cannot believe that You—to whom many songs of love were written, the richest of which is codified in Your holy books as the Song of Songs—would forbid that sort of experience.

King David, in the book of Psalms, wrote, "You bring joy into our hearts" and "You have changed my lamentations into dancing…you have girded me with joy." This is how Dani makes me feel.

I've known love from my parents, from my siblings. I've even known love of a sort from Dalia. But with Dani…his love for me feels different from all the others. His love, even before he expressed it in words, was obvious to me. His love for me transcends the physical acts of intimacy we engage in; he shows me love in his caring. He expressed his love in the ways he helped me out after my bicycle accident, even in the face of Ima and Abba's clear dislike for his presence. And he shows me love

daily, checking in with me to find out how my day was, or to tell me something funny he heard at work. Our love is more than how we physically express it.

Yet it's that physical expression of our love that is so complicated, not just for us as a couple in the community in which I live, but in my own head. I am working through the process of retraining myself, to rethink what I was taught, to reframe Your laws in a way that does not invalidate my feelings, invalidate my being. *And Dani shows his love yet again by standing by me, by being patient while I figure out what I am comfortable with. And I have faith that he will continue to stand with me and love me regardless of what I decide.*

V'ahavtcha, al tassir mimenu l'olamim—*and Your love, may You forever not remove it from us. Please help us to find our way as we navigate our love, through Your love.*

coffee—the breakfast of champions

WHEN DANI'S PHONE ALARM WENT off, he blearily grabbed for the phone and smacked it until the ringing stopped. He stumbled to the bathroom, leaving his glasses on the bedside table. He used the bathroom and took a quick shower, and then wrapped a towel around his waist and went back to the bedroom for his glasses, underwear, and a T-shirt. Once he'd put it all on, he went to the kitchen, mentally blessing whoever had invented the coffeemaker with an internal timer. He toasted himself a bagel as he drank his first cup and then poured himself a refill after spreading the cream cheese. Taking his plate and his mug, he settled at the table and started reading his way through his standard news websites.

"What day is it?" Jake's very tired voice came from the kitchen doorway behind Dani.

Dani jumped, nearly dropping his tablet on the floor; he hadn't realized there was anyone else in Avi's house.

"Uh… Tuesday?" The first cup of coffee hadn't hit yet—even though Dani was well into the second cup—so he wasn't really sure himself, but it *seemed* like Tuesday. And based on Dani's—admittedly somewhat foggy—recollection of the previous day, he was confident that, in fact, this was Tuesday. They'd come back from Vermont a week and a few days ago, so, yeah. Must be Tuesday. Of course, since he and his coworkers

started the crazed dance that was involved with bidding for the Potential Really Big Client, days of the week had lost most of their differentiating characteristics.

"Could be. Yeah. Tuesday. That sounds right." Jake rummaged through cabinets. "Where the fuck did you hide the coffee?"

"The pot on the warmer is no more than twenty minutes old, so it should still be fresh. And the coffee's in the freezer, where it always is."

Jake finally turned around and did a double-take when he saw that the other occupant of the kitchen wasn't who he had expected. "Dani?"

Dani would have thought that the three-inch height difference between Avi and himself, not to mention their totally different voices, would've made it obvious to Jake that he wasn't Avi, but maybe Jake really was really that oblivious before his first cup. "Yup."

"Is Avi still asleep?"

"Avi went to Shacharit, so he was up and out by six thirty. And he's working near the Aquarium today, so his plan was to go downtown straight from shul."

"What time is it now?"

Dani looked at the clock on the kitchen wall. "Just about seven forty-five. On a normal Tuesday I'd be leaving right around now, but I was in the office until ten thirty last night, so I'm working from home this morning and then going into the office for the afternoon." Okay, so maybe it was a liberal definition of "from home," but Avi's house was beginning to be more and more like home to Dani.

"Fuck. I'm supposed to be on shift starting in fifteen minutes. Eh, what are they gonna do, fire me? And they didn't page me, so they're probably doing fine. Not what they were claiming last night, but eh, fuck 'em."

"Rough night?" Dani asked. Jake was still rummaging in cabinets, and Dani probably knew where whatever Jake was looking for was, but Dani was half afraid to ask just what he was seeking.

"Rough week. The ED was busier than usual, due to kids being on winter break and taking the free time as an opportunity to be randomly stupid. The snowstorm last week means more ED visits because of the standard snow blower-related injuries, heart attacks, and slip-and-falls.

And if that wasn't enough, there was a twenty-four-car pileup on 93 yesterday afternoon. From the time I went on-shift at seven yesterday morning, I didn't leave the department for more than ten minutes, and I didn't make it out of the hospital until four thirty this morning. Didn't want to go all the way home for the couple of hours of sleep I'd get."

"Seems reasonable," Dani said. Avi's house was on the same street as most of the major Boston hospitals, so even though Jake's apartment was less than a mile away from Avi's place, it made sense that Jake would consider Avi's house a better option.

"I didn't hear you come in," Dani said. "Of course, I was pretty wiped out by the time Avi and I went to sleep the previous night, so that was no big surprise."

"Do I want to know this about my brother's love life?" Jake asked. "More to the point, would Avi want me to know?"

"It's nothing like that. My work is crazy right now, too, and I've been working late, as I said. So by the time I got here, and Avi gave me a snack—because of course he did—and we got to bed, it was almost midnight. How Avi was then up and out by six forty-five I don't know, but he seems to function on less sleep than almost anyone else I know."

Jake finally found what he was looking for—cold cereal, as it turned out. He pulled the box, a bowl, and a coffee mug out of various cabinets and started putting his breakfast together. After filling his mug, he took a long drink then turned to Dani. "Oh, this is good. I should get you to teach Avi to make a decent cup of coffee. Or you should be the one to make it every morning."

Dani liked that idea. Making coffee at Avi's every morning was a very nice thing to consider.

"Anyway," Jake said, "I really should be getting my ass in gear and getting back to the hospital. Just because they haven't come looking for me doesn't mean that they won't hold me responsible for time I should have been there and wasn't. Have a good day." He put his coffee cup on the counter and grabbed his bag and coat from the corner of the kitchen—where he'd apparently left them when he came in earlier that morning—and in a minute or so, Dani heard the front door close.

He poured himself another cup of coffee and sat down at the kitchen table to assess what had just happened. It was most definitely odd. Good odd, but odd nonetheless. Not expected, that was for sure. And it might have future repercussions. He would have to wait and see.

Dani sipped his coffee as he contemplated what he should tell Avi about the morning. There was no question that he would tell Avi at least some details; this was the sort of information Avi needed, especially if Jake said something to Ilana.

He was spared additional contemplation when his phone rang with a snippet of "Abanibi," the ringtone he'd set for Avi.

"Hey, motek. You on your way downtown?"

"Yeah," Avi said. "We had to wait a bit for a minyan, so I'm running a few minutes behind my planned schedule, but I'll still make it before my scheduled time. Even with Government Center Station closed I should make it. I hope I didn't wake you when I left."

"I felt you leave the bed, but I didn't really wake up, if that makes any sense. I fell back asleep and then got up for real around seven thirty."

"And how has your morning been so far?" Avi asked.

"Not bad. Well, a bit weird in one sense, but otherwise fine. I'm just having my coffee before settling in to work for a couple of hours."

"Weird *how*, Dani?"

"Well, I learned this morning that your brother can't tell the difference between you and me before he has had coffee."

"You saw Jake?"

"Jake was here this morning when I woke up. He said he came in around four thirty and crashed on the sofa for a couple of hours."

"Yeah, he does that sometimes. I had no clue he was there this morning; if I'd known, I would've left you a note."

"I appreciate that. But I probably startled him as much as he startled me." Dani chuckled. "You should've seen his face when he realized I wasn't you."

"The fact that you're his height and I'm, well, *not* didn't give it away?"

"To be fair, he was pre-coffee. He stumbled into the kitchen, drank some coffee, had some cereal, and then was out the door. I'm not totally

convinced he was completely awake; I hope he wasn't driving, given how asleep he seemed."

"He's very good at going from dead asleep to completely awake and functional in seconds; he says it's a job requirement. But on nights like the one he apparently had last night, he either walks or gets a ride, so no need to worry."

"Good to know," Dani said. "Anyway, I just thought you might want to know that Jake knows I spent the night here, even though I didn't specifically tell him."

"Jake's a smart guy; he will figure out from context clues that you slept over." Avi paused. "You… you were wearing pants when he found you in the kitchen, right?"

"Well, not pants, but I was in my boxers and T-shirt, not just a towel. Is that okay?" Dani asked, a laugh tingeing his voice.

"That's fine; I just had a mental image of you and Jake conversing while you were wearing nothing but a towel, and, well… not a comfortable image."

"That would've been awkward, yeah," Dani said. "And would probably remove all plausible deniability, if you wanted such a thing."

"I'm not ashamed that you sleep over. I'm not embarrassed that you are spending nights in my bed or that I'm spending nights in yours. I just don't want our sleeping arrangements to be the subject of *lashon hara* amongst my family."

"But whatever they might talk about would be true—I *am* spending the night in your bed, and Jake *did* catch me without pants in your kitchen at seven thirty in the morning. There's little else that they could speculate about us that would make any sense."

"Lashon hara is always true; otherwise it's *motzei shem ra*," Avi said. "But that's neither here nor there. Jake probably won't say anything to Ima and Abba. It's more than likely that he called Dalia right after he left the house and FaceTimed with her as he walked back to the hospital, which means that Chava will know, as well. Chava may say something to Ima and Abba, but it's more likely that she'll just squee about it with Dalia."

"Squee?" Dani asked.

"Ugh. I'm picking up vocabulary from my sister. It's best described as a high-pitched squealing noise that is used by some people to express unbounded joy."

"I'm not sure if that pleases me or worries me," Dani said.

"They're happy for us. I'd consider that a good thing."

"You're right, motek. I'm glad they're happy for us."

"And if Chava has her way, my parents will come around to being happy for us." Though Avi and Dani hadn't talked about it a lot, at least not in the past few months, Avi's parents were still slow to accept their relationship. They could spend time together amicably, and Yoni and Ilana had fewer objections to Dani's presence in Avi's life every time they interacted with Dani, but they still had not completely embraced the idea of Dani as Avi's partner.

"I don't want to think about how your parents might react to finding out we sleep together regularly," Dani said. "And their knowing that we spend nights together would not make them at all happy."

"I don't want to think about my parents thinking about my sex life," Avi countered.

"Okay, I'll give you that."

"I'm almost at work; I should go. But don't worry, chamudi. Jake knowing we're sleeping together shouldn't matter, but I'll give him a call on my first break, just to be sure."

"Thanks, motek."

"So, you're okay with Jake knowing? Should I tell him to forget that he saw you? He'd really do it. Well, not forget it for real, but he'd never mention it again, not to anyone, not even to you or me."

"No, I'm all right with him knowing. I just didn't want your life to get harder because I offered Jake coffee."

"I appreciate that, chamudi. Anyway, I really must go; I'm starting in about fifteen minutes and I need to get up to the room and look at the setup."

"Have a good day, motek. I'll talk to you later."

"Thanks, Dani. You, too."

They hung up, and Dani started to get ready for work. After talking to Avi, he wasn't so worried about Jake saying anything. But part of him wanted it known. After all, it was time that Avi's family knew that this relationship was real, that Dani was not going anywhere.

In the week since they returned from Vermont, he and Avi had even begun talking around the idea of Dani moving in when his lease was up in September. So something was going have to be said soon, or the situation might become even more awkward.

The next time, after all, it might be Avi's mother who found Dani in Avi's kitchen, clad in just his boxers and a T-shirt, so early in the morning.

going out and being out

"So what do I wear to something like this?" Dani asked, looking at the invitation in his hand. It had arrived in the day's mail, which he had picked up when he came home from work. He'd stuck it in his bag on his way out the door to Avi's. Now, sitting at Avi's kitchen table and staring at the card for about ten minutes, he still didn't know exactly what to make of it.

"Does it say anything about dress?"

"No, all it says is that your family's shul is having its annual dinner, that a bunch of people are being honored, and the date and time. I'm assuming from the fact that one arrived addressed to me that you want me to go with you."

"I was hoping that I'd get a chance to talk to you before the invitation arrived, but yes. My mother asked me this morning if you were coming with me, and I said I'd have to ask you."

"Okay, so we'll talk later about why you didn't tell me this was even a thing until now, but yes. I would love to go with you if it's something you want to do."

"I desperately want to you to come with me, chamudi. There is little I dread more than a room full of people I don't know but who know who I am, all asking me questions that I don't know the answer to. Your presence

at this shindig will be the only thing that will make it at all tolerable." Avi walked over to the kitchen table and gave Dani a kiss. "And I want you there for my own selfish reasons beyond as a buffer. I want you to meet some people that will likely be there. I want to introduce people to my magnificent boyfriend."

"All right, if you're sure."

"I'm sure," Avi said, giving Dani a deeper kiss than the first.

"Then I will be honored to go with you."

As THEY WALKED TO THE front door of the hotel, Dani stopped and pulled his hand from Avi's grip. "You're still sure you want me here?"

"More than anything, chamudi," Avi said.

"Then here we go," Dani said, taking a deep breath and reaching again for Avi's hand. It was unusual, how jittery he was feeling. But this was an unusual situation; he'd never been the guest of the son of honorees at a fancy dinner, especially one where a significant percentage of the people in attendance might be predisposed to hostility toward him purely for being the guest of the aforementioned son of the honorees.

"Everyone will love you," Avi said, uncannily reading Dani's mind.

"If you're sure, motek."

"I am. And? Free food. Very good food, at that, if the rumors I heard about who is catering this thing are true."

"All right, let's go," Dani said, finally opening the door and walking into the hotel lobby. A sign pointed attendees to the ballroom where the dinner was being held, and another sign pointed people to the coat room. In silent agreement, Dani and Avi headed to check their coats before trying to find Avi's parents.

They were four feet from the coat check when they were stopped for the first time. "Avi?"

Avi turned but did not let go of Dani's hand. "Mr. and Mrs. Rosen! It's so good to see you!"

"How many times do we have to remind you to call us Bob and Lisa?" the wife—Lisa—said.

"I'm sorry; old habits and all," Avi said, a slight blush rising on his cheeks. "Dani, Lisa and Bob's daughter babysat me from when I was about five until I was about ten. Lisa, Bob, this is my boyfriend, Dani Perez."

"Nice to meet you, Dani," Bob said. "We'll have to tell Gabi we saw you, Avi."

"Please do send her my regards."

Bob and Lisa headed off, and Dani and Avi made it to the coat check without further interruption. On their way from the coat check to the ballroom, however, a similar scenario played out four or five times; Dani lost count. As they walked down the long corridors toward their destination, they would encounter a person or a couple that Avi knew. He would say hello, they would say hello, he would introduce Dani— always as his boyfriend—pleasantries would be exchanged, and they would continue on their way.

"I'm not going to remember any of these people, motek," Dani said as they stopped at the table holding place cards at the entry of the ballroom.

"Don't worry, chamudi," Avi said. "Most of these people remember me more than I remember them. I only remember the names of half of them. In fact, if you don't mind, I'm going to use you as a method to be reminded of people's names when they approach me."

"Fine with me," Dani said.

They found their place cards, not surprised to find themselves sitting at the table next to that of the honorees, and entered the big room. Dani looked around to see whom he might recognize in the crowd and was happy to see Jake and Chava near the bar.

"My parents are over there," Avi said, gesturing at a corner of the room across from the doorway. "I should go say hello before we do anything else."

Though relations with Avi's parents had improved significantly in the past few months, Dani still found himself a bit nervous as he and Avi approached Ilana and Yoni. He let Avi precede him slightly so that Avi was the one that his parents saw first.

163

"Avi! You're here!" Ilana said, interrupting the conversation she was involved in and turning to give Avi a big hug. When she released Avi, she said, "And Dani! It's wonderful to have you here. I'm glad you could come." Ilana pulled Dani into a hug while Yoni hugged Avi.

"*Mazal tov*, Ilana," Dani said. He turned to Yoni and shook his hand. "Mazal tov to both of you."

"If it were up to me," Yoni said with a grin, "they would've just given me an *aliyah* to the Torah on Shabbat in shul and skipped the whole *gantze megillah*, but first of all it's not up to me; second, it's a good fundraiser for the shul; and third, Ilana deserves a night to dress up and be feted for all that she does for this community."

"You both deserve it, Abba," Avi said. "You do as much as Ima does; you just don't like to get any publicity for it."

"You know that's true, Yoni," Ilana said. "Boys, Jake and Chava are here. They'll be glad to know you've arrived."

"I saw them near the drinks when we came in," Dani said. "If you'll excuse us, we should go say hello."

"Go, mingle," Ilana said. "We'll see you when dinner starts."

Avi gave his parents each one more hug and then he took Dani's hand and walked toward the bar.

They made it halfway across the room before they were approached again. Dani figured they were wearing enough of an "I'm desperate for something to drink" look that people didn't want to derail them from their mission, but one couple clearly didn't get the message.

"Avi!" The voice came from their left, and Dani and Avi turned to see who it was. The guy who had called to them was short, slightly heavyset, with light brown, curly hair and hazel eyes. His broad smile displayed his dimples as he bounded toward Avi and Dani.

"Noam? I can't believe it!" He grinned, and Dani was suddenly very interested to know who could put a look like that on Avi's face.

"I'm only in town for a couple more days; I flew in yesterday, and then I'll be here through Shabbat, and then I'm flying out Sunday morning. I'm so glad I'm getting a chance to see you here; online conversation is great, but it's not the same."

164

Dani squeezed Avi's hand, and Avi turned to him. "Oh! Dani! This is Noam! Noam, this is Dani, my boyfriend."

"Nice to meet you," Dani said, extending his free hand but not letting go of Avi's.

Noam took the proffered hand. "I'm Noam. Avi and I have been friends since middle school."

"And he was the bass in the four-man a cappella group I started over the summer between ninth and tenth grade. And, when I started looking back, I realized he was the first guy I had a serious crush on."

"You did?" Noam asked, smiling. "That must've been bizarre."

"It would have been both bizarre and embarrassing if I had realized at the time what it was. All I thought it was back then, though, was envy. I wanted to be your partner for every group project we did in high school, wanted to be part of every club you were part of."

"You must've hated Dalia, then."

"Dalia?" Dani asked. "Like, Dalia-Dalia?"

Avi laughed. "Actually," he said to Noam, "it was when you and Dalia started dating that she and I became really close."

"Really? I totally missed that. And then she and I broke up, and then after graduation I moved to Israel and ultimately decided to stay and make aliyah. She and I kept in touch for a bit, but it was hard once I was in the army and there wasn't really any good means of visual communication."

"I'll have to tell her I saw you," Avi said.

"Please do. And let her know I'll be in touch very soon. I need to send her a YouTube video or something. It's been a while, and I have stuff I need to tell her."

As they were talking, Jake and Chava walked up. Jake put his hand on Dani's shoulder. "Hey, Dani," he said.

"Hey, Jake. Managed to get the night off?"

"I told them a couple of months ago that there was no way I could work tonight because I had a family obligation. They're not so flexible about scheduling, but they understand the wrath of snubbed moms. So, here I am."

"Makes sense to me," Dani said. He turned to Chava and very haltingly signed, {Good to see you}.

Chava smiled and signed something back that Dani couldn't understand.

{Slower. Sorry. Please}, Dani signed back.

"Want me to interpret for you?" Jake asked, signing to Chava as well.

Dani had only been studying ASL for about two months, and while he had pretty good skill at learning languages, ASL was still kicking his ass. "Yes, please," he said.

Chava nodded and repeated the signs she had made before.

"I didn't know you signed at all."

"I'm learning," Dani said. "I figured it was the only way I could hold my own with you and Dalia."

"You thought right," Chava said.

Avi grinned. "I promised I wouldn't tell anyone that he was learning; I knew you'd all be excited, but he wanted to wait until he had a bit of fluency before he revealed it."

"'A bit of fluency' is an exaggeration," Dani said. "I have some basic sentences and a couple of useful terms, and that's about it. But I'm committed to becoming fluent as soon as I can."

"It's a useful language to know," Noam said. "Jake, it's great to see you again." He signed to Chava, who grinned back at him.

"Where are you sitting, Noam?" Jake asked.

"Table three," Noam said.

"Oh, excellent," Avi said. "That seems to be the table of honorees' relatives; you'll be sitting with Dani and me."

"And Chava and me," Jake added.

"You didn't bring anyone?" Avi asked his siblings.

"I'm not dating anyone seriously enough at the moment to bring to this sort of event," Jake said.

"And Jeremy is teaching tonight and couldn't get anyone to cover his class," Chava added.

"You up for an almost undiluted evening of Levine siblings?"

"I've missed you guys," Noam said. "And, Dani, from what I've seen just now, you seem to mesh perfectly with this bunch."

"Oh, I desperately hope so," Dani said.

"Jake?" Avi said, "We were on our way to get something to drink when we ran into Noam. Can you all go stake out seats at the table for us, and we'll be along momentarily?"

"Sure, Avi," Jake said. "Come on, let's go see which other honorees' relatives will be subjected to the Levine siblings tonight."

As they walked away, Dani took Avi's hand again. "Thanks, motek."

"You were putting out 'I need a break' vibes, whether you know it or not."

"Wasn't the plan that I would be here to keep *you* from having too-many-people stress?"

"Plans are adjustable. And being the odd man out during Old Home Week can be really stressful."

"I like Noam, from what I've seen of him. I hope to get a chance to talk to him over dinner."

"Just don't pump him for embarrassing stories about me from high school. There are tons of them, and they all make me cringe."

"Let's just get our drinks, and then we'll head over for the opportunity to eat way too much good food and listen to boring speeches," Dani said with a grin.

"… If it weren't for their kindness and generosity, Miriam and I wouldn't have had Shabbat dinner the night after our son was born, and in the twenty years since then they have never turned down a request for hospitality, nor have they ever asked for anything in return. So please help me give a heartfelt thank you to Ilana and Yoni, the recipients of this year's Foundation award."

Applause and cheers ushered Yoni and Ilana up to the stage. Dani watched as they walked up to the microphone and Yoni pulled an index card out of his pocket.

Yoni and Ilana had a brief whispered conversation, and then Yoni took the microphone out of its stand and moved the stand toward the back of the stage. Ilana stood where the microphone stand had been.

"Good evening," Yoni said, and Ilana interpreted his words into ASL. "Thank you all for this honor; we are thrilled to be here. We have a couple of thank-yous we want to make sure to give. First, we want to thank the board of directors and the dinner committee for this lovely event. We are honored and humbled to be a part of it."

He paused to let Ilana finish signing the first section before he continued.

"We would like to thank our parents, *zichronam livracha*, for teaching us how to fulfill the *mitzvah* of *Hachnasat orchim*. We do not see ourselves as doing anything special; we are just carrying on the traditions of our predecessors. And we would like to recognize our children, who are, in their own homes, bringing the traditions to the next generation. In their continuing to open their homes to both friends and strangers, they show their commitment to one of the mitzvot for which, as we say every morning in Shacharit, we get reward both in this life and in the life to come. And so to our children, Avi and Dani, Chava and Jeremy, and Ya'akov, may you continue to fulfill this mitzvah, and may you have as wonderful a community as we do to support you in this endeavor. Thank you."

There was thunderous applause in the room, but Dani was too shocked to pay attention. "Did they…"

"Welcome to the family, Dani," Jake said, reaching across Avi to shake Dani's hand.

On their way off the stage, Yoni and Ilana stopped at what the people sitting there had, during dinner, come to call "the children's table."

"Mazal tov again, Ima and Abba," Avi said, rising to his feet and giving his parents each a hug.

"Thank you," Ilana said. "I hope…"

"It was a beautiful speech," Avi said.

"Yes, it was," Jake said, also getting to his feet.

Dani rose as well. "Yoni, Ilana…"

"I hope we didn't embarrass you too much, Dani. We wanted to make sure that you know that we consider you one of our children, as we do Jeremy."

"Thank you," Dani said. "I hope I can live up to that designation."

"You love Avi?" Yoni asked.

"Beyond the telling of it," Dani replied.

"Then that's enough for us."

"Abba, you're embarrassing him," Avi said.

"I'm sorry, Dani; I'll go back to embarrassing my other kids now," Yoni said, giving Dani a hug.

Ilana gave Dani a hug, as well, startling him. She and Yoni greeted the rest of the people at the table and then returned to their seats.

"That was… unexpected," Dani said.

"But good?" Avi asked.

"Oh, yes. Very good."

TEFILAH: I LIFT MY EYES TO THE MOUNTAINS
FROM WHICH MY HELP WILL COME

Hashem, *You have always sent aid to those who need You, when they need it most. I come to You at a moment of crisis, at a moment of questioning, at a moment of anguish.*

Your great scholars, the ancient rabbis of blessed memory, set a path for us to walk after the destruction of Your Holy Temple. But how could they know what modern people would face?

So you imbued great scholars throughout the generations, so that Your Torah's laws could be adapted to modern times, no matter what those modern times were. You gave men the intelligence to interpret Your laws.

But while You are without flaw, humans are flawed. Which means that their interpretations of Your laws may be flawed. Yet we have to live with those flawed interpretations.

I cannot believe that You would allow for some flaws but condemn human beings for others.

The rabbis, in their wisdom, never legislated against thoughts, just actions. I understand the separation of feelings from acts. But I cannot live as a whole person in that bifurcated mindset. I cannot say to myself that I can be gay and have gay urges but never act on them. But at the same time, how is that any different from craving non-kosher food but still refraining from it because I know it's forbidden?

Can I still call myself an Orthodox Jew if I don't abstain from having anal sex with Dani?

We believe that you are rewarded for each mitzvah you perform and are held responsible for every sin you commit. But in Kohelet, Shlomo says there is no one who is always righteous and never sins.

What if I make the choice that certain sexual acts are a vital part of my life with Dani? I will be making the conscious decision to commit a sin and not do true teshuvah *for doing so.*

Again, I go to Shlomo, but this time to Mishlei, *the book of Proverbs. He wrote, "In all of your ways, know God." The holy scholars of the Gemarah interpreted that to mean that we should know You even when we are committing a sin.*

And what about Yom Kippur? How can I repent, how can I say the prayers asking You for forgiveness when I know I have no intention of changing my ways in certain circumstances?

But as we say on the High Holy Days, we are only flesh and blood. So we ask You for guidance in making our decisions and for forgiveness for the times when we made a decision we shouldn't have.

Perhaps the solution is that there is no solution. Perhaps the answer is that there is no answer. Perhaps the path that is right for me and for Dani is not the path that is right for another person, for another couple.

Essah einei el heharim, me'ayin yavo ezri. *I lift my eyes up to the mountains, from where my help comes. Please, Hashem, help me find a path for Dani and me to walk.* Ezri me'im Hashem, oseh shamayim va'aretz. *My help comes from You, the creator of Heaven and Earth.*

wisdom affords strength to the wise

It was the last Sunday in February, and the weather was finally beginning to clear up enough that they could consider making plans that didn't run the risk of being canceled due to snow or rain. Dani sat at Avi's kitchen table trying to make a plan for the day while Avi was emptying the dishwasher. He remembered that they had discussed their weekend plans earlier in the week, and he remembered that Avi was getting together with his siblings, but he couldn't remember exactly what Avi had scheduled for the day.

"Hey, Avi? What's this on your calendar, 'Manot and museums with the Gang of Three'?"

"Purim preparations, and then a trip to the MFA and/or Isabella Stewart Gardner, depending on what we feel like. Why?"

"Dudu and I have been trying to schedule a squash date for a while, and we're both free today, unless you and I are doing something that I'm not remembering."

"Nope, unless you want to come along. You're more than welcome, you know."

"Yes, and I appreciate that, but if it's all the same I'm going to instead participate in a societally accepted method of beating up my brother."

Avi laughed. "If it's all right with Dudu, it's all right with me."

"And I can give you a lift to Jake's on my way to Dudu's, if you want."

"That would be great."

After they both got ready, Dani drove Avi over to Jake's. He pulled into a parking space and turned off the car.

"Have a good time," Dani said. "Give all of them my love."

"Thanks," Avi said. "Give Dudu my love and tell him I said not to let you beat him unless you earned it."

"I've been beating him on the squash court since college," Dani said. "He should be used to it by now." He gave Avi a kiss. "Have a good time with the Wiseguys. Talk to them about whatever is bothering you. And don't get angry at Chava if—sorry, when—she says something that cuts too close to the bone."

"What do you mean?" Avi said, his expression blank, though Dani could tell it was taking a lot to keep it that way.

"I know you're struggling with something, motek. And when you struggle, you tend to seek their advice. Take this opportunity, Avi. Talk to them about whatever you need. Listen to them; they're smart people, and they have your best interests at heart. And then come talk to me when you're ready. I love you, motek. And nothing is going to change that."

"I love you, too," Avi said. "Don't get hurt." He grabbed his bag, got out of the car, and headed over to Jake's building. Dani watched him walk away and then started the car again and pulled back out onto the street.

AVI SEEMED HAPPY IF SOMEWHAT subdued when Dani picked him up a couple of hours later. As they drove back from Jake's, they discussed the drubbing that Dudu had experienced at Dani's hands on the squash court.

"So," Dani asked as they pulled into Avi's driveway, "did you have a good afternoon?"

"I did," Avi said. "You were right about talking to them. It was awkward and embarrassing, as I probably should have anticipated, but good. There's stuff I'd like us to talk about, though, when you've got time."

"I'm glad it went well," Dani said. "And my time is totally free for the rest of the day. I just need to do a couple of quick things when we get inside, and then I'm totally yours."

They got out of the car and headed into the house. "I bought some fresh mint today while we were out shopping for Purim, and I was going to put up some *nana* tea," I said.

"Ooh, make me some, too, please?

"Of course. Meet me in the living room?"

"Sure, motek." Dani gave Avi a kiss, went to Avi's room to put his dirty clothes in the laundry, then headed back out into the hallway with his squash bag. Opening the closet in the entryway, he moved his running shoes aside and set his equipment bag next to the bicycle pump. Hearing the kettle start to whistle, he straightened up and walked to the kitchen.

"I need a few more minutes, is that okay? I got a quick shower at the club, enough that I don't completely stink, but I'd really like to just jump in the shower if you don't mind."

"No, that's fine," Avi said. "The tea will need time to steep."

"Thanks, motek. I'll be right back," Dani said, and then showered after a stop in the bedroom for fresh clothes.

When he was out of the shower, Dani headed back down to the kitchen to find Avi, but he wasn't there. "Motek?"

"In the living room."

Dani followed Avi's voice and found him sitting on the sofa. While he'd been in the shower, Avi had set out some snacks on a tray and brought it into the living room along with the teapot and mugs.

Dani sat down on the sofa next to Avi and laid his arm across the back. "Is everything all right, motek?" he asked, worry in his voice.

"I hope so," Avi said. "I…" He paused.

"Whatever it is, we'll figure it out. It's what we do," Dani said.

"Well, you know that I've been learning with Rabbi Berger these past few months, and that I've been striving to find an answer to how we can have a complete sex life."

"As I've said before, I have no problem with our sex life the way it is."

"I appreciate that, chamudi. I truly do. But please let me talk this through."

Dani nodded, so Avi continued.

173

"I'd been hoping, as you know, to find a modern halachic authority who had ruled that we could do everything that a gay couple may want to do and still be within the bounds of halacha. Or, barring that, some way that I could reconcile going against the majority halachic opinion and still consider myself a fully halachic, 'Torah-true' Jew, much as I hate that phrase. That's huge, Dani; that knowledge that I am still acting within the bounds of the community norms, or, if not completely within them, that I'd still be close enough to stay within the community, that's my mental safety net."

Dani nodded, but he didn't speak.

"I've been searching for months, and I'm afraid that I cannot reconcile the two." Avi's tone was very tight, very controlled, as if he was fighting back a torrent of emotions. "I… I don't think I can do everything that you expect from me, that you want from me." At that point, whatever control Avi was exerting cracked, and he put his face in his hands.

Dani moved his arm down from behind Avi and put his hand on Avi's knee. "Motek, look at me," he said. Avi turned his head and looked at Dani. "Avi, relax. I… I sort of expected this to be coming, especially once you started learning every week with Rabbi Berger. I started doing a little bit of learning myself. To be honest, I started it to see if I could outsmart the rabbis. I was determined to find the answer, just as you were. But the more I learned, the more I looked, the more I realized that the two cannot be neatly reconciled. There are no easy answers when it comes to this. So maybe right now there is no way that we can find within a halachic context that you will be comfortable with anal sex. But who knows—the rabbis who interpret the texts in modern times have found ways to make all sorts of other long-standing prohibited acts permissible. Who's to say that in ten, twenty years the rabbis won't find an interpretation that makes it allowable? And if that happens, it's you that I want by my side to celebrate with."

Avi slid over and rested his head on Dani's shoulder. "You amaze me, you know that?"

"I love you, Avi. And that's all there is to it."

They sat in silence for a few minutes, enjoying the closeness. Then Dani said, "The tea's going to get cold. And tepid nana tea just isn't the same."

"We can't be having that now, can we?" Avi joked back, sitting up to start pouring.

"Not at all," Dani said, accepting the mug Avi passed him.

Things weren't completely settled, of course. That's what life is; life is messy at times. And Dani and Avi both knew they would have more discussions in the weeks—months, years, hopefully—to come. But this was them; this was how they worked.

And they would be just fine.

epilogue
the season of our freedom

"C'MON, AVI, THE ZMAN ENDS at just about eleven thirty. That gives us less than two hours to get out to the fire station to burn the *chametz*!"

It was *erev Pesach*, the day before the first Passover that Dani was going to be celebrating since he and Avi started living together. And he wanted to make sure everything went perfectly—or, at least, that nothing went sufficiently wrong as to undo all the hard work they'd done over the past few weeks preparing the house for Passover. All of the kitchen and dining room surfaces had been thoroughly cleaned, and all of the chametz—any food items containing any leavening—had been removed.

Now all that was left was to burn the chametz they had found during the ritual search. And then they could get down to the business of getting ready for the Seder. To celebrate their first Pesach together in the house, Dani and Avi had volunteered to host, which in this case meant preparing a meal for fifteen people. Almost everyone had offered to bring something, to take some of the pressure off, but there were still a lot of details to work on.

"I'm coming," Avi said. "I just wanted to make sure I'd gone through my shaving kit and removed any potential chametz. That's the one place I forget to check until right before."

Dani grabbed the bag of chametz for burning, and they drove to the fire station in Brighton where almost everyone in the community came to burn their chametz. It had started as a service offered to one community, but through word of mouth it had turned into the place to

be on the morning before the Seder, and it had taken on something of a block party atmosphere.

They said hello to the friends who were there, burned their chametz, gave a donation to the organizers, and then went back to the house. When they arrived, they found that Dalia, Chava, and Ilana had arrived to start putting the food together while Jake and Yoni were picking up the last of the supplies needed to set the table.

As Avi went to the basement to carry up some of the serving dishes and other items that were used only for the Seder, Dani pulled Ilana aside.

"Is everything set?" he asked.

"Not *everything*, but everything that can be organized ahead has been organized, yes," she said. "Dalia put everything where we discussed, and you should be able to find it all when you're ready."

"Thanks," Dani said. "And Avi has no idea?"

"He hasn't said anything, not to me or to Yoni or to Chava and Dalia. If he said anything to Jake, well, that I can't know since Jake hasn't mentioned anything, but I think you're in good shape."

"Excellent," Dani said. "Thanks so much to all of you for your help."

"We're looking forward to watching it all play out. What's your plan?"

Dani paused, listening for Avi's footfalls on the basement stairs. He knew Avi would be coming up momentarily. "I'm thinking right before *Tzafun*, once we've all eaten but before the *Afikoman*."

"That sounds perfect," Ilana said just as the doorbell rang.

Avi came running back up the stairs carrying a box marked "*Haggadot*." Dani was glad to know that Avi had remembered where they had put that box of books needed for the Passover Seder when they put away all of the Passover stuff last year. Everyone would want one so that they could follow along as the Seder proceeded.

"Ima," Avi said, "can you put these on the sideboard? I know everyone has their favorite, but if we put out one standard one that everyone will have, people can then choose a second or third or whatever to enhance the conversation." Along with having twenty-five of one style so that everyone could find the place and page numbers could be called, Avi had collected a large number of more elaborate Haggadot. While each one contained

the traditional text used for the Seder, each also had commentary or stories designed to add more depth to the codified text.

Avi thrust the box at Ilana and went to the entryway to let in the latest arrivals. Dani followed on his heels, figuring that Avi might want his help. When he got to the doorway, he found he was right—his parents stood at the front door holding a bunch of bags and boxes.

Dani held the door for his parents as they entered and for Avi, who had taken some of the parcels from Penina and Ben.

"Hi, Ima; hi, Abba. Thanks for coming so early," Dani said, kissing his parents' cheeks as they walked by him.

"We're so glad you invited us, we're happy to help with whatever you need," Penina said. "We picked up the *matzah shmurah* and a couple of bottles of grape juice, though I know you've probably got a lot."

"Never enough grape juice," Ilana said, coming out of the kitchen. "I'm likely to switch to grape juice after the second cup, and even if we don't use it all tonight or tomorrow at the *Sedarim*, it'll get used for Shabbat or whenever." She gave Penina a hug. "It's good to see you again."

"It's good to see you, as well," Penina said, hugging back.

The two mothers walked toward the living room and Avi went to the kitchen with the boxes of matzah. Ben put the case of grape juice on the floor and said, "Dani, how are you?"

"I'm doing well, Abba," Dani said.

"Nervous?"

"A bit," Dani admitted. "It's the first Seder I've ever co-hosted, though we've been doing them my whole life."

"Well, yes, that, but I was also thinking of —" He stopped when Avi came back into the hallway and picked up the case of grape juice.

"What were you thinking of?" Avi asked as he shifted the grape juice into a comfortable position.

"I was thinking of the fact that this is Dani's first year doing two Sedarim. We usually only do one, since that's what we did in Israel, and all of our Israeli friends only do one. This year, he's doing two with you, which must be odd."

"Not so odd," Dani said. "I did two last year, too, because Avi and I were dating already by Pesach."

"Oh, you're right," Ben said. "We were in Israel for Pesach, so I forgot."

"Uh, okay," Avi said. "I'm just going to take this box and put it somewhere. Dani, I'll be wherever Ima needs me if you're looking for me." Avi and Dani might have been the hosts of the Seder, but Penina and Ilana, being more experienced with running the setup, were totally in charge of the goings-on before the holiday started.

Avi left the hallway, and after Dani heard his footsteps fade, he hissed at his father, "You totally almost blew it, Abba."

"I'm sorry, Dani. I'll be more careful."

"He might be suspicious that *something* is going on, but if I can keep him focused on getting ready for the Seder I think I can surprise him. And once we get started with the actual Seder, I think he'll be too busy to notice any shenanigans that I or anyone else might be pondering."

"That sounds reasonable."

"Anyway," Dani said, "Ima is making lunch, and then we really have to get started setting things up. There's so much to do and not as much time as you might think. I'm going to eat quickly and then I need to work on getting everything ready. I'm told I'm in charge of making *charoset*; we're making both the traditional Ashkenazi version with apples and walnuts and also a Sepharadi version with dates as the main fruit."

"Need an extra set of hands?" Ben asked. "I'm told I make a decent sous chef."

"Of course," Dani said, heading toward the kitchen. "I can always use your help."

Six hours later, everything was set that could be done ahead. The table was beautiful, the ritual items were all arranged, and, knowing that the Seder could easily go until one in the morning and cleanup until two or later, all of the family had taken the opportunity to have a rest before the evening got underway.

"Did anyone talk to the Steinbergs and make sure they knew what they were getting themselves into?" Avi asked, looking around the living

room. All of the Perezes and Levines were present, as was Chava's fiancé, Jeremy. The only guests that were missing were a family that had recently moved to the community and that had asked for hospitality for the holiday from the synagogue. Since Ilana and Yoni usually hosted at least one family, Avi and Dani had extended a similar invitation.

"I spoke to them yesterday afternoon," Ilana said. "They said they'd walk over after candle lighting; they live about six blocks from here, so they'll probably show up while we're doing the last of the setup."

During the next hour, the last details that had to be taken care of before the holiday were all attended to. And then, right around seven all of the women plus Avi and Jeremy gathered around the sideboard to light the candles for the holiday. They said the blessing to usher in the holiday plus the *Shehechiyanu*, the blessing said on every holiday that expresses thankfulness for arriving at the holiday season.

After they lit candles, everyone started putting out the ritual foods that would be needed for the Seder. Chava set up the plate containing the six ritual items that would be used as symbols during the Seder. Avi washed and prepared the lettuce that would be used for the bitter herb twice during the evening, and Dani made salt water and chopped the vegetables to be used at the beginning of the ritual. As they were finishing, there was a knock at the front door.

"Oh, that's probably the Steinbergs," Yoni called from the living room. "I'll go let them in."

A few minutes later, Yoni led a couple in their late twenties and two young children into the dining room. "Malka, Shlomo, this is everyone. Everyone, these are Malka and Shlomo and their kids, Lior and Hadassah."

"It's lovely to meet you all," Penina said. "I'm Penina and I'm Dani's mother. Don't worry if you don't remember all our names; there are a lot of us."

Malka leaned down to the small girl clinging to her leg and started to slowly sign Penina's name.

"Oh!" Ilana exclaimed. "They didn't tell us that —"

"It's not… We didn't tell the shul; we hope it's not a problem if we translate things for her."

Yoni laughed. "You have nothing to worry about here." He called out toward the kitchen. "Hey, Avi? C'mere, if you're free. And bring Chava, too."

In just a minute, Avi, Chava, and Dani came out of the kitchen, Avi still drying his hands. "Yes, Abba? We'll be ready in just a couple more minutes."

"Priority override," Yoni said. "Avi, Dani, Chava, this is Hadassah, her parents, Malka and Shlomo, and her brother Lior," he said and signed.

Chava immediately crouched down and started signing to Hadassah; Avi interpreted for the non-signers in the group. "*Chag Sameach*, Hadassah. Have you learned the four questions? I'm tired of being the youngest at the table and having to ask them."

"I know them," Hadassah responded. "But I'm nervous."

"I'll ask them with you, if you want," Chava said.

"I'd like that," Hadassah said, moving away from her mother and walking closer to Chava.

Once everyone was seated according to Ilana's seating chart, with Avi and Dani anchoring the table at each end, they started the Seder. Dani, Avi, and Yoni took turns doing the parts of the ritual traditionally done by the head of the household.

When the four questions were asked, Chava and Hadassah signed them while Avi interpreted them into Hebrew. After that, as was traditional in Dani's family, they went around the table asking the questions in whatever other languages people felt like bringing. Dudu asked them in Ladino, while Yoni asked them in Yiddish. They also did most of the other traditional songs in a combination of voice and ASL, because Hadassah wanted to join in. She especially wanted to repeat the chorus of "*Dayenu*"—"it would be enough."

By the time the *Maggid* section of the *Haggadah* had been completed, and everyone around the table prepared for the ritual hand washing before eating the matzah for the first time at the Seder, the Steinbergs were laughing and joking with everyone else as if they were long lost family. Chava, Dalia, and Hadassah had become fast friends despite the

age difference, and Jeremy and Malka had bonded over their shared love of obscure 1980s television shows. By the time dinner was finished, Lior was asleep on Dudu's shoulder, and Hadassah was slumped in Dalia's lap, struggling to keep her eyes open.

{Dassy? Do you want to search for the afikoman?} Malka asked.

{Sleepy}, Hadassah answered. {Can Dalia help?}

{Sure}, Dalia said.

They left the table hand in hand with the one guideline that the special piece of matzah was hidden somewhere on the first floor, so there was no need to go upstairs. After a few minutes, everyone in the dining room heard a triumphant giggle and then the sound of a child's running feet followed by an adult walking slightly more slowly.

{We found it!} Hadassah said, waving the afikoman bag in the air.

{Give it to Avi}, Yoni said, looking quickly at Dani.

Dani nodded. "Yes, give it to Avi," he said.

"Uh, okay," Avi said. "I'm happy to distribute the afikoman. I just figured we'd make it sort of free-form."

"This way we can make sure everyone gets the right amount," Dani said, though he knew that wasn't a logical statement.

It being late at night and there still being about an hour left of the seder to go, Dani hoped Avi wouldn't argue, and he didn't. He took the bag and unzipped it.

{I'm afraid the afikoman broke when Hadassah found the bag}, Dalia said.

{Don't worry}, Avi replied, {I was about to break it into pieces for everyone anyway.}

He pulled out pieces of matzah of varying sizes. As he collected enough pieces to make a proper portion for each person, he passed the matzah around the table.

"Remember, this is 'dessert,' according to the Talmud," Penina said.

"The rabbis of the Talmud should've learned to be pastry chefs. This is the most boring dessert I've ever eaten," Yoni said, nibbling on his piece of matzah.

{Abba, you say that every year}, Chava said. {Somehow I doubt it will ever get funnier.}

As Avi got closer to handing everyone their portion of afikoman, Dani began to get nervous. The whole plan hinged on this. He had originally come up with a plan that involved someone barging in when they opened the door after *birkat hamazon* to, among other things, invite *Eliyahu ha Navi* to join the gathering, but then he realized that people at the table might get freaked out if there was someone lurking outside. So he settled for this plan. Which he still thought was brilliant. And which would work if only Avi would find what he was supposed to.

Finally, the only person left at the table who was still awake and waiting for a piece of afikoman was Avi. He reached his hand into the bag one more time. "I did pretty well this year—I didn't overwhelm or short anyone, but I'm not stuck eating a huge amount so that we finish it all." He pulled out the remaining pieces of matzah and put them on his plate and then put the empty bag next to it.

There was a faint clanging noise.

"Uh… matzah crumbs don't usually make a noise," Avi said. He stuck his hand into the bag one more time and felt around. Within seconds, he pulled his hand back out, a thin gold band looped around his pinky. "What… what's this?"

"Ah!" said Yoni. "I always thought Jake was the Simple Son."

"Hey!" Jake exclaimed, but there was no heat in it.

Dani moved around the table to where Avi was sitting. Avi was still staring at the ring and didn't notice Dani's approach at first, but then he looked up.

"Chamudi, what's this?" He held out the ring, and Dani took it in his right hand.

Dani had considered for quite a long time exactly what he would say, and now that the moment was here, he wanted his words to be perfect. He wanted them to be right, to express what he meant without sounding too legalistic. He still wasn't sure he had it right, but it was close enough.

"Avi, my love. My bashert. Will you marry me according to the laws of the Commonwealth of Massachusetts?" As contrasted, he knew, to the

laws of Moses and Israel, which were the words spoken at a traditional Jewish wedding.

Avi gasped and said, "Yes! Of course!" He stood up from his chair and hugged Dani close.

"Mazal tov!" everyone around the table said.

{You should have a summer wedding}, Dalia said, grinning.

"Logistics after sleep, Dal," Avi said. "And sleep doesn't come until after the end of the Seder. So let's move along."

They finished eating the afikoman and moved along in the haggadah, completing the ancient ritual that had endured for centuries.

It was close to one a.m. when they concluded the Seder with the traditional songs that were intended to keep the children engaged late at night. In this case, the children were both long asleep and many of the adults were fighting not to drift off, but Dani felt invigorated.

"Thank you for saying yes," he whispered to Avi as they walked to the closet to get the Steinbergs their coats.

"Like I would say no," Avi said with a tired laugh. "In the morning, we can discuss all the reasons why you should know I would never say no."

"In the morning, I will be asleep. We can discuss in the afternoon, over a late lunch."

"If I'm awake, I'll go to shul in the morning. But yes. Talk in the afternoon."

The Steinbergs were the first to leave, the children not waking at all as their parents bundled them into their coats and then into their stroller.

"Thank you for having us," Malka said at the door. "Thank you for including Hadassah so seamlessly. And thank you for letting us join in your simcha."

"Thank you for coming. You should come back for a Shabbat meal. We'll be in touch after Pesach."

They said goodnight and watched the Steinbergs walk down the path and then closed the door and went into the kitchen.

"The Steinbergs heading home?" Penina asked.

"Yeah," Dani said. "And you all should, too. The dishes and all can wait."

"We helped make the mess; we'll help clean it up. Anyway, you can't kick family out."

"It's late, Ima. And you've got a bit of a trip home."

"We're staying overnight with Ilana and Yoni. If we're going to be *mechutanim*, we should get to know each other better."

Dani thought about the word his mother used, mechutanim. In Yiddish and Hebrew, it described the relationship between parents whose children are married to one another.

"Hey, Avi," he said with the clarity that can only come from having been awake for close to twenty hours.

"Mm?" Avi responded from the table, where he was organizing the items they'd need for the next night's Seder.

"Y'know how there's no English equivalent to describe the relationship between your mother and mine, so in some ways it's a relationship without terminology? In the same way, we're creating a relationship without terminology."

"That's really profound, Dani," Avi said, his tone betraying his amusement. "But I think we can learn something else. Just as the Seder has a ritual but everyone brings their own spin to it, so too will we bring our own spin to a ritual when we get married."

"That's so cheesy," Dani said, leaning into Avi. "I love it. I love you."

"I love you, too." Avi said, kissing Dani on the head. "And it can't be cheesy; we're *fleishig*."

"You pun even when you're completely exhausted."

"I pun worse when I'm completely exhausted. You should know that now before you commit to being with me for the rest of your life."

"Too late. I think I made that commitment the day we met."

"Now who's being cheesy?" Avi asked.

They stood in silence for a minute, holding each other close.

"It's Pesach. Zman cheirutainu," Avi whispered. "The time of our freedom."

"Freedom to be us, together."

"Dayenu."

glossary
of Jewish religious and cultural terms

H = Hebrew
Y = Yiddish
L = Latin
A = Aramaic
Pronunciation note: ch is pronounced as in "Bach" or "Loch."

Abba (H)—Dad.

Acharei Mot (H)—Literally, "After the death." The weekly Torah portion that contains the list of forbidden sexual unions. Includes Leviticus 18: 22.

Afikoman (H)—A broken piece of matzah that is set aside at the beginning of the Passover Seder and then eaten after the main meal.

Al neteilat yadayim (H)—The blessing said over the ritual washing of hands before eating bread.

Aliyah (H)—Literally, "the act of going up." Refers both to being called to the Torah for an honor and to the act of moving to Israel to settle there.

Ani Ma'amin (H)—Literally, "I believe." A song expressing hope for the Messianic era, based on the twelfth of Maimonides' Thirteen Principles of Faith.

Arayot (H)—The forbidden sexual unions outlined in Leviticus.

Ashkenazi (H)—A Jew of Eastern European descent.

Assur (H)—Forbidden.

Aufruf (Y)—The celebration where a groom is called up to the Torah before his wedding. Traditionally this happens on a Saturday, during the Shabbat services. Most occur either the week before or the day before the wedding.

Aveinu Malkeinu (H)—Literally, "Our Father, Our King." A supplication said on fast days and on the High Holy Days of Rosh Hashanah and Yom Kippur.

B'li neder (H)—Without making a vow. Said reflexively by observant Jews when they promise something mundane so as to not have it as a sacred vow in case something prevents them from fulfilling their promise.

Bar mitzvah (H)—The ceremony that takes place when a Jewish boy turns thirteen and becomes responsible for his own actions.

Baruch Hashem (H)—Literally, "blessed is God." Idiomatically, "Thank goodness."

Bashert (Y)—Destined. Commonly used to refer to one's beloved.

Beged (H)—An article of clothing. Commonly used to refer to the four-cornered garment to which ritual fringes (tzitzit) are attached.

Beit din (H)—Religious court.

Bentcher (Y)—Booklet containing the Grace After Meals.

Bentching (Y)—Literally, "blessing." The act of saying the Grace After Meals.

Beraishit (H)—The book of Genesis.

Birkat hamazon (H)—Grace After Meals.

Birkon (H)—Booklet containing the Grace After Meals.

Chag Sameach (H)—Happy holiday.

Chalavi (H)—Containing dairy.

Chametz (H)—Containing leavened ingredients. Food forbidden on Passover.

Chamudi (H)—Honey, term of endearment.

Chas v'shalom (H)—God forbid.

Chillul Hashem (H)—Blasphemy. Also refers to an action that brings a bad name to Jews or Judaism. For example, a prominent Jew doing something illegal and getting caught is considered chillul Hashem.

Chol hamoed (H)—The intermediate days between the sacred days of the eight-day holidays of Passover and Sukkot. Work can be performed on these days, unlike on the sacred days. The first two days and the last two days are sacred; the intermediate four days are chol hamoed.

Chutzpah (H)—Nerve, gall.

Dati (H)—Religiously observant

Dayenu (H)—Literally, "It would have been enough." A song that is part of the Passover Seder.

Divrei Torah (H) (singular: d'var torah)—Short talks on religious texts.

Drash (Y)—Short talk on religious texts. Yiddish equivalent of "d'var torah."

Eliyahu ha Navi (H)—Elijah the Prophet. Traditionally, the return of Elijah is a harbinger of the Messianic era.

Erev (H)—Evening. Commonly used to describe the day before a holiday or the evening that begins the Sabbath or a holiday.

Erev Shel Shoshanim (H)—A popular Hebrew love song first recorded in 1957.

Fleishig (Y)—Containing meat ingredients.

Frum (Y)—Religiously observant.

Gantze megillah (Y)—A whole big deal.

Gemarah (A)—Rabbinic commentary on the oral law ("Mishna"), codified approximately 500 CE.

Hachnasat orchim (H)—The welcoming of visitors.

Gut Shabbos (Y) —Good Sabbath. A traditional Sabbath greeting.

Haggadah (H) (plural: Haggadot)—Book containing the service for the Passover Seder.

Halacha (H)—Literally, "the path." Jewish law and jurisprudence.

Halacha l'ma'a'seh (H)—Practical application of Jewish law.

Halachic (H)—Of or pertaining to Jewish law

Hamotzei (H)—The blessing said before eating bread

Hashem (H)—Literally, "The Name." Observant Jews use this as a euphemism for God to avoid blasphemy in casual conversation.

Hashgacha (H)—Kosher certification.

Havdallah (H)—Ritual marking the end of the Sabbath

Ibn Ezra (H)—Abraham Ibn Ezra (1089-1167), a Jewish poet, philosopher, and biblical commentator.

Ima (H)—Mom.

Issur (H)—Something that is forbidden

Kah Ribon (A)——A song frequently sung at Sabbath meal times. Originally published in 1600 in Vienna, it was composed by the sixteenth century poet Rabbi Israel ben Moshe Najara.

Kashrut (H)—Jewish dietary laws

Kiddush (H)—Blessing over wine on the Sabbath and holidays. Colloquially, includes the light meal served at the synagogue after prayers at which the blessing is said.

Kippah (plural: kippot) (H)—skullcap

Kohelet (H)—The book of Ecclesiastes

Lashon hara (H)—Literally, "bad speech." Commonly used to refer to derogatory speech or gossip. It is considered a sin and is something that religious people work to avoid.

M'dakdek (H)—Painstaking, precise.

Macher (Y)—An important or influential person.

Maggid (H)—The part of the Passover Seder that includes the story of the Exodus from Egypt.

Matzah shmurah (H)—Unleavened bread used for Passover. Its preparation is carefully overseen to make sure that no leavening substance is introduced from the time that the wheat is harvested. Contrasted with standard matzah, which is overseen from the time that the wheat is ground into flour.

Mazal tov (H)—Congratulations.

Mechitzah (H)—The physical divider that separates between the men's section and the women's section in the sanctuary of an Orthodox synagogue.

Mechutanim (H)—The relationship between one spouse's parents and the other spouse's parents.

Megillah (H)—Any of the five biblical books of Ruth, Esther, Ecclesiastes, Lamentations, or Song of Songs.

Miluim (H)—Reserve duty in the Israeli army.

Mincha (H)—The daily afternoon prayer service.

Minyan (H) —A religious quorum of ten men.

Mishlei (H)—The biblical book of Proverbs.

Mishloach manot (H)—Packages of food given out at Purim to friends and neighbors.

Mitzvah (H)—A commandment. Colloquially, a good deed.

Motek (H) —Sweetheart.

Motzei shem ra (H) —Literally, "spreading a bad name." Slander.

Nana (H)—Mint, the herb.

Nehedar (H)—Magnificent.

Nu (H)—(Interrogatory) "Well?" or "And so…?"

P'ru u'rvu (H)—"Be fruitful and multiply." The biblical command to procreate.

Pareve (Y)—Food containing neither meat nor dairy ingredients.

Passuk (H)—A biblical verse.

Paytanim (H)—Jewish liturgical poets.

Pesach (H)—Passover.

Pikuach nefesh (H)—Saving a life. One violates the restrictions of the Sabbath or holidays when someone's health or life is at risk (such as using a telephone to call 911).

Responsa (L)—Written decisions by rabbis in response to questions regarding Jewish law.

Schlep (Y)—To drag or haul. Colloquially, to move with effort or reluctance.

Schlump (Y)—A sloppily dressed person.

Seder (H)—Literally, "Order." The ritual held, usually in the home, on the first two nights of Passover, during which the Exodus from Egypt is discussed in depth. Plural: Sedarim.

Sefer Vayikkra (H)—The book of Leviticus.

Sepharadi (H)—Descended from Jews who lived in the Iberian Peninsula prior to the expulsion from Spain in 1492. The term has also come to include other Jewish groups who are not from Eastern Europe, such as those from North Africa.

Shabbat shalom (H)—Good Sabbath. A traditional Sabbath greeting.

Shabbat (H)—The Jewish Sabbath, observed from Friday evening through Saturday night.

Shabbos (Y)—The Jewish Sabbath, observed from Friday evening through Saturday night.

Shacharit (H)—Daily morning services.

Shas (H)—The six books that contain the Mishna, the written compendium of the oral law. Shas is an abbreviation for "shisha sidrei," meaning "six volumes."

Shehechiyanu (H)—The blessing said the first time one performs an act or when celebrating a joyous occasion.

Shir HaShirim (H)—The Song of Songs.

Shomer negiah (H) (feminine: shomeret negiah)—Observant of religious rules regarding refraining from touching adults of the opposite sex who are not married to one another.

Shul (Y)—Synagogue.

Simcha (H)—Celebration, happy occasion.

Sufganiah (H)—Doughnut, specifically a style of jelly doughnut traditional for Chanukah.

Sukkah (H) (plural: Sukkot)—Temporary outdoor structure in which one lives as much as possible during the holiday of Sukkot. Representative of the booths the Jews built in the desert after the Exodus from Egypt. Observant Jews eat their meals and live as much of their lives as possible in the sukkah during Sukkot.

Talmud (H)— The written compendium of Jewish laws and traditions, codified in the eighth century CE. It comprises the Mishna and the Gemarah.

Tanach (H)—An acronym for the Hebrew Bible, containing the Torah (Five Books of Moses), the Prophets, and the Writings (Hagiographa).

Tchotchkes (Y)—Knickknacks.

Teshuvah (H)—Literally, "return." Repentance.

Teshuvot (H)—Answers. Specifically, rabbinic answers regarding Jewish law and practice.

Tzafun (H)—Literally, "hidden." The section of the Passover Seder in which the hidden matzah piece, the Afikoman, is eaten.

Tzahal (H)—The Israeli army.

Tzitzit—(H)—Ritual fringes that hang from the corners of a four-cornered garment (beged).

Tzuris (Y)—Trouble.

Ushpizin (A)—Guests. Specifically, the biblical characters (Abraham, Isaac, Jacob, Joseph, Moses, Aaron, and David) metaphorically invited to the sukkah on the holiday of Sukkot.

Vayikkra (H)—The book of Leviticus.

Yarmulke (Y)—Skullcap.

Yenta (Y)—A busybody. Also, a matchmaker.

Yom tov (H)—Literally, "a good day." A religious holiday.

Yomim nora'im (H)—Literally, "Days of Awe." The High Holidays of Rosh Hashana and Yom Kippur.

Zichronam livracha (H)—May their memories be for a blessing. Said after mentioning people who have died.

Zman (H)—Time.

Zman cheirutainu (H)—The time of our freedom. Another name for the holiday of Passover.

Zman simchateinu (H)—The time of our celebration. Another name for the holiday of Sukkot.

acknowledgments

DANI AND AVI HAVE BEEN with me for a very long time; they appeared unannounced and unceremoniously in the back of my brain and wouldn't be quiet until I wrote down their words. But bringing them into actual book form was only possible with the support of others. I am forever grateful to Beth, who first told me to pay attention to the noisy characters in my head. Writing encouragement also came from many others; I must especially acknowledge Jen's support from five time zones away and Gail, Cindy, and Mary from just a couple of miles away.

Lorna and Shawn, without you I never would've thought I could be a published fiction writer; thank you for being you and for creating what you created.

CB, thanks for the late-night chats that I never wanted to end even though we both needed sleep. It may have only been one weekend almost ten years ago, but your enthusiasm—and your continued cheerleading since then—helped me find my own voice in a way that I might not have otherwise.

Jodi and Chris, you may not realize what working with you on your writing did to build my confidence in my own writing; I look forward to our future endeavors, whatever they may be.

I got my first electric typewriter for my bat mitzvah; I remember typing stories that went only into a box under my bed. My parents and sister had faith in me, however, and encouraged me to find my path as a professional word nerd, be it as a professional editor, a technical writer, or a fiction writer.

I am grateful to all of my teachers and keep in memory my teacher Miss S., who taught me how to craft a meaningful sentence and how to get my intended meaning out of my brain and onto the page. I also have to thank all the rabbis who taught me over the years. You showed me how to be analytical and questioning while still staying on the derech.

To Annie and Candy, thank you for taking a chance on me and on Avi and Dani. Thank you for seeing their potential and encouraging me to explore them more deeply than I thought I could. And CB, your cover art is magnificent. Thank you for just getting it, despite my inability to describe anything coherent in the beginning.

Finally, my deepest thanks to Michael, E, and Y. Each in your own way, you helped me bring this book to reality. Without your steadfast faith in my ability to write and juggle everything else, I wouldn't have had the confidence to even attempt this. Michael, I literally couldn't have finished this book without you. And, girls, Mommy loves you and promises that this book is finished. (No promises about the next one, though.)

about the author

E.M. BEN SHAUL LIVES IN many communities. An Orthodox Jew and
writer of gay fiction, E.M. lives in the simultaneously gay-friendly and
Jewish-friendly Boston area with her husband and twin daughters. A
technical writer by day and freelance editor by nights and weekends,
E.M. likes to knit, cook, and coin neologisms. E.M. seeks to explore
the seeming conflict between religious teachings and the heart's desires.

interlude**press**™

 interludepress.com
 @InterludePress
 interludepress
 store.interludepress.com

interlude press™
you may also like...

Idlewild

Named one of Kirkus Reviews' Best Books of 2016

In a last ditch effort to revive the downtown Detroit gastropub he opened with his late husband, Asher Schenck hires a new staff. Among them is Tyler Heyward, a recent college graduate working his way toward med school. When they fall for each other, it's not race or class that challenges their love, but the ghosts and expectations of their pasts.

ISBN (print) 978-1-945053-07-8 | (eBook) 978-1-945053-08-5

What It Takes

Publishers Weekly Starred Review Recipient

Milo met Andrew moments after moving to Cape Cod—launching a lifelong friendship of deep bonds, secret forts and plans for the future. When Milo goes home for his father's funeral, he and Andrew finally act on their attraction—but doubtful of his worth, Milo severs ties. They meet again years later, and their long-held feelings will not be denied. Will they have what it takes to find lasting love?

ISBN (print) 978-1-941530-59-7 | (eBook) 978-1-941530-60-3

And It Came to Pass by Laura Stone

Adam Young is a devout Mormon following the pious path set forth for him by his church and family. But when his mission trajectory sends him to Barcelona, Spain, with a handsome mission companion named Brandon Christensen, Adam discovers there may be more to life and love than he ever expected.

ISBN (print) 978-1-945053-15-3 | (eBook) 978-1-945053-35-1

The
Ghasting

XIII

UF

The Ghastling

2021   BOOK 13

Tales of Ghosts, the Macabre and the Oh-So Strange

G

THE FETCH would like to thank Patreon supporter, AARON SPINK, for sponsoring his omen and keeping impending death alive...

THE FETCH
ILLUSTRATION BY ANDREW ROBINSON

EDITOR
Rebecca Parfitt

ASSISTANT EDITOR
Rhys Owain Williams

GRAPHIC DESIGNER
Wallace McBride

SPECIAL THANKS

Reid Britt, J&C Parfitt, Andrew Robinson,
Esther Stephenson & Karen Boissonneault-Gauthier

CONTACT THE GHASTLING

EDITOR@THEGHASTLING.COM
WWW.THEGHASTLING.COM
SOCIAL MEDIA: @THEGHASTLING

ISSN: 2514-815X
ISBN: 978-1-8381891-1-2

The Ghastling gratefully acknowledges the financial support of the Books Council of Wales.

EDITORIAL

REBECCA PARFITT

ILLUSTRATION BY KAREN BOISSONNEAULT-GAUTHIER

We have arrived at 2021 and there is a feeling of change in the air: people are retreating into the country (if they can reach it), into books, into music, into films, into creative spaces, into Zoom calls and virtual realities and, while we cannot travel, our minds can take us anywhere. Inside the pages of this edition you'll find a nursery bogie, dogs that can see ghosts, doubles and others; alternate versions of the self; lost souls stuck watching their bodies decay. We are, after all, spending a lot more time with ourselves these days and I wonder if some of these themes are the writer's subconscious dealing with the alternate universe: the 'normal' vs 'now' – remembering our lives *before* and *after*. It is bound to tap into the psyche one way or another and I certainly got a feeling of this when reading through the latest stack of submissions.

Superstitions were another feature, often serving as warnings and deterrents against misfortune, passed down by voices lost to the depth of time. I wonder if new forms of superstition and folklore might arise from this time of crises – looking for the presence of something else in the ordinary. I'd be very interested to read some folk horror from the future if anybody has some...

To conclude, anxious times can also bring about immense creativity and rejuvenation and there are a lot of people creating some wonderful things right now. I am happy to introduce the following stories for your enjoyment:

Have you ever wondered what visits us when we sleep? What is it in the doorway that your dog growls at? What do your cat's eyes follow across the room? What is it that comes for you? A disturbing 'truth' is revealed in EMILY RUTH VERONA's tale 'The Dog Lives in This One'.

In WILLIAM BURTON MCCORMICK's uncanny story 'The Bell Keep's Tale', we travel to old Riga and hear the grand old cathedral's bell keeper recount a dark and disturbing story of a curse and the night some strange visitors arrive at the cathedral. Tip: you'll need to read this in a quiet place so you can listen for the echo...

MEGAN STANNARD's 'Slack Water' is a grotesque, tragic and darkly-comic story of two dead junkies that haunt the riverside waiting for their bodies to be found. This story explores the very real horrors of drug abuse, addiction and the lives that get swept away in its tide.

KAITLYNN MCSHEA retells the story of Pinnochio in 'Mojigangas'. It is the 17th century in San Miguel El Grande, Mexico. An artist and giant-maker, Alonso, is given the much-longed-for news that his wife is expecting their first child. But their lives take a tragic and macabre turn as they exhibit their 'Mojigangas' at the annual city festival.

DAMIEN B. RAPHAEL's 'Grubble' is a disturbing folk horror about a girl who finds a 'boggleboe' – an animate doll that feeds on cloth and garments. She brings it home, feeds it, cares for it as if it were her very own child. But she is deemed mad, possessed and is locked away in an attempt to 'starve' her of the boggleboe (and it from her), until the day her father returns and marries her off…

In LENA NG's story 'The King of the Rats', a young doctor receives a letter one day from a long-lost uncle, wishing to put his 'affairs' in order. Dr William Hughes makes the journey to visit the ailing uncle only to find his 'inheritance' is little more than a crumbling mansion. This story escalates deliciously into a pure horror that will delight those with a strong stomach and a penchant for the charming, clever and magnificent creature that is the rat…

In BEANIE AURORA WHITE's story '1000 Rabbits', Father Yakob sets a peculiar and gory goal to skin a thousand rabbits. His village community watches with awe, believing the thousandth will bring them luck and good fortune. But there is a price to pay for taking and killing for sport, and something is watching them…

Charles, a bingo caller working in, what was, a Victorian theatre, is not having much luck these days. Alone and with redundancy imminent, he's missing the good old days when the bingo hall was

his side. Things appear to be moving on and yet, the ghosts of his past seem to be missing him too, in NICK RYLE WRIGHT's eerie tale 'Unlucky for Some'.

And finally, in ANN WUEHLER's story 'Jimmy's Jar Collection', a bored kid, Park, joins their older cousin in his strange pastime of catching ghosts in a local cemetery. All it takes is a little patience and a jar…

We are also delighted to introduce our newest member at Ghastling Towers: WALLACE McBRIDE. He has taken over the role of graphic designer with this issue. Coming from a background in newspapers he has a wealth of experience in publishing and design (please see Wallace's bio for more info on his current projects). We were very keen to return the magazine to its former roots in the Victorian penny dreadful and we are very much looking forward to working with him on developing the look of the magazine.

I hope you enjoy this issue as much as we have enjoyed putting it together. I want to thank all of our subscribers and patrons for being here, and anyone who has bought a copy of this magazine. Things are tough for a lot of us so it means a great deal to have you. Patreon is the only regular, reliable source of income I have for this magazine so if you like what we do, please consider supporting us on there. Our rewards range from mentions in the magazine, artwork giveaways, t-shirts, bags, magazines, writing prompts, writing feedback and a chill-wind blowing your letterbox open… Patreon.com/TheGhastling

Be well and I hope you enjoy this latest edition.

With thanks,
REBECCA PARFITT
Editor

THE MILKY WAY ABYSS INCLINES

UF

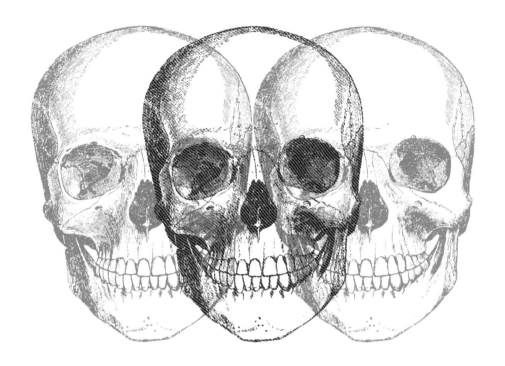

GRUBBLE

by Damien B. Raphael

ILLUSTRATION BY REID BRITT

You were no more *than a babe when I found you by the river. A thing born of stitches and bobbins, a patchwork body sewn together under the glow of a lace maker's lamp. Your hessian skin was caked in silt. Your glass bead lips eager to suckle. Wrapped in my shawl, you smiled, an unruly tongue of horsehair peeking out, defiant.*

There were many places for us to hide in my father's townhouse. My choice: an unused garret, high atop the south tower. The safest place. You seemed so happy in your nest of feather pillows and eiderdowns, yet feeding time was so troublesome. You'd turn your little head at every scrap pilfered from the kitchen, crumbs of cheese, honey-fried dates. As you were born by the river, I thought fish would suit you best, but pike and eel proved in vain. When offered chub, your hands of straw and branches would only scratch the scales, enthralled by the fatty clumps

of silver. Perhaps you lacked the sense to eat, the sense to think. You knew hunger though, the keening to be fed unmistakable. Unrelenting.

To my shame, I cursed you. Fetched my sewing box to stitch your mouth shut and end your wailing for good. Before the needle was threaded, though, you'd rummaged through my wares, gorging upon a ribbon of green silk. Did your sunken eyes blink then? Did they threaten tears? Searching around for more there lay a scrap of pillow lace. You devoured it, and then a button. You loved those most of all. Buttons of bone and vegetable ivory, and mother of pearl as well, it mattered not. Your teeth crushed them like egg-shells, fast and gluttonous.

Soon, with the stolen supplies from Mother's stores, you'd doubled in size. A full-sized mannequin, itching to stir. During my tapestry lessons, I heard you crawling above us, and pricked my finger when something tumbled over. I yelped and laughed, scrambling to make light of my clumsiness. Our seamstress merely frowned and tapped her wrist in annoyance, as my sisters exchanged guarded looks, raw with scorn.

How had they not heard?

Weeds of gossip grew untamed and servants began avoiding me, leaving only swirls of dust in half-cleaned, half-abandoned grates when I'd dare to enter rooms. Each night, I'd stroke your hair of golden thread reassuring myself that others would love you too, had I only the courage to parade you as my own. But doubts slipped into my mind like playing cards against crushed velvet. *Would they throw you on a bonfire if they found you? Let hunting dogs tear your body of fabrics to pieces?*

Mother would know best.

On Midsummer Eve, beside a gar-

"AT CHRISTMAS, WHEN THE HOUSE WAS FEASTING AND THE GUESTS PLAYED COSTUMES, YOU TOOK YOUR LAST BREATH, ONE LAST PUFF OF MIST FROM YOUR WOOLLEN LUNGS."

landed hearth, I broke down in front of her and begged forgiveness for bringing an imp inside the house, a boggleboe.

Mother's face paled whiter than powder. 'A boggleboe? What is this nonsense?'

'Its name is Grubble—'

The slap across my face stung less than the blessing she gave herself, the bitter look of repulsion. She squeezed my wrist, dragged me through the house and up to your quarters demanding to be shown, my skirt rustling in protest. Mother didn't see you, though. Not even after my frantic screams, and pointing at you on the floor. Not even after stamping across the remnants of your button dinners.

She shut the door in my face, locking it from outside. 'There is a sickness in you, child. Never speak of this again, else you tar our name with madness.' Before pummelling my hands against the oak that sealed me in, her shoes echoed off and away, clacking down the stairwell.

The new regime began the next day. A knock on the door after sunrise, a plate of gruel left outside, a glass of milk. A chamber pot. Sometimes I caught sight of servants through the keyhole. It was like being visited by mourners, their eyes downcast. And no amount of flattery could tempt their mouths to speak. I had become as invisible to them, as you to Mother.

Begging for your sustenance, for any scrap of cotton or cambric, was hopeless. The chambermaids thought my ravings woeful, my pleas nothing but an impulse of bad blood. *I'm sorry, Beatrice*, said a servant through the door, *your mother has forbidden any such folly*. In desperation I cut up my filthy dress, and tried to feed you by hand. But you'd cough it back up, disgusted with its taste.

The weeks unspooled into months and you wasted away, your plump legs withering flat. At Christmas, when the house was feasting and the guests played costumes, you took your last breath, one last puff of mist from your woollen lungs. I hugged you then, or what remained of you, bunched in my white-knuckled grip, and plucked a golden thread from your leathern scalp, twisted it between my thumb and finger, marvelling at its shimmer. And in your honour, in your memory, threaded my needle with it, and vowed never to speak of you or anything else again. Piercing my bottom lip, my eyes fluttered with pain, blood inking fingers. The top lip was awful too, but soon the horror was done. Studying my reflection in the window, my stitching had rambled like the work of a blind spider. Yet who would know? Who could see your fibre, but I?

Not a morsel of food was eaten in the following months, only mere sips of broth. I spent my days pouncing patterns, cutting up the fabric of my dress, re-tailoring every piece. Nights would be for tapping the floorboards under which you were buried, daring to hope that you'd knock back. You never did.

By the first summer of my imprisonment, Father had returned to the house from his business abroad. He roared my name, searching through the house and barged down the garret door staring at me agape, a ghost of his former daughter. He swept me up in his arms, crushing me against fine garments of linen and brocade, his beard smelling of spiced ale, tobacco and cold. That afternoon Father explained Mother's meaning, how she thought my solitude would help and how she had, in secret, told the chandler to carve bundles of tallow candles in my image, left guttering under St Frideswide tomb. *Forgive your Mother's superstitions*, he said, *she did her best for you*.

I nodded, my smile straining against secrets.

Father did away with my seclusion, and reintroduced me into the house once

more. My hair was cut and washed. New dresses made. As the weeks passed, even Mother began to forget my years of abandonment. But I did not, and prayed for the day she would be made accountable for your neglect.

A year passed quickly, and my sisters were soon wed. Father explained my betrothal wasn't possible, at least not until I'd proved myself. *A Lord has offered to take your hand*, Father said, *consider this the chance to impress*. Nodding without a single word, Father kissed my forehead, and he thanked God for blessing him with a daughter so diligent.

My first night at Minister Hall, the steward welcomed us into the great hall itself. Father looked over parchment documents, pressing his signet ring into a bubbling splodge of wax. The seal took a second to form, a blink of an eye in exchange for a lifetime. Inspecting the mark through an orbed crystal pendant, the steward inclined his head. The deed was complete.

A banquet followed with platters of gravied meats and baskets toppling over with doorstops of bread. Minstrels played songs and mummers juggled eggs.

My plate went untouched, however, my food gone cold. I thought of you, then. How you would have feasted upon the banners adorning the walls, the standards stitched with every beast and bird imaginable.

Before I had time to shrug away your memory, a tapping on the table had silenced the din. I glanced around, but it was too late. The Lord had skewered me with an indignant stare.

'Is the food not to your liking, my sweet?'

The entire gathering sat with bated breath, their gold-threaded garments dazzling in the candlelight. How I would have liked to feed them to you, every last piece of material. And there sat Mother, watching, across from me. Her expres-

sion cracked like ice as she ground her teeth, an ounce of that same repulsion in the garret. It was as good as that room, the hall: to be swept away from Mother's eyes, out of sight.

Hidden.

I stood up, my chair scraping along the flagstones. Picking up a knife, I hacked away the thread from my mouth. People coughed in displeasure. But so be it, for when at last my lips were freed, something tickled at them, grown long in the years of my silence. A tongue of horsehair.

And with that tongue, I told them of you.

Of my baby lying under the boards, forgotten.

Of you, my boggleboe. My Grubble.

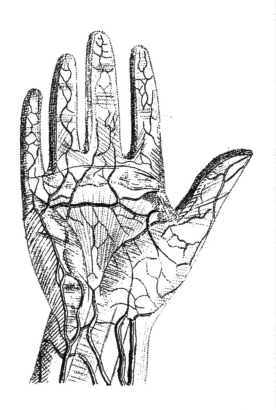

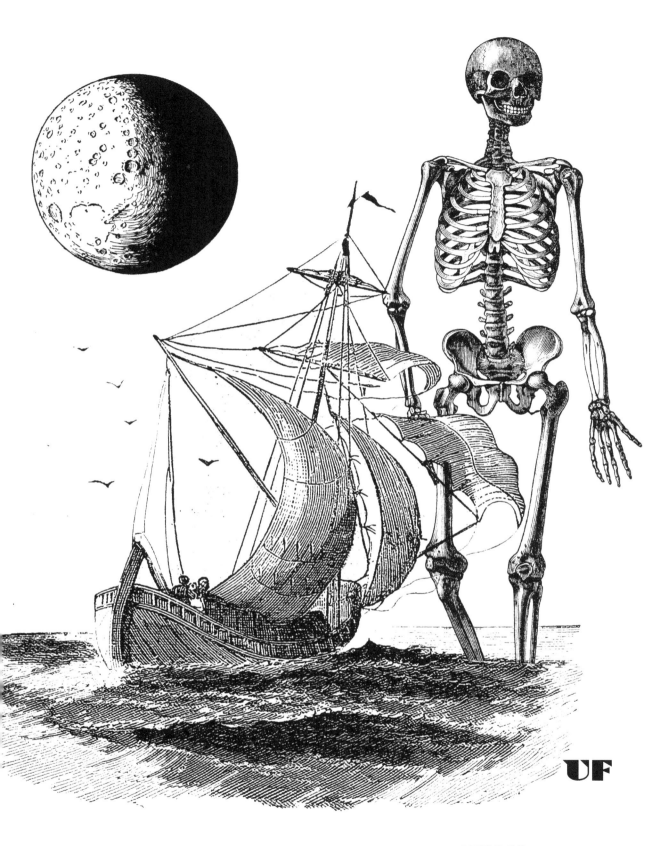

A SWEEPING STATEMENT, YOU SAY. THAT IS TRUE, BUT PROOF OF
THE STATEMENT IS TO BE FOUND EVERYWHERE.

THE KING OF THE RATS

by Lena Ng

ILLUSTRATION BY Esther Stephenson

*T**hat day started* *out like any ordinary one where I was enjoying a rare day off. I was finishing up my tea and toast, lei-
surely grazing over the headlines, when I heard the metallic rattle
of the mail slot and the soft swish of landing letters.*

I left the breakfast table, tight-
ening the belt of my paisley robe, to
gather the arriving correspondence.
I separated any letters addressed
directly to me—Dr. William Hughes—
before tossing the remainders in the
wastepaper basket beside the foyer table and trundling back to the cooling
dregs of my tea.

My half-moon reading glasses
slipped down my Roman nose as
I cut open the envelopes with my
silver letter opener. Several invoices
for services performed some weeks

ago, a few cheques for services I had
rendered, a cheery postcard from a
friend who was on a driving tour of
the Continent.

I had to adjust my reading glasses
to read the last letter. It was a single
translucent page, not in standard
business format, but written in a
shaky, child-like scrawl, as from
someone unpracticed at holding a
pen.

Dear Dr. Hughes, it read. *I have,
through sleuthing by my solicitor, at
long-last traced your whereabouts.*

My name is Thomas Rathburn and it is of utmost importance that I meet with you. You likely have little knowledge of your family history; from my source, it is to my understanding you were adopted at birth. I am one of your uncles, an unproductive branch, unfortunately, on our convoluted family tree. I have not much time left, though this will be of great benefit to you, and it is time for me to settle my affairs. Although we have not met, I trust in your absolute discretion, since I have no wish to argue my affairs with any other members of our quarrelsome kin. Please come as quickly as you are able, Thomas Rathburn.

The letter ended with an address and rather rudimentary directions to his country house. I went to a shelf and pulled out a map. Judging from the distance, it looked like a day's worth of motoring through the English countryside. I scratched my chin. What about my practice? My waiting room was always filled with ailing patients. Would my medical partner be able to cover them? Other doubts churned over in my mind. Could this be a hoax? But, if so, what would he have to gain?

Later that day, I discussed the coverage of my practice with my medical partner. Although I was of course interested in my claim as an heir to this strange uncle, I was far more intrigued with learning about my personal genealogy. Mr. Rathburn—*Uncle Rathburn? Uncle Thomas?*—was correct in his assessment of my orphan status. The friars, however, ensured me a proper education, and although they were disappointed I didn't take the vows myself, they were supportive of my calling to heal the sick.

My medical partner—Dr. Samuel Davies, one of my mentors during my residency training—willingly obliged with my request, and I left to pack a few changes of clothes.

It was well into dusk when I drove the long, dirt road to my mysterious uncle's

estate. The sun's last rays were cooling over the horizon and I squinted into the gloom to see where I could park. My car, which was coasting on the empty tank of petrol fumes, gave a last shudder before it died. I had driven along circuitous back routes of dales and rolling landscapes of manicured green, passing many crumbling farmhouses before stopping for a quick bite at one of the pubs and to fill up the car. I had continued my journey for many hours; my uncle's estate, however, was so remote that I didn't find another stop to replenish the tank and I could only hope he could provide some petrol for the trip back.

After I had parked, I was shutting the

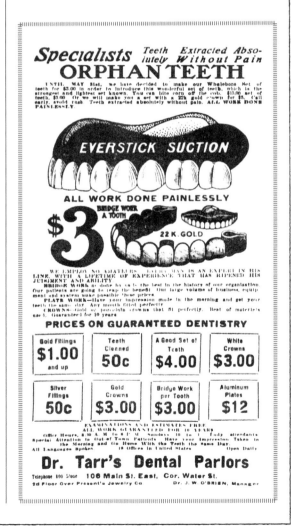

car door when I had the creeping feeling of being watched. A shadow passed overhead as a cloud obscured the moon. A rustle and wave of shrubbery. Twin pinpoints of lights, several pairs at ankle height, peered at me through the overgrown vegetation. I felt a sweeping chill as I realised I was being spied upon by a crew of skulking creatures hiding in the bushes.

With a sense of revulsion, I hurried up the stone steps to my uncle's estate. When the door was opened, it was the stench that hit me first. It hit me directly in my face and instinctively I drew my hand to protect my nose. The powerful odour of waste and animal reek. My gut churned and I couldn't hide an expression of disgust.

'Welcome,' said a mottled voice, distracting me briefly from my revulsion. 'Dear nephew, how glad I am to see you.'

'Uncle, I—' I didn't know what to say. How could I express the horror that I felt at his living conditions? I tried to let the clinical side of my nature take over until I could find out what my uncle needed.

'Yes, yes,' he said, impatiently, 'Hurry up and get in. Wouldn't want the poor dears to catch their deaths.' He waved me in, and I stepped over the threshold so he could shut the door.

The floors were scurrying. Large furry bodies of various shades of white, black, and brown explored every corner and baseboard of the room. Twitching white or grey whiskers. Pink little feet. A mass of wandering rats with full run of the house. A big pink nose sniffed at my shoe as I tried to squeeze my way closer to the walls.

My uncle turned, and with a disjointed, shuffling gait, made his way from the foyer—no type of walk I could diagnose. Not shuffling enough for Parkinson's. Not the asymmetric walk of scoliosis either. A walk of legs working peculiarly—independently, instead of as a pair. Strange

thing after strange thing ever since I received his letter. I tentatively tried to follow through the vermin sea.

As I walked through the marble-floor foyer, besides the rat hoard, I felt something else amiss. I bent my head to the side. The walls seemed not to line up properly with the floor, but tilted on an angle. With the smell heightening my dizziness, I felt as if I were walking through a carnival funhouse.

It was then I realised—all the paintings on the walls were not level. They were all bent at some haphazard slant. And what odd paintings they were. One of a rat wearing a pink dress with a bow. Another painting bursting with fat, rodent bodies: black, glistening eyes peering from the piece; bodies dissolving into a brown mass at the bottom of the canvas. It looked like the plague brought to life. The biggest picture was of my uncle's portrait done in oil—on his head a plain gold crown, his figure striking a classical pose...with a large rat standing on hindlegs on an outstretched forearm.

As I arrived into the living room, my uncle shooed away a furry body with a pillow so I could sit on the couch. I kept my knees clenched together as more pink noses sniffed the hem of my pants. My uncle was clearly insane. Living in isolation on such a huge estate must have driven him mad. If I could suppress my shuddering feelings of dread, I could convince my uncle this was no way to live and get him appropriate help.

'Uncle,' I said, leaning forward on the edge of the couch. 'Things have obviously gotten out of control. From two pets, these rats have spiraled into a horde.' I felt a flush rise to my face as a big, brown-and-white rat leapt onto the coffee table and began sniffing my knee. 'You cannot live amongst these vermin.'

My uncle's face twitched in a very rat-like gesture. 'Vermin?' he asked. 'You see these charming, clever, magnificent

creatures as vermin? I would argue the opposite of this position—that mankind is the vermin of the earth, consuming all its resources, breeding without limits, polluting their homes, their air...' His ranting continued despite the stony obstinance on my face.

All I could see were the carriers of the bubonic plague. 'Uncle, these things are foul. You are projecting your need for company on these things—'

My uncle waved a swollen hand. I thought I saw a ripple of movement under the skin before the length of his sleeve covered it. 'I prefer the rats' company over people. They are good companions. Sweet and affectionate. Clever. The world would be a much better place if the rats ruled the earth. I have taught them reading and writing. Even speaking.' He put out the bloated hand. An albino rat with bright pink eyes scampered up his arm to rest on his shoulder. My uncle leaned his head as the rat whispered into his ear. 'Eh? Speak up, Nibbles! You know how my hearing in that frequency has gone.'

I heard a high-pitched squeaking, but I couldn't believe my uncle understood what that rat was saying. The hour was late and I didn't have the strength to argue with a madman. In the morning, I would try to ascertain my uncle's needs, search for some petrol, then after consultation with my colleagues, get him the appropriate medication and counselling. Even institutionalisation if necessary.

I rose from the frayed, satin-striped sofa. 'Uncle, it's been a long day. Let's get some rest and we'll sort out your business in the morning.'

My uncle imitated my action, rising as well from his chair. 'Of course, my boy. You must be tired. Don't mind me; now that things have changed, I find I've turned nocturnal. Nibbles will show you to your room.'

The big, albino rat sniffed at me before jumping from my uncle's shoulder. It waited for me to follow, then led me down an ugly red hall with peeling wallpaper that had seen better days. Big splotches of mould bloomed from the paper. The albino rat waited outside a particular room. Once my hand was on the doorknob, it squeaked and ambled back in the direction from which we came, likely to rejoin my bizarre uncle.

The bedroom brought no more comfort than the rest of the house. Looming portraits of my uncle covered in rats with their black, beady eyes. The burning stench of rat droppings, their round balls of waste dotting the carpet. And instead of a bed, there was shredded material on the floor, strips of torn fabric gathered in the corner. I was to sleep in a rat's nest.

I couldn't lay down in this horrible bed. Instead I propped myself up in a corner of the room. Above me, scurrying, the scratch of small feet running from one end of the ceiling to the other. The pitter-patter of multitudes of bodies in the walls. How could I sleep amongst all these squeaky, infernal bodies?

The night was long as I sat there, and after many hours, the heaviness of sleep overcame me. I dreamt of a monstrous

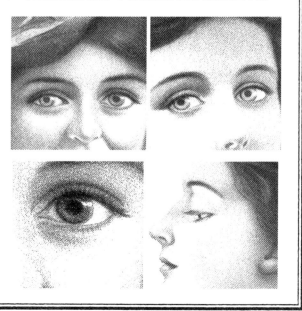

rat king with red glowing eyes. It was seated upon a throne, mangy, dirty, eyes as empty as the sockets of a skull. I awoke with a start. The fabric of the nest beside me was moving and I kicked out a foot as the rat came too close to investigate. It gave an angry hiss and I got up to find another room.

I put my hands out to try to find the light switch. When I flicked it on, the room remained dark. I opened the door into the hall, and saw a flicker of light.

Following the light, I walked down the hall to the last room on the floor. When I entered the room, my hair stood on end. My clinical detachment fled and my heart thumped heavily in my chest. My uncle was seated upon a large gold chair, a throne, surrounded by the light of many candles. The floor was covered in rats, all stone still, watching me. Upon his head was a crown of burnished gold. His black, beady eyes bulged. 'Still up, my boy?'

In silence, I stood in front of this eerie scene.

My uncle's face twisted into an expression of gleeful madness. 'Rat's got your tongue? We can discuss the business at hand.'

My jaw loosened and I was able to croak out, 'My inheritance?'

My uncle stood. His skin rippled as though insects scuttled through his veins. He pointed at me with a bloated, death-mottled finger. 'More than that, my boy. You have been chosen. I've called upon you to witness my coronation. Bow down to me!'

The rats launched themselves at my legs, nipped at my ankles. I tried to turn but the weight of these bodies caused me to stumble and fall. On my hands and knees, I looked up at the shining throne.

My uncle started a choking, guttural laughing. It started deeply, but the laughter grew higher and higher until the sound resembled the triumphant squeal of thousands of rodents. His smile grew too wide; his skin stretched out as though small hands pulled at his mouth's corners until they met ear, until his mouth resembled an elastic gash with lips. His mouth split open and out dropped...a rat. Rat after rat poured forth from his mouth. The skin of his cheeks seemed to sink in from their escape.

Soon his voice dissolved until no human sound remained, only high-pitched squeaks as the rats no longer used his voice box for sound amplification. The skin of his face, a yellowing, hardening mask from rigor mortis, fell away. His golden crown dropped upon the floor. Instead of flesh, there ran the squirming bodies of a human-sized mountain of rats. They disbanded from his body like fleeing maggots from a corpse. A monstrous horde of rats had controlled my uncle's body from within.

I was frozen. I couldn't run despite the outpouring of these hideous rodents all over my body. Up my pant legs, crawling down my collar, creeping into my sleeves. I opened my mouth to scream and choked as a flea-ridden body scurried down my throat. I could feel its claws scrabbling, the thump of its long, worm-like tail. Another rat jumped into my oral cavity. I felt it peering out from behind my eyes.

In a terrifying moment, I realised I would inherit my poor uncle's fate. I picked up the fallen crown and placed it upon my head. I lifted my hands to the air and surveyed my scurrying kingdom. My face twisted in gleeful madness.

All hail the new King of the Rats!

UF

MOJIGANGAS

by Kaitlynn McShea

*T*he autumnal sun blazed *over San Miguel El Grande, Mexico, as Alonso bent over his work table. They said that God made the sun blaze on Sundays so that men, women, and children stayed indoors, and praying their rosaries at that, to honor the Sabbath. But Alonso could claim neither manhood, as his heart was too soft, nor womanhood, as his heart was not soft enough, and his wiry beard and fine wrinkles excluded him from childhood, which was most unfortunate.*

No, no, not a man. Alonso was an artist.

At least, that's what Alonso called himself. His wife called him a sinner.

At the thought, Alonso glanced at the icon of Guadalupe that lived on his wall. Trails of slimy, warm *papel maché* lingered on his skin as he traced the sign of the cross: forehead (a sin that he didn't have more wrinkles like his field-working father), chest (a sin that he didn't yet have a son, or any child), left shoulder (a sin that he only felt holy at his workbench and not at church), right shoulder (a sin that he wanted his spirit to live on in his work), and lips (a sin that he shirked his own cross to bear). The supplication was brief but intense; if Alonso put enough feeling behind his sparse worship, he needn't go to church or receive Holy Communion.

He huddled back over the *mojiganga*, his two-meter-long creation. He stretched his neck back and forth to toss the sins away and allowed his breath to steady. After dipping his fingers into the tub of pulped paper, plaster, and clay, Alonso traced a loose but steady hand against his *mojiganga's* already formed fea-

tures: bulbous eyes, a wide nose, an open-mouthed grin, a thick mustache. The day's work was done; tomorrow, he would paint. He wiped his hands and stepped back.

Feet wide, hands in pockets, he observed.

Mojiganga.

Giant.

A crash broke his reverie. Alonso turned to see his wife steadying herself against a work table with one hand and holding her stomach with another.

A chunk of *papel maché*, the culprit of her trip, rested at her feet. Stepping over the naked busts of discarded *mojigangas*, she wagged her finger at him. 'I swear it, Alonso, you're trying to kill me! Why won't you pick these things up?' She pulled away from the work table as she wobbled closer.

He gave a sad smile. 'Ah, Magdalena, you know I can't.' Indeed, his workshop was filled with *mojigangas* in various stages of work: some only formed with *papel maché*, some half-painted, some finished...but they were all "wrong." Imperfect. Lifeless. If he cleaned up the failures, his current works-in-progress were doomed to the same existence.

Her eyes flashed and her nostrils flared. 'Ay, it's a sin to choose your dolls over your wife!'

'Magdalena...Lena.' He reached for her hands and brought them to his lips. They were rough, too rough, for her age, dried up from years of cleaning houses. 'I do this for you, *mi querida*.' He widened his eyes and held her gaze. Her eyes shifted from a fiery intensity to melted honey.

She kissed his hands then swatted him. He pulled back, chuckling. 'All lies,' she said, but she was laughing, too.

Fortune, Jesus, or Guadalupe surely smiled on him the day that Magdalena became his wife. Her brown skin flushed with the fall heat, and her off-kilter *mantilla* revealed her still-brown hair.

The *mantilla*, once parakeet-blue, was now faded to the cool blue of a winter sky. Blue...the exact color his *mojiganga's* suit should be.

Before he could fix Magdalena's *mantilla*, she fixed it herself.

'So, Alonso, tell me about this pair of *mojigangas*. Are they joining the graveyard?'

'What do you think?' He cocked his head at her.

'You know I think they're always acceptable.'

He threw his hands in the air. 'I don't want acceptable! I want magnificent!' He pulled at his hair. Claws pierced his heart and squeezed. He sighed; they would never be perfect.

Magdalena touched his shoulder. 'Yes, I know. Tell me their story.'

She kissed his hands then swatted him. He pulled back, chuckling. 'All lies,' she said, but she was laughing, too.

He let his hands fall to his sides. Jutting his chin towards his work table, he started. 'This one, his name is Jose Berrera. He once thought he'd be a monk, but then he met Damiana Sánchez.' His gaze caught on the bride hanging from the corner of his workshop. She was finished, except for her dress. Her green eyes, her wide smile...yes, he had truly *created* something here.

'And what of Damiana?' Magdalena approached Damiana. Her hands reached towards the *mojiganga*, but she didn't touch. Not yet.

'Damiana is *peninsulares*. She wasn't going to stay in Mexico, thinking she'd return to Spain to marry. But then, she met Jose.'

'And how did they meet?' She hovered to Jose now, taking in his still-forming features.

'At church.'

The spell ended; Magdalena whirled around. 'So even these *mojigangas* go to church, but you won't?'

He rolled his eyes. 'Not unless you want me to meet someone else. Now let me finish.'

'Fine, fine.' She turned back around. 'So this former monk and *peninsulares*, what do they do now?'

'Damiana, cast out from her family, started to make tortillas during the day, while Jose worked in the mines.'

'And are they happy?'

'Yes, magnificently so.'

'And do they have children?' She was still speaking to the wall.

'Yes, five. One for each year they've been married. A sixth is on the way.'

She shifted to look at the icon of Guadalupe. 'What if I told you,' she said, her voice muffled, 'That Damiana and I have this in common?'

He took a step forward. 'What?'

She turned. A lone tear streaked down her face, but she was smiling. She approached, slowly, carefully, as if cajoling a stray dog to not run away.

He wanted to take another step forward, to meet her halfway, but he was frozen.

When she was close enough, Magdalena took his hands. Her lips tickled his palms as she kissed them. One by one, she placed them on her stomach.

Her *round* stomach. Small, but round nonetheless.

Gasping, he fell to his knees, placing his lips, his ears to her stomach.

His child. *Their* child.

He stood, pulling Magdalena into a tight embrace. This time, he purposefully moved her *mantilla* so he could stroke her magnolia-scented hair. 'Oh, Magdalena, I'm the happiest man alive.' The claws in his heart retracted. He felt weightless.

After some time, they stepped apart.

A thought struck through his happiness.

'Oh, Magdalena, but should you be in the festival this year?'

'Yes, of course. Who else can wear the *mojiganga* and not make a fool of themselves?'

'You're sure?'

'Yes, I'm sure. Your wife is always sure. Now, let's get some dinner before you get back to work.'

Hand in hand, they stepped through his workshop's graveyard, making their way to the kitchen.

A radiant spring sunset filtered into the kitchen. Magdalena sat at the kitchen table: legs wide, hands on stomach. Across from her sat Jose in one chair and Damiana in another. Alonso busied himself with the dishes while they rested.

'Did you fix Damiana?' Magdalena didn't worry about the festival until it was close enough to slap them in the face, and this year was no different.

'Yes, my love.' During the last fitting, Damiana proved to be too slim for Magdalena and her nine-month belly.

He placed the last bowl from their supper in the cabinet. It was time.

Chest light, legs even lighter, he bounded over to Magdalena. He tugged at his beard. 'Are you ready?'

She smiled. 'Only if you help me stand.'

He heaved her up and brought Damiana to her. Together, they tugged on the *mojiganga*. It was a tight fit.

It took him just a moment to put Jose on, and then, they were off.

Torches lit up the night. Under the stars, the bright colors of his city faded to nothing. At this night every year, San Miguel El Grande suspended itself in time. It could be any city, really, when it looked like this: any city in New Spain, any city in the New World. Maybe it even looked like Barcelona.

Alonso stared out between the buttons of Jose's blue shirt. At two meters high, his *mojiganga* was only slightly taller than Magdalena's. He turned towards her, allowing Jose to bump into Damiana.

Magdalena grinned at him through Damiana's patterned shirt.

Love.

He loved his wife, his *mojigangas*, this festival.

And he liked the money.

Music filtered through the air, and Alonso led Magdalena closer to the hubbub. They danced through the now growing crowd. Some people smiled and clapped their hands when they saw the pair, but more people licked their lips and backed away or brought their hands to their faces, turning pale.

Mojigangas.
Giants.

They saw them every year, but Alonso's *mojigangas* always managed to evoke the same emotions from his people: joy, fear, and wonderment.

They stopped near the city centre, still swaying to the band's music. Smoking maize and heated tortillas filtered through the air, and he could have sworn he saw Damiana smile.

An hour passed as they huddled with their neighbours. The crowd, now as heavy as a wet cloak, jostled and screamed. Everyone had something of value, something that might strike attention: food, jewels, family heirlooms... *mojigangas.*

Finally, Viceroy Bucareli clopped into the market upon his black horse, surrounded by his guards.

The crowd paused: the silence before the cannon.

At the front of the line, the Viceroy threw a silver cob at a couple holding out emerald earrings. A guard tucked the earrings away, and the couple held the silver to the light of the torches, grinning. Along with the rest of the crowd, Alonso felt his feet move towards the couple. Before, one with the crowd. Now, surrounded by the crowd.

Sweat dropped from Alonso's brow to his lips. He watched the Viceroy stop two more times before pausing in front of Alonso and Magdalena; Jose and Damiana.

He rubbed one of his many medals and chuckled. 'Ah, my favorite pair! *Los mojigangas*, as magnificent as always!' Alonso grinned despite himself. 'Ah, but I recently saw a marionette show. You know that word, Alonso? Marionette?' Alonso nodded his head as his stomach sunk, causing Jose's torso to bend. 'Next year, no *mojigangas*. Marionettes instead, okay?' Alonso, Jose moved up and down again. 'Now you and your beautiful wife can take those off to get your payment. Twice as much this year, yes? For you to get new supplies for the marionettes I'll see next year.'

As Alonso wrestled off his *mojiganga*, he felt the crowd step closer. Panicked, he thrust Jose off, not worrying about damage. A piece of the *mojiganga* caught on his forehead, and Alonso could do nothing but feel the hardened *papel maché* slice through his skin.

Magdalena also tore off Damiana, and her wide eyes caught his.

The crowd jostled, pushing Magdalena into him. He stepped forward.

The Viceroy handed him a heavy pouch of coins. They could buy more than materials for marionettes. These coins would buy a life for their child. He pocketed them and then handed Jose to one of the Viceroy's guards. As he passed Damiana over, someone stumbled and knocked into Alonso's shoulder. Upright before, Damiana now keeled at her invisible waist, knocking her large, grotesque nose into the horse's eye.

The horse nickered and reared. The guardsman clutched at its neck with white knuckles. Eyes wide with panic, he shouted as its hooves rammed into Damiana, knocking the *mojiganga* out of his grip. Alonso tripped onto his knees, feeling his pants rip. Sweat and hair stung his eyes.

With Damiana out of the way, the horse's hooves lowered towards Magdalena.

Like a typhoon, Alonso's senses pummeled at him, rooting him.

Later, much later, he would remember what happened. The horse's hooves landing on Magdalena's chest, his frozen body, the pooling blood, and her eyes, her open eyes, staring at the endless sky.

But now, at present, when he could move his body again, he lunged towards Magdalena. His foot caught on a rock, and he fell onto his knees beside her.

'Magdalena. Magdalena! It's time to go home!' He shook her. She didn't move.

Leaning over, he stared into her eyes, waiting for them to go from anger to melted honey. He kept staring, willing the fire of life to appear, but instead, a drop fell from his face onto her cheek. Not the clear liquid of tears, but the rusty red of blood. Oh, yes. The scratch from earlier.

He wiped the bloody drop away from her face, tracing his hand over her eyebrows, her nose, her lips, down her chest, her stomach.

Her stomach.

He brought his ear down. Life. He could hear life.

He scooped her up, held her close. Someone put a hand on his arm, and he started.

'Alonso, you need to get your wife to a priest.' Alonso ignored the distant voice. One of his neighbours.

'No! No.' He jerked away, bumping into a guardsman. The guardsman stepped back, eyes wide. Alonso stepped to the right, but the crowd blocked his way. So he ran left, stumbling past the solemn crowd.

He ran through the night, knocking into the walls of the city. The streets, usually familiar to him, twisted and turned, coming to life like a coiled snake.

Finally, finally, Alonso lurched into his yard. He entered his house, passed the kitchen, and crashed through the graveyard. He laid Magdalena down on his favourite work table. He checked her pulse one more time.

Nothing.

So, he began.

First, he unclothed Magdalena from the waist down. Then, grabbing a knife from his supplies, he plunged it into his beloved wife's flesh, and pulled.

And, when it was time, he stretched his fingers and bent them into claws. He scratched right over his breast and pulled out the strings of his heart.

Over the years, after the silver ran out and the food supply disappeared, people came to visit. Knocking on the door, peering through the windows. They left two plates of food in the evening, only to find the plates clean and waiting in the morning.

They kept knocking and peering, but Alonso wouldn't come out. Not until they were perfect.

The heart strings lengthened, the

bond grew.

And still, Alonso waited. Waited for perfection.

On the seventh anniversary of Magdalena's death, he knew they were ready. He waited until the sun set and torches lit the night.

They crept through the city, trying to evade the neighbours. Every corner was a reminder of Alonso's past life, but also a promise for the life to come.

Finally, they reached the square. The Viceroy and his guards had their backs to them. They crept to the fountain, being careful to stay in the shadows until it was time.

When the Viceroy finished his canter around the square, they stepped into the light of a torch. And waited. A minute passed. Two.

And then, a gasp. A woman pointed to them, and as one, the Viceroy and his guards turned their way.

'Are my eyes deceiving me, or is that Alonso? Alonso the scoundrel, Alonso who is six years past due?'

Alonso smiled, willing them to come closer. He raised his hands, and beside him, Lorenzo moved.

The frowning Viceroy dismounted his horse and walked until he was a step below them on the fountain.

'After seven years, I would expect amazing work, Alonso. And you did it. You made the best marionette I've ever seen.'

Alonso smiled and nodded, bringing his hands in the air. From each finger trailed a sinuous string. He started his performance.

With every twitch of his finger, the boy moved, or sang, or spoke. He had Lorenzo tell a story, he had Lorenzo dance. He had Lorenzo breathe.

For the first hour of their performance, Lorenzo sang a ballad about an outlaw who disappeared for seven years. Once the Viceroy's frown disappeared, they moved to theatre. They performed *La Vida es Sueño*, one of Alonso's favourite plays. The play lasted until the torches flickered out and the sky glowed with the dawn.

During the sunrise, they danced the *chinelos*, circling each other with care. His neighbours joined in, adding music and circling with reckless abandon until the song ended with a high, sharp note. Lorenzo and Alonso smiled at one another, the crowd, the Viceroy.

At last, the Viceroy spoke. 'Amazing, Alonso, amazing. How much? It is your price to give.'

'What?'

'How much do you want for your marionette? It is beautiful, breathtaking. So full of life.'

He shook his head. 'No, no. Not for sale.'

'Then why come? Of course, you want to sell it.'

He shook his head, backing himself and Lorenzo away. He met Lorenzo's eyes. They were wide with fear.

'I paid you to make the marionette. Now, of course, you will give him to me.'

Alonso's heart raced. He couldn't speak, couldn't breathe.

'Guards, bring me my sword.' The Viceroy held out his hand until a sword appeared in it. 'Now, Alonso, one last chance.'

Alonso's head spun. Before he could even think of moving, the Viceroy brandished his sword and arced it down, cutting through the strings attaching Alonso to Lorenzo, Lorenzo to Alonso.

Both father and son screamed.

Alonso landed hard on the ground below the fountain. His hands and chest blossomed with pain.

Lorenzo landed a metre away. Alonso stared at him until their eyes met. A lump rose in his throat, and despite the pain, he clawed his way to Lorenzo. A heartbeat later, Lorenzo began to do the same.

They crawled to each other over the rough ground, through the strings filled with heart's blood. The risen sun, now fierce, blazed on the bloodied ground. Alonso, limbs as heavy as lead, stopped crawling. He reached towards Lorenzo, cradling his son's bloodied hands in his own. He allowed a faint trail of blood to drip to his forehead, chest, left shoulder, right shoulder, and mouth.

He breathed into his son's hands. '*Mojiganga*. Giant.'

UF

SLACK WATER

by Megan Stannard

*T*here were better rivers to die in.
Somewhere there were woodland streams so clear that in the shallows you could see right down to the sandy bed. Ophelia drifting with her flowers. Reeds and frogs and minnows. Handsome men in billowing shirts and tight pants, ready to kiss a rusalka's cold lips and break her curse or come join her on the bottom.

Somewhere there were rivers that weren't home to shoals of carrier bags and the bobbing corpses of rats bloated up to football size. Rivers that didn't stink like they were dead themselves.

But this wasn't one of those rivers and right now Marnie was watching a guy in an Adidas tracksuit throw up into her water.

It wasn't even real Adidas.

There wasn't much else to do though, so she and Rosa sprawled out on the concrete embankment next to him and watched the oily bile drift downstream.

'Did you ever play Pooh Sticks as a kid?' Rosa asked and Marnie snorted.

'Our toilet used to back up all the time. Same difference, right?'

A raft of scum circled the handle of a shopping cart, jutting proud from the water, and Marnie heard Rosa take a breath she no longer needed. They both looked from the ripples

back to the guy, who was finished and wiping his mouth on his sleeve, but with a grunt and without a second glance he straightened up and staggered away across the cement.

'Next time, honey,' said Marnie and carefully aligned her cold hand with Rosa's shoulder.

When Marnie had ODed in the vacant lot behind the Dollar Tree, her boyfriend – her dealer, really – had found her a week later, down jacket foul and heavy with all the puke and decomposition fluid it'd soaked up. He'd wrapped her up in her sleeping bag, weighed it down with chunks of rubble, and rolled her into the river.

She still didn't know why he bothered.

Rosa had been down there already, shrouded in trash bags, cradled in the wire basket of a shopping cart, wondering if her family even knew she was dead. She'd been wondering for years.

It worked out pretty well because Marnie knew the answer. Knew Rosa to the point she'd got tongue-tied when she'd finally put the pieces together. It was like meeting George Clooney in a coffee shop but George Clooney was, at least, widely accepted to be alive.

Marnie knew Rosa from the TV spots and articles when she first went missing, her pale, pretty face gazing from front pages, and then the books and podcasts and forum posts, trying to piece together her final night alive. The world loved a mystery and it loved a woman that couldn't talk back even more. A dead girl wrapped up in a story like it was a shroud.

Rosa had died back before it was chic to say you had a favourite murder, and the concept fascinated her. 'Was *I* your favourite?' she asked coyly when Marnie explained, a shadow of a smile upon her shadow of a face.

'Nah,' Marnie told her. 'There was a missing cave diver I liked better. I loved those shows, but I kind of hated them too. Everyone sits around guessing whether it

was the boyfriend or the stepdad or Ted Bundy.' Personally, Marnie had always thought it was the boyfriend, but she was still surprised at her own disappointment when Rosa confirmed it. The mysterious disappearance of Rosa Dawes was much more fun than the mundanely horrible truth. 'And everyone's like 'she was so sweet' and 'she had so much potential', but never 'she used to crunch up Doritos into powder and then drink them out of the bag like an animal'. *That's* what I want to be remembered for.'

'That's gross, though,' said Rosa as if Marnie, bloated and ravaged by rot and fish, hadn't found a whole new level of gross. 'Maybe you deserved to die,' she teased.

The sun was setting, all grease and smoke, dripping over the horizon like an over-fried egg, but the industrial estate was far enough from the city lights that Marnie could look up now and see the stars. She regretted a lot of things, but one of them was that she'd never learned anything about the constellations. Rosa could just about do Orion, and even then only the belt.

'We're never going to eat Doritos again,' Rosa said sadly. A gust of wind blew through her, leaving her hair and clothes untouched but sending a swirl of dead leaves through her chest. 'I'm never going to graduate or go to Paris or have kids. And I didn't even want kids! I don't even *like* Doritos. My death's going to be the most interesting thing about me. That's all anyone's going to remember.'

That was true, so Marnie just shrugged and said, 'You know what I regret?'

She regretted so many things. She regretted the time her brother had let her crash on his couch and she'd stolen his Macbook. She regretted not staying clean. She regretted that her own death was the most interesting thing about her and it wasn't even interesting. She could already see the headlines. *Rosa Dawes Found Under A Dead Junkie.*

Marnie wondered if there was ever a time she could have been Rosa. Rosa had done drugs too, had been high as shit the night she died, might've passed out and puked herself to death just like Marnie had if fate and a shitty boyfriend hadn't intervened. But Marnie would never have been rich or pretty or blonde enough, and she didn't think even a better death would have saved her. It had been six months and she was pretty sure no one was even looking. If she'd been her brother, she wouldn't have bothered. She'd have been glad.

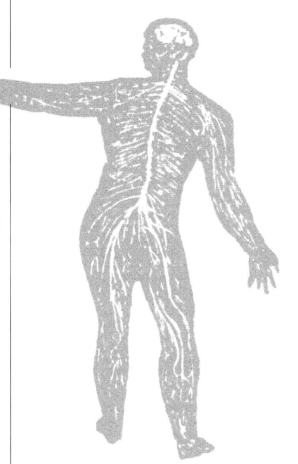

'What I regret most,' she said. 'is never trying that one coffee they make by having cats shit out the beans. You know the stupidly expensive one? I always wanted to see if catshit really did make it magically good or if someone was running a scam.'

Rosa checked the water level every day. She pretended she didn't and Marnie pretended she didn't notice. As July gave way to a sticky August, it sank low enough to show the shopping cart's wire ribcage, cradling a shroud of dripping trash bags. If you squinted, you could maybe see the blue-green blur of Marnie's sleeping bag lying next to it.

From the bottom of the river, the light drifted down, green and gold and brown, and if you squinted so as not to see the trash caught in the current, it was beautiful. Sometimes Rosa would sink down to where her body lay in its swaddling of trash bags, and try to fit herself back into those damp bones and clumps of sloughing, waterlogged flesh. She'd line up her pale, translucent fingers with the clawed remains, the ruins of a French manicure still clinging to its nails.

'That's creepy,' Marnie told her, floating next to her, tilted so she wouldn't see her own putrefying body.

'I'm a ghost. Creepy's my deal. Woooo.' Rosa fluttered her fingers between her own bones. 'I've been thinking about horror movies. Ghosts there get to *do* things. Murder people. I would murder the shit out of Colin if I had ghost powers.'

Despite ten years of concerted effort, Rosa hadn't yet managed to possess or force choke anyone. She insisted she could summon a chill and haunting wind, just strong enough to blow an old gum wrapper into their water, but Marnie thought it had probably been a regular breeze.

'I dunno that I want to murder anyone,' she said.

'Give it ten years. You'll get there.'

Marnie bit the inside of her cheek and felt no pain. 'I heard that if you die before your time, you gotta spend the whole rest of how long you would have had as a ghost

before you get to move on. That's all this is. Using up dead time.'

'I wish I hadn't done so much cardio,' said Rosa. 'I've got another forty years, I bet.'

Forty years staring at the weed-strung wire of the shopping cart while time blurred their faces. Forty years of watching weeds push up through cracks in the concrete and losing her mind with excitement whenever a duck had the misfortune to land here. Forty years on top of the ten Rosa had already spent here. Marnie didn't know how she'd survived it alone.

'That's not narratively satisfying, though,' Rosa went on thoughtfully. 'I think we move on when we resolve things. When they find me and catch him. When the people that did this to us are brought to justice. You know?'

Sometimes, when her foster mom was scolding or the teachers had called on her for an answer she didn't know, Marnie would wish she could sink right into the ground.

'Sure,' she said, and the one good thing about being a ghost was that now she could fall right through the river's sludgy bed until the mud closed over her head and it was just her and the worms and the horrible envy gnawing through her guts.

The months rolled on. The days got colder. The water crept up over Rosa's tomb. Marnie watched its progress with a mixture of relief and regret.

Two dead girls killing time together was something she could live with. Or the opposite of that. But when they found Rosa, buried her proper, sent her boyfriend down for life, where did that leave Marnie? Part of her was scared the police wouldn't know how she'd died, that if they did they wouldn't care, that if they cared they'd never find out who'd sold her the smack that'd stopped her heart. The greater part of her was sure it didn't matter. The person that'd left her dead in an empty lot beside a stinking trickle of a river was already doing time.

When three teenage boys slouched along the embankment, sneakers scuffing through her where she lay stretched out on the concrete, she didn't bother sitting up.

They stopped and huddled round, their bodies a windbreak as one of them began inexpertly rolling a joint. He had a buzzcut that made him look like a new chick, half-

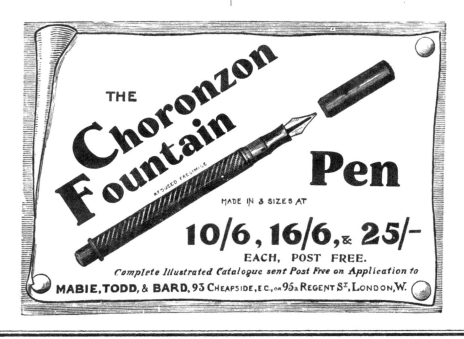

formed and tufty, and Marnie sat up and floated closer, so she could hear them talk in case it was about movies or something.

It was about their new English teacher and what a massive fuckwad he was, which was still the most exciting gossip Marnie had heard in a year, so she stayed huddled in, trying and failing to catch the fug of weed.

The boy with the bad haircut ran it under his nose – 'Shit, that's dank' – and handed it off to a friend to light.

The friend had a cheap Bic lighter, the kind Marnie had held so many times she could feel the phantom weight in her hand, the scrape of the spark wheel against the pad of her thumb.

Without stopping to think, she leaned over his shoulder and blew on the flame. The breeze flared up and the fire flicked out.

'What're you doing?' said Rosa, sitting up. In the afternoon sun, she was almost invisible, a blur of a girl in a torn green halterneck.

'Shh.'

'Are we using ghost powers to bully children?' She drifted to her feet. 'I'm into it.'

'Shh,' said Marnie and blew out the flame again before the boy could get a cherry going.

'Fuckhead,' one of the other boys said in a friendly tone and took the lighter and the joint.

She snatched the flame away from him too. This was the worst idea she'd had since she took the baggie AJ gave her without asking where he'd got it or what he'd cut it with, because if Rosa was wrong and this didn't save her then it would break her. And if she was right, it would break Marnie.

Marnie had been a kid once, the kind of kid that snuck off to smoke shitty weed and graffiti empty buildings. The kind of kid that had a short attention span and liked to make a mark.

No adult was going to look twice at a pile of trash half sunk in a dirty river, but the leader was bored now, looking away from the group and out over his kingdom of weeds and cracked concrete. His eyes skimmed the much-tagged back wall of the old Dollar Tree and settled on the river, on the gas-bloated bags that lay like a hippo in the shallows. Expression calculating, he picked up a chip of loose cement and threw it overarm at the hippo's algae-streaked flank.

'I can't watch,' Rosa said, blue eyes wide in her pale face.

Marnie didn't want to. Marnie was dead and monstrous with it because she already regretted what she'd done. She hoped the boys walked away, she hoped their bones stayed buried.

The rock hit the bag and bounced off, sinking into the water with a blorp.

One of the boys cheered sarcastically. Rosa clutched at Marnie's hand, palms pressing through each other.

Another boy picked up a rock but his throw clanged off the metal of the cart.

The leader narrowed his eyes, something to prove now. The missile he chose this time was heavier, a jagged iron staple sticking from its side. He took the time to line up his shot.

The bag split.

In a gush of gas and stinking water, the river let them go.

Jimmy's Jar Collection

by Ann Wuehler

I happened across my cousin, Jimmy David Cubison, near the corner of the old graveyard that my grandmother's house overlooks. Nobody gets buried there much anymore. It's mostly pioneers and old babies. John Gabriel Smith, born 1878, died 1879 of fever. There's so many of those little gravestones just like that. It's not creepy, just kind of sad. Jimmy was sat near a very old statue of an angel whose face was mostly worn away.

The grave the angel guarded had a date closer to the Civil War than the one with the Nazis. 'Fredrick Gimmel' read the name, in what had once been very grand letters. Now it looked like dogs had been chewing on the marble. I tried to recall if there were any Gimmels still here in Council. Maybe they had moved down the road to Weiser.

'Don't bother me, Park.' Jimmy did not take his eyes from the grave or the shorn grass around it. He held a Mason jar in his right hand, with some gunk at the bottom. There was a lid nearby that he could grab if he had to. 'I'm busy.' The air seemed as if it were full of snow – cottonwood fluff sparkled as if dipped in pale glitter.

'What are you trying to catch?' I scratched at my cheek, getting a sunburn. The big storm the lying weather

rats promised had never showed up.

'A ghost,' he said, huddling his long body up into more of a ball, eyes flicking toward me. 'He shows up every day, sits here, then disappears. As if he's waiting for something.'

I admit, a sick little thrill went through me. This seemed more fun than trying to get someone to drive me up to Mann Creek to look for the Mann Creek Ape (it's like a snipe hunt but fun, my Uncle Chris had said – I had forgotten to ask what a snipe was). 'There's no ghosts,' I ventured and Jimmy gave me a look. A look that said just try asking for a ride into the trees. 'But you never know…Hey, what's a snipe?'

'You don't know,' he said, almost under his breath. 'It's a bird. You're so dumb. Look. Go away. I'm busy. Or help me out. Grab some ghost lure, a jar – maybe it doesn't matter who holds it.'

I sat nearby, because I had heard the Council Cubisons were batshit crazy. My mother's words. Crazy seemed more interesting than Grandma Barb's speeches on how prices at the grocery store were due to globalists who all worked for the Clintons. 'Sure. I can hold a jar. What's ghost lure?'

Jimmy handed me his jar. I got a whiff of dill pickles, dirt, something like horses. 'Don't sniff it. It doesn't work as well if you sniff it. I don't know why.' He slouched off toward his bicycle. I looked at the jar. The mixture had an odd, oily sheen here and there. A thickness like spit or runny snot. I watched the grave of Fredrick Gimmel but I just saw sunshine, old leaves and the fluff from the cottonwoods that were all around. Seeds, I guess. Ghosts liked the smell? Jimmy slouched back holding a lidded Mason jar and a small covered container. His jeans barely clung to his hips, his t-shirt proclaimed him a fan of John Deere, his haircut had been done with a bowl and very dull scissors, but he also looked like a movie star. Which one I was not sure, maybe the ones from the black-and-white movies? My mother and Aunt Perri discussed the rest of the family in our north Boise apartment kitchen, when they were not planning on how to make it big. My mother would tell me to go along now, Park, if she caught me listening. He looks a bit like if Tyrell Powers had a baby with Ermine Flynn, I had overheard my mom say. At least I think those were the names.

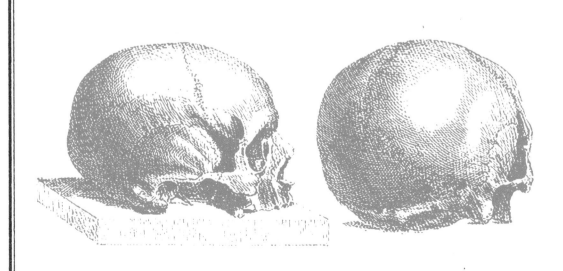

This was why I was here with Grandma Barb for a bit. So Mom and Aunt Perri could travel to cities to play their music. They were opening for a band that pretended it was some other band. Confusing to me, but they both seemed over the moon about their real shot to get a foot in the door.

After making me take the second jar, Jimmy sat down again. He set the container close to his hip. 'Stop watching me. Watch the grave. Gimmel musta thought no one would care if he showed up to take a look around.'

'Sorry. You know they all say you look like a movie star? The baby of Tyrell Powers and something Flynn? I'm not sure of the names.'

'Jesus, that shit again?' He made a huffy sound, leaned forward. 'He's late today. Who says that? I do not look like Tyrone Power. Do I look like freaking Robin Hood? Jesus!'

'No. You look like you.' I heard things, I passed them on. Mom knew this. It's why she made sure I was elsewhere when she and her sister held one of their intense it's-gonna-happen sessions. 'What's the smelly stuff?'

'Mostly dirt.' He tilted his head, turned it, as if listening. 'Shh.'

'Sure,' I said, waving my jar a bit. I looked over my shoulder at the decaying lines of gravestones, statues and markers for the dead. A big field full of dead people, rimmed with pine, locust, and cottonwood trees. Grandma Barb's small house was behind the big wall of locust trees. 'There's just nothing to do here. Grandma doesn't have Internet, says she doesn't need it.'

'Read a book,' he said. 'Don't wave that about. Hold it steady. You can walk up the road there, there's a creek. Don't kids like creeks?'

I perked up at once. I actually did like creeks. 'Is it far? Maybe we can go on the Gator. Look for that ape. Or was it Bigfoot?'

'Just walk there. You got feet. They're pulling your leg, Park. Little kids are sure dumb.' The black of his eyes reminded me of wet poster paint. 'Now be quiet. I gotta concentrate. Just hold the jar on the ground if your arm's tired. It has to come to the jar and go in by itself. Then you

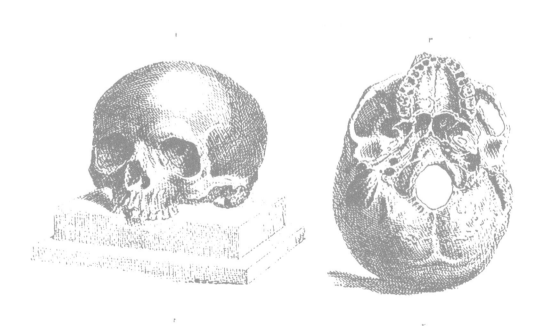

slam the lid on.'

'I don't have a lid. So it's like a mouse-trap? Except for ghosts? How many do you have?'

'Eighteen jars of em.' He put a finger to his lips and I swear on my mother's old Casio keyboard I saw, for just a second, the outline of a big fat man sitting on the rounded top of the Gimmel gravestone. Not the jiggly fat, but a solid fat man who could rip your arms off – like a wrestler. Then just air and birds fighting over something in the far corner of the place. Jimmy leaned close, his breath cinnamon farts. 'He's been here the whole time. Just be still. I'll take you for a ride in the Gator. Just sit here, be quiet, be still.'

For a long moment, I saw other out-

fluff that comes off the cottonwood trees floated toward me and Jimmy, who did not even blink. That fluff caught at the edge of Jimmy's jar, then fell downward. Jimmy slammed the lid on and then threw that jar as the other outlines drew near and nearer still. The jar seemed to ripple. The grass beneath the jar turned brown, as if the glass had gone very hot. 'It's never done that,' he clutched at my arm and I patted him. Skinny. His shoulder had so many bones. 'Go get it.'

'No,' I very sensibly said. The inside of that Mason jar had turned weird. Like it was stuffed full with a tutu. I had always wanted to dance about with one of those on but my mom said ballet was for rich people. 'You get it. It's your jar.'

lines in the graveyard. Not very many, like thirteen or so. Thirteen was the number my brain insisted on. An old lady who put her finger to her lips. A little girl who turned into sparkling sunlight and back again. A tall man who lifted his hat at me very politely. A ghost in a hat. A ghost in a hat! My head hurt, I closed my eyes momentarily. The smell of the ghost lure was so strong. I was offended by that smell. It made me want to sniff flowers and candy bars just so I'd remember there were good smells left. The big fat man faded. What looked like the

'Just go get it,' Jimmy shoved at me. I shoved back. He might just be made of lots of bones but he was awful strong. Still, I was not about to put up with that from some no-account Council Cubinson, as my Aunt Perri had said once on her third glass of cheap box wine. Cheap box wine for cheap boxes, which had made my mom and aunt laugh. 'You agreed to help me. So help me! Go get that damn jar.'

'Fine!' I slapped the top of his black head, and he pinched me before I could get out of reach. Fair was fair. The jar moved

and shifted without me touching it. The lid bulged a bit. The fluff glowed. I looked back at Jimmy, who gaped at the jar. 'What the hell did you catch in there?' A sliver of a crack grew up the side. Jimmy stood by my side now, both of us staring down at the possessed Mason jar full of Mr. Gimmel. I had chills and thrills. I heard breathing just over my shoulder. Maybe the other ghosts were curious as well. A hand crept into mine – the little girl or one of the dead babies that were buried here. I could not let go of the cool hand fitted into mine. Jimmy jerked his head at me, then stepped back. My feet stumbled backward as well. My aching eyeballs continued staring at the jar, which now had a river of cracks – a delta of cracks. I had learned about deltas, the end of the rivers. That's what the cracking on the glass looked like.

Jimmy gripped my arms, yanked me back just as the jar exploded.

It went like someone had chucked a big firework inside. Glass went everywhere. Glass pieces hit me even as Jimmy tossed us both to the mowed grass. Glass rained on my back. And a smell of old flower-pot dirt, like the mould I had once smelled on bread, and something else that was just foul and rank. Jimmy was shivering, his arm holding my head down. Then nothing. Just the birds calling back and forth, the barking of the big dog that had to live chained up guarding a falling-down trailer house. The burr of someone's chainsaw. 'You okay?' Jimmy sat up, glass bits falling from him. They fell from me as well. What remained of the jar could have fit in a mouse's ear. The ground where it had been thrown was burned brown-black, as if someone had tried to light a fire there. Jimmy's bike now lay on the ground, his backpack torn to shreds. His finger traced along my cheek and came away dark with my blood. I felt the press of that little girl's hand in mine, then just my hand and my

blood on my cousin's finger, his black eyes shocked and very wide.

'I didn't know it would do that. The others just sort of sat at the bottom.'

'You should probably let them all go,' someone whispered in my ear, a very low man's voice, sounding like my Uncle Chris when he had a cold. 'You do as I tell you, girl.'

'You should let them go, too,' I said, very obedient for once in my life. My cheek stung now. Jimmy stared over my shoulder and I just knew the man who had been sitting on the Gimmel gravestone was standing right behind me.

'And if I don't?' Jimmy asked.

Nothing was said back – I just heard the wind, that lonely sound of branches rubbing against each other. Jimmy stared at the ground, his sunburned face almost white he was so angry and scared. 'Maybe they don't like being caught. I'll have to try something else. Something stronger. Grandma's gonna shit herself. Your face got cut up.'

'I'll blame the Clintons,' I said very wisely and he laughed and laughed. Then we picked up his bike, then decided to leave it as it was twisted into a pretzel. His backpack was a total loss too, his ghost lure dumped out and oozing into the ground.

'You can't tell none of this, Park.'

What could I tell? Had I really seen a Mason jar explode like a bomb? I had the cut on my face. Had a little ghost held my hand as the big ghost went after my cousin for jailing them? My dad would be coming home soon from Los Angeles. He'd been hauling freight down that way. Otherwise, I'd still be in Boise, playing Pet Mountain and drinking from a juice box. Mango melon was my favourite. I had no wish to tell any of this to anyone just yet. 'Sure,' I promised and almost meant it.

The DOG LIVES IN THIS ONE

by Emily Ruth Verona

There is a woman who likes to stand all alone in the corner of the room. She skulks in the loose, blank space between the chipped red dresser and the fan that buzzes all night long like an army of angry bees. My Mindy does not see this woman, but I do.

It happens like this almost every night. The same as dinnertime arriving or the sun going down. Night arrives and sinks its teeth in and as the hours grow late—long after my Mindy has brushed her teeth and washed her face, turned off the lights and gone to sleep—I get up and sit at the foot of the bed and wait for the woman to appear. It doesn't always happen right away, but it does happen. You can be sure. You can always rely on uninvited guests, can't you?

By one or two in the morning, just when my eyes are feeling sleep-iest, I start to notice something. But not just something. *Her.* The woman only takes shape in the shadows, putting her pieces together one at a time. They don't always fit so easily. Some-times she has to force the joints to make them work, which you'd think would make a *clicking* or *popping* sound at least, but it doesn't. Because she is sneaky. And patient. So very patient. She has spent a long, long time doing whatever it is she does and practice has made her mindful.

When she's finally made herself whole—a little nicked in spots, but as

solid as she's going to get—she approaches the bed and this is always when I sit up, arch forward and growl like a hound twice my size. My growl is big enough, even if I am not—but growling alone doesn't always do it. So, if I need to snap and nip, I snap and nip. Or bark. Barking is usually effective. Once, I even let out my very fiercest howl—just to show her how I meant business. A piercing, screeching, sob of a howl. That's right! Only, my Mindy gets real mad about the barking—and she got even madder at the howling. Made a big fuss because I woke her up and scared her so; but the shadow-shaped woman would scare her more, I think—the woman who looks like a person but does not smell like one. What does she smell like? How would you know her? I'm not sure. She smells like...like something mouldy and maybe damp. Porous and mushy. Like when my Mindy throws wet paper towels in the trash on top of old takeout boxes half-filled with expired noodles. That kind of smell. Like abandonment or something equally awful. Not that I know of such a thing. What could possibly be worse than that?

The woman in the corner is tall, disjointed the way skeletons are, with hair all a mess and lips so thin they resemble a crooked line drawn in crayon more than they do a mouth. And her hands, they are rough and bony and stained with this pink rust color. It stains her dress all over, from her high collar all the way down to her pale, delicate ankles. Blood. But it doesn't smell like blood. It should, I know, but it doesn't. She's such a strange not-person—yes, she looks wrong and smells wrong, but it's the way she makes the room feel that scares me most. When she comes, the air goes still. It thins to the point of flaking. It's hard to breathe, at times—like the room and everyone in it is less real when she's around.

She has these eyes, too—have I mentioned her eyes? No? They aren't the kind of eyes you'd expect to see in anyone. They are nothing like my Mindy's eyes. Not in the least. It's hard to see them in the dark, but sometimes a car will pass on the street and the headlights will wash up against the window, through the blinds. When this happens, the flash ignites the woman's gaze and makes those wide eyes glitter like scales in a cruel, frozen sea. There is something wrong with the color too—the whites are yellow and there are no pupils in the centre. How does she see? I know she can. She watches my every move. The slightest shift, however silent, makes her head turn with intrinsic accuracy. Her eyes work like those of a hawk. Or an eagle. Or a dog in the dark.

She's been showing up more and more, the woman in the corner, but she hasn't gotten what she's come for yet. At least, I have come to believe that she hasn't. If she'd found what she wanted then she surely would have left us alone by now. Gone off and bothered someone else's Mindy. But she hasn't. Which means she's not done with us yet.

That's why it's so important that I stay sharp. Stay focused. No matter how late it gets or how tired I get. I'm good at keeping watch, you see. My Mindy likes to call me her lapdog—her *loopy little lapdog*. She sing-songs those words when she strokes my ears and stares deep, deep, deep into my face. But I am more than that. I can be more for her, if she needs me to be. I would do anything for my Mindy. No matter how scary. Even if it means facing the pink-handed woman with her drawn-on face and yellow scaley eyes.

The woman in the corner isn't the only one I've seen in the apartment. There are others who come to visit, just as unwelcome as she. There's a little boy who will sit at the breakfast table

sometimes, counting coins as they drop into a piggy bank, and a man who paces the hallway in the evening like he's expecting someone who is never going to show up. My Mindy usually hears his hard, narrow feet, pounding on the floor in his sturdy, shiny leather shoes. She blames the noise on me—she thinks the pacing is because I'm restless and hungry and want to eat. And I do want to eat, so I never complain when she gets up to pour dinner in my bowl, but I am not the one walking back and forth and back again. Not in the hallway. Not me. That's the old man. He's restless—always restless. I don't like him, that's for sure. He's tried to trick me twice now—coax me over with a smile or a soft gesture of the hand only to kick one of those big foot-ed shoes in my face. But I am fast. I know how to escape him. I always scamper free. And I won't let him into the bedroom. No matter what he does or how many times he tries to kick me. Not while my Mindy is in there. He's exactly like the woman who lurks in the corner. His eyes don't have any pupils. He smells like a not-person—like flat, stale air. His scent does not taste like that of a predator, but he feels like one anyway. He must think my Mindy is easy prey. But she's not. I'm around to see that she's not. And when I bare my teeth at that mean, old man, fear burns in his hollow cheeks and he cowers like the lonely creature that he is. Slinking and twitching and popping at the joints. His bones never make a sound, either. They are silent. Quiet. Sneaky. There's just the *thump, thump, thump* of his feet. Impatient and unforgiving.

The little boy, he never makes a sound but he gets frustrated with his counting. He goes through this big pile of silver coins, one by one, and when they are all in the painted, porcelain bank his face twists up and he dumps the money out again. Waves his fists. Starts all over

from the beginning. He smells like the woods sometimes smell—my Mindy took me hiking one summer, and as it got late you could taste firewood burning somewhere off in the distance. That's what the boy reminds me of, that smoky wood. His eyes are without pupils like the others and the look in his face so often reminds me of the old man's stern expression. Every so often the boy turns away from his coins and pouts at my Mindy, like whatever has made him mad is her fault. He looks so jealous. I can tell. It's the way I get when I see my Mindy out the window petting another dog on the sidewalk. I can almost smell the jealousy in his smokiness and that envy smoldering until it looks like he might even strike my Mindy, but he doesn't. Because deep down, he's afraid to do it. Not because of me I don't think. But because he's small and not quite all together and my Mindy is big and strong and whole.

Sometimes, early in the morning—when the sun is just a tiny dot at the edge of the sky—an old lady comes into the bedroom and sits at the foot of the bed. I don't trust the others, but this lady is different. She doesn't smell wet or stale or smoky. She doesn't smell like anything, in fact. Her pupils are missing but her eyes don't have that same hard look in them that sits heavy in the old man's eyes. She doesn't seem to want to hurt my Mindy. All she's ever done is watch her sleep. That's all. And I can't blame her just for watching. I do the very same. My Mindy is a good sleeper, or she would be—if I wasn't always waking her with the yelping and the growling, pawing protectively at the comforter, making it all bumpy and uneven with loose threads. My Mindy says she can't get a new blanket because I'd ruin that one like I've ruined this one. She's right and I'm sorry she's right, but I have to look mean. Like a fighter. For the woman in the corner with the scaley eyes. The little boy who watches my Mindy

drink her coffee. The man who stomps around the hallway, angry—always angry. How can anyone be so angry? I don't know. Just like I don't know why my Mindy doesn't see them, but that's all right. I see them for her. And I watch them to make sure they don't try to take my Mindy away. Because that's what they want—when all is said and done. I can tell. They are drawn to her, ache for her. It's true. They want her to go where they go. To be like them. But that will never happen. She is my Mindy. A lapdog can only have one person, I think, so why should I have to share? My Mindy wouldn't share me if she saw them, no matter what the woman in the corner says.

She talks sometimes, you know. She's the only one of the not-people who does it. Sometimes she'll whisper low all the reasons my Mindy will leave me but mostly she just repeats my Mindy's name over and over in a limp, cracked voice. She never gives her own name. Or says mine. Perhaps she doesn't know it. Sometimes I think maybe she isn't really scared of me, but if that were it then she would have made a move by now. And she hasn't.

So, you see: I'm what keeps her in the corner. Keeps her off the bed. It is my job and I do it well. She can stand there all alone as long as she wants. She can stare and glare and watch with those yellow, empty eyes. Whisper lies and croon my person's name.

It won't matter. She can't have my Mindy. No. Because my Mindy smells like herself. My Mindy has pupils and parts and she doesn't disappear the second I turn my head. My Mindy is good. And kind. My Mindy loves me, just as I love her.

These strangers cannot have my Mindy. My Mindy is mine.

XIII

the Seas of Infinity

UNLUCKY FOR SOME

by Nick Ryle Wright

*C**harles clears his throat** and angles his head towards the microphone.*

'Four and seven, forty-seven.'

It unsettles him, the way his amplified voice, devoid of the enthusiasm that once came so naturally to him, echoes around the hall.

Even for a wet Thursday afternoon in late November, the turnout is poor: half a dozen sullen pensioners, a handful of sniggering students and a couple of off-season tourists in search of something to do.

The computer flashes into life, throws up a new number.

'All the fives, fifty-five.'

Charles misses the old days. He misses the metallic creak of the cage as he rotated it, the sound the numbered balls made as they churned around inside it. But most of all he misses the happy repartee he enjoyed with the public. *His* public. But that was before the takeover. Now, his new bosses prefer him to replicate the cheerless and formulaic approach of the chain's larger, more profitable halls. *Keep it simple*, they say, when his tone becomes too familiar. *Stick to the script.*

'Two little ducks, twenty-two.'

'Bingo!' A tattooed man, wedged awkwardly into a mobility scooter, waves his dabber in the air as his wife affectionately squeezes his

fleshy arm.

Charles slides his glasses down from the top of his head and consults the page of notes taped to the side of the computer screen. After reading aloud a few perfunctory, preapproved words of congratulation to the winner, he draws the session to a close and wishes everyone a safe journey home. It takes a few minutes for the hall to empty, and when it does, Charles gathers his things and descends the stage.

'They don't deserve you.'

Charles startles at the sight of an ashen-faced lady in a dated, violet-coloured coat, sitting alone beside the door. He doesn't remember seeing her a moment ago, and he's pretty sure she wasn't an active participant in the last game.

'Bloody disgrace, if you ask me. A man of your talents forced to work in such conditions. It's unconscionable.'

Wrongfooted, Charles struggles to form a meaningful response, and is saved by his boss Marcela, who pushes through the doors, and, somewhat forebodingly, invites him to follow her into her office for a chat.

'Don't worry,' the ashen-faced lady calls out after him. 'It won't be long now.'

'It's not good news, I'm afraid,' Marcela says, leaning back in her expensive-looking director's chair. Her face free of emotion, she informs Charles that the hall is losing money and that tough decisions will need to be taken. As a result, she'll henceforth be conducting a review of all the hall's employees. Redundancies, she says gravely, cannot be ruled out.

It's not lost on Charles that his superiors regard him as something of a relic. Too old, too set in his ways, his outdated style is at odds with company philosophy.

'I'd like to stress that no decisions have yet been taken,' Marcela says.

It was in this very office some forty-two years ago that Charles was first interviewed for the job of trainee caller by the hall's then owner, Mrs Bartholomew. Concerned that he was too young at only nineteen years of age to command the respect and attention of a large crowd, the old lady – a well-known and well-respected local businesswoman – offered him a week-long trial. But Charles, an amateur magician accustomed to playing support slots in working men's clubs, was confident in his abilities, and so persuasive was his obvious rapport with the hall's loyal customers, that the notoriously *hard to please* Mrs Bartholomew offered him the job after just three days. If David were here now, he'd implore Charles to put up a fight. *Sell yourself! Tell her what you're worth!* But David's gone, and, in his absence, all Charles can muster is a timid and submissive nod of the head.

'Right,' he says. 'I see.'

A shadowy figure sits, head in lap, beside the residents' mailboxes as Charles ascends the staircase up to his first-floor flat. There was a time when he'd have enquired as to the individual's wellbeing. But not now. Now you're better off turning a blind eye. The neighbourhood's slow decline was one of the reasons David left. Upon the death of Charles' mother, he'd implored him to sell up so that they might move to a more salubrious part of town. But Charles wasn't keen. He'd grown up in the flat and he liked the fact that it was only a short walk from his front door to the old Victorian theatre in which the bingo hall was housed. When, eventually, David asked him to choose between him and the flat, Charles chose the flat.

But now, three years later, Charles feels David's absence more acutely than ever. What he wouldn't give to feel his arm around him now, to hear him whisper words of encouragement into his ear as he turns the key in the lock and he pushes open the door.

For a while, he sits in front of the TV, a fast-cooling microwave meal-for-one

resting on a tray on his lap. All around him are his mother's things: her crockery, her paintings, her rugs and throws. Ten years dead, and still he hasn't gotten around to removing them. Sometimes he sees her – or *thinks* that he sees her – sitting beside him in her chair, cigarette in one hand, glass of sherry in the other. Occasionally, he finds himself asking her about his father, whom he never knew. But just as she did in life, his mother says nothing. 'Sometimes,' she once told him, 'it's better not to know.'

Tonight, however, his mother's chair remains empty, and, his appetite having vanished, he scrapes what's left of his food into the bin, turns off the lights and retires to his bed.

The following morning, busy preparing for the first session of the day, Charles is greeted by the unexpected, yet vaguely familiar face of a bald-headed man in late middle-age, sitting outside the staff toilet.

'Hope you don't mind me saying so,' the man says, his grey, lifeless eyes fixed unblinkingly upon Charles, 'but you're wasted around here.'

'Well,' Charles says modestly, 'I don't know about that.'

'Don't do yourself down,' the man says. 'You're the mutt's nuts. You always

were.'

Charles checks his appearance in the long mirror opposite the toilet door, and straightens his bow tie.

'Are you here to play?' he asks the man.

A wry grin appears on the man's face. 'Not as such,' he says, looking over Charles' shoulder. 'You might say I'm just here to observe.'

Charles laughs, though in truth he's suddenly and inexplicably beset by an uneasy feeling. 'Observe?' he asks.

'Yes,' the man says, opening out his arms. 'We all are.'

When Charles wakes, he's lying flat on his back by the toilet door, Marcela and one of her assistants standing over him, concern etched on their faces.

'Are you OK?' Marcela asks.

Feeling a little nauseous and fuzzy-headed, Charles struggles to get back to his feet. 'Yes,' he lies, 'Never better.'

Marcela and her assistant share a doubtful look.

'Are you sure?' the assistant asks. 'You don't look too good. What happened?'

His mind a blank, Charles once again regards himself in the mirror as he attempts to straighten himself out. 'I

tripped,' he says, in lieu of a more be-
lievable explanation. 'Nothing more.'

Charles does his best to get
through the rest of the day in one
piece, but it troubles him that he can't
remember how it was he came to pass
out beside the toilet door. Distracted
by these vexatious thoughts, he blun-
ders his way through game after game
until a complaint is lodged and Marcela
appears, mid-session, to relieve him of
his duties.

'I want you to take some time off,'
his boss says, backstage.

Once again, Charles insists he's
fine. But the more he protests, the
worse things look, and eventually he's
forced to accept that Marcela's suggestion is less a request than an order.

That night, lost in a fog of depres-
sion, Charles drinks the bottle of champagne he and David had been saving
for a special occasion that, in the end,
never happened. It isn't long before
he's leaving his former lover a succes-
sion of nonsensical voicemails. The
following morning, severely hungover
and wracked with regret, he calls him
again. This time David picks up.

'I'm sorry,' Charles says. 'I was
drunk. I didn't know what I was saying.'

David sighs. 'It's OK,' he says in a
soft, understanding voice. 'It doesn't
matter.'

'No,' Charles says. 'It does. It does
matter. I shouldn't be troubling you
with my problems.'

David snorts out a wry laugh. 'Never stopped you before.'

'How dare you!' Charles retorts,
playfully.

They go on like this for a few
minutes before Charles tells David he
misses him.

'I was stubborn,' he says. 'I can see
that now. But I'm ready to move on.'

'Charles, listen – '

'Please,' Charles says, cutting him off. 'Hear me out. I'm going to sell the flat.'

'Don't do that.'

'But I need to. It's important. I'm going to box up my mother's things, take them to the charity shop. Then I'm going to put the place on the market, just like you wanted. And I was thinking, if you still want to, perhaps the two of us can give it another go.'

'Charles, I'm married.'

Charles feels his heart sink. 'I'm sorry?'

'His name's Alistair. He's a retired doctor.'

Charles' mouth dries up, as do his words.

'I just thought you should know,' David says.

'Right,' Charles says. 'I'm sorry. I shouldn't have called.'

'No, don't be silly. It's nice to hear from you. How's things?' David asks. 'How's work?'

Without saying another word, Charles ends the call, lays his phone on the table and goes off in search of something significantly stronger than champagne.

The following Monday, sleep-deprived and hungover, Charles returns to work. He does his best to avoid the prying eyes of Marcela and her beady-eyed assistants-cum-spies as he goes about his business. If he can get through the week unscathed, he thinks, any previous indiscretions might be forgotten.

As it is, the first few hours pass without incident. But then, as Charles steps outside onto the fire escape for a cigarette between sessions, he startles at the sound of a shrill and unexpected voice.

'If only you knew how much

you're missed.'

The voice, Charles discovers, belongs to a small lady of about sixty, standing to his right. To his left, there's a man of about the same age and height with cauliflower ears and a tattoo of a black cat on his neck. Both seem vaguely familiar to him.

'You can say that again,' the man says.

'It's not been the same without you,' remarks the woman.

Charles feels his temperature rising.

'Who are you and what do you want from me?' he shouts.

The woman smiles, revealing a mouth full of cracked, yellow teeth. 'We want what you want,' she says.

Charles hears the creak of a door somewhere behind him, closely followed by slow and purposeful footsteps.

'You don't recognise us, do you?' the man asks.

'Should I?'

The woman lays her wrinkled hand on Charles' arm. Curiously, he doesn't feel a thing. 'It doesn't have to be this way,' she says. 'We can help you.'

'How?' Charles asks, by now close to tears. 'How can you possibly help me?'

'Be here at midnight,' the man says, 'and you'll see for yourself.'

Just then, the door opens and Marcela steps out onto the fire escape.

'Is everything all right?' she asks. 'Only, I thought I heard you shouting.'

'No,' Charles says defensively. 'We were just talking, that's all.'

'*We?*' Marcela asks, confused.

Charles looks around. The man and the woman are nowhere to be seen.

That night, Charles tosses and turns in his bed, unable to sleep.

Don't worry. It won't be long now.

Most likely, Charles thinks, Marcela's already made the call to head office, already recommended him for the chop on account of his fast-unravelling mind. And what if she's right? What will become of him without his work?

Drenched in sweat, Charles throws back the covers, steps into the bathroom and splashes cold water over his face. Glancing at himself in the mirror, he sees an old man with his mother's eyes. What, he wonders, would she say if she could see him now?

If only you knew how much you're missed.

Charles wanders back to the bedroom, gets dressed in the dark, and walks out of the flat. A bitter wind, coming in off the sea, stings his skin as he pushes through the communal entrance and steps out into the street. It's a quarter to twelve and the pavements are clogged with solitary, sad-eyed alkies, and clusters of swaying, gibberish-spouting students. Charles gives them a wide berth as he makes his way

The **Ghastling**

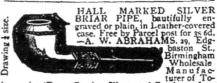

towards the hall.

Be here at midnight and you'll see for yourself.

When he gets there, he pauses, stares up at the imposing red brick façade. It occurs to him that he's never seen the hall – formerly the Grandison Theatre – in the dark before. Above the arched cathedral-like doorway is the new garish neon sign, unsubtly flashing the word BINGO into the night. Hands in pockets, Charles walks up and down the pavement, furtively checking for any sign of the man and woman he met – or thought he met – on the fire escape. He feels foolish, and once again questions his grip on reality. But then, as he's about to give up and head to a nearby dive bar, he notices that the main entrance, previously closed, is now open.

'Hello?' Charles calls into the darkness. 'Is anyone there?'

When no reply ensues, Charles steps over the threshold.

A little further. You know the way.

He edges forward, one hand outstretched in front of him, the other brushing against the cold wall to his right.

Nearly there.

Charles feels his way to the swing doors that open out into the main hall.

Go on. Open them. Step inside…

A swirling breeze circles the hall, brings with it a profusion of familiar, perfumed scents.

What took you so long?

Charles scrabbles around for a light switch. But before he's able to locate one, the pervading darkness slowly gives way to a warm yellow light. Suddenly, Charles discovers that he's not alone – that, just like it always used to be, the hall is packed to the rafters with expectant players.

Paralysed by a mixture of fear and disbelief, Charles says nothing. Is what he sees before him real or a figment of his compromised imagination?

As one, the crowd begins to clap and chant his name.

Come now. Let us begin.

Panicked, Charles turns on his heels and moves in the direction of the door through which he's just walked. But the door's no longer there, replaced by a thick, featureless wall.

Don't be afraid. We're all friends here. Do what you do best. We're waiting…

Before he knows what he's doing, Charles finds himself moving towards the stage. As he does so, he observes that the seated players are made up of his crowds of old; people he knew well, people he once regarded as friends. They're all here; the woman in the violet-coloured coat; the bald-headed man; the couple on the fire escape. Even his mother is present, sat at the front beside old Mrs Bartholomew.

There's a hearty cheer as Charles climbs up to the stage. The set-up is just as he remembers it: a long grey table, an egg-shaped cage full of numbered balls, and an ancient microphone, crudely held together by gaffer tape.

One more game. For old time's sake…

Charles turns the handle that protrudes from the side of the cage. Goose pimples rise up on his arms as the plastic balls begin to churn around inside it, clicking against each other in a strangely satisfying way.

The weight of expectation pressing down upon his shoulders, Charles picks out the first ball to slide out of the runway at the bottom of the cage. Pinching it between his thumb and forefinger, he holds it up to the light. Energised by the crowd's unbridled enthusiasm, he takes a deep breath, angles his head towards the microphone and says, 'Unlucky for some…'

Go on. Say it!

'…one and three…'

Thirteen! a polyphony of long-dead voices cries out in uncanny unison.

1000 RABBITS

by Beanie Aurora White

Father Yakob starts, as he always does, by giving the carcass a deft dunk into the wooden pail of water to the left of his work-bench. 'To stop the fur from sticking to the meat,' he says to the large crowd that have gathered outside the shop to watch him at work. Of course, Yessie already knows all 7 steps, she has observed him many times and she likes to take note of numbers. She sits on the stool, tucked away behind Father's bench swinging her legs backwards and forward, toes skimming the ground. Freeing her hand from beneath her buttocks she thrusts two of her fingers sky-ward to indicate the second step.

Father ties a white cord round each of the rabbit's feet before securing it to the narrow wooden beam that runs across the top of the shop window. He takes a knife and this is when Yessie swivels to face the other direction. She knows almost exactly how long it takes Father to finish the job. Approximately 20 seconds to wring the legs, she clutches her stomach and counts under her breath. Another 20 to disconnect the tail bone, she can feel his disapproving eyes on her back. 15 to pull the skin to the sleeves.

'Yessie, won't you help?' The onlookers laugh as she shakes her head furiously and continues to count, her lips mouthing the numbers into solid shapes. 25 to de-sleeve, she hates this part because rabbits don't have sleeves. It takes a final 28 seconds to work the skin all the way down past the head, Father is always very gentle with this step. He likes to keep the ears intact. *26, 27, 28,* a small ripple of applause scatters through the crowd accompanied by some gasps of satisfaction. Yessie knows they are marvelling at Father Yakob's clean and skilful method.

'It is done. Yessie, will you do the honours?' She scoots back round and over to the chalkboard propped against Father Yakob's bench. The fat nub of chalk leaves a fine white powder in its wake as Yessie writes the number *1000*. The crowd erupts, becoming a sea of hands waving bags full of coins aloft like little clinking flags.

Father had set up shop this time last year and had vowed to reach 1000 skinned rabbits by its first anniversary. Nobody had quite believed him and this attitude had attached itself to the 1000th rabbit in the form of superstition. The townspeople now believe that this rabbit will bring them luck, so the head of each and every family had ventured out to claim it. Yessie doesn't think the rabbit is lucky, in fact, the number 1000 sits heavy in her stomach. Too many rabbits in such a short amount of time. She sits beside the chalkboard and watches the crowd. Through the mess of eager features, she spots a face unknown to her. That of a young boy, perhaps around her age, 11. His hair is unkempt and his face unwashed. The crowd parts a little and she sees that he is wearing a brown linen shirt and matching trousers. His feet are bare. The boy stares back at Yessie and parts his lips to smile. He seems wrong, his front teeth are too long and his eyes are too black. Yessie turns away and counts down from 5, to calm herself. By the time she glances back he has disappeared.

Yessie counts out the glass beads, separating them by colour. A green column, followed by red, then yellow and finally blue.

Father holds his tankard and watches her from his chair by the hearth. 'Your mother used to make jewellery from those beads. She would paint them with flowers and animals.'

Yessie doesn't respond. She is going to lose her place: *58, 59, 60–*

'You could have a go? Make a necklace?'

61, 62, 63, 64–

Father pulls a small burlap sack from his pocket. 'The Garricks let me keep this. It's yours, for luck.' The Garricks are the wealthiest family in town. Mr Garrick is

RABBITS, RABBITS,

the mayor and he had offered Father five times as many coins as the second highest offer.

65, 66, 67–

'Yessie?' Father proffers her the sack, it swings between them for a moment whilst she counts the last of the beads.

68, 69, 70.

She takes it and looks inside. Her stomach drops. She looks at Father Yakob, on his face hangs an expectant grin.

'I don't want this, Father.' She pulls the rabbits foot from the sack, taking particular care to touch only the loop of black string it is fastened to. 'This is not lucky.'

She dangles it over the steadily burning firewood. The flames jump up and taste it with eager orange tongues. Father makes a sound somewhere between a snarl and a sob. He snatches it from her hand and throws the string over her head so that the foot rests just above her navel. She stares down at it; the fur has been carefully stitched back into place but Yessie knows the raw pink is inside. The beads have left her mind, in their place sits the number *1000*. Too many rabbits.

Father returns from his hunt the next morning in bad spirits. Usually, he and his apprentice come home with sacks full of meat, two or three rabbits slung across their shoulders. Today, nothing. Yessie can see that Father is worried. She listens outside the backroom of the shop.

'This is my own doing,' she hears Father say, 'I never should have sold the rabbit.'

She goes and stands behind the counter but the shop is empty, devoid of both people and carcasses. The metallic scent of flesh that normally fills the air is gone too. Father joins her and they watch like sentient statues as the townspeople bustle past the wood-frame window.

'Where's the rabbit's foot, Yessie?' Father asks. She had hoped he wouldn't notice. She pulls it from her apron and

puts it back round her neck. She spots the boy from yesterday across the square, he is outside the tavern standing very still. He watches them with unblinking black eyes. Yessie thinks she can see his nose twitching gently like he might be catching a scent.

She turns to Father. 'Who is that?' She points towards where the boy had been standing. He is gone.

Yessie is woken by a cacophony of fists pounded on wooden doors, of strangled screams and urgent footsteps. The Garrick house is on fire. Sure enough, she can see it over the tops of the other roofs, burning violently against the sunrise. The smoke tickles her lungs and catches in her throat. Father carries two barrels full of water, one under each arm. The light from the flames illuminates the expression of quiet terror on his face. She has never seen Father afraid. Townsfolk are throwing pails of water against the rich orange haze but the fire roars on. It is like a beast consuming the house in its flickering maw. Although Yessie stays over by the gates, she can feel its presence catching in her throat. Father runs forward with his barrels trying to catch the root of the flames.

A voice rings out from the crowd, 'You need to leave and take your young witch with you!' Father whips around, stunned.

'What spell did she put on that rabbit?'

'She's always counting and chanting under her breath, what unlucky curse did she place upon that poor creature?'

The accusations seem to catch Father off balance, he stumbles and drops the barrels. The wasted water creeps across the charred grass and pools at his feet.

'Where is the girl?'

'Find her and see what she has to say for herself.'

Yessie ducks behind the gate, heart racing, counting steadily under her breath: *1, 2, 3, 4, 5.* The voices overlap now, growing in anger. Yessie creeps over to the low

stone wall that surrounds the Garrick land and peeps over. The townsfolk are swarming around Father, pushing him ever closer to the biting flames. *6, 7, 8, 9–*

'*1000,*' whispers a voice from behind her. Yessie slowly looks round. There he is again, standing in amongst the trees, fire dancing in the depths of his black eyes. This time he beckons to her, she can see that his hand has no fingers. It looks to her like a fleshy paw. She can hear a group of townsfolk heading towards the gate. They are calling for her but they aren't using her name.

'WITCH.'

Keeping low she sprints over to the boy and takes his paw. Together they flee further into the belly of the forest.

'I HAVE to go back for Father,' Yessie protests. The boy ignores her, guiding her under tree-branch tunnels and splashing through hidden creeks. She tilts her head back, the sun must have risen high into the sky by now but in the forest, it is always dusk. The canopy of green has locked the world out and thrown away the key. The sounds and sights of the forest stay secret between the trees, that is what Father always told her. He never took her hunting. She tries to get a closer look at the boy, he keeps his head down, shaggy hair billowing slightly in the breeze. He is nimble, leaping over rocks where Yessie stumbles and ducking under vines that catch in her hair. He knows his way around; she can see that. The boy slows as they reach a tangled thicket of felled trees. He crouches and crawls underneath. Yessie hesitates and he turns to regard her, head tilted, unblinking.

'*Come,*' he says, and his small V-shaped nose begins to twitch. She follows him inside. Twigs claw at her face. The deeper they crawl, the darker it becomes until Yessie is sure that she is no longer in a thicket. She puts her hands out to the sides and they brush earthy surfaces. She straightens

up and her head grazes that same yielding earth. She is heading underground. Despite this realisation she feels calm, counting out the rhythm of her hands and knees: *Right hand 1, then left knee 2, left hand 3, then right knee 4.* She cannot see the boy ahead but she knows he is there. He stops suddenly and she hears him drop from the tunnel and land on solid ground. A faint glow enters her vision. She comes to the end of the tunnel and slides over the edge. The height is greater than she expected and she lands on her knees, hitting her head on cold, stone floor.

Yessie comes to. She is surrounded by robed figures, their faces concealed by hoods. The boy is standing directly over her. He twitches his nose and squeaks. Disorientated, she looks around; they appear to be in some sort of circular chamber. It is dimly lit by an unseen source of light. She is frightened now. The figures take down their hoods. The faces that stare down at her are all wrong. Human...but not quite. Patches of fur are scattered across skin, whiskers poke through fleshy cheeks, black eyes blink sparingly. Long round-tipped ears break through their scalps. The boy looks more like them than before. He opens his mouth and all she hears is garbled squeaking. She strains her ears, focusing on the shapes his mouth is trying to form, pretending they are numbers and that's when she hears it.

'*We warned him. Do not take advantage of the bounty of this forest. Do not take the 1000th.*' Yessie cannot tear her eyes from their faces, she is starting to understand.

'*We must restore the balance. You must restore the balance Yessie.*' They reach out and place fleshy paws onto Yessie's body. She begins to transform. If Father Yakob is still alive, she wonders whether he will hunt her and skin her, like the rest of them.

RANGCIAU 'SPRING-HEEL JA

YR ARFON AID MEWN YCHRYN.

ENGYS fod y erson dirge odd a adna
enw 'Sprin hynoc ddo ei hun
nnill cym o'r diwedd wedi gwr
eraill o'r s sir Gaernarf
ngosiad y yn mysg y trig
aw a dych ankel fergoelus o honynt.
y rbai mw wn wedi peri y fat
ngosiad y bo modd hyrwyddw
d, meddir, fe trefol o amg
leol Porthma a'i fod i'
su fod Jack wedi ei ddal r gl
achfa o amn yd ddeg—
onullai tyfiac dd lliosog
dd ynddo ddyn euange wedi
myned trwy ei glen. Ond y
mddengys fod y braw yn mysg
Dychryn personat
d a'r llwybrau ; tra yr ymddygir yr un
eithwyr ag sydd yn myned at eu gwaith
mân y boreu. Dywedir fod un fone
dd yn beryglus wael oddi wrth effaith

THE
Bell Keep's
TALE

by William Burton McCormick

I am not a man prone to visions, nightmares or fantasies. Let me assure you, friend, if I were a dreamer with a penchant for phantasms, I could not work where I do: seventy feet above the cobblestone streets of the Old City's centre. The crumbling cathedral I toil upon is little more than a ruin nowadays, reduced from its ancient majesty by age and abandonment.

A neglect sown in a communal dread of the great church, a fear the locals imagine seeped into every stone, pooling under every silent archway. Unending exposure to the gusting Baltic winds has made its roof a treacherous slope and even the most sure-footed are hesitant to ascend it, despite the magnificent view the climb affords. The steeple and belfry are in comparatively tolerable condition for I, the aged bell keep and caretaker of the highest levels, maintain them. It takes steady footsteps and steely nerve to work up here so high above the Rīga streets, balanced on centuries-slickened stones and scaffoldings of weather-warped wood, while repairing the jutting spires, fixing broken teeth of carnivorous gargoyles, and cleaning the tonnage of the six great black bells which, despite their weight, clang and peal against each other at the slightest vibration in the air.

Snowstorm or thunderous tempest, I labour here in my duties. So, you will understand my intuitions are correct, yes? A man who cannot trust his senses will not survive such conditions. Indeed, many have perished at my vocation over the centuries,

and it has only enhanced the grim legend concerning the cathedral being haunted or, worse, accursed. Despite its location in the very apex of a sprawling port city, the temple has no congregation and neither the clergy nor the common man will tarry here after nightfall, nor linger inside even in daylight if the great front doors are closed. Fanatical pilgrims come on holidays but even those devotees grow rarer with every decade. Sailors and merchants from foreign ports, wholly ignorant of the legend, occasion the dark altar, making prayers for safe homewards journeys. I always wonder how those return voyages fair, for these travelers are seldom witnessed in our nave again. Thus, mainly in isolation, I serve my penance above the busy streets maintaining what I can of the building's facade. There is no living man who knows the cathedral or its haunts as I do. So, listen to what I say and be assured I speak truth.

There were rumours of live burials and fiery immolations on the church grounds in past eons, but the first documented death associated with the cathedral was a bell ringer of the fifteenth century. In those days it was thought that the vibrations of the massive bells could disperse storms. It was common for a brave ringer to battle the unyielding sea gales, the cathedral's thunderous bells alternating with the Baltic's genuine thunder in titanic conflicts as well-remembered in our lands as the clash of any battlefield armies throughout history. This war between man's six bells and God's four elements went on for generations until three ringers fell to their deaths during consecutive storms in one terrible month. The last victim's body was immersed in flames from a lightning strike to the steeple, a human comet or meteor plummeting to the streets to land at the feet of the aghast city mayor himself. This plunging man's image is a frequent subject in the paintings of artisans

high and low throughout the town to this day. Many a tourist has brought home a curio carved in fiery Baltic amber depicting the 'Bell Keep's Fall' thinking it only legend and souvenir. To us it is truth. After the three timely bell ringer deaths, the practice of storm dispersal was banned citywide forever. In the centuries afterwards, poor Rīga has endured the gales as other cities along the Baltic coast must: unarmed and without resistance.

But whatever haunts this place, whether it is the fallen bell ringer's spirit or something older and more insidious, the malevolence within needs no storm to materialise. Since that fiery fall, five have perished on the calmest evenings, when no inland breeze turns the protective weathercocks on Rīga's spires. Over a span of eighty years – when something walked within these walls more often than perhaps it does now – a monk, two priests, a Swedish sailor and finally a skeptic, who strove to disprove the curse by spending a night within the cathedral, fell victim. All were found hanged among the belfry ropes, their corpses drumming lightly against the bell-sides in the morning light.

Such is the fate of any who spend the night within the locked cathedral. To avert tragedy one of the two massive front doors is left open all hours and in all weather. That great door was even kept ajar during the tempest of 1805 when the sea winds tore the shingles from every roof for thirty miles. I remember that storm and my youthful prayers to live through it. My predecessor did not survive. The gale slammed shut the entrance as he was securing the cathedral windows and he too was found the next morning hanging in the belfry. I, his boy assistant, took on the mantle afterwards. Sixty years have passed and I have cleaned these bells twice a week ever since.

The sights I have witnessed over the years from my precipitous heights would

surprise you. I have seen, in the open squares of the city and on the narrow roads that run beside the church, all aspects of humanity. Mobs and protests of every kind in the plazas. Victorious and defeated armies invading and retreating over the bridges spanning the Daugava River. Winter celebrations and summer holiday gatherings. Marriages, parties and funeral processions. Love and life, hatred and loss of life. These are the visions that haunt my memory, not the occasional apparition stirring in the darkest corner of the tower nor an odd gleam in a statue's eye near the altar. As long as that great front door remains ajar, I have nothing to fear from the supernatural world. The weathered collapsing stone, the rotting rafters, the slippery downwards sloping stairs – *these* threaten me, not any Peter the Painter glimpsed over my shoulder at midnight.

So, you will see what I report to you must be exceptional, though it may not seem so at the beginning. I would not retell of a chance sighting or strange noises. Best to save those 'bump-in-the-night' yarns for fireside gatherings in the shuttered inns of the seacoast. Indeed,

the encounter I relay has me rethinking my own stay in a cathedral so late at night. But where could I go after so much time? Who would take in an old man ill-starred? There are forces here beyond my paltry strength.

I first sighted *them* on a warm August night when the mists were following the Daugava inland leaving most of Rīga enshrouded in fog. The city's citizenry were reduced to stifled shades shuffling through the gloom below while I slaved away on my slim cathedral lattices and polished the bells, wielding a tattered rag at hand since childhood – my oldest possession save the locked finger ring I have worn, it seems, almost from conception. It was the absence of sound from the city beneath that attuned my other senses and took my gaze from the bell skin to the cathedral's yard. Two figures, walking closely together and hunched as if in conversation, crossed the stones towards the ever-opened door. They made no sounds as they moved, I heard no footsteps nor stray words from my position and in the mists few details could be ascertained. By their size, I guessed them male, though even that was not a certainty.

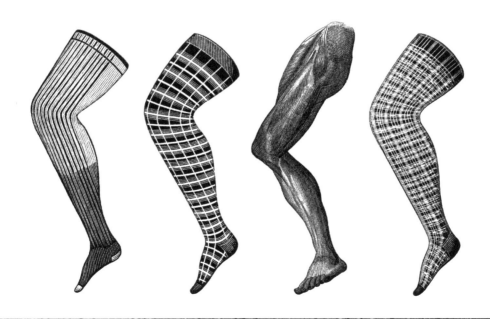

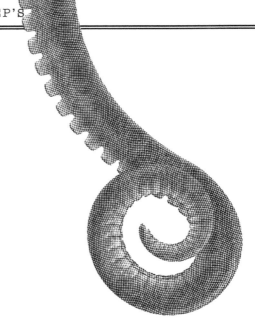

I abandoned my lattice and slipped inside the belfry, sliding down my rope to its lowest level to observe them from the church rafters if they dared enter.

They *did* enter, though their hesitation and furtive manner made me suspect these were not ignorant travelers. The strangers knew something of the cathedral's reputation or, at the least, feared discovery in their intrusion. They stepped through the solitary opened door into the shadows of the nave, the mists flowing in with them. These foggy tendrils would have given even the most benign figures an ethereal or supernatural cast but, even without the mysterious atmosphere, something in their manner raised the hairs along the back of my head. Their nature disturbed me, a distaste magnified by my discovery that they carried within their jackets the tools of excavation. What they hoped to extract from our ancient church I could not guess, but the knowledge that they were thieves or relic hunters roused protective instincts. By personal inclination, rather than official capacity, I felt responsibility for all areas of the church.

I watched these rogues as they pressed deeper inside, down the wide nave with its rotten pews in the direction of the altar. By slight gestures and inclinations of their hooded heads, I could tell they were still conversing, though not a discernible word could be heard from my high perch. My inability to hear any sound from the pair troubled me more than potential thefts. Curiosity, protectiveness – and memories of the peculiar vocal qualities associated with haunts of the cathedral – brought an end to my patience. I stole down from my rafter perch to the slanting stones of the spiral staircase and crept lower.

Fortune was against me. A stray pebble struck by my foot rattled down the stairs, heralding my advance.

They fled into the night through the fog-filled doorway. I followed them to the courtyard, but grew disorientated within the mists, a dizziness and weakness that dissuaded pursuit. I returned to the interior and eventually resumed my work.

It would have not been a notable encounter if not for subsequent events, friend. At the time, I barely thought of the rogues, my mind lingering more on my confusion in a courtyard I knew so well, a reeling loss of orientation seldom encountered even in the heights of my belfry. This curious effect raised the possibility of spell or hypnosis in the presence of the mystical, that it had somehow been a supernatural encounter.

Still, there was little to be done about it.

They returned the next night. I watched them again. Heard their footsteps this time and the occasional clank of their metallic digging tools. It eased my concerns somewhat, but weight and sound did not disqualify them as apparitions. Many spirits are known to open doors, move objects, or string up a man from his neck in the belfry. The dead, especially the dreaded doppelgänger, were indistinguishable from the living in all ways save one. As surely as the vampire makes no reflection in polished glass, the doppelgänger's voice

does not echo. Though the monster does not know it, he and his words are not of this world. A trait unique to the spirits of our region.

For this reason, I wished to be closer, to examine their speech carefully. I once more descended the staircase, cautiously, not wishing to betray my position as before. There was no error this time. I did not stumble, no stone was kicked. Nothing to reveal my approach.

Yet some paranormal sense alerted them. Again they fled. Again I lost them in the yard. Into the din of night the thieves, or spirits of thieves, once more escaped.

The third evening was most revealing.

The summer storms returned. The ominous clouds conjured up the old fears of working in the cathedral's tower as lightning branched through the skies, struck the rods and steeples of the other great churches of Rīga. I had just left the storm-shaken belfry to seek surer shelter when the two appeared on the nave floor, furtive and hunched as always.

I was prepared for their return. Instead of traversing the tortuous staircase, I had a long spindly rope ready that I descended undetected between the lightning flashes to the nave floor tiles, a rope's end I kept at hand should I need a quick return to the rafters. Their attention focused on a bare spot of wall off the apse, the invaders did not seem to sense my approach.

But the undead often lay traps for the living.

Row by row, pew by pew, I moved closer. They would not slip away from me this time. Not until I knew their nature and discovered if their words reverberated through these halls. Despite the peals of thunder and the clanging of my own bells in the storm winds, I was just within reach of their whispered exchanges as the two gestured towards the bare wall.

I thought the words German.

I crept nearer, listening attentively for any echo in their speech. Any hint of reverberation. Were they doppelgängers of life? Unknowing imitations of the living?

One lifted his excavation tool – a great hammer – high and struck the wall. A second blow. A third. The cracking of stone alternating with God's thunder overhead. A hole opened, a recess behind. From this cavity fell a corpse, a skeleton in the remnants of a monk's tunic. On its boney finger, a ring in black enamel.

I gasped. I wore the same ring.

Yet, mine had disappeared from my hand. Lost in descent, surely.

The hammer-wielder turned at my cry, his face contorted in surprise. He nudged his fellow, who stared wide-eyed through the gloom and lightning flashes. Their mouths moved, yet no audible sound passed their lips.

'Speak!' I shouted. 'Who is that man? Why are you here?'

One mute raised a crucifix.

'Speak!' I repeated, twisting my escape rope into a slipknot. 'Say something! Anything!'

'Your voice,' whispered the crucifix holder at last.

'It does not echo.'

we are alone in the universe

CONTRIBUTORS

★ ★ ★

REID BRITT is a self-taught artist from the haunted foothills of North Carolina, USA, where he was raised – and still subsists – on a heady blend of monstrous films, ghostly tales, and heavy metal. He invites you enter freely and of your own will at *instagram.com/spooky-wolffe* or *facebook.com/spookywolffe*

KAREN BOISSONNEAULT-GAUTHIER is a visual artist, writer and photographer. Most recently she's been a cover artist for Arachne Press, *Pretty Owl Poetry*, *Wild Musette*, *Existere Journal*, *Vine Leaves Literary Journal*, *Gigantic Sequins*, *Ottawa Arts Journal* and more. When she's not walking her two huskies, she's also designing with Art of Where and writing poetry. Karen now uses some of her artwork on non-medical face masks, hoping to be a better global citizen. *www.kcbgphoto.com*

WILLIAM BURTON McCORMICK is a native of Nevada, USA, who currently lives in Rīga, Latvia. His fiction has appeared in Alfred Hitchcock's Mystery Magazine, Sherlock Holmes Mystery Magazine, Curiosities 3, The Saturday Evening Post, Ellery Queen's Mystery Magazine, Lovecraftiana, Black Mask and elsewhere. His novel of revolution in the Baltic States, *Lenin's Harem* (Lume Books), was published in both English and Latvian and became the first work of fiction added to the permanent library at the Latvian War Museum in Rīga.

KAITLYNN McSHEA is a teacher and writer from Indiana, USA. In 2019, she graduated with her MA in Creative Writing from the University of Limerick, Ireland. She is a co-founder of the Heartland Society of Women Writers (*hlwomenwriters.com*). When she isn't teaching or writing, you can find her sipping on a matcha latte or in the corner of a library. Discover more at *kaitlynnmcshea.wordpress.com*

LENA NG scuttles around Toronto, Canada, and is an eight-legged member of the Horror Writers Association. She has curiosities published in over fifty tomes, including *Amazing Stories* and the anthology *We Shall Be Monsters*, which was a finalist for the 2019 Prix Aurora Award. Her forthcoming 2021 publications include *The Half That You See*, *Polar Borealis*, *Love Letters to Poe*, *Selene Quarterly*, *The Gallery of Curiosities*, *Green Inferno*, *Dread Imaginings*, *The Quiet Reader*, *Boneyard Soup*, *Death Throes Webzine* and *Sage Cigarettes*. Her short story collection *Under an Autumn Moon* was published in 2014, and she is currently seeking a publisher for her novel *Darkness Beckons*, a gothic romance.

DAMIEN B. RAPHAEL lives and works in Oxfordshire, England. His fascination with the supernatural probably stems back to Halloween 1992, when he was scared witless by *Ghostwatch* on the BBC. Damien has had three stories ap-

pear in previous *Ghastlings*: 'The Sculpture' in Book Eight, 'Rupert's Little Brother' in Book Nine and 'Firstborn' in Book Twelve.

ANDREW ROBINSON is a printmaker and graphic designer. A self-taught artist specialising in linocut prints, his interests and influences stem from wildlife, mythology, and all things creepy or otherworldly. Andrew hails from the east coast of Canada and now lives in Oxford, England, with his partner and daughters. A selection of his work can be seen at *monografik. ca* and on Instagram *@eaglesnakefight.*

MEGAN STANNARD has a BSc in Psychology and Zoology from the University of Bristol, England, and now works as a conservationist and environmental journalist. She is currently writing a series of articles for the platform *Mongabay*. Megan is represented by Saritza Hernandez of the Andrea Brown Literary Agency, and her first novel is currently out on submission.

ESTHER STEPHENSON is originally from Lincoln, England, and studied at the University of Gloucestershire where she gained a BA and MA in illustration. She is now based in London where she works as a freelance illustrator and runs her own small business. Her practice encompasses numerous styles and processes, but she favours traditional media – such as printmaking, painting and drawing. Through her work she explores the aesthetic qualities of nostalgia, as well as its emotional connection to herself and to other people.

EMILY RUTH VERONA received her Bachelor of Arts in Creative Writing and Cinema Studies from the State University of New York at Purchase. She is the recipient of the 2014 Pinch Literary Award in Fiction, and is a Jane Austen Short Story Award finalist and a Luke Bitmead Bursary finalist. Her previous publication credits include fiction featured in *The*

Pinch, Lamplight Magazine, Indigo Rising and *New Legends*, as well as essays/articles written for *Bookbub, Medium,* and *BUST.com*. She lives in New Jersey, USA, with a very small dog. *www.emilyruthverona.com*

BEANIE AURORA WHITE is a writer from Wiltshire, England. She has recently graduated from Royal Holloway University with an MA in Creative Writing, and is currently working on a YA horror/fantasy series and an anthology of short fiction looking at women and trauma under the guise of surrealist-based horror. Beanie is heavily inspired by music, film and nature, constantly stumbling upon ideas in the strangeness of everyday life.

NICK RYLE WRIGHT is a writer of short fiction, currently based in the New Forest, Hampshire, England. He has been lucky enough to have had stories published in a number of anthologies, journals and magazines, both online and in print, including *The Nottingham Review, The Occulum, Open Pen, The Fiction Pool, Here Comes Everyone, Nothing Is As It Was* and *Firewords*. He is currently at work on a novel and can be found on Twitter: *@nickrylew*

ANN WUEHLER is a writer from Oregon, USA. A collection of her short stories, *Oregon Gothic*, was published by KGHH Publishing in 2015, and she has since published two novels: *House on Clark Boulevard* (KGHH Publishing, 2017) and *Aftermath: Boise, Idaho* (Poe Boy Publishing, 2020). Her latest novel, *Remarkable Women of Brokenheart Lane*, will be published later this year. Ann's plays have also been performed widely, including at the Ilkley Playhouse, England, in September 2018. Her short story 'The Little Visitors' appeared in *The Ghastling's* Book Ten.

REBECCA PARFITT has worked in pub-

lishing for over a decade. Her debut poetry collection, *The Days After*, was published by Listen Softly London in 2017. She is currently working on a book of macabre short stories for which she won a Writers' Bursary from Literature Wales in 2020. Two stories from this collection were published in *The New Gothic Review* in 2020. Her first film, *Feeding Grief to Animals*, was recently commissioned by the BBC & FfilmCymruWales. She lives in the Llynfi Valley, Wales, with her partner and daughter. *rebeccaparfitt.com*

RHYS OWAIN WILLIAMS is a writer and editor from Swansea, Wales. His first poetry collection, *That Lone Ship*, was published by Parthian in 2018. Rhys also runs *The Crunch* – a multimedia poetry magazine (*crunchpoetry. com*). In addition to all things ghastly, Rhys is interested in folklore, urban myth and psychogeography. He lives in a terraced house near the

sea with his partner and a black cat named Poe. *rhysowainwilliams.com*

WALLACE McBRIDE is a graphic designer from South Carolina, USA. His work has been featured in *Fangoria*, The Sleepy Hollow International Film Festival, The Boston Comedy Festival, the Associated Press and dozens of newspapers in the United States, and also used on official merchandise for *The Prisoner* and *Star Trek*. He is the creator of The Collinsport Historical Society, a website dedicated to the cult television series *Dark Shadows*. Since its launch in 2012, The Collinsport Historical Society has been recognised numerous times by The Rondo Hatton Classic Horror Awards, and received The Silver Bolo Award in 2020 from Shudder's *The Last Drive-In with Joe Bob Briggs*. Wallace sometimes uses the handle 'Unlovely Frankenstein', which is either a pseudonym or just the name of his Etsy store. He isn't sure yet. *www.unlovelyfrankenstein.com*

LAST NAME OF AUTHOR

Issue 13
The Ghastling

BOOK TITLE